The Count of Monte Cristo

Volume Two

Alexandre Dumas

Saymton Solutions

Contents

Chapter 1

The Prison Register

The day after that in which the scene we have just described had taken place on the road between Bellegarde and Beaucaire, a man of about thirty or two-and-thirty, dressed in a bright blue frock coat, nankeen trousers, and a white waistcoat, having the appearance and accent of an Englishman, presented himself before the mayor of Marseilles.

"Sir," said he, "I am chief clerk of the house of Thomson & French, of Rome. We are, and have been these ten years, connected with the house of Morrel & Son, of Marseilles. We have a hundred thousand francs or thereabouts loaned on their securities, and we are a little uneasy at reports that have reached us that the firm is on the brink of ruin. I have come, therefore, express from Rome, to ask you for information."

"Sir," replied the mayor. "I know very well that during the last four or five years misfortune has seemed to pursue M. Morrel. He has lost four or five vessels, and suffered by three or four bankruptcies; but it is not for me, although I am a creditor myself to the amount of ten thousand francs, to give any information as to the state of his finances. Ask of me, as mayor, what is my opinion of M. Morrel, and I shall say that he is a man honorable to the last degree, and who has up to this time fulfilled every engagement with scrupulous punctuality. This is all I can say, sir; if you wish to learn more, address yourself to M. de Boville, the inspector of prisons, No. 15, Rue de Nouailles; he has, I believe, two hundred thousand francs in Morrel's hands, and if there be any grounds for apprehension, as this is a greater amount than mine, you will most probably find him better informed than myself."

The Englishman seemed to appreciate this extreme delicacy, made his bow and went away, proceeding with a characteristic British stride towards the street mentioned.

M. de Boville was in his private room, and the Englishman, on perceiving him, made a gesture of surprise, which seemed to indicate that it was not the first time he had been in his presence. As to M. de Boville, he was in such a state of despair, that it was evident all the faculties of his mind, absorbed in the thought which occupied him at the moment, did not allow either his memory or his imagination to stray to the past.

The Englishman, with the coolness of his nation, addressed him in terms nearly similar to those with which he had accosted the mayor of Marseilles.

"Oh, sir," exclaimed M. de Boville, "your fears are unfortunately but too well founded, and you see before you a man in despair. I had two hundred thousand francs placed in the hands of Morrel & Son; these two hundred thousand francs were the dowry of my daughter, who was to be married in a fortnight, and these two hundred thousand francs were payable, half on the 15th of this month, and the other half on the

15th of next month. I had informed M. Morrel of my desire to have these payments punctually, and he has been here within the last half-hour to tell me that if his ship, the *Pharaon*, did not come into port on the 15th, he would be wholly unable to make this payment."

"But," said the Englishman, "this looks very much like a suspension of payment."

"It looks more like bankruptcy!" exclaimed M. de Boville despairingly.

The Englishman appeared to reflect a moment, and then said, "From which it would appear, sir, that this credit inspires you with considerable apprehension?"

"To tell you the truth, I consider it lost."

"Well, then, I will buy it of you!"

"You?"

"Yes, I!"

"But at a tremendous discount, of course?"

"No, for two hundred thousand francs. Our house," added the Englishman with a laugh, "does not do things in that way."

"And you will pay "

"Ready money."

And the Englishman drew from his pocket a bundle of banknotes, which might have been twice the sum M. de Boville feared to lose. A ray of joy passed across M. de Boville's countenance, yet he made an effort at self-control, and said:

"Sir, I ought to tell you that, in all probability, you will not realize six per cent of this sum."

"That's no affair of mine," replied the Englishman, "that is the affair of the house of Thomson & French, in whose name I act. They have, perhaps, some motive to serve in hastening the ruin of a rival firm. But all I know, sir, is, that I am ready to hand you over this sum in exchange for your assignment of the debt. I only ask a brokerage."

"Of course, that is perfectly just," cried M. de Boville. "The commission is usually one and a half; will you have two three five per cent, or even more? Whatever you say."

"Sir," replied the Englishman, laughing, "I am like my house, and do not do such things no, the commission I ask is quite different."

"Name it, sir, I beg."

"You are the inspector of prisons?"

"I have been so these fourteen years."

"You keep the registers of entries and departures?"

"I do."

"To these registers there are added notes relative to the prisoners?"

"There are special reports on every prisoner."

"Well, sir, I was educated at Rome by a poor devil of an abbé, who disappeared suddenly. I have since learned that he was confined in the Château d'If, and I should like to learn some particulars of his death."

"What was his name?"

"The Abbé Faria."

"Oh, I recollect him perfectly," cried M. de Boville; "he was crazy."

"So they said."

"Oh, he was, decidedly."

"Very possibly; but what sort of madness was it?"

"He pretended to know of an immense treasure, and offered vast sums to the government if they would liberate him."

"Poor devil! and he is dead?"

"Yes, sir, five or six months ago, last February."

"You have a good memory, sir, to recollect dates so well."

"I recollect this, because the poor devil's death was accompanied by a singular incident."

"May I ask what that was?" said the Englishman with an expression of curiosity, which a close observer would have been astonished at discovering in his phlegmatic countenance.

"Oh dear, yes, sir; the abbé's dungeon was forty or fifty feet distant from that of one of Bonaparte's emissaries, one of those who had contributed the most to the return of the usurper in 1815, a very resolute and very dangerous man."

"Indeed!" said the Englishman.

"Yes," replied M. de Boville; "I myself had occasion to see this man in 1816 or 1817, and we could only go into his dungeon with a file of soldiers. That man made a deep impression on me; I shall never forget his countenance!"

The Englishman smiled imperceptibly.

"And you say, sir," he interposed, "that the two dungeons "

"Were separated by a distance of fifty feet; but it appears that this Edmond Dantès "

"This dangerous man's name was "

"Edmond Dantès. It appears, sir, that this Edmond Dantès had procured tools, or made them, for they found a tunnel through which the prisoners held communication with one another."

"This tunnel was dug, no doubt, with an intention of escape?"

"No doubt; but unfortunately for the prisoners, the Abbé Faria had an attack of catalepsy, and died."

"That must have cut short the projects of escape."

"For the dead man, yes," replied M. de Boville, "but not for the survivor; on the contrary, this Dantès saw a means of accelerating his escape. He, no doubt, thought that prisoners who died in the Château d'If were interred in an ordinary burial-ground, and he conveyed the dead man into his own cell, took his place in the sack in which they had sewed up the corpse, and awaited the moment of interment."

"It was a bold step, and one that showed some courage," remarked the Englishman.

"As I have already told you, sir, he was a very dangerous man; and, fortunately, by his own act disembarrassed the government of the fears it had on his account."

"How was that?"

"How? Do you not comprehend?"

"No."

"The Château d'If has no cemetery, and they simply throw the dead into the sea, after fastening a thirty-six-pound cannon-ball to their feet."

"Well?" observed the Englishman as if he were slow of comprehension.

"Well, they fastened a thirty-six-pound ball to his feet, and threw him into the sea."

"Really!" exclaimed the Englishman.

"Yes, sir," continued the inspector of prisons. "You may imagine the amazement of the fugitive when he found himself flung headlong over the rocks! I should like to have seen his face at that moment."

"That would have been difficult."

"No matter," replied De Boville, in supreme good-humor at the certainty of recovering his two hundred thousand francs, "no matter, I can fancy it." And he shouted with laughter.

"So can I," said the Englishman, and he laughed too; but he laughed as the English do, "at the end of his teeth."

"And so," continued the Englishman who first gained his composure, "he was drowned?"

"Unquestionably."

"So that the governor got rid of the dangerous and the crazy prisoner at the same time?"

"Precisely."

"But some official document was drawn up as to this affair, I suppose?" inquired the Englishman.

"Yes, yes, the mortuary deposition. You understand, Dantès' relations, if he had any, might have some interest in knowing if he were dead or alive."

"So that now, if there were anything to inherit from him, they may do so with easy conscience. He is dead, and no mistake about it."

"Oh, yes; and they may have the fact attested whenever they please."

"So be it," said the Englishman. "But to return to these registers."

"True, this story has diverted our attention from them. Excuse me."

"Excuse you for what? For the story? By no means; it really seems to me very curious."

"Yes, indeed. So, sir, you wish to see all relating to the poor abbé, who really was gentleness itself."

"Yes, you will much oblige me."

"Go into my study here, and I will show it to you."

And they both entered M. de Boville's study. Everything was here arranged in perfect order; each register had its number, each file of papers its place. The inspector begged the Englishman to seat himself in an armchair, and placed before him the register and documents relative to the Château d'If, giving him all the time he desired for the examination, while De Boville seated himself in a corner, and began to read his newspaper. The Englishman easily found the entries relative to the Abbé Faria; but it seemed that the history which the inspector had related interested him greatly, for after having perused the first documents he turned over the leaves until he reached the deposition respecting Edmond Dantès. There he found everything arranged in due order, the accusation, examination, Morrel's petition, M. de Villefort's marginal notes. He folded up the accusation quietly, and put it as quietly in his pocket; read the examination, and saw that the name of Noirtier was not mentioned in it; perused, too, the application dated 10th April, 1815, in which Morrel, by the deputy procureur's advice, exaggerated with the best intentions (for Napoleon was then on the throne) the services Dantès had rendered to the imperial cause services which Villefort's certificates rendered indisputable. Then he saw through the whole thing. This petition to Napoleon, kept back by Villefort, had become, under the second restoration, a terrible weapon against him in the hands of the king's attorney. He was no longer astonished when he searched on to find in the register this note, placed in a bracket against his name:

Edmond Dantès.

An inveterate Bonapartist; took an active part in the return from the Island of Elba.

To be kept in strict solitary confinement, and to be closely watched and guarded.

Beneath these lines was written in another hand: "See note above nothing can be done."

He compared the writing in the bracket with the writing of the certificate placed beneath Morrel's petition, and discovered that the note in the bracket was the same writing as the certificate that is to say, was in Villefort's handwriting.

As to the note which accompanied this, the Englishman understood that it might have been added by some inspector who had taken a momentary interest in Dantès' situation, but who had, from the remarks we have quoted, found it impossible to give any effect to the interest he had felt.

As we have said, the inspector, from discretion, and that he might not disturb the Abbé Faria's pupil in his researches, had seated himself in a corner, and was reading *Le Drapeau Blanc*. He did not see the Englishman fold up and place in his pocket the accusation written by Danglars under the arbor of La Réserve, and which had the postmark, "Marseilles, 27th February, delivery 6 o'clock, P.M."

But it must be said that if he had seen it, he attached so little importance to this scrap of paper, and so much importance to his two hundred thousand francs, that he would not have opposed whatever the Englishman might do, however irregular it might be.

"Thanks," said the latter, closing the register with a slam, "I have all I want; now it is for me to perform my promise. Give me a simple assignment of your debt; acknowledge therein the receipt of the cash, and I will hand you over the money."

He rose, gave his seat to M. de Boville, who took it without ceremony, and quickly drew up the required assignment, while the Englishman counted out the bank-notes on the other side of the desk.

Chapter 2

The House of Morrel & Son

Anyone who had quitted Marseilles a few years previously, well acquainted with the interior of Morrel's warehouse, and had returned at this date, would have found a great change. Instead of that air of life, of comfort, and of happiness that permeates a flourishing and prosperous business establishment instead of merry faces at the windows, busy clerks hurrying to and fro in the long corridors instead of the court filled with bales of goods, re-echoing with the cries and the jokes of porters, one would have immediately perceived all aspect of sadness and gloom. Out of all the numerous clerks that used to fill the deserted corridor and the empty office, but two remained. One was a young man of three or four-and-twenty, who was in love with M. Morrel's daughter, and had remained with him in spite of the efforts of his friends to induce him to withdraw; the other was an old one-eyed cashier, called "Cocles," or "Cock-eye," a nickname given him by the young men who used to throng this vast now almost deserted bee-hive, and which had so completely replaced his real name that he would not, in all probability, have replied to anyone who addressed him by it.

Cocles remained in M. Morrel's service, and a most singular change had taken place in his position; he had at the same time risen to the rank of cashier, and sunk to the rank of a servant. He was, however, the same Cocles, good, patient, devoted, but inflexible on the subject of arithmetic, the only point on which he would have stood firm against the world, even against M. Morrel; and strong in the multiplication-table, which he had at his fingers' ends, no matter what scheme or what trap was laid to catch him.

In the midst of the disasters that befell the house, Cocles was the only one unmoved. But this did not arise from a want of affection; on the contrary, from a firm conviction. Like the rats that one by one forsake the doomed ship even before the vessel weighs anchor, so all the numerous clerks had by degrees deserted the office and the warehouse. Cocles had seen them go without thinking of inquiring the cause of their departure. Everything was as we have said, a question of arithmetic to Cocles, and during twenty years he had always seen all payments made with such exactitude, that it seemed as impossible to him that the house should stop payment, as it would to a miller that the river that had so long turned his mill should cease to flow.

Nothing had as yet occurred to shake Cocles' belief; the last month's payment had been made with the most scrupulous exactitude; Cocles had detected an overbalance of fourteen sous in his cash, and the same evening he had brought them to M. Morrel, who, with a melancholy smile, threw them into an almost empty drawer, saying:

"Thanks, Cocles; you are the pearl of cashiers."

Cocles went away perfectly happy, for this eulogium of M. Morrel, himself the pearl of the honest men of Marseilles, flattered him more than a present of fifty crowns. But since the end of the month M. Morrel had passed many an anxious hour. In order to meet the payments then due; he had collected all his resources, and, fearing lest the report of his distress should get bruited abroad at Marseilles when he was known to be reduced to such an extremity, he went to the Beaucaire fair to sell his wife's and daughter's jewels and a portion of his plate. By this means the end of the month was passed, but his resources were now exhausted. Credit, owing to the reports afloat, was no longer to be had; and to meet the one hundred thousand francs due on the 15th of the present month, and the one hundred thousand francs due on the 15th of the next month to M. de Boville, M. Morrel had, in reality, no hope but the return of the *Pharaon*, of whose departure he had learnt from a vessel which had weighed anchor at the same time, and which had already arrived in harbor.

But this vessel which, like the *Pharaon*, came from Calcutta, had been in for a fortnight, while no intelligence had been received of the *Pharaon*.

Such was the state of affairs when, the day after his interview with M. de Boville, the confidential clerk of the house of Thomson & French of Rome, presented himself at M. Morrel's. Emmanuel received him; this young man was alarmed by the appearance of every new face, for every new face might be that of a new creditor, come in anxiety to question the head of the house. The young man, wishing to spare his employer the pain of this interview, questioned the new-comer; but the stranger declared that he had nothing to say to M. Emmanuel, and that his business was with M. Morrel in person.

Emmanuel sighed, and summoned Cocles. Cocles appeared, and the young man bade him conduct the stranger to M. Morrel's apartment. Cocles went first, and the stranger followed him. On the staircase they met a beautiful girl of sixteen or seventeen, who looked with anxiety at the stranger.

"M. Morrel is in his room, is he not, Mademoiselle Julie?" said the cashier.

"Yes; I think so, at least," said the young girl hesitatingly. "Go and see, Cocles, and if my father is there, announce this gentleman."

"It will be useless to announce me, mademoiselle," returned the Englishman. "M. Morrel does not know my name; this worthy gentleman has only to announce the confidential clerk of the house of Thomson & French of Rome, with whom your father does business."

The young girl turned pale and continued to descend, while the stranger and Cocles continued to mount the staircase. She entered the office where Emmanuel was, while Cocles, by the aid of a key he possessed, opened a door in the corner of a landing-place on the second staircase, conducted the stranger into an antechamber, opened a second door, which he closed behind him, and after having left the clerk of the house of Thomson & French alone, returned and signed to him that he could enter.

The Englishman entered, and found Morrel seated at a table, turning over the formidable columns of his ledger, which contained the list of his liabilities. At the sight of the stranger, M. Morrel closed the ledger, arose, and offered a seat to the stranger; and when he had seen him seated, resumed his own chair. Fourteen years had changed the worthy merchant, who, in his thirty-sixth year at the opening of this history, was now in his fiftieth; his hair had turned white, time and sorrow had ploughed deep furrows on his brow, and his look, once so firm and penetrating, was now irresolute and wandering, as if he feared being forced to fix his attention on some particular thought or person.

The Englishman looked at him with an air of curiosity, evidently mingled with interest. "Monsieur," said Morrel, whose uneasiness was increased by this examination, "you wish to speak to me?"

"Yes, monsieur; you are aware from whom I come?"

"The house of Thomson & French; at least, so my cashier tells me."

"He has told you rightly. The house of Thomson & French had 300,000 or 400,000 francs to pay this month in France; and, knowing your strict punctuality, have collected all the bills bearing your signature, and charged me as they became due to present them, and to employ the money otherwise."

Morrel sighed deeply, and passed his hand over his forehead, which was covered with perspiration.

"So then, sir," said Morrel, "you hold bills of mine?"

"Yes, and for a considerable sum."

"What is the amount?" asked Morrel with a voice he strove to render firm.

"Here is," said the Englishman, taking a quantity of papers from his pocket, "an assignment of 200,000 francs to our house by M. de Boville, the inspector of prisons, to whom they are due. You acknowledge, of course, that you owe this sum to him?"

"Yes; he placed the money in my hands at four and a half per cent nearly five years ago."

"When are you to pay?"

"Half the 15th of this month, half the 15th of next."

"Just so; and now here are 32,500 francs payable shortly; they are all signed by you, and assigned to our house by the holders."

"I recognize them," said Morrel, whose face was suffused, as he thought that, for the first time in his life, he would be unable to honor his own signature. "Is this all?"

"No, I have for the end of the month these bills which have been assigned to us by the house of Pascal, and the house of Wild & Turner of Marseilles, amounting to nearly 55,000 francs; in all, 287,500 francs."

It is impossible to describe what Morrel suffered during this enumeration. "Two hundred and eighty-seven thousand five hundred francs," repeated he.

"Yes, sir," replied the Englishman. "I will not," continued he, after a moment's silence, "conceal from you, that while your probity and exactitude up to this moment are universally acknowledged, yet the report is current in Marseilles that you are not able to meet your liabilities."

At this almost brutal speech Morrel turned deathly pale.

"Sir," said he, "up to this time and it is now more than four-and-twenty years since I received the direction of this house from my father, who had himself conducted it for five-and-thirty years never has anything bearing the signature of Morrel & Son been dishonored."

"I know that," replied the Englishman. "But as a man of honor should answer another, tell me fairly, shall you pay these with the same punctuality?"

Morrel shuddered, and looked at the man, who spoke with more assurance than he had hitherto shown.

"To questions frankly put," said he, "a straightforward answer should be given. Yes, I shall pay, if, as I hope, my vessel arrives safely; for its arrival will again procure me the credit which the numerous accidents, of which I have been the victim, have deprived me; but if the *Pharaon* should be lost, and this last resource be gone "

The poor man's eyes filled with tears.

"Well," said the other, "if this last resource fail you?"

"Well," returned Morrel, "it is a cruel thing to be forced to say, but, already used to misfortune, I must habituate myself to shame. I fear I shall be forced to suspend payment."

"Have you no friends who could assist you?"

Morrel smiled mournfully.

"In business, sir," said he, "one has no friends, only correspondents."

"It is true," murmured the Englishman; "then you have but one hope."

"But one."

"The last?"

"The last."

"So that if this fail "

"I am ruined, completely ruined!"

"As I was on my way here, a vessel was coming into port."

"I know it, sir; a young man, who still adheres to my fallen fortunes, passes a part of his time in a belvedere at the top of the house, in hopes of being the first to announce good news to me; he has informed me of the arrival of this ship."

"And it is not yours?"

"No, she is a Bordeaux vessel, *La Gironde*; she comes from India also; but she is not mine."

"Perhaps she has spoken to the *Pharaon*, and brings you some tidings of her?"

"Shall I tell you plainly one thing, sir? I dread almost as much to receive any tidings of my vessel as to remain in doubt. Uncertainty is still hope." Then in a low voice Morrel added, "This delay is not natural. The *Pharaon* left Calcutta the 5th of February; she ought to have been here a month ago."

"What is that?" said the Englishman. "What is the meaning of that noise?"

"Oh, my God!" cried Morrel, turning pale, "what is it?"

A loud noise was heard on the stairs of people moving hastily, and half-stifled sobs. Morrel rose and advanced to the door; but his strength failed him and he sank into a chair. The two men remained opposite one another, Morrel trembling in every limb, the stranger gazing at him with an air of profound pity. The noise had ceased; but it seemed that Morrel expected something something had occasioned the noise, and something must follow. The stranger fancied he heard footsteps on the stairs; and that the footsteps, which were those of several persons, stopped at the door. A key was inserted in the lock of the first door, and the creaking of hinges was audible.

"There are only two persons who have the key to that door," murmured Morrel, "Cocles and Julie."

At this instant the second door opened, and the young girl, her eyes bathed with tears, appeared. Morrel rose tremblingly, supporting himself by the arm of the chair. He would have spoken, but his voice failed him.

"Oh, father!" said she, clasping her hands, "forgive your child for being the bearer of evil tidings."

Morrel again changed color. Julie threw herself into his arms.

"Oh, father, father!" murmured she, "courage!"

"The *Pharaon* has gone down, then?" said Morrel in a hoarse voice. The young girl did not speak; but she made an affirmative sign with her head as she lay on her father's breast.

"And the crew?" asked Morrel.

"Saved," said the girl; "saved by the crew of the vessel that has just entered the harbor."

Morrel raised his two hands to heaven with an expression of resignation and sublime gratitude.

"Thanks, my God," said he, "at least thou strikest but me alone."

A tear moistened the eye of the phlegmatic Englishman.

"Come in, come in," said Morrel, "for I presume you are all at the door."

Scarcely had he uttered those words when Madame Morrel entered weeping bitterly. Emmanuel followed her, and in the antechamber were visible the rough faces of seven or eight half-naked sailors. At the sight of these men the Englishman started and advanced a step; then restrained himself, and retired into the farthest and most obscure corner of the apartment. Madame Morrel sat down by her husband and took one of his hands in hers, Julie still lay with her head on his shoulder, Emmanuel stood in the centre of the chamber and seemed to form the link between Morrel's family and the sailors at the door.

"How did this happen?" said Morrel.

"Draw nearer, Penelon," said the young man, "and tell us all about it."

An old seaman, bronzed by the tropical sun, advanced, twirling the remains of a hat between his hands.

"Good-day, M. Morrel," said he, as if he had just quitted Marseilles the previous evening, and had just returned from Aix or Toulon.

"Good-day, Penelon," returned Morrel, who could not refrain from smiling through his tears, "where is the captain?"

"The captain, M. Morrel, he has stayed behind sick at Palma; but please God, it won't be much, and you will see him in a few days all alive and hearty."

"Well, now tell your story, Penelon."

Penelon rolled his quid in his cheek, placed his hand before his mouth, turned his head, and sent a long jet of tobacco-juice into the antechamber, advanced his foot, balanced himself, and began.

"You see, M. Morrel," said he, "we were somewhere between Cape Blanc and Cape Boyador, sailing with a fair breeze, south-south-west after a week's calm, when Captain Gaumard comes up to me I was at the helm I should tell you and says, 'Penelon, what do you think of those clouds coming up over there?' I was just then looking at them myself. 'What do I think, captain? Why I think that they are rising faster than they have any business to do, and that they would not be so black if they didn't mean mischief.' 'That's my opinion too,' said the captain, 'and I'll take precautions accordingly. We are carrying too much canvas. Avast, there, all hands! Take in the studding-sails and stow the flying jib.' It was time; the squall was on us, and the vessel began to heel. 'Ah,' said the captain, 'we have still too much canvas set; all hands lower the mainsail!' Five minutes after, it was down; and we sailed under mizzen-topsails and top-gallant sails. 'Well, Penelon,' said the captain, 'what makes you shake your head?' 'Why,' I says, 'I still think you've got too much on.' 'I think you're right,' answered he, 'we shall have a gale.' 'A gale? More than that, we shall have a tempest, or I don't know what's what.' You could see the wind coming like the dust at Montredon; luckily the captain understood his business. 'Take in two reefs in the top-sails,' cried the captain; 'let go the bowlin's, haul the brace, lower the top-gallant sails, haul out the reef-tackles on the yards.'"

"That was not enough for those latitudes," said the Englishman; "I should have taken four reefs in the topsails and furled the spanker."

His firm, sonorous, and unexpected voice made everyone start. Penelon put his hand over his eyes, and then stared at the man who thus criticized the manœuvres of his captain.

"We did better than that, sir," said the old sailor respectfully; "we put the helm up to run before the tempest; ten minutes after we struck our top-sails and scudded under bare poles."

"The vessel was very old to risk that," said the Englishman.

"Eh, it was that that did the business; after pitching heavily for twelve hours we sprung a leak. 'Penelon,' said the captain, 'I think we are sinking, give me the helm, and go down into the hold.' I gave him the helm, and descended; there was already three feet of water. 'All hands to the pumps!' I shouted; but it was too late, and it seemed the more we pumped the more came in. 'Ah,' said I, after four hours' work, 'since we are sinking, let us sink; we can die but once.' 'Is that the example you set, Penelon?' cries the captain; 'very well, wait a minute.' He went into his cabin and came back with a brace of pistols. 'I will blow the brains out of the first man who leaves the pump,' said he."

"Well done!" said the Englishman.

"There's nothing gives you so much courage as good reasons," continued the sailor; "and during that time the wind had abated, and the sea gone down, but the water kept rising; not much, only two inches an hour, but still it rose. Two inches an hour does not seem much, but in twelve hours that makes two feet, and three we had before, that makes five. 'Come,' said the captain, 'we have done all in our power, and M. Morrel will have nothing to reproach us with, we have tried to save the ship, let us now save ourselves. To the boats, my lads, as quick as you can.' Now," continued Penelon, "you see, M. Morrel, a sailor is attached to his ship, but still more to his life, so we did not wait to be told twice; the more so, that the ship was sinking under us, and seemed to say, 'Get along save yourselves.' We soon launched the boat, and all eight of us got into it. The captain descended last, or rather, he did not descend, he would not quit the vessel; so I took him round the waist, and threw him into the boat, and then I jumped after him. It was time, for just as I jumped the deck burst with a noise like the broadside of a man-of-war. Ten minutes after she pitched forward, then the other way, spun round and round, and then good-bye to the *Pharaon*. As for us, we were three days without anything to eat or drink, so that we began to think of drawing lots who should feed the rest, when we saw *La Gironde*; we made signals of distress, she perceived us, made for us, and took us all on board. There now, M. Morrel, that's the whole truth, on the honor of a sailor; is not it true, you fellows there?" A general murmur of approbation showed that the narrator had faithfully detailed their misfortunes and sufferings.

"Well, well," said M. Morrel, "I know there was no one in fault but destiny. It was the will of God that this should happen, blessed be his name. What wages are due to you?"

"Oh, don't let us talk of that, M. Morrel."

"Yes, but we will talk of it."

"Well, then, three months," said Penelon.

"Cocles, pay two hundred francs to each of these good fellows," said Morrel. "At another time," added he, "I should have said, Give them, besides, two hundred francs over as a present; but times are changed, and the little money that remains to me is not my own, so do not think me mean on this account."

Penelon turned to his companions, and exchanged a few words with them.

"As for that, M. Morrel," said he, again turning his quid, "as for that "

"As for what?"

"The money."

"Well "

"Well, we all say that fifty francs will be enough for us at present, and that we will wait for the rest."

"Thanks, my friends, thanks!" cried Morrel gratefully; "take it take it; and if you can find another employer, enter his service; you are free to do so."

These last words produced a prodigious effect on the seaman. Penelon nearly swallowed his quid; fortunately he recovered.

"What, M. Morrel!" said he in a low voice, "you send us away; you are then angry with us!"

"No, no," said M. Morrel, "I am not angry, quite the contrary, and I do not send you away; but I have no more ships, and therefore I do not want any sailors."

"No more ships!" returned Penelon; "well, then, you'll build some; we'll wait for you."

"I have no money to build ships with, Penelon," said the poor owner mournfully, "so I cannot accept your kind offer."

"No more money? Then you must not pay us; we can scud, like the *Pharaon*, under bare poles."

"Enough, enough!" cried Morrel, almost overpowered; "leave me, I pray you; we shall meet again in a happier time. Emmanuel, go with them, and see that my orders are executed."

"At least, we shall see each other again, M. Morrel?" asked Penelon.

"Yes; I hope so, at least. Now go." He made a sign to Cocles, who went first; the seamen followed him and Emmanuel brought up the rear. "Now," said the owner to his wife and daughter, "leave me; I wish to speak with this gentleman."

And he glanced towards the clerk of Thomson & French, who had remained motionless in the corner during this scene, in which he had taken no part, except the few words we have mentioned. The two women looked at this person whose presence they had entirely forgotten, and retired; but, as she left the apartment, Julie gave the stranger a supplicating glance, to which he replied by a smile that an indifferent spectator would have been surprised to see on his stern features. The two men were left alone. "Well, sir," said Morrel, sinking into a chair, "you have heard all, and I have nothing further to tell you."

"I see," returned the Englishman, "that a fresh and unmerited misfortune has overwhelmed you, and this only increases my desire to serve you."

"Oh, sir!" cried Morrel.

"Let me see," continued the stranger, "I am one of your largest creditors."

"Your bills, at least, are the first that will fall due."

"Do you wish for time to pay?"

"A delay would save my honor, and consequently my life."

"How long a delay do you wish for?"

Morrel reflected. "Two months," said he.

"I will give you three," replied the stranger.

"But," asked Morrel, "will the house of Thomson & French consent?"

"Oh, I take everything on myself. Today is the 5th of June."

"Yes."

"Well, renew these bills up to the 5th of September; and on the 5th of September at eleven o'clock (the hand of the clock pointed to eleven), I shall come to receive the money."

"I shall expect you," returned Morrel; "and I will pay you or I shall be dead." These last words were uttered in so low a tone that the stranger could not hear them. The bills were renewed, the old ones destroyed, and the poor ship-owner found himself with three months before him to collect his resources. The Englishman received his thanks with the phlegm peculiar to his nation; and Morrel, overwhelming him with grateful blessings, conducted him to the staircase. The stranger met Julie on the stairs; she pretended to be descending, but in reality she was waiting for him. "Oh, sir" said she, clasping her hands.

"Mademoiselle," said the stranger, "one day you will receive a letter signed 'Sinbad the Sailor.' Do exactly what the letter bids you, however strange it may appear."

"Yes, sir," returned Julie.

"Do you promise?"

"I swear to you I will."

"It is well. Adieu, mademoiselle. Continue to be the good, sweet girl you are at present, and I have great hopes that Heaven will reward you by giving you Emmanuel for a husband."

Julie uttered a faint cry, blushed like a rose, and leaned against the baluster. The stranger waved his hand, and continued to descend. In the court he found Penelon, who, with a rouleau of a hundred francs in either hand, seemed unable to make up his mind to retain them. "Come with me, my friend," said the Englishman; "I wish to speak to you."

Chapter 3

The Fifth of September

The extension provided for by the agent of Thomson & French, at the moment when Morrel expected it least, was to the poor shipowner so decided a stroke of good fortune that he almost dared to believe that fate was at length grown weary of wasting her spite upon him. The same day he told his wife, Emmanuel, and his daughter all that had occurred; and a ray of hope, if not of tranquillity, returned to the family. Unfortunately, however, Morrel had not only engagements with the house of Thomson & French, who had shown themselves so considerate towards him; and, as he had said, in business he had correspondents, and not friends. When he thought the matter over, he could by no means account for this generous conduct on the part of Thomson & French towards him; and could only attribute it to some such selfish argument as this: "We had better help a man who owes us nearly 300,000 francs, and have those 300,000 francs at the end of three months than hasten his ruin, and get only six or eight per cent of our money back again."

Unfortunately, whether through envy or stupidity, all Morrel's correspondents did not take this view; and some even came to a contrary decision. The bills signed by Morrel were presented at his office with scrupulous exactitude, and, thanks to the delay granted by the Englishman, were paid by Cocles with equal punctuality. Cocles thus remained in his accustomed tranquillity. It was Morrel alone who remembered with alarm, that if he had to repay on the 15th the 50,000 francs of M. de Boville, and on the 30th the 32,500 francs of bills, for which, as well as the debt due to the inspector of prisons, he had time granted, he must be a ruined man.

The opinion of all the commercial men was that, under the reverses which had successively weighed down Morrel, it was impossible for him to remain solvent. Great, therefore, was the astonishment when at the end of the month, he cancelled all his obligations with his usual punctuality. Still confidence was not restored to all minds, and the general opinion was that the complete ruin of the unfortunate shipowner had been postponed only until the end of the month.

The month passed, and Morrel made extraordinary efforts to get in all his resources. Formerly his paper, at any date, was taken with confidence, and was even in request. Morrel now tried to negotiate bills at ninety days only, and none of the banks would give him credit. Fortunately, Morrel had some funds coming in on which he could rely; and, as they reached him, he found himself in a condition to meet his engagements when the end of July came.

The agent of Thomson & French had not been again seen at Marseilles; the day after, or two days after his visit to Morrel, he had disappeared; and as in that city he had had no intercourse but with the mayor, the inspector of prisons, and M. Morrel, his departure left no trace except in the memories of these three persons. As to the sailors of the *Pharaon*, they must have found snug berths elsewhere, for they also had disappeared.

Captain Gaumard, recovered from his illness, had returned from Palma. He delayed presenting himself at Morrel's, but the owner, hearing of his arrival, went to see him. The worthy shipowner knew, from Penelon's recital, of the captain's brave conduct during the storm, and tried to console him. He brought him also the amount of his wages, which Captain Gaumard had not dared to apply for.

As he descended the staircase, Morrel met Penelon, who was going up. Penelon had, it would seem, made good use of his money, for he was newly clad. When he saw his employer, the worthy tar seemed much embarrassed, drew on one side into the corner of the landing-place, passed his quid from one cheek to the other, stared stupidly with his great eyes, and only acknowledged the squeeze of the hand which Morrel as usual gave him by a slight pressure in return. Morrel attributed Penelon's embarrassment to the elegance of his attire; it was evident the good fellow had not gone to such an expense on his own account; he was, no doubt, engaged on board some other vessel, and thus his bashfulness arose from the fact of his not having, if we may so express ourselves, worn mourning for the *Pharaon* longer. Perhaps he had come to tell Captain Gaumard of his good luck, and to offer him employment from his new master.

"Worthy fellows!" said Morrel, as he went away, "may your

new master love you as I loved you, and be more fortunate than I have been!"

August rolled by in unceasing efforts on the part of Morrel to renew his credit or revive the old. On the 20th of August it was known at Marseilles that he had left town in the mailcoach, and then it was said that the bills would go to protest at the end of the month, and that Morrel had gone away and left his chief clerk Emmanuel, and his cashier Cocles, to meet the creditors. But, contrary to all expectation, when the 31st of August came, the house opened as usual, and Cocles appeared behind the grating of the counter, examined all bills presented with the usual scrutiny, and, from first to last, paid all with the usual precision. There came in, moreover, two drafts which M. Morrel had fully anticipated, and which Cocles paid as punctually as the bills which the shipowner had accepted. All this was incomprehensible, and then, with the tenacity peculiar to prophets of bad news, the failure was put off until the end of September.

On the 1st, Morrel returned; he was awaited by his family with extreme anxiety, for from this journey to Paris they hoped great things. Morrel had thought of Danglars, who was now immensely rich, and had lain under great obligations to Morrel in former days, since to him it was owing that Danglars entered the service of the Spanish banker, with whom he had laid the foundations of his vast wealth. It was said at this moment that Danglars was worth from six to eight millions of francs, and had unlimited credit. Danglars, then, without taking a crown from his pocket, could save Morrel; he had but to pass his word for a loan, and Morrel was saved. Morrel had long thought of Danglars, but had kept away from some instinctive motive, and had delayed as long as possible availing himself of this last resource. And Morrel was right, for he returned home crushed by the humiliation of a refusal.

Yet, on his arrival, Morrel did not utter a complaint, or say one harsh word. He embraced his weeping wife and daughter, pressed Emmanuel's hand with friendly warmth, and then going to his private room on the second floor had sent for Cocles.

"Then," said the two women to Emmanuel, "we are indeed ruined."

It was agreed in a brief council held among them, that Julie should write to her brother, who was in garrison at Nîmes, to come to them as speedily as possible. The poor women felt instinctively that they required all their strength to support the blow that impended. Besides, Maximilian Morrel, though hardly two-and-twenty, had great influence over his father.

He was a strong-minded, upright young man. At the time when he decided on his profession his father had no desire to choose for him, but had consulted young Maximilian's taste. He had at once declared for a military life, and had in consequence studied hard, passed brilliantly through the Polytechnic School, and left it as sub-lieutenant of the 53rd of the line. For a year he had held this rank, and expected promotion on the first vacancy. In his regiment Maximilian Morrel was noted for his rigid observance, not only of the obligations imposed on a soldier, but also of the duties of a man; and he thus gained the name of "the stoic." We need hardly say that many of those who gave him this epithet repeated it because they had heard it, and did not even know what it meant.

This was the young man whom his mother and sister called to their aid to sustain them under the serious trial which they felt they would soon have to endure. They had not mistaken the gravity of this event, for the moment after Morrel had entered his private office with Cocles, Julie saw the latter leave it pale, trembling, and his features betraying the utmost consternation. She would have questioned him as he passed by her, but the worthy creature hastened down the staircase with unusual precipitation, and only raised his hands to heaven and exclaimed:

"Oh, mademoiselle, mademoiselle, what a dreadful misfortune! Who could ever have believed it!"

A moment afterwards Julie saw him go upstairs carrying two

or three heavy ledgers, a portfolio, and a bag of money.

Morrel examined the ledgers, opened the portfolio, and counted the money. All his funds amounted to 6,000 or 8,000 francs, his bills receivable up to the 5th to 4,000 or 5,000, which, making the best of everything, gave him 14,000 francs to meet debts amounting to 287,500 francs. He had not even the means for making a possible settlement on account.

However, when Morrel went down to his dinner, he appeared very calm. This calmness was more alarming to the two women than the deepest dejection would have been. After dinner Morrel usually went out and used to take his coffee at the club of the Phocéens, and read the *Semaphore*; this day he did not leave the house, but returned to his office.

As to Cocles, he seemed completely bewildered. For part of the day he went into the courtyard, seated himself on a stone with his head bare and exposed to the blazing sun. Emmanuel tried to comfort the women, but his eloquence faltered. The young man was too well acquainted with the business of the house, not to feel that a great catastrophe hung over the Morrel family. Night came, the two women had watched, hoping that when he left his room Morrel would come to them, but they heard him pass before their door, and trying to conceal the noise of his footsteps. They listened; he went into his sleeping-room, and fastened the door inside. Madame Morrel sent her daughter to bed, and half an hour after Julie had retired, she rose, took off her shoes, and went stealthily along the passage, to see through the keyhole what her husband was doing.

In the passage she saw a retreating shadow; it was Julie, who, uneasy herself, had anticipated her mother. The young lady went towards Madame Morrel.

"He is writing," she said.

They had understood each other without speaking. Madame Morrel looked again through the keyhole, Morrel was writing; but Madame Morrel remarked, what her daughter had not observed, that her husband was writing on stamped paper. The terrible idea that he was writing his will flashed across her; she shuddered, and yet had not strength to utter a word.

Next day M. Morrel seemed as calm as ever, went into his office as usual, came to his breakfast punctually, and then, after dinner, he placed his daughter beside him, took her head in his arms, and held her for a long time against his bosom. In the evening, Julie told her mother, that although he was apparently so calm, she had noticed that her father's heart beat violently.

The next two days passed in much the same way. On the evening of the 4th of September, M. Morrel asked his daughter for the key of his study. Julie trembled at this request, which seemed to her of bad omen. Why did her father ask for this key which she always kept, and which was only taken from her in childhood as a punishment? The young girl looked at Morrel.

"What have I done wrong, father," she said, "that you should take this key from me?"

"Nothing, my dear," replied the unhappy man, the tears starting to his eyes at this simple question, "nothing, only I want it."

Julie made a pretence to feel for the key. "I must have left it in my room," she said.

And she went out, but instead of going to her apartment she hastened to consult Emmanuel.

"Do not give this key to your father," said he, "and tomorrow morning, if possible, do not quit him for a moment."

She questioned Emmanuel, but he knew nothing, or would not say what he knew.

During the night, between the 4th and 5th of September, Madame Morrel remained listening for every sound, and, until three o'clock in the morning, she heard her husband pacing the room in great agitation. It was three o'clock when he threw himself on the bed. The mother and daughter passed the night together. They had expected Maximilian since the previous evening. At eight o'clock in the morning Morrel entered their chamber. He was calm; but the agitation of the night was legible in his pale and careworn visage. They did not dare to ask him how he had slept. Morrel was kinder to his wife, more affectionate to his daughter, than he had ever been. He could not cease gazing at and kissing the sweet girl. Julie, mindful of Emmanuel's request, was following her father when he quitted the room, but he said to her quickly:

"Remain with your mother, dearest." Julie wished to accompany him. "I wish you to do so," said he.

This was the first time Morrel had ever so spoken, but he said it in a tone of paternal kindness, and Julie did not dare to disobey. She remained at the same spot standing mute and motionless. An instant afterwards the door opened, she felt two arms encircle her, and a mouth pressed her forehead. She looked up and uttered an exclamation of joy.

"Maximilian, my dearest brother!" she cried.

At these words Madame Morrel rose, and threw herself into her son's arms.

"Mother," said the young man, looking alternately at Madame Morrel and her daughter, "what has occurred what has happened? Your letter has frightened me, and I have come hither with all speed."

"Julie," said Madame Morrel, making a sign to the young man, "go and tell your father that Maximilian has just arrived."

The young lady rushed out of the apartment, but on the first step of the staircase she found a man holding a letter in his hand.

"Are you not Mademoiselle Julie Morrel?" inquired the man, with a strong Italian accent.

"Yes, sir," replied Julie with hesitation; "what is your pleasure? I do not know you."

"Read this letter," he said, handing it to her. Julie hesitated. "It concerns the best interests of your father," said the messenger. The young girl hastily took the letter from him. She opened it quickly and read:

"Go this moment to the Allées de Meilhan, enter the house No. 15, ask the porter for the key of the room on the fifth floor, enter the apartment, take from the corner of the mantelpiece a purse netted in red silk, and give it to your father. It is important that he should receive it before eleven o'clock. You promised to obey me implicitly. Remember your oath.

"Sinbad the Sailor."

The young girl uttered a joyful cry, raised her eyes, looked round to question the messenger, but he had disappeared. She cast her eyes again over the note to peruse it a second time, and saw there was a postscript. She read:

"It is important that you should fulfil this mission in person and alone. If you go accompanied by any other person, or should anyone else go in your place, the porter will reply that he does not know anything about it."

This postscript decreased greatly the young girl's happiness. Was there nothing to fear? was there not some snare laid for her? Her innocence had kept her in ignorance of the dangers that might assail a young girl of her age. But there is no need to know danger in order to fear it; indeed, it may be observed, that it is usually unknown perils that inspire the greatest terror.

Julie hesitated, and resolved to take counsel. Yet, through a singular impulse, it was neither to her mother nor her brother that she applied, but to Emmanuel. She hastened down and told him what had occurred on the day when the agent of Thomson & French had come to her father's, related the scene on the staircase, repeated the promise she had made, and showed him the letter.

"You must go, then, mademoiselle," said Emmanuel.

"Go there?" murmured Julie.

"Yes; I will accompany you."

"But did you not read that I must be alone?" said Julie.

"And you shall be alone," replied the young man. "I will await you at the corner of the Rue du Musée, and if you are so long absent as to make me uneasy, I will hasten to rejoin you, and woe to him of whom you shall have cause to complain to me!"

"Then, Emmanuel?" said the young girl with hesitation, "it is your opinion that I should obey this invitation?"

"Yes. Did not the messenger say your father's safety depended upon it?"

"But what danger threatens him, then, Emmanuel?" she asked.

Emmanuel hesitated a moment, but his desire to make Julie decide immediately made him reply.

"Listen," he said; "today is the 5th of September, is it not?"

"Yes."

"Today, then, at eleven o'clock, your father has nearly three hundred thousand francs to pay?"

"Yes, we know that."

"Well, then," continued Emmanuel, "we have not fifteen thousand francs in the house."

"What will happen then?"

"Why, if today before eleven o'clock your father has not found someone who will come to his aid, he will be compelled at twelve o'clock to declare himself a bankrupt."

"Oh, come, then, come!" cried she, hastening away with the young man.

During this time, Madame Morrel had told her son everything. The young man knew quite well that, after the succession of misfortunes which had befallen his father, great changes had taken place in the style of living and housekeeping; but he did not know that matters had reached such a point. He was thunderstruck. Then, rushing hastily out of the apartment, he ran upstairs, expecting to find his father in his study, but he rapped there in vain.

While he was yet at the door of the study he heard the bedroom door open, turned, and saw his father. Instead of going direct to his study, M. Morrel had returned to his bedchamber, which he was only this moment quitting. Morrel uttered a cry of surprise at the sight of his son, of whose arrival he was ignorant. He remained motionless on the spot, pressing with his left hand something he had concealed under his coat. Maximilian sprang down the staircase, and threw his arms round his father's neck; but suddenly he recoiled, and placed his right hand on Morrel's breast.

"Father," he exclaimed, turning pale as death, "what are you going to do with that brace of pistols under your coat?"

"Oh, this is what I feared!" said Morrel.

"Father, father, in Heaven's name," exclaimed the young man, "what are these weapons for?"

"Maximilian," replied Morrel, looking fixedly at his son, "you are a man, and a man of honor. Come, and I will explain to you."

And with a firm step Morrel went up to his study, while Maximilian followed him, trembling as he went. Morrel opened the door, and closed it behind his son; then, crossing the ante-room, went to his desk on which he placed the pistols, and pointed with his finger to an open ledger. In this ledger was made out an exact balance-sheet of his affairs. Morrel had to pay, within half an hour, 287,500 francs. All he possessed was 15,257 francs.

"Read!" said Morrel.

The young man was overwhelmed as he read. Morrel said not a word. What could he say? What need he add to such a desperate proof in figures?

"And have you done all that is possible, father, to meet this disastrous result?" asked the young man, after a moment's pause.

"I have," replied Morrel.

"You have no money coming in on which you can rely?"

"None."

"You have exhausted every resource?"

"All."

"And in half an hour," said Maximilian in a gloomy voice, "our name is dishonored!"

"Blood washes out dishonor," said Morrel.

"You are right, father; I understand you." Then extending his hand towards one of the pistols, he said, "There is one for you and one for me thanks!"

Morrel caught his hand. "Your mother your sister! Who will support them?"

A shudder ran through the young man's frame. "Father," he said, "do you reflect that you are bidding me to live?"

"Yes, I do so bid you," answered Morrel, "it is your duty. You have a calm, strong mind, Maximilian. Maximilian, you are no ordinary man. I make no requests or commands; I only ask you to examine my position as if it were your own, and then judge for yourself."

The young man reflected for a moment, then an expression of sublime resignation appeared in his eyes, and with a slow and sad gesture he took off his two epaulets, the insignia of his rank.

"Be it so, then, my father," he said, extending his hand to Morrel, "die in peace, my father; I will live."

Morrel was about to cast himself on his knees before his son, but Maximilian caught him in his arms, and those two noble hearts were pressed against each other for a moment.

"You know it is not my fault," said Morrel.

Maximilian smiled. "I know, father, you are the most honorable man I have ever known."

"Good, my son. And now there is no more to be said; go and rejoin your mother and sister."

"My father," said the young man, bending his knee, "bless me!"

Morrel took the head of his son between his two hands, drew him forward, and kissing his forehead several times said:

"Oh, yes, yes, I bless you in my own name, and in the name of three generations of irreproachable men, who say through me, 'The edifice which misfortune has destroyed, Providence may build up again.' On seeing me die such a death, the most inexorable will have pity on you. To you, perhaps, they will accord the time they have refused to me. Then do your best to keep our name free from dishonor. Go to work, labor, young man, struggle ardently and courageously; live, yourself, your mother and sister, with the most rigid economy, so that from day to day the property of those whom I leave in your hands may augment and fructify. Reflect how glorious a day it will be, how grand, how solemn, that day of complete restoration, on which you will say in this very office, 'My father died because he could not do what I have this day done; but he died calmly and peaceably, because in dying he knew what I should do.'"

"My father, my father!" cried the young man, "why should you not live?"

"If I live, all would be changed; if I live, interest would be converted into doubt, pity into hostility; if I live I am only a man who has broken his word, failed in his engagements in fact, only a bankrupt. If, on the contrary, I die, remember, Maximilian, my corpse is that of an honest but unfortunate man. Living, my best friends would avoid my house; dead, all Marseilles will follow me in tears to my last home. Living, you would feel shame at my name; dead, you may raise your head and say, 'I am the son of him you killed, because, for the first time, he has been compelled to break his word.'"

The young man uttered a groan, but appeared resigned.

"And now," said Morrel, "leave me alone, and endeavor to keep your mother and sister away."

"Will you not see my sister once more?" asked Maximilian. A last but final hope was concealed by the young man in the effect of this interview, and therefore he had suggested it.

Morrel shook his head. "I saw her this morning, and bade her adieu."

"Have you no particular commands to leave with me, my father?" inquired Maximilian in a faltering voice.

"Yes; my son, and a sacred command."

"Say it, my father."

"The house of Thomson & French is the only one who, from humanity, or, it may be, selfishness it is not for me to read men's hearts has had any pity for me. Its agent, who will in ten minutes present himself to receive the amount of a bill of 287,500 francs, I will not say granted, but offered me three months. Let this house be the first repaid, my son, and respect this man."

"Father, I will," said Maximilian.

"And now, once more, adieu," said Morrel. "Go, leave me; I would be alone. You will find my will in the secretaire in my bedroom."

The young man remained standing and motionless, having but the force of will and not the power of execution.

"Hear me, Maximilian," said his father. "Suppose I were a soldier like you, and ordered to carry a certain redoubt, and you knew I must be killed in the assault, would you not say to me, as you said just now, 'Go, father; for you are dishonored by delay, and death is preferable to shame!'"

"Yes, yes," said the young man, "yes;" and once again embracing his father with convulsive pressure, he said, "Be it so, my father."

And he rushed out of the study. When his son had left him, Morrel remained an instant standing with his eyes fixed on the door; then putting forth his arm, he pulled the bell. After a moment's interval, Cocles appeared.

It was no longer the same man the fearful revelations of the three last days had crushed him. This thought the house of Morrel is about to stop payment bent him to the earth more than twenty years would otherwise have done.

"My worthy Cocles," said Morrel in a tone impossible to describe, "do you remain in the antechamber. When the gentleman who came three months ago the agent of Thomson & French arrives, announce his arrival to me."

Cocles made no reply; he made a sign with his head, went into the anteroom, and seated himself. Morrel fell back in his chair, his eyes fixed on the clock; there were seven minutes left, that was all. The hand moved on with incredible rapidity, he seemed to see its motion.

What passed in the mind of this man at the supreme moment of his agony cannot be told in words. He was still comparatively young, he was surrounded by the loving care of a devoted family, but he had convinced himself by a course of reasoning, illogical perhaps, yet certainly plausible, that he must separate himself from all he held dear in the world, even life itself. To form the slightest idea of his feelings, one must have seen his face with its expression of enforced resignation and its tear-moistened eyes raised to heaven. The minute hand moved on. The pistols were loaded; he stretched forth his hand, took one up, and murmured his daughter's name. Then he laid it down, seized his pen, and wrote a few words. It seemed to him as if he had not taken a sufficient farewell of his beloved daughter. Then he turned again to the clock, counting time now not by minutes, but by seconds.

He took up the deadly weapon again, his lips parted and his eyes fixed on the clock, and then shuddered at the click of the trigger as he cocked the pistol. At this moment of mortal anguish the cold sweat came forth upon his brow, a pang stronger than death clutched at his heart-strings. He heard the door of the staircase creak on its hinges the clock gave its warning to strike eleven the door of his study opened. Morrel did not turn round he expected these words of Cocles, "The agent of Thomson & French."

He placed the muzzle of the pistol between his teeth. Suddenly he heard a cry it was his daughter's voice. He turned and saw Julie. The pistol fell from his hands.

"My father!" cried the young girl, out of breath, and half dead with joy "saved, you are saved!" And she threw herself into his arms, holding in her extended hand a red, netted silk purse.

"Saved, my child!" said Morrel; "what do you mean?"

"Yes, saved saved! See, see!" said the young girl.

Morrel took the purse, and started as he did so, for a vague remembrance reminded him that it once belonged to himself. At one end was the receipted bill for the 287,000 francs, and at the other was a diamond as large as a hazel-nut, with these words on a small slip of parchment: *Julie's Dowry.*

Morrel passed his hand over his brow; it seemed to him a dream. At this moment the clock struck eleven. He felt as if each stroke of the hammer fell upon his heart.

"Explain, my child," he said, "Explain, my child," he said, "explain where did you find this purse?"

"In a house in the Allées de Meilhan, No. 15, on the corner of a mantelpiece in a small room on the fifth floor."

"But," cried Morrel, "this purse is not yours!" Julie handed to her father the letter she had received in the morning.

"And did you go alone?" asked Morrel, after he had read it.

"Emmanuel accompanied me, father. He was to have waited for me at the corner of the Rue du Musée, but, strange to say, he was not there when I returned."

"Monsieur Morrel!" exclaimed a voice on the stairs; "Monsieur Morrel!"

"It is his voice!" said Julie. At this moment Emmanuel entered, his countenance full of animation and joy.

"The *Pharaon*!" he cried; "the *Pharaon*!"

"What! what! the *Pharaon*! Are you mad, Emmanuel? You know the vessel is lost."

"The *Pharaon*, sir they signal the *Pharaon*! The *Pharaon* is entering the harbor!"

Morrel fell back in his chair, his strength was failing him; his understanding weakened by such events, refused to comprehend such incredible, unheard-of, fabulous facts. But his son came in.

"Father," cried Maximilian, "how could you say the *Pharaon* was lost? The lookout has signalled her, and they say she is now coming into port."

"My dear friends," said Morrel, "if this be so, it must be a miracle of heaven! Impossible, impossible!"

But what was real and not less incredible was the purse he held in his hand, the acceptance receipted the splendid diamond.

"Ah, sir," exclaimed Cocles, "what can it mean? the *Pharaon*?"

"Come, dear ones," said Morrel, rising from his seat, "let us go and see, and Heaven have pity upon us if it be false intelligence!"

They all went out, and on the stairs met Madame Morrel, who had been afraid to go up into the study. In a moment they were at the Canebière. There was a crowd on the pier. All the crowd gave way before Morrel. "The *Pharaon*! the *Pharaon*!"

said every voice.

And, wonderful to see, in front of the tower of Saint-Jean, was a ship bearing on her stern these words, printed in white letters, "The *Pharaon*, Morrel & Son, of Marseilles." She was the exact duplicate of the other *Pharaon*, and loaded, as that had been, with cochineal and indigo. She cast anchor, clued up sails, and on the deck was Captain Gaumard giving orders, and good old Penelon making signals to M. Morrel. To doubt any longer was impossible; there was the evidence of the senses, and ten thousand persons who came to corroborate the testimony.

As Morrel and his son embraced on the pier-head, in the presence and amid the applause of the whole city witnessing this event, a man, with his face half-covered by a black beard, and who, concealed behind the sentry-box, watched the scene with delight, uttered these words in a low tone:

"Be happy, noble heart, be blessed for all the good thou hast done and wilt do hereafter, and let my gratitude remain in obscurity like your good deeds."

And with a smile expressive of supreme content, he left his hiding-place, and without being observed, descended one of the flights of steps provided for debarkation, and hailing three times, shouted "Jacopo, Jacopo, Jacopo!"

Then a launch came to shore, took him on board, and conveyed him to a yacht splendidly fitted up, on whose deck he sprung with the activity of a sailor; thence he once again looked towards Morrel, who, weeping with joy, was shaking hands most cordially with all the crowd around him, and thanking with a look the unknown benefactor whom he seemed to be seeking in the skies.

"And now," said the unknown, "farewell kindness, humanity, and gratitude! Farewell to all the feelings that expand the heart! I have been Heaven's substitute to recompense the good now the god of vengeance yields to me his power to punish the wicked!"

At these words he gave a signal, and, as if only awaiting this signal, the yacht instantly put out to sea.

Chapter 4

Italy: Sinbad the Sailor

T owards the beginning of the year 1838, two young men belonging to the first society of Paris, the Viscount Albert de Morcerf and the Baron Franz d'Épinay, were at Florence. They had agreed to see the Carnival at Rome that year, and that Franz, who for the last three or four years had inhabited Italy, should act as cicerone to Albert.

As it is no inconsiderable affair to spend the Carnival at Rome, especially when you have no great desire to sleep on the Piazza del Popolo, or the Campo Vaccino, they wrote to Signor Pastrini, the proprietor of the Hôtel de Londres, Piazza di Spagna, to reserve comfortable apartments for them. Signor Pastrini replied that he had only two rooms and a parlor on the third floor, which he offered at the low charge of a louis per diem. They accepted his offer; but wishing to make the best use of the time that was left, Albert started for Naples. As for Franz, he remained at Florence, and after having passed a few days in exploring the paradise of the Cascine, and spending two or three evenings at the houses of the Florentine nobility, he took a fancy into his head (having already visited Corsica, the cradle of Bonaparte) to visit Elba, the waiting-place of Napoleon.

One evening he cast off the painter of a sailboat from the iron ring that secured it to the dock at Leghorn, wrapped himself in his coat and lay down, and said to the crew, "To the Island of Elba!"

The boat shot out of the harbor like a bird and the next morning Franz disembarked at Porto-Ferrajo. He traversed the island, after having followed the traces which the footsteps of the giant have left, and re-embarked for Marciana.

Two hours after he again landed at Pianosa, where he was assured that red partridges abounded. The sport was bad; Franz only succeeded in killing a few partridges, and, like every unsuccessful sportsman, he returned to the boat very much out of temper.

"Ah, if your excellency chose," said the captain, "you might have capital sport."

"Where?"

"Do you see that island?" continued the captain, pointing to a conical pile rising from the indigo sea.

"Well, what is this island?"

"The Island of Monte Cristo."

"But I have no permission to shoot over this island."

"Your excellency does not require a permit, for the island is uninhabited."

"Ah, indeed!" said the young man. "A desert island in the midst of the Mediterranean must be a curiosity."

"It is very natural; this island is a mass of rocks, and does not contain an acre of land capable of cultivation."

ALEXANDRE DUMAS

"To whom does this island belong?"

"To Tuscany."

"What game shall I find there!"

"Thousands of wild goats."

"Who live upon the stones, I suppose," said Franz with an incredulous smile.

"No, but by browsing the shrubs and trees that grow out of the crevices of the rocks."

"Where can I sleep?"

"On shore in the grottos, or on board in your cloak; besides, if your excellency pleases, we can leave as soon as you like we can sail as well by night as by day, and if the wind drops we can use our oars."

As Franz had sufficient time, and his apartments at Rome were not yet available, he accepted the proposition. Upon his answer in the affirmative, the sailors exchanged a few words together in a low tone. "Well," asked he, "what now? Is there any difficulty in the way?"

"No." replied the captain, "but we must warn your excellency that the island is an infected port."

"What do you mean?"

"Monte Cristo although uninhabited, yet serves occasionally as a refuge for the smugglers and pirates who come from Corsica, Sardinia, and Africa, and if it becomes known that we have been there, we shall have to perform quarantine for six days on our return to Leghorn."

"The deuce! That puts a different face on the matter. Six days! Why, that's as long as the Almighty took to make the world! Too long a wait too long."

"But who will say your excellency has been to Monte Cristo?"

"Oh, I shall not," cried Franz.

"Nor I, nor I," chorused the sailors.

"Then steer for Monte Cristo."

The captain gave his orders, the helm was put up, and the boat was soon sailing in the direction of the island. Franz waited until all was in order, and when the sail was filled, and the four sailors had taken their places three forward, and one at the helm he resumed the conversation. "Gaetano," said he to the captain, "you tell me Monte Cristo serves as a refuge for pirates, who are, it seems to me, a very different kind of game from the goats."

"Yes, your excellency, and it is true."

"I knew there were smugglers, but I thought that since the capture of Algiers, and the destruction of the regency, pirates existed only in the romances of Cooper and Captain Marryat."

"Your excellency is mistaken; there are pirates, like the bandits who were believed to have been exterminated by Pope Leo XII., and who yet, every day, rob travellers at the gates of Rome. Has not your excellency heard that the French *chargé d'affaires* was robbed six months ago within five hundred paces of Velletri?"

"Oh, yes, I heard that."

"Well, then, if, like us, your excellency lived at Leghorn, you would hear, from time to time, that a little merchant vessel, or an English yacht that was expected at Bastia, at Porto-Ferrajo, or at Civita Vecchia, has not arrived; no one knows what has become of it, but, doubtless, it has struck on a rock and foundered. Now this rock it has met has been a long and narrow boat, manned by six or eight men, who have surprised and plundered it, some dark and stormy night, near some desert and gloomy island, as bandits plunder a carriage in the recesses of a forest."

"But," asked Franz, who lay wrapped in his cloak at the bottom of the boat, "why do not those who have been plundered complain to the French, Sardinian, or Tuscan governments?"

"Why?" said Gaetano with a smile.

"Yes, why?"

"Because, in the first place, they transfer from the vessel to their own boat whatever they think worth taking, then they bind the crew hand and foot, they attach to everyone's neck a four-and-twenty-pound ball, a large hole is chopped in the vessel's bottom, and then they leave her. At the end of ten minutes the vessel begins to roll heavily and settle down. First one gun'l goes under, then the other. Then they lift and sink again, and both go under at once. All at once there's a noise like a cannon that's the air blowing up the deck. Soon the water rushes out of the scupper-holes like a whale spouting, the vessel gives a last groan, spins round and round, and disappears, forming a vast whirlpool in the ocean, and then all is over, so that in five minutes nothing but the eye of God can see the vessel where she lies at the bottom of the sea. Do you understand now," said the captain, "why no complaints are made to the government, and why the vessel never reaches port?"

It is probable that if Gaetano had related this previous to proposing the expedition, Franz would have hesitated, but now that they had started, he thought it would be cowardly to draw back. He was one of those men who do not rashly court danger, but if danger presents itself, combat it with the most unalterable coolness. Calm and resolute, he treated any peril as he would an adversary in a duel, calculated its probable method of approach; retreated, if at all, as a point of strategy and not from cowardice; was quick to see an opening for attack, and won victory at a single thrust.

"Bah!" said he, "I have travelled through Sicily and Calabria I have sailed two months in the Archipelago, and yet I never saw even the shadow of a bandit or a pirate."

"I did not tell your excellency this to deter you from your project," replied Gaetano, "but you questioned me, and I have answered; that's all."

"Yes, and your conversation is most interesting; and as I wish to enjoy it as long as possible, steer for Monte Cristo."

The wind blew strongly, the boat made six or seven knots an hour, and they were rapidly reaching the end of their voyage. As they drew near the island seemed to lift from the sea, and the air was so clear that they could already distinguish the rocks heaped on one another, like cannon balls in an arsenal, with green bushes and trees growing in the crevices. As for the sailors, although they appeared perfectly tranquil yet it was evident that they were on the alert, and that they carefully watched the glassy surface over which they were sailing, and on which a few fishing-boats, with their white sails, were alone visible.

They were within fifteen miles of Monte Cristo when the sun began to set behind Corsica, whose mountains appeared against the sky, showing their rugged peaks in bold relief; this mass of rock, like the giant Adamastor, rose dead ahead, a formidable barrier, and intercepting the light that gilded its massive peaks so that the voyagers were in shadow. Little by little the shadow rose higher and seemed to drive before it the last rays of the expiring day; at last the reflection rested on the summit of the mountain, where it paused an instant, like the fiery crest of a volcano, then gloom gradually covered the summit as it had covered the base, and the island now only appeared to be a gray mountain that grew continually darker; half an hour after, the night was quite dark.

Fortunately, the mariners were used to these latitudes, and knew every rock in the Tuscan Archipelago; for in the midst of this obscurity Franz was not without uneasiness Corsica had long since disappeared, and Monte Cristo itself was invisible; but the sailors seemed, like the lynx, to see in the dark, and the pilot who steered did not evince the slightest hesitation.

An hour had passed since the sun had set, when Franz fancied he saw, at a quarter of a mile to the left, a dark mass, but he could not precisely make out what it was, and fearing to excite the mirth of the sailors by mistaking a floating cloud for land, he remained silent; suddenly a great light appeared on the strand; land might resemble a cloud, but the fire was not a meteor.

"What is this light?" asked he.

"Hush!" said the captain; "it is a fire."

"But you told me the island was uninhabited?"

"I said there were no fixed habitations on it, but I said also that it served sometimes as a harbor for smugglers."

"And for pirates?"

"And for pirates," returned Gaetano, repeating Franz's words. "It is for that reason I have given orders to pass the island, for, as you see, the fire is behind us."

"But this fire?" continued Franz. "It seems to me rather re-assuring than otherwise; men who did not wish to be seen would not light a fire."

"Oh, that goes for nothing," said Gaetano. "If you can guess the position of the island in the darkness, you will see that the fire cannot be seen from the side or from Pianosa, but only from the sea."

"You think, then, this fire indicates the presence of unpleasant neighbors?"

"That is what we must find out," returned Gaetano, fixing his eyes on this terrestrial star.

"How can you find out?"

"You shall see."

Gaetano consulted with his companions, and after five minutes' discussion a manœuvre was executed which caused the vessel to tack about, they returned the way they had come, and in a few minutes the fire disappeared, hidden by an elevation of the land. The pilot again changed the course of the boat, which rapidly approached the island, and was soon within fifty paces of it. Gaetano lowered the sail, and the boat came to rest. All this was done in silence, and from the moment that their course was changed not a word was spoken.

Gaetano, who had proposed the expedition, had taken all the responsibility on himself; the four sailors fixed their eyes on him, while they got out their oars and held themselves in readiness to row away, which, thanks to the darkness, would not be difficult. As for Franz, he examined his arms with the utmost coolness; he had two double-barrelled guns and a rifle; he loaded them, looked at the priming, and waited quietly.

During this time the captain had thrown off his vest and shirt, and secured his trousers round his waist; his feet were naked, so he had no shoes and stockings to take off; after these preparations he placed his finger on his lips, and lowering himself noiselessly into the sea, swam towards the shore with such precaution that it was impossible to hear the slightest sound; he could only be traced by the phosphorescent line in his wake. This track soon disappeared; it was evident that he had touched the shore.

Everyone on board remained motionless for half an hour, when the same luminous track was again observed, and the swimmer was soon on board.

"Well?" exclaimed Franz and the sailors in unison.

"They are Spanish smugglers," said he; "they have with them two Corsican bandits."

"And what are these Corsican bandits doing here with Spanish smugglers?"

"Alas," returned the captain with an accent of the most profound pity, "we ought always to help one another. Very often the bandits are hard pressed by gendarmes or carbineers; well, they see a vessel, and good fellows like us on board, they come and demand hospitality of us; you can't refuse help to a poor hunted devil; we receive them, and for greater security we stand out to sea. This costs us nothing, and saves the life, or at least the liberty, of a fellow-creature, who on the first occasion returns the service by pointing out some safe spot where we can land our goods without interruption."

"Ah!" said Franz, "then you are a smuggler occasionally, Gaetano?"

"Your excellency, we must live somehow," returned the other, smiling impenetrably.

"Then you know the men who are now on Monte Cristo?"

"Oh, yes, we sailors are like freemasons, and recognize each other by signs."

"And do you think we have nothing to fear if we land?"

"Nothing at all; smugglers are not thieves."

"But these two Corsican bandits?" said Franz, calculating the chances of peril.

"It is not their fault that they are bandits, but that of the authorities."

"How so?"

"Because they are pursued for having made a stiff, as if it was not in a Corsican's nature to revenge himself."

"What do you mean by having made a stiff? having assassinated a man?" said Franz, continuing his investigation.

"I mean that they have killed an enemy, which is a very different thing," returned the captain.

"Well," said the young man, "let us demand hospitality of these smugglers and bandits. Do you think they will grant it?"

"Without doubt."

"How many are they?"

"Four, and the two bandits make six."

"Just our number, so that if they prove troublesome, we shall be able to hold them in check; so, for the last time, steer to Monte Cristo."

"Yes, but your excellency will permit us to take all due precautions."

"By all means, be as wise as Nestor and as prudent as Ulysses; I do more than permit, I exhort you."

"Silence, then!" said Gaetano.

Everyone obeyed. For a man who, like Franz, viewed his position in its true light, it was a grave one. He was alone in the darkness with sailors whom he did not know, and who had no reason to be devoted to him; who knew that he had several thousand francs in his belt, and who had often examined his weapons, which were very beautiful, if not with envy, at least with curiosity. On the other hand, he was about to land, without any other escort than these men, on an island which had, indeed, a very religious name, but which did not seem to Franz likely to afford him much hospitality, thanks to the smugglers and bandits. The history of the scuttled vessels, which had appeared improbable during the day, seemed very probable at night; placed as he was between two possible sources of danger, he kept his eye on the crew, and his gun in his hand.

The sailors had again hoisted sail, and the vessel was once more cleaving the waves. Through the darkness Franz, whose

eyes were now more accustomed to it, could see the loom-
ing shore along which the boat was sailing, and then, as they
rounded a rocky point, he saw the fire more brilliant than
ever, and about it five or six persons seated. The blaze illumined the sea for a hundred paces around. Gaetano skirted the
light, carefully keeping the boat in the shadow; then, when
they were opposite the fire, he steered to the centre of the
circle, singing a fishing song, of which his companions sung
the chorus.

At the first words of the song the men seated round the fire
arose and approached the landing-place, their eyes fixed on
the boat, evidently seeking to know who the new-comers
were and what were their intentions. They soon appeared satisfied and returned (with the exception of one, who remained
at the shore) to their fire, at which the carcass of a goat was
roasting. When the boat was within twenty paces of the shore,
the man on the beach, who carried a carbine, presented arms
after the manner of a sentinel, and cried, "Who comes there?"
in Sardinian.

Franz coolly cocked both barrels. Gaetano then exchanged a
few words with this man which the traveller did not understand, but which evidently concerned him.

"Will your excellency give your name, or remain *incognito*?"
asked the captain.

"My name must rest unknown," replied Franz; "merely say I
am a Frenchman travelling for pleasure."

As soon as Gaetano had transmitted this answer, the sentinel
gave an order to one of the men seated round the fire, who rose
and disappeared among the rocks. Not a word was spoken,
everyone seemed occupied, Franz with his disembarkment,
the sailors with their sails, the smugglers with their goat; but
in the midst of all this carelessness it was evident that they
mutually observed each other.

The man who had disappeared returned suddenly on the opposite side to that by which he had left; he made a sign with
his head to the sentinel, who, turning to the boat, said, "*S'ac-*

commodi." The Italian *s'accommodi* is untranslatable; it means at once, "Come, enter, you are welcome; make yourself at home; you are the master." It is like that Turkish phrase of Molière's that so astonished the bourgeois gentleman by the number of things implied in its utterance.

The sailors did not wait for a second invitation; four strokes of the oar brought them to land; Gaetano sprang to shore, exchanged a few words with the sentinel, then his comrades disembarked, and lastly came Franz. One of his guns was swung over his shoulder, Gaetano had the other, and a sailor held his rifle; his dress, half artist, half dandy, did not excite any suspicion, and, consequently, no disquietude. The boat was moored to the shore, and they advanced a few paces to find a comfortable bivouac; but, doubtless, the spot they chose did not suit the smuggler who filled the post of sentinel, for he cried out:

"Not that way, if you please."

Gaetano faltered an excuse, and advanced to the opposite side, while two sailors kindled torches at the fire to light them on their way.

They advanced about thirty paces, and then stopped at a small esplanade surrounded with rocks, in which seats had been cut, not unlike sentry-boxes. Around in the crevices of the rocks grew a few dwarf oaks and thick bushes of myrtles. Franz lowered a torch, and saw by the mass of cinders that had accumulated that he was not the first to discover this retreat, which was, doubtless, one of the halting-places of the wandering visitors of Monte Cristo.

As for his suspicions, once on *terra firma*, once that he had seen the indifferent, if not friendly, appearance of his hosts, his anxiety had quite disappeared, or rather, at sight of the goat, had turned to appetite. He mentioned this to Gaetano, who replied that nothing could be more easy than to prepare a supper when they had in their boat, bread, wine, half a dozen partridges, and a good fire to roast them by.

"Besides," added he, "if the smell of their roast meat tempts you, I will go and offer them two of our birds for a slice."

"You are a born diplomat," returned Franz; "go and try."

Meanwhile the sailors had collected dried sticks and branches with which they made a fire. Franz waited impatiently, inhaling the aroma of the roasted meat, when the captain returned with a mysterious air.

"Well," said Franz, "anything new? do they refuse?"

"On the contrary," returned Gaetano, "the chief, who was told you were a young Frenchman, invites you to sup with him."

"Well," observed Franz, "this chief is very polite, and I see no objection the more so as I bring my share of the supper."

"Oh, it is not that; he has plenty, and to spare, for supper; but he makes one condition, and rather a peculiar one, before he will receive you at his house."

"His house? Has he built one here, then?"

"No, but he has a very comfortable one all the same, so they say."

"You know this chief, then?"

"I have heard talk of him."

"Favorably or otherwise?"

"Both."

"The deuce! and what is this condition?"

"That you are blindfolded, and do not take off the bandage until he himself bids you."

Franz looked at Gaetano, to see, if possible, what he thought of this proposal. "Ah," replied he, guessing Franz's thought, "I know this is a serious matter."

"What should you do in my place?"

"I, who have nothing to lose, I should go."

"You would accept?"

"Yes, were it only out of curiosity."

"There is something very peculiar about this chief, then?"

"Listen," said Gaetano, lowering his voice, "I do not know if what they say is true" he stopped to see if anyone was near.

"What do they say?"

"That this chief inhabits a cavern to which the Pitti Palace is nothing."

"What nonsense!" said Franz, reseating himself.

"It is no nonsense; it is quite true. Cama, the pilot of the *Saint Ferdinand*, went in once, and he came back amazed, vowing that such treasures were only to be heard of in fairy tales."

"Do you know," observed Franz, "that with such stories you make me think of Ali Baba's enchanted cavern?"

"I tell you what I have been told."

"Then you advise me to accept?"

"Oh, I don't say that; your excellency will do as you please; I should be sorry to advise you in the matter."

Franz pondered the matter for a few moments, concluded that a man so rich could not have any intention of plundering him of what little he had, and seeing only the prospect of a good supper, accepted. Gaetano departed with the reply. Franz was prudent, and wished to learn all he possibly could concerning his host. He turned towards the sailor, who, during this dialogue, had sat gravely plucking the partridges with the air of a man proud of his office, and asked him how these men had landed, as no vessel of any kind was visible.

"Never mind that," returned the sailor, "I know their vessel."

"Is it a very beautiful vessel?"

"I would not wish for a better to sail round the world."

"Of what burden is she?"

"About a hundred tons; but she is built to stand any weather. She is what the English call a yacht."

"Where was she built?"

"I know not; but my own opinion is she is a Genoese."

"And how did a leader of smugglers," continued Franz, "venture to build a vessel designed for such a purpose at Genoa?"

"I did not say that the owner was a smuggler," replied the sailor.

"No; but Gaetano did, I thought."

"Gaetano had only seen the vessel from a distance, he had not then spoken to anyone."

"And if this person be not a smuggler, who is he?"

"A wealthy signor, who travels for his pleasure."

"Come," thought Franz, "he is still more mysterious, since the two accounts do not agree."

"What is his name?"

"If you ask him, he says Sinbad the Sailor; but I doubt if it be his real name."

"Sinbad the Sailor?"

"Yes."

"And where does he reside?"

"On the sea."

"What country does he come from?"

"I do not know."

"Have you ever seen him?"

"Sometimes."

"What sort of a man is he?"

"Your excellency will judge for yourself."

"Where will he receive me?"

"No doubt in the subterranean palace Gaetano told you of."

"Have you never had the curiosity, when you have landed and found this island deserted, to seek for this enchanted palace?"

"Oh, yes, more than once, but always in vain; we examined the grotto all over, but we never could find the slightest trace of any opening; they say that the door is not opened by a key, but a magic word."

"Decidedly," muttered Franz, "this is an Arabian Nights' adventure."

"His excellency waits for you," said a voice, which he recognized as that of the sentinel. He was accompanied by two of the yacht's crew.

Franz drew his handkerchief from his pocket, and presented it to the man who had spoken to him. Without uttering a word, they bandaged his eyes with a care that showed their apprehensions of his committing some indiscretion. Afterwards he was made to promise that he would not make the least attempt to raise the bandage. He promised.

Then his two guides took his arms, and he went on, guided by them, and preceded by the sentinel. After going about thirty paces, he smelt the appetizing odor of the kid that was roasting, and knew thus that he was passing the bivouac; they then led him on about fifty paces farther, evidently advancing towards that part of the shore where they would not allow Gaetano to go a refusal he could now comprehend.

Presently, by a change in the atmosphere, he knew that they were entering a cave; after going on for a few seconds more he heard a crackling, and it seemed to him as though the atmosphere again changed, and became balmy and perfumed. At length his feet touched on a thick and soft carpet, and his guides let go their hold of him. There was a moment's silence, and then a voice, in excellent French, although, with a foreign accent, said:

"Welcome, sir. I beg you will remove your bandage."

It may be supposed, then, Franz did not wait for a repetition of this permission, but took off the handkerchief, and found himself in the presence of a man from thirty-eight to forty years of age, dressed in a Tunisian costume, that is to say, a red cap with a long blue silk tassel, a vest of black cloth embroidered with gold, pantaloons of deep red, large and full gaiters of the same color, embroidered with gold like the vest, and yellow slippers; he had a splendid cashmere round his waist, and a small sharp and crooked cangiar was passed through his girdle.

Although of a paleness that was almost livid, this man had a remarkably handsome face; his eyes were penetrating and sparkling; his nose, quite straight, and projecting direct from the brow, was of the pure Greek type, while his teeth, as white as pearls, were set off to admiration by the black moustache that encircled them.

His pallor was so peculiar, that it seemed to pertain to one who had been long entombed, and who was incapable of resuming the healthy glow and hue of life. He was not particularly tall, but extremely well made, and, like the men of the South, had small hands and feet. But what astonished Franz, who had treated Gaetano's description as a fable, was the splendor of the apartment in which he found himself.

The entire chamber was lined with crimson brocade, worked with flowers of gold. In a recess was a kind of divan, surmounted with a stand of Arabian swords in silver scabbards, and the handles resplendent with gems; from the ceiling hung a lamp of Venetian glass, of beautiful shape and color, while the feet rested on a Turkey carpet, in which they sunk to the instep; tapestry hung before the door by which Franz had entered, and also in front of another door, leading into a second apartment which seemed to be brilliantly illuminated.

The host gave Franz time to recover from his surprise, and, moreover, returned look for look, not even taking his eyes off him.

"Sir," he said, after a pause, "a thousand excuses for the precaution taken in your introduction hither; but as, during the greater portion of the year, this island is deserted, if the secret of this abode were discovered, I should doubtless, find on my return my temporary retirement in a state of great disorder, which would be exceedingly annoying, not for the loss it occasioned me, but because I should not have the certainty I now possess of separating myself from all the rest of mankind at pleasure. Let me now endeavor to make you forget this temporary unpleasantness, and offer you what no doubt you did not expect to find here that is to say, a tolerable supper and pretty comfortable beds."

"*Ma foi*, my dear sir," replied Franz, "make no apologies. I have always observed that they bandage people's eyes who penetrate enchanted palaces, for instance, those of Raoul in the *Huguenots*, and really I have nothing to complain of, for what I see makes me think of the wonders of the *Arabian Nights*."

"Alas! I may say with Lucullus, if I could have anticipated the honor of your visit, I would have prepared for it. But such as is my hermitage, it is at your disposal; such as is my supper, it is yours to share, if you will. Ali, is the supper ready?"

At this moment the tapestry moved aside, and a Nubian, black as ebony, and dressed in a plain white tunic, made a sign to his master that all was prepared in the dining-room.

"Now," said the unknown to Franz, "I do not know if you are of my opinion, but I think nothing is more annoying than to remain two or three hours together without knowing by name or appellation how to address one another. Pray observe, that I too much respect the laws of hospitality to ask your name or title. I only request you to give me one by which I may have the pleasure of addressing you. As for myself, that I may put you at your ease, I tell you that I am generally called 'Sinbad the Sailor.'"

"And I," replied Franz, "will tell you, as I only require his wonderful lamp to make me precisely like Aladdin, that I see no reason why at this moment I should not be called Aladdin. That will keep us from going away from the East whither I am tempted to think I have been conveyed by some good genius."

"Well, then, Signor Aladdin," replied the singular Amphitryon, "you heard our repast announced, will you now take the trouble to enter the dining-room, your humble servant going first to show the way?"

At these words, moving aside the tapestry, Sinbad preceded his guest. Franz now looked upon another scene of enchantment; the table was splendidly covered, and once convinced of this important point he cast his eyes around him. The dining-room was scarcely less striking than the room he had just left; it was entirely of marble, with antique bas-reliefs of priceless value; and at the four corners of this apartment, which was oblong, were four magnificent statues, having baskets in their hands. These baskets contained four pyramids of most splendid fruit; there were Sicily pine-apples, pomegranates from Malaga, oranges from the Balearic Isles, peaches from France, and dates from Tunis.

The supper consisted of a roast pheasant garnished with Corsican blackbirds; a boar's ham with jelly, a quarter of a kid with tartar sauce, a glorious turbot, and a gigantic lobster. Between these large dishes were smaller ones containing various dainties. The dishes were of silver, and the plates of Japanese china.

Franz rubbed his eyes in order to assure himself that this was not a dream. Ali alone was present to wait at table, and acquitted himself so admirably, that the guest complimented his host thereupon.

"Yes," replied he, while he did the honors of the supper with much ease and grace "yes, he is a poor devil who is much devoted to me, and does all he can to prove it. He remembers that I saved his life, and as he has a regard for his head, he feels some gratitude towards me for having kept it on his shoulders."

Ali approached his master, took his hand, and kissed it.

"Would it be impertinent, Signor Sinbad," said Franz, "to ask you the particulars of this kindness?"

"Oh, they are simple enough," replied the host. "It seems the fellow had been caught wandering nearer to the harem of the Bey of Tunis than etiquette permits to one of his color, and he was condemned by the Bey to have his tongue cut out, and his hand and head cut off; the tongue the first day, the hand the second, and the head the third. I always had a desire to have a mute in my service, so learning the day his tongue was cut out, I went to the Bey, and proposed to give him for Ali a splendid double-barreled gun, which I knew he was very desirous of having. He hesitated a moment, he was so very desirous to complete the poor devil's punishment. But when I added to the gun an English cutlass with which I had shivered his highness's yataghan to pieces, the Bey yielded, and agreed to forgive the hand and head, but on condition that the poor fellow never again set foot in Tunis. This was a useless clause in the bargain, for whenever the coward sees the first glimpse of the shores of Africa, he runs down below, and can only be induced to appear again when we are out of sight of that quarter of the globe."

Franz remained a moment silent and pensive, hardly knowing what to think of the half-kindness, half-cruelty, with which his host related the brief narrative.

"And like the celebrated sailor whose name you have assumed," he said, by way of changing the conversation, "you pass your life in travelling?"

"Yes. I made a vow at a time when I little thought I should ever be able to accomplish it," said the unknown with a singular smile; "and I made some others also which I hope I may fulfil in due season."

Although Sinbad pronounced these words with much calmness, his eyes gave forth gleams of extraordinary ferocity.

"You have suffered a great deal, sir?" said Franz inquiringly.

Sinbad started and looked fixedly at him, as he replied, "What makes you suppose so?"

"Everything," answered Franz, "your voice, your look, your pallid complexion, and even the life you lead."

"I? I live the happiest life possible, the real life of a pasha. I am king of all creation. I am pleased with one place, and stay there; I get tired of it, and leave it; I am free as a bird and have wings like one; my attendants obey my slightest wish. Sometimes I amuse myself by delivering some bandit or criminal from the bonds of the law. Then I have my mode of dispensing justice, silent and sure, without respite or appeal, which condemns or pardons, and which no one sees. Ah, if you had tasted my life, you would not desire any other, and would never return to the world unless you had some great project to accomplish there."

"Revenge, for instance!" observed Franz.

The unknown fixed on the young man one of those looks which penetrate into the depth of the heart and thoughts. "And why revenge?" he asked.

"Because," replied Franz, "you seem to me like a man who, persecuted by society, has a fearful account to settle with it."

"Ah!" responded Sinbad, laughing with his singular laugh, which displayed his white and sharp teeth. "You have not guessed rightly. Such as you see me I am, a sort of philosopher, and one day perhaps I shall go to Paris to rival Monsieur Appert, and the man in the little blue cloak."

"And will that be the first time you ever took that journey?"

"Yes; it will. I must seem to you by no means curious, but I assure you that it is not my fault I have delayed it so long it will happen one day or the other."

"And do you propose to make this journey very shortly?"

"I do not know; it depends on circumstances which depend on certain arrangements."

"I should like to be there at the time you come, and I will endeavor to repay you, as far as lies in my power, for your liberal hospitality displayed to me at Monte Cristo."

"I should avail myself of your offer with pleasure," replied the host, "but, unfortunately, if I go there, it will be, in all probability, *incognito*."

The supper appeared to have been supplied solely for Franz, for the unknown scarcely touched one or two dishes of the splendid banquet to which his guest did ample justice. Then Ali brought on the dessert, or rather took the baskets from the hands of the statues and placed them on the table. Between the two baskets he placed a small silver cup with a silver cover. The care with which Ali placed this cup on the table roused Franz's curiosity. He raised the cover and saw a kind of greenish paste, something like preserved angelica, but which was perfectly unknown to him. He replaced the lid, as ignorant of what the cup contained as he was before he had looked at it, and then casting his eyes towards his host he saw him smile at his disappointment.

"You cannot guess," said he, "what there is in that small vase, can you?"

"No, I really cannot."

"Well, then, that green preserve is nothing less than the ambrosia which Hebe served at the table of Jupiter."

"But," replied Franz, "this ambrosia, no doubt, in passing through mortal hands has lost its heavenly appellation and assumed a human name; in vulgar phrase, what may you term this composition, for which, to tell the truth, I do not feel any particular desire?"

"Ah, thus it is that our material origin is revealed," cried Sinbad; "we frequently pass so near to happiness without seeing, without regarding it, or if we do see and regard it, yet without recognizing it. Are you a man for the substantials, and is gold your god? taste this, and the mines of Peru, Guzerat, and Golconda are opened to you. Are you a man of imagination a poet? taste this, and the boundaries of possibility disappear; the fields of infinite space open to you, you advance free in heart, free in mind, into the boundless realms of unfettered reverie. Are you ambitious, and do you seek after the greatnesses of the earth? taste this, and in an hour you will be a king, not a king of a petty kingdom hidden in some corner of Europe like France, Spain, or England, but king of the world, king of the universe, king of creation; without bowing at the feet of Satan, you will be king and master of all the kingdoms of the earth. Is it not tempting what I offer you, and is it not an easy thing, since it is only to do thus? look!"

At these words he uncovered the small cup which contained the substance so lauded, took a teaspoonful of the magic sweetmeat, raised it to his lips, and swallowed it slowly with his eyes half shut and his head bent backwards. Franz did not disturb him whilst he absorbed his favorite sweetmeat, but when he had finished, he inquired:

"What, then, is this precious stuff?"

"Did you ever hear," he replied, "of the Old Man of the Mountain, who attempted to assassinate Philippe Auguste?"

"Of course I have."

"Well, you know he reigned over a rich valley which was overhung by the mountain whence he derived his picturesque name. In this valley were magnificent gardens planted by Hassen-ben-Sabah, and in these gardens isolated pavilions. Into these pavilions he admitted the elect, and there, says Marco Polo, gave them to eat a certain herb, which transported them to Paradise, in the midst of ever-blooming shrubs, ever-ripe fruit, and ever-lovely virgins. What these happy persons took for reality was but a dream; but it was a dream so soft, so voluptuous, so enthralling, that they sold themselves body and soul to him who gave it to them, and obedient to his orders as to those of a deity, struck down the designated victim, died in torture without a murmur, believing that the death they underwent was but a quick transition to that life of delights of which the holy herb, now before you, had given them a slight foretaste."

"Then," cried Franz, "it is hashish! I know that by name at least."

"That is it precisely, Signor Aladdin; it is hashish the purest and most unadulterated hashish of Alexandria, the hashish of Abou-Gor, the celebrated maker, the only man, the man to whom there should be built a palace, inscribed with these words, *A grateful world to the dealer in happiness*."

"Do you know," said Franz, "I have a very great inclination to judge for myself of the truth or exaggeration of your eulogies."

"Judge for yourself, Signor Aladdin judge, but do not confine yourself to one trial. Like everything else, we must habituate the senses to a fresh impression, gentle or violent, sad or joyous. There is a struggle in nature against this divine substance, in nature which is not made for joy and clings to pain. Nature subdued must yield in the combat, the dream must succeed to reality, and then the dream reigns supreme, then the dream becomes life, and life becomes the dream. But what changes occur! It is only by comparing the pains of actual being with the joys of the assumed existence, that you would desire to live no longer, but to dream thus forever. When you return to this mundane sphere from your visionary world, you would seem to leave a Neapolitan spring for a Lapland winter to quit paradise for earth heaven for hell! Taste the hashish, guest of mine taste the hashish."

Franz's only reply was to take a teaspoonful of the marvellous preparation, about as much in quantity as his host had eaten, and lift it to his mouth.

"*Diable!*" he said, after having swallowed the divine preserve.

"I do not know if the result will be as agreeable as you describe, but the thing does not appear to me as palatable as you
say."
"Because your palate his not yet been attuned to the sublim-
ity of the substances it flavors. Tell me, the first time you
tasted oysters, tea, porter, truffles, and sundry other dainties which you now adore, did you like them? Could you
comprehend how the Romans stuffed their pheasants with
assafœtida, and the Chinese eat swallows' nests? Eh? no! Well,
it is the same with hashish; only eat for a week, and nothing in
the world will seem to you to equal the delicacy of its flavor,
which now appears to you flat and distasteful. Let us now go
into the adjoining chamber, which is your apartment, and Ali
will bring us coffee and pipes."
They both arose, and while he who called himself Sinbad and
whom we have occasionally named so, that we might, like his
guest, have some title by which to distinguish him gave some
orders to the servant, Franz entered still another apartment.
It was simply yet richly furnished. It was round, and a large
divan completely encircled it. Divan, walls, ceiling, floor,
were all covered with magnificent skins as soft and downy as
the richest carpets; there were heavy-maned lion-skins from
Atlas, striped tiger-skins from Bengal; panther-skins from the
Cape, spotted beautifully, like those that appeared to Dante;
bear-skins from Siberia, fox-skins from Norway, and so on; and
all these skins were strewn in profusion one on the other, so
that it seemed like walking over the most mossy turf, or reclining on the most luxurious bed.
Both laid themselves down on the divan; chibouques with jas-
mine tubes and amber mouthpieces were within reach, and all
prepared so that there was no need to smoke the same pipe
twice. Each of them took one, which Ali lighted and then retired to prepare the coffee.
There was a moment's silence, during which Sinbad gave himself up to thoughts that seemed to occupy him incessantly,
even in the midst of his conversation; and Franz abandoned

himself to that mute reverie, into which we always sink when smoking excellent tobacco, which seems to remove with its fume all the troubles of the mind, and to give the smoker in exchange all the visions of the soul. Ali brought in the coffee.

"How do you take it?" inquired the unknown; "in the French or Turkish style, strong or weak, sugar or none, cool or boiling? As you please; it is ready in all ways."

"I will take it in the Turkish style," replied Franz.

"And you are right," said his host; "it shows you have a tendency for an Oriental life. Ah, those Orientals; they are the only men who know how to live. As for me," he added, with one of those singular smiles which did not escape the young man, "when I have completed my affairs in Paris, I shall go and die in the East; and should you wish to see me again, you must seek me at Cairo, Bagdad, or Ispahan."

"*Ma foi*," said Franz, "it would be the easiest thing in the world; for I feel eagle's wings springing out at my shoulders, and with those wings I could make a tour of the world in four-and-twenty hours."

"Ah, yes, the hashish is beginning its work. Well, unfurl your wings, and fly into superhuman regions; fear nothing, there is a watch over you; and if your wings, like those of Icarus, melt before the sun, we are here to ease your fall."

He then said something in Arabic to Ali, who made a sign of obedience and withdrew, but not to any distance.

As to Franz a strange transformation had taken place in him. All the bodily fatigue of the day, all the preoccupation of mind which the events of the evening had brought on, disappeared as they do at the first approach of sleep, when we are still sufficiently conscious to be aware of the coming of slumber. His body seemed to acquire an airy lightness, his perception brightened in a remarkable manner, his senses seemed to redouble their power, the horizon continued to expand; but it was not the gloomy horizon of vague alarms, and which he had seen before he slept, but a blue, transparent, unbounded horizon, with all the blue of the ocean, all the spangles of the sun, all the perfumes of the summer breeze; then, in the midst of the songs of his sailors, songs so clear and sonorous, that they would have made a divine harmony had their notes been taken down, he saw the Island of Monte Cristo, no longer as a threatening rock in the midst of the waves, but as an oasis in the desert; then, as his boat drew nearer, the songs became louder, for an enchanting and mysterious harmony rose to heaven, as if some Loreley had decreed to attract a soul thither, or Amphion, the enchanter, intended there to build a city.

At length the boat touched the shore, but without effort, without shock, as lips touch lips; and he entered the grotto amidst continued strains of most delicious melody. He descended, or rather seemed to descend, several steps, inhaling the fresh and balmy air, like that which may be supposed to reign around the grotto of Circe, formed from such perfumes as set the mind a-dreaming, and such fires as burn the very senses; and he saw again all he had seen before his sleep, from Sinbad, his singular host, to Ali, the mute attendant; then all seemed to fade away and become confused before his eyes, like the last shadows of the magic lantern before it is extinguished, and he was again in the chamber of statues, lighted only by one of those pale and antique lamps which watch in the dead of the night over the sleep of pleasure.

They were the same statues, rich in form, in attraction, and poesy, with eyes of fascination, smiles of love, and bright and flowing hair. They were Phryne, Cleopatra, Messalina, those three celebrated courtesans. Then among them glided like a pure ray, like a Christian angel in the midst of Olympus, one of those chaste figures, those calm shadows, those soft visions, which seemed to veil its virgin brow before these marble wantons.

Then the three statues advanced towards him with looks of love, and approached the couch on which he was reposing, their feet hidden in their long white tunics, their throats bare, hair flowing like waves, and assuming attitudes which the gods could not resist, but which saints withstood, and looks inflexible and ardent like those with which the serpent charms the bird; and then he gave way before looks that held him in a torturing grasp and delighted his senses as with a voluptuous kiss.

It seemed to Franz that he closed his eyes, and in a last look about him saw the vision of modesty completely veiled; and then followed a dream of passion like that promised by the Prophet to the elect. Lips of stone turned to flame, breasts of ice became like heated lava, so that to Franz, yielding for the first time to the sway of the drug, love was a sorrow and voluptuousness a torture, as burning mouths were pressed to his thirsty lips, and he was held in cool serpent-like embraces. The more he strove against this unhallowed passion the more his senses yielded to its thrall, and at length, weary of a struggle that taxed his very soul, he gave way and sank back breathless and exhausted beneath the kisses of these marble goddesses, and the enchantment of his marvellous dream.

Chapter 5

The Waking

When Franz returned to himself, he seemed still to be in a dream. He thought himself in a sepulchre, into which a ray of sunlight in pity scarcely penetrated. He stretched forth his hand, and touched stone; he rose to his seat, and found himself lying on his bournous in a bed of dry heather, very soft and odoriferous. The vision had fled; and as if the statues had been but shadows from the tomb, they had vanished at his waking.

He advanced several paces towards the point whence the light came, and to all the excitement of his dream succeeded the calmness of reality. He found that he was in a grotto, went towards the opening, and through a kind of fanlight saw a blue sea and an azure sky. The air and water were shining in the beams of the morning sun; on the shore the sailors were sitting, chatting and laughing; and at ten yards from them the boat was at anchor, undulating gracefully on the water.

There for some time he enjoyed the fresh breeze which played on his brow, and listened to the dash of the waves on the beach, that left against the rocks a lace of foam as white as silver. He was for some time without reflection or thought for the divine charm which is in the things of nature, specially after a fantastic dream; then gradually this view of the outer world, so calm, so pure, so grand, reminded him of the illusiveness of his vision, and once more awakened memory. He recalled his arrival on the island, his presentation to a smuggler chief, a subterranean palace full of splendor, an excellent supper, and a spoonful of hashish.

It seemed, however, even in the very face of open day, that at least a year had elapsed since all these things had passed, so deep was the impression made in his mind by the dream, and so strong a hold had it taken of his imagination. Thus every now and then he saw in fancy amid the sailors, seated on a rock, or undulating in the vessel, one of the shadows which had shared his dream with looks and kisses. Otherwise, his head was perfectly clear, and his body refreshed; he was free from the slightest headache; on the contrary, he felt a certain degree of lightness, a faculty for absorbing the pure air, and enjoying the bright sunshine more vividly than ever.

He went gayly up to the sailors, who rose as soon as they perceived him; and the patron, accosting him, said:

"The Signor Sinbad has left his compliments for your excellency, and desires us to express the regret he feels at not being able to take his leave in person; but he trusts you will excuse him, as very important business calls him to Malaga."

"So, then, Gaetano," said Franz, "this is, then, all reality; there exists a man who has received me in this island, entertained me right royally, and has departed while I was asleep?"

"He exists as certainly as that you may see his small yacht

with all her sails spread; and if you will use your glass, you will, in all probability, recognize your host in the midst of his crew."

So saying, Gaetano pointed in a direction in which a small vessel was making sail towards the southern point of Corsica. Franz adjusted his telescope, and directed it towards the yacht. Gaetano was not mistaken. At the stern the mysterious stranger was standing up looking towards the shore, and holding a spy-glass in his hand. He was attired as he had been on the previous evening, and waved his pocket-handkerchief to his guest in token of adieu. Franz returned the salute by shaking his handkerchief as an exchange of signals. After a second, a slight cloud of smoke was seen at the stern of the vessel, which rose gracefully as it expanded in the air, and then Franz heard a slight report.

"There, do you hear?" observed Gaetano; "he is bidding you adieu."

The young man took his carbine and fired it in the air, but without any idea that the noise could be heard at the distance which separated the yacht from the shore.

"What are your excellency's orders?" inquired Gaetano.

"In the first place, light me a torch."

"Ah, yes, I understand," replied the patron, "to find the entrance to the enchanted apartment. With much pleasure, your excellency, if it would amuse you; and I will get you the torch you ask for. But I too have had the idea you have, and two or three times the same fancy has come over me; but I have always given it up. Giovanni, light a torch," he added, "and give it to his excellency."

Giovanni obeyed. Franz took the lamp, and entered the subterranean grotto, followed by Gaetano. He recognized the place where he had awaked by the bed of heather that was there; but it was in vain that he carried his torch all round the exterior surface of the grotto. He saw nothing, unless that, by traces of smoke, others had before him attempted the same thing, and, like him, in vain. Yet he did not leave a foot of this granite wall, as impenetrable as futurity, without strict scrutiny; he did not see a fissure without introducing the blade of his hunting sword into it, or a projecting point on which he did not lean and press in the hopes it would give way. All was vain; and he lost two hours in his attempts, which were at last utterly useless. At the end of this time he gave up his search, and Gaetano smiled.

When Franz appeared again on the shore, the yacht only seemed like a small white speck on the horizon. He looked again through his glass, but even then he could not distinguish anything.

Gaetano reminded him that he had come for the purpose of shooting goats, which he had utterly forgotten. He took his fowling-piece, and began to hunt over the island with the air of a man who is fulfilling a duty, rather than enjoying a pleasure; and at the end of a quarter of an hour he had killed a goat and two kids. These animals, though wild and agile as chamois, were too much like domestic goats, and Franz could not consider them as game. Moreover, other ideas, much more enthralling, occupied his mind. Since, the evening before, he had really been the hero of one of the tales of the *Thousand and One Nights*, and he was irresistibly attracted towards the grotto.

Then, in spite of the failure of his first search, he began a second, after having told Gaetano to roast one of the two kids. The second visit was a long one, and when he returned the kid was roasted and the repast ready. Franz was sitting on the spot where he was on the previous evening when his mysterious host had invited him to supper; and he saw the little yacht, now like a sea-gull on the wave, continuing her flight towards Corsica.

"Why," he remarked to Gaetano, "you told me that Signor Sinbad was going to Malaga, while it seems he is in the direction of Porto-Vecchio."

"Don't you remember," said the patron, "I told you that among the crew there were two Corsican brigands?"

"True; and he is going to land them," added Franz.

"Precisely so," replied Gaetano. "Ah, he is one who fears nei-ther God nor Satan, they say, and would at any time run fifty leagues out of his course to do a poor devil a service."

"But such services as these might involve him with the au-thorities of the country in which he practices this kind of phil-anthropy," said Franz.

"And what cares he for that," replied Gaetano with a laugh, "or any authorities? He smiles at them. Let them try to pursue him! Why, in the first place, his yacht is not a ship, but a bird, and he would beat any frigate three knots in every nine; and if he were to throw himself on the coast, why, is he not certain of finding friends everywhere?"

It was perfectly clear that the Signor Sinbad, Franz's host, had the honor of being on excellent terms with the smugglers and bandits along the whole coast of the Mediterranean, and so enjoyed exceptional privileges. As to Franz, he had no longer any inducement to remain at Monte Cristo. He had lost all hope of detecting the secret of the grotto; he consequently despatched his breakfast, and, his boat being ready, he has-tened on board, and they were soon under way. At the mo-ment the boat began her course they lost sight of the yacht, as it disappeared in the gulf of Porto-Vecchio. With it was effaced the last trace of the preceding night; and then supper, Sinbad, hashish, statues, all became a dream for Franz.

The boat sailed on all day and all night, and next morning, when the sun rose, they had lost sight of Monte Cristo.

When Franz had once again set foot on shore, he forgot, for the moment at least, the events which had just passed, while he finished his affairs of pleasure at Florence, and then thought of nothing but how he should rejoin his companion, who was awaiting him at Rome.

He set out, and on the Saturday evening reached the Place de la Douane by the mail-coach. An apartment, as we have said, had been retained beforehand, and thus he had but to go to Si-gnor Pastrini's hotel. But this was not so easy a matter, for the streets were thronged with people, and Rome was already a prey to that low and feverish murmur which precedes all great events; and at Rome there are four great events in every year, the Carnival, Holy Week, Corpus Christi, and the Feast of St. Peter.

All the rest of the year the city is in that state of dull apathy, between life and death, which renders it similar to a kind of station between this world and the next a sublime spot, a resting-place full of poetry and character, and at which Franz had already halted five or six times, and at each time found it more marvellous and striking.

At last he made his way through the mob, which was continually increasing and getting more and more turbulent, and reached the hotel. On his first inquiry he was told, with the impertinence peculiar to hired hackney-coachmen and innkeepers with their houses full, that there was no room for him at the Hôtel de Londres. Then he sent his card to Signor Pastrini, and asked for Albert de Morcerf. This plan succeeded; and Signor Pastrini himself ran to him, excusing himself for having made his excellency wait, scolding the waiters, taking the candlestick from the porter, who was ready to pounce on the traveller and was about to lead him to Albert, when Morcerf himself appeared.

The apartment consisted of two small rooms and a parlor. The two rooms looked on to the street a fact which Signor Pastrini commented upon as an inappreciable advantage. The rest of the floor was hired by a very rich gentleman who was supposed to be a Sicilian or Maltese; but the host was unable to decide to which of the two nations the traveller belonged.

"Very good, signor Pastrini," said Franz; "but we must have some supper instantly, and a carriage for tomorrow and the following days."

"As to supper," replied the landlord, "you shall be served immediately; but as for the carriage "

"What as to the carriage?" exclaimed Albert. "Come, come, Signor Pastrini, no joking; we must have a carriage."

"Sir," replied the host, "we will do all in our power to procure you one this is all I can say."

"And when shall we know?" inquired Franz.

"Tomorrow morning," answered the innkeeper.

"Oh, the deuce! then we shall pay the more, that's all, I see plainly enough. At Drake's or Aaron's one pays twenty-five lire for common days, and thirty or thirty-five lire a day more for Sundays and feast days; add five lire a day more for extras, that will make forty, and there's an end of it."

"I am afraid if we offer them double that we shall not procure a carriage."

"Then they must put horses to mine. It is a little worse for the journey, but that's no matter."

"There are no horses."

Albert looked at Franz like a man who hears a reply he does not understand.

"Do you understand that, my dear Franz no horses?" he said, "but can't we have post-horses?"

"They have been all hired this fortnight, and there are none left but those absolutely requisite for posting."

"What are we to say to this?" asked Franz.

"I say, that when a thing completely surpasses my comprehension, I am accustomed not to dwell on that thing, but to pass to another. Is supper ready, Signor Pastrini?"

"Yes, your excellency."

"Well, then, let us sup."

"But the carriage and horses?" said Franz.

"Be easy, my dear boy; they will come in due season; it is only a question of how much shall be charged for them." Morcerf then, with that delighted philosophy which believes that nothing is impossible to a full purse or well-lined pocketbook, supped, went to bed, slept soundly, and dreamed he was racing all over Rome at Carnival time in a coach with six horses.

Chapter 6

Roman Bandits

The next morning Franz woke first, and instantly rang the bell. The sound had not yet died away when Signor Pastrini himself entered.

"Well, excellency," said the landlord triumphantly, and without waiting for Franz to question him, "I feared yesterday, when I would not promise you anything, that you were too late there is not a single carriage to be had that is, for the three last days"

"Yes," returned Franz, "for the very three days it is most needed."

"What is the matter?" said Albert, entering; "no carriage to be had?"

"Just so," returned Franz, "you have guessed it."

"Well, your Eternal City is a nice sort of place."

"That is to say, excellency," replied Pastrini, who was desirous of keeping up the dignity of the capital of the Christian world in the eyes of his guest, "that there are no carriages to be had from Sunday to Tuesday evening, but from now till Sunday you can have fifty if you please."

"Ah, that is something," said Albert; "today is Thursday, and who knows what may arrive between this and Sunday?"

"Ten or twelve thousand travellers will arrive," replied Franz, "which will make it still more difficult."

"My friend," said Morcerf, "let us enjoy the present without gloomy forebodings for the future."

"At least we can have a window?"

"Where?"

"In the Corso."

"Ah, a window!" exclaimed Signor Pastrini, "utterly impossible; there was only one left on the fifth floor of the Doria Palace, and that has been let to a Russian prince for twenty sequins a day."

The two young men looked at each other with an air of stupefaction.

"Well," said Franz to Albert, "do you know what is the best thing we can do? It is to pass the Carnival at Venice; there we are sure of obtaining gondolas if we cannot have carriages."

"Ah, the devil, no," cried Albert; "I came to Rome to see the Carnival, and I will, though I see it on stilts."

"Bravo! an excellent idea. We will disguise ourselves as monster pulchinellos or shepherds of the Landes, and we shall have complete success."

"Do your excellencies still wish for a carriage from now to Sunday morning?"

"*Parbleu!*" said Albert, "do you think we are going to run about on foot in the streets of Rome, like lawyers' clerks?"

"I hasten to comply with your excellencies' wishes; only, I tell you beforehand, the carriage will cost you six piastres a day."

"And, as I am not a millionaire, like the gentleman in the next apartments," said Franz, "I warn you, that as I have been four times before at Rome, I know the prices of all the carriages; we will give you twelve piastres for today, tomorrow, and the day after, and then you will make a good profit."

"But, excellency" said Pastrini, still striving to gain his point.

"Now go," returned Franz, "or I shall go myself and bargain with your *affettatore*, who is mine also; he is an old friend of mine, who has plundered me pretty well already, and, in the hope of making more out of me, he will take a less price than the one I offer you; you will lose the preference, and that will be your fault."

"Do not give yourselves the trouble, excellency," returned Signor Pastrini, with the smile peculiar to the Italian speculator when he confesses defeat; "I will do all I can, and I hope you will be satisfied."

"And now we understand each other."

"When do you wish the carriage to be here?"

"In an hour."

"In an hour it will be at the door."

An hour after the vehicle was at the door; it was a hack conveyance which was elevated to the rank of a private carriage in honor of the occasion, but, in spite of its humble exterior, the young men would have thought themselves happy to have secured it for the last three days of the Carnival.

"Excellency," cried the *cicerone*, seeing Franz approach the window, "shall I bring the carriage nearer to the palace?"

Accustomed as Franz was to the Italian phraseology, his first impulse was to look round him, but these words were addressed to him. Franz was the "excellency," the vehicle was the "carriage," and the Hôtel de Londres was the "palace." The genius for laudation characteristic of the race was in that phrase.

Franz and Albert descended, the carriage approached the palace; their excellencies stretched their legs along the seats; the *cicerone* sprang into the seat behind.

"Where do your excellencies wish to go?" asked he.

"To Saint Peter's first, and then to the Colosseum," returned Albert. But Albert did not know that it takes a day to see Saint

Peter's, and a month to study it. The day was passed at Saint Peter's alone.

Suddenly the daylight began to fade away; Franz took out his watch it was half-past four. They returned to the hotel; at the door Franz ordered the coachman to be ready at eight. He wished to show Albert the Colosseum by moonlight, as he had shown him Saint Peter's by daylight. When we show a friend a city one has already visited, we feel the same pride as when we point out a woman whose lover we have been.

He was to leave the city by the Porta del Popolo, skirt the outer wall, and re-enter by the Porta San Giovanni; thus they would behold the Colosseum without finding their impressions dulled by first looking on the Capitol, the Forum, the Arch of Septimus Severus, the Temple of Antoninus and Faustina, and the Via Sacra.

They sat down to dinner. Signor Pastrini had promised them a banquet; he gave them a tolerable repast. At the end of the dinner he entered in person. Franz thought that he came to hear his dinner praised, and began accordingly, but at the first words he was interrupted.

"Excellency," said Pastrini, "I am delighted to have your approbation, but it was not for that I came."

"Did you come to tell us you have procured a carriage?" asked Albert, lighting his cigar.

"No; and your excellencies will do well not to think of that any longer; at Rome things can or cannot be done; when you are told anything cannot be done, there is an end of it."

"It is much more convenient at Paris, when anything cannot be done, you pay double, and it is done directly."

"That is what all the French say," returned Signor Pastrini, somewhat piqued; "for that reason, I do not understand why they travel."

"But," said Albert, emitting a volume of smoke and balancing his chair on its hind legs, "only madmen, or blockheads like us, ever do travel. Men in their senses do not quit their hotel in the Rue du Helder, their walk on the Boulevard de Gand, and the Café de Paris."

It is of course understood that Albert resided in the aforesaid street, appeared every day on the fashionable walk, and dined frequently at the only restaurant where you can really dine, that is, if you are on good terms with its waiters.

Signor Pastrini remained silent a short time; it was evident that he was musing over this answer, which did not seem very clear.

"But," said Franz, in his turn interrupting his host's meditations, "you had some motive for coming here, may I beg to know what it was?"

"Ah, yes; you have ordered your carriage at eight o'clock precisely?"

"I have."

"You intend visiting *Il Colosseo*."

"You mean the Colosseum?"

"It is the same thing. You have told your coachman to leave the city by the Porta del Popolo, to drive round the walls, and re-enter by the Porta San Giovanni?"

"These are my words exactly."

"Well, this route is impossible."

"Impossible!"

"Very dangerous, to say the least."

"Dangerous! and why?"

"On account of the famous Luigi Vampa."

"Pray, who may this famous Luigi Vampa be?" inquired Albert; "he may be very famous at Rome, but I can assure you he is quite unknown at Paris."

"What! do you not know him?"

"I have not that honor."

"You have never heard his name?"

"Never."

"Well, then, he is a bandit, compared to whom the Decesaris and the Gasparones were mere children."

"Now then, Albert," cried Franz, "here is a bandit for you at last."

"I forewarn you, Signor Pastrini, that I shall not believe one word of what you are going to tell us; having told you this, begin. 'Once upon a time' Well, go on."

Signor Pastrini turned toward Franz, who seemed to him the more reasonable of the two; we must do him justice, he had had a great many Frenchmen in his house, but had never been able to comprehend them.

"Excellency," said he gravely, addressing Franz, "if you look upon me as a liar, it is useless for me to say anything; it was for your interest I "

"Albert does not say you are a liar, Signor Pastrini," said Franz, "but that he will not believe what you are going to tell us, but I will believe all you say; so proceed."

"But if your excellency doubt my veracity "

"Signor Pastrini," returned Franz, "you are more susceptible than Cassandra, who was a prophetess, and yet no one believed her; while you, at least, are sure of the credence of half your audience. Come, sit down, and tell us all about this Signor Vampa."

"I had told your excellency he is the most famous bandit we have had since the days of Mastrilla."

"Well, what has this bandit to do with the order I have given the coachman to leave the city by the Porta del Popolo, and to re-enter by the Porta San Giovanni?"

"This," replied Signor Pastrini, "that you will go out by one, but I very much doubt your returning by the other."

"Why?" asked Franz.

"Because, after nightfall, you are not safe fifty yards from the gates."

"On your honor, is that true?" cried Albert.

"Count," returned Signor Pastrini, hurt at Albert's repeated doubts of the truth of his assertions, "I do not say this to you, but to your companion, who knows Rome, and knows, too, that these things are not to be laughed at."

"My dear fellow," said Albert, turning to Franz, "here is an admirable adventure; we will fill our carriage with pistols, blunderbusses, and double-barrelled guns. Luigi Vampa comes to take us, and we take him we bring him back to Rome, and present him to his holiness the Pope, who asks how he can repay so great a service; then we merely ask for a carriage and a pair of horses, and we see the Carnival in the carriage, and doubtless the Roman people will crown us at the Capitol, and proclaim us, like Curtius and Horatius Cocles, the preservers of their country."

Whilst Albert proposed this scheme, Signor Pastrini's face assumed an expression impossible to describe.

"And pray," asked Franz, "where are these pistols, blunderbusses, and other deadly weapons with which you intend filling the carriage?"

"Not out of my armory, for at Terracina I was plundered even of my hunting-knife. And you?"

"I shared the same fate at Aquapendente."

"Do you know, Signor Pastrini," said Albert, lighting a second cigar at the first, "that this practice is very convenient for bandits, and that it seems to be due to an arrangement of their own."

Doubtless Signor Pastrini found this pleasantry compromising, for he only answered half the question, and then he spoke to Franz, as the only one likely to listen with attention. "Your excellency knows that it is not customary to defend yourself when attacked by bandits."

"What!" cried Albert, whose courage revolted at the idea of being plundered tamely, "not make any resistance!"

"No, for it would be useless. What could you do against a dozen bandits who spring out of some pit, ruin, or aqueduct, and level their pieces at you?"

"Eh, *parbleu!* they should kill me."

The innkeeper turned to Franz with an air that seemed to say, "Your friend is decidedly mad."

"My dear Albert," returned Franz, "your answer is sublime, and worthy the '*Let him die*,' of Corneille, only, when Horace made that answer, the safety of Rome was concerned; but, as for us, it is only to gratify a whim, and it would be ridiculous to risk our lives for so foolish a motive."

Albert poured himself out a glass of *lacryma Christi*, which he sipped at intervals, muttering some unintelligible words.

"Well, Signor Pastrini," said Franz, "now that my companion is quieted, and you have seen how peaceful my intentions are, tell me who is this Luigi Vampa. Is he a shepherd or a nobleman? young or old? tall or short? Describe him, in order that, if we meet him by chance, like Jean Sbogar or Lara, we may recognize him."

"You could not apply to anyone better able to inform you on all these points, for I knew him when he was a child, and one day that I fell into his hands, going from Ferentino to Alatri, he, fortunately for me, recollected me, and set me free, not only without ransom, but made me a present of a very splendid watch, and related his history to me."

"Let us see the watch," said Albert.

Signor Pastrini drew from his fob a magnificent Bréguet, bearing the name of its maker, of Parisian manufacture, and a count's coronet.

"Here it is," said he.

"*Peste!*" returned Albert, "I compliment you on it; I have its fellow" he took his watch from his waistcoat pocket "and it cost me 3,000 francs."

"Let us hear the history," said Franz, motioning Signor Pastrini to seat himself.

"Your excellencies permit it?" asked the host.

"*Pardieu!*" cried Albert, "you are not a preacher, to remain standing!"

The host sat down, after having made each of them a respectful bow, which meant that he was ready to tell them all they wished to know concerning Luigi Vampa.

"You tell me," said Franz, at the moment Signor Pastrini was about to open his mouth, "that you knew Luigi Vampa when he was a child he is still a young man, then?"

"A young man? he is only two-and-twenty; he will gain himself a reputation."

"What do you think of that, Albert? at two-and-twenty to be thus famous?"

"Yes, and at his age, Alexander, Cæsar, and Napoleon, who have all made some noise in the world, were quite behind him."

"So," continued Franz, "the hero of this history is only two-and-twenty?"

"Scarcely so much."

"Is he tall or short?"

"Of the middle height about the same stature as his excellency," returned the host, pointing to Albert.

"Thanks for the comparison," said Albert, with a bow.

"Go on, Signor Pastrini," continued Franz, smiling at his friend's susceptibility. "To what class of society does he belong?"

"He was a shepherd-boy attached to the farm of the Count of San-Felice, situated between Palestrina and the Lake of Gabri; he was born at Pampinara, and entered the count's service when he was five years old; his father was also a shepherd, who owned a small flock, and lived by the wool and the milk, which he sold at Rome. When quite a child, the little Vampa displayed a most extraordinary precocity. One day, when he was seven years old, he came to the curate of Palestrina, and asked to be taught to read; it was somewhat difficult, for he could not quit his flock; but the good curate went every day to say mass at a little hamlet too poor to pay a priest and which, having no other name, was called Borgo; he told Luigi that he might meet him on his return, and that then he would give him a lesson, warning him that it would be short, and that he must profit as much as possible by it. The child accepted joyfully. Every day Luigi led his flock to graze on the road that leads from Palestrina to Borgo; every day, at nine o'clock in the morning, the priest and the boy sat down on a bank by the wayside, and the little shepherd took his lesson out of the priest's breviary. At the end of three months he had learned to read. This was not enough he must now learn to write. The priest had a writing teacher at Rome make three alphabets one large, one middling, and one small; and pointed out to him that by the help of a sharp instrument he could trace the letters on a slate, and thus learn to write. The same evening, when the flock was safe at the farm, the little Luigi hastened to the smith at Palestrina, took a large nail, heated and sharpened it, and formed a sort of stylus. The next morning he gathered an armful of pieces of slate and began. At the end of three months he had learned to write. The curate, astonished at his quickness and intelligence, made him a present of pens, paper, and a penknife. This demanded new effort, but nothing compared to the first; at the end of a week he wrote as well with this pen as with the stylus. The curate related the incident to the Count of San-Felice, who sent for the little shepherd, made him read and write before him, ordered his attendant to let him eat with the domestics, and to give him two piastres a month. With this, Luigi purchased books and pencils. He applied his imitative powers to everything, and, like Giotto, when young, he drew on his slate sheep, houses, and trees. Then, with his knife, he began to carve all sorts of objects in wood; it was thus that Pinelli, the famous sculptor, had commenced.

"A girl of six or seven that is, a little younger than Vampa tended sheep on a farm near Palestrina; she was an orphan, born at Valmontone and was named Teresa. The two children met, sat down near each other, let their flocks mingle together, played, laughed, and conversed together; in the evening they separated the Count of San-Felice's flock from those of Baron Cervetri, and the children returned to their respective farms, promising to meet the next morning. The next day they kept their word, and thus they grew up together. Vampa was twelve, and Teresa eleven. And yet their natural disposition revealed itself. Beside his taste for the fine arts, which Luigi had carried as far as he could in his solitude, he was given to alternating fits of sadness and enthusiasm, was often angry and capricious, and always sarcastic. None of the lads of

Pampinara, Palestrina, or Valmontone had been able to gain any influence over him or even to become his companion. His disposition (always inclined to exact concessions rather than to make them) kept him aloof from all friendships. Teresa alone ruled by a look, a word, a gesture, this impetuous character, which yielded beneath the hand of a woman, and which beneath the hand of a man might have broken, but could never have been bended. Teresa was lively and gay, but coquettish to excess. The two piastres that Luigi received every month from the Count of San-Felice's steward, and the price of all the little carvings in wood he sold at Rome, were expended in ear-rings, necklaces, and gold hairpins. So that, thanks to her friend's generosity, Teresa was the most beautiful and the best-attired peasant near Rome.

"The two children grew up together, passing all their time with each other, and giving themselves up to the wild ideas of their different characters. Thus, in all their dreams, their wishes, and their conversations, Vampa saw himself the captain of a vessel, general of an army, or governor of a province. Teresa saw herself rich, superbly attired, and attended by a train of liveried domestics. Then, when they had thus passed the day in building castles in the air, they separated their flocks, and descended from the elevation of their dreams to the reality of their humble position.

"One day the young shepherd told the count's steward that he had seen a wolf come out of the Sabine mountains, and prowl around his flock. The steward gave him a gun; this was what Vampa longed for. This gun had an excellent barrel, made at Brescia, and carrying a ball with the precision of an English rifle; but one day the count broke the stock, and had then cast the gun aside. This, however, was nothing to a sculptor like Vampa; he examined the broken stock, calculated what change it would require to adapt the gun to his shoulder, and made a fresh stock, so beautifully carved that it would have fetched fifteen or twenty piastres, had he chosen to sell it. But nothing could be farther from his thoughts.

"For a long time a gun had been the young man's greatest ambition. In every country where independence has taken the place of liberty, the first desire of a manly heart is to possess a weapon, which at once renders him capable of defence or attack, and, by rendering its owner terrible, often makes him feared. From this moment Vampa devoted all his leisure time to perfecting himself in the use of his precious weapon; he purchased powder and ball, and everything served him for a mark the trunk of some old and moss-grown olive-tree, that grew on the Sabine mountains; the fox, as he quitted his earth on some marauding excursion; the eagle that soared above their heads: and thus he soon became so expert, that Teresa overcame the terror she at first felt at the report, and amused herself by watching him direct the ball wherever he pleased, with as much accuracy as if he placed it by hand.

"One evening a wolf emerged from a pine-wood near which they were usually stationed, but the wolf had scarcely advanced ten yards ere he was dead. Proud of this exploit, Vampa took the dead animal on his shoulders, and carried him to the farm. These exploits had gained Luigi considerable reputation. The man of superior abilities always finds admirers, go where he will. He was spoken of as the most adroit, the strongest, and the most courageous *contadino* for ten leagues around; and although Teresa was universally allowed to be the most beautiful girl of the Sabines, no one had ever spoken to her of love, because it was known that she was beloved by Vampa. And yet the two young people had never declared their affection; they had grown together like two trees whose roots are mingled, whose branches intertwined, and whose intermingled perfume rises to the heavens. Only their wish to see each other had become a necessity, and they would have preferred death to a day's separation.

"Teresa was sixteen, and Vampa seventeen. About this time, a band of brigands that had established itself in the Lepini mountains began to be much spoken of. The brigands have never been really extirpated from the neighborhood of Rome.

Sometimes a chief is wanted, but when a chief presents himself he rarely has to wait long for a band of followers.

"The celebrated Cucumetto, pursued in the Abruzzo, driven out of the kingdom of Naples, where he had carried on a regular war, had crossed the Garigliano, like Manfred, and had taken refuge on the banks of the Amasine between Sonnino and Juperno. He strove to collect a band of followers, and followed the footsteps of Decesaris and Gasparone, whom he hoped to surpass. Many young men of Palestrina, Frascati, and Pampinara had disappeared. Their disappearance at first caused much disquietude; but it was soon known that they had joined Cucumetto. After some time Cucumetto became the object of universal attention; the most extraordinary traits of ferocious daring and brutality were related of him.

"One day he carried off a young girl, the daughter of a surveyor of Frosinone. The bandit's laws are positive; a young girl belongs first to him who carries her off, then the rest draw lots for her, and she is abandoned to their brutality until death relieves her sufferings. When their parents are sufficiently rich to pay a ransom, a messenger is sent to negotiate; the prisoner is hostage for the security of the messenger; should the ransom be refused, the prisoner is irrevocably lost. The young girl's lover was in Cucumetto's troop; his name was Carlini. When she recognized her lover, the poor girl extended her arms to him, and believed herself safe; but Carlini felt his heart sink, for he but too well knew the fate that awaited her. However, as he was a favorite with Cucumetto, as he had for three years faithfully served him, and as he had saved his life by shooting a dragoon who was about to cut him down, he hoped the chief would have pity on him. He took Cucumetto one side, while the young girl, seated at the foot of a huge pine that stood in the centre of the forest, made a veil of her picturesque head-dress to hide her face from the lascivious gaze of the bandits. There he told the chief all his affection for the prisoner, their promises of mutual fidelity, and how every night, since he had been near, they had met in some neighboring ruins.

"It so happened that night that Cucumetto had sent Carlini to a village, so that he had been unable to go to the place of meeting. Cucumetto had been there, however, by accident, as he said, and had carried the maiden off. Carlini besought his chief to make an exception in Rita's favor, as her father was rich, and could pay a large ransom. Cucumetto seemed to yield to his friend's entreaties, and bade him find a shepherd to send to Rita's father at Frosinone.

"Carlini flew joyfully to Rita, telling her she was saved, and bidding her write to her father, to inform him what had occurred, and that her ransom was fixed at three hundred piastres. Twelve hours' delay was all that was granted that is, until nine the next morning. The instant the letter was written, Carlini seized it, and hastened to the plain to find a messenger. He found a young shepherd watching his flock. The natural messengers of the bandits are the shepherds who live between the city and the mountains, between civilized and savage life. The boy undertook the commission, promising to be in Frosinone in less than an hour. Carlini returned, anxious to see his mistress, and announce the joyful intelligence. He found the troop in the glade, supping off the provisions exacted as contributions from the peasants; but his eye vainly sought Rita and Cucumetto among them.

"He inquired where they were, and was answered by a burst of laughter. A cold perspiration burst from every pore, and his hair stood on end. He repeated his question. One of the bandits rose, and offered him a glass filled with Orvietto, saying, 'To the health of the brave Cucumetto and the fair Rita.' At this moment Carlini heard a woman's cry; he divined the truth, seized the glass, broke it across the face of him who presented it, and rushed towards the spot whence the cry came. After a hundred yards he turned the corner of the thicket; he found Rita senseless in the arms of Cucumetto. At the sight of Carlini, Cucumetto rose, a pistol in each hand. The two brigands looked at each other for a moment the one with a smile of lasciviousness on his lips, the other with the pallor of death on his brow. A terrible battle between the two men seemed imminent; but by degrees Carlini's features relaxed, his hand, which had grasped one of the pistols in his belt, fell to his side. Rita lay between them. The moon lighted the group.

"'Well,' said Cucumetto, 'have you executed your commission?'

"'Yes, captain,' returned Carlini. 'At nine o'clock tomorrow Rita's father will be here with the money.'

"'It is well; in the meantime, we will have a merry night; this young girl is charming, and does credit to your taste. Now, as I am not egotistical, we will return to our comrades and draw lots for her.'

"'You have determined, then, to abandon her to the common law?' said Carlini.

"'Why should an exception be made in her favor?'

"'I thought that my entreaties'

"'What right have you, any more than the rest, to ask for an exception?'

"'It is true.'

"'But never mind,' continued Cucumetto, laughing, 'sooner or later your turn will come.' Carlini's teeth clenched convulsively.

"'Now, then,' said Cucumetto, advancing towards the other bandits, 'are you coming?'

"'I follow you.'

"Cucumetto departed, without losing sight of Carlini, for, doubtless, he feared lest he should strike him unawares; but nothing betrayed a hostile design on Carlini's part. He was standing, his arms folded, near Rita, who was still insensible. Cucumetto fancied for a moment the young man was about to take her in his arms and fly; but this mattered little to him now Rita had been his; and as for the money, three hundred piastres distributed among the band was so small a sum that he cared little about it. He continued to follow the path to the glade; but, to his great surprise, Carlini arrived almost as soon as himself.

"'Let us draw lots! let us draw lots!' cried all the brigands, when they saw the chief.

"Their demand was fair, and the chief inclined his head in sign of acquiescence. The eyes of all shone fiercely as they made their demand, and the red light of the fire made them look like demons. The names of all, including Carlini, were placed in a hat, and the youngest of the band drew forth a ticket; the ticket bore the name of Diavolaccio. He was the man who had proposed to Carlini the health of their chief, and to whom Carlini replied by breaking the glass across his face. A large wound, extending from the temple to the mouth, was bleeding profusely. Diavolaccio, seeing himself thus favored by fortune, burst into a loud laugh.

"'Captain,' said he, 'just now Carlini would not drink your health when I proposed it to him; propose mine to him, and let us see if he will be more condescending to you than to me.'

"Everyone expected an explosion on Carlini's part; but to their great surprise, he took a glass in one hand and a flask in the other, and filling it,

"'Your health, Diavolaccio,' said he calmly, and he drank it off, without his hand trembling in the least. Then sitting down by the fire, 'My supper,' said he; 'my expedition has given me an appetite.'

"'Well done, Carlini!' cried the brigands; 'that is acting like a good fellow;' and they all formed a circle round the fire, while Diavolaccio disappeared.

"Carlini ate and drank as if nothing had happened. The bandits looked on with astonishment at this singular conduct until they heard footsteps. They turned round, and saw Diavolaccio bearing the young girl in his arms. Her head hung back, and her long hair swept the ground. As they entered the circle, the bandits could perceive, by the firelight, the unearthly pallor of the young girl and of Diavolaccio. This apparition was so strange and so solemn, that everyone rose, with the exception of Carlini, who remained seated, and ate and drank calmly. Diavolaccio advanced amidst the most profound silence, and laid Rita at the captain's feet. Then everyone could understand the cause of the unearthly pallor in the young girl and the bandit. A knife was plunged up to the hilt in Rita's left breast. Everyone looked at Carlini; the sheath at his belt was empty.

"'Ah, ah,' said the chief, 'I now understand why Carlini stayed behind.'

"All savage natures appreciate a desperate deed. No other of the bandits would, perhaps, have done the same; but they all understood what Carlini had done.

"'Now, then,' cried Carlini, rising in his turn, and approaching the corpse, his hand on the butt of one of his pistols, 'does anyone dispute the possession of this woman with me?'

"'No,' returned the chief, 'she is thine.'

"Carlini raised her in his arms, and carried her out of the circle of firelight. Cucumetto placed his sentinels for the night, and the bandits wrapped themselves in their cloaks, and lay down before the fire. At midnight the sentinel gave the alarm, and in an instant all were on the alert. It was Rita's father, who brought his daughter's ransom in person.

"'Here,' said he, to Cucumetto, 'here are three hundred piastres; give me back my child.

"But the chief, without taking the money, made a sign to him to follow. The old man obeyed. They both advanced beneath the trees, through whose branches streamed the moonlight. Cucumetto stopped at last, and pointed to two persons grouped at the foot of a tree.

"'There,' said he, 'demand thy child of Carlini; he will tell thee what has become of her;' and he returned to his companions.

"The old man remained motionless; he felt that some great and unforeseen misfortune hung over his head. At length he advanced toward the group, the meaning of which he could not comprehend. As he approached, Carlini raised his head, and the forms of two persons became visible to the old man's eyes. A woman lay on the ground, her head resting on the knees of a man, who was seated by her; as he raised his head, the woman's face became visible. The old man recognized his child, and Carlini recognized the old man.

"'I expected thee,' said the bandit to Rita's father.

"'Wretch!' returned the old man, 'what hast thou done?' and he gazed with terror on Rita, pale and bloody, a knife buried in her bosom. A ray of moonlight poured through the trees, and lighted up the face of the dead.

"'Cucumetto had violated thy daughter,' said the bandit; 'I loved her, therefore I slew her; for she would have served as the sport of the whole band.' The old man spoke not, and grew pale as death. 'Now,' continued Carlini, 'if I have done wrongly, avenge her;' and withdrawing the knife from the wound in Rita's bosom, he held it out to the old man with one hand, while with the other he tore open his vest.

"'Thou hast done well!' returned the old man in a hoarse voice; 'embrace me, my son.'

Carlini threw himself, sobbing like a child, into the arms of his mistress's father. These were the first tears the man of blood had ever wept.

"'Now,' said the old man, 'aid me to bury my child.' Carlini fetched two pickaxes; and the father and the lover began to dig at the foot of a huge oak, beneath which the young girl was to repose. When the grave was formed, the father embraced her first, and then the lover; afterwards, one taking the head, the other the feet, they placed her in the grave. Then they knelt on each side of the grave, and said the prayers of the dead. Then, when they had finished, they cast the earth over the corpse, until the grave was filled. Then, extending his hand, the old man said; 'I thank you, my son; and now leave me alone.'

"'Yet' replied Carlini.

"'Leave me, I command you.'

"Carlini obeyed, rejoined his comrades, folded himself in his cloak, and soon appeared to sleep as soundly as the rest. It had been resolved the night before to change their encampment. An hour before daybreak, Cucumetto aroused his men, and gave the word to march. But Carlini would not quit the forest, without knowing what had become of Rita's father. He went toward the place where he had left him. He found the old man suspended from one of the branches of the oak which shaded his daughter's grave. He then took an oath of bitter vengeance over the dead body of the one and the tomb of the other. But he was unable to complete this oath, for two days afterwards, in an encounter with the Roman carbineers, Carlini was killed. There was some surprise, however, that, as he was with his face to the enemy, he should have received a ball between his shoulders. That astonishment ceased when one of the brigands remarked to his comrades that Cucumetto was stationed ten paces in Carlini's rear when he fell. On the morning of the departure from the forest of Frosinone he had followed Carlini in the darkness, and heard this oath of vengeance, and, like a wise man, anticipated it.

"They told ten other stories of this bandit chief, each more singular than the other. Thus, from Fondi to Perusia, everyone trembles at the name of Cucumetto.

"These narratives were frequently the theme of conversation between Luigi and Teresa. The young girl trembled very much at hearing the stories; but Vampa reassured her with a smile, tapping the butt of his good fowling-piece, which threw its ball so well; and if that did not restore her courage, he pointed to a crow, perched on some dead branch, took aim, touched the trigger, and the bird fell dead at the foot of the tree. Time passed on, and the two young people had agreed to be married when Vampa should be twenty and Teresa nineteen years of age. They were both orphans, and had only their employers' leave to ask, which had been already sought and obtained. One day when they were talking over their plans for the future, they heard two or three reports of firearms, and then suddenly a man came out of the wood, near which the two young persons used to graze their flocks, and hurried towards them. When he came within hearing, he exclaimed:

'I am pursued; can you conceal me?'

"They knew full well that this fugitive must be a bandit; but there is an innate sympathy between the Roman brigand and the Roman peasant and the latter is always ready to aid the former. Vampa, without saying a word, hastened to the stone that closed up the entrance to their grotto, drew it away, made a sign to the fugitive to take refuge there, in a retreat unknown to everyone, closed the stone upon him, and then went and resumed his seat by Teresa. Instantly afterwards four carbineers, on horseback, appeared on the edge of the wood; three of them appeared to be looking for the fugitive, while the fourth dragged a brigand prisoner by the neck. The three carbineers looked about carefully on every side, saw the young peasants, and galloping up, began to question them. They had seen no one.

"'That is very annoying,' said the brigadier; for the man we are looking for is the chief.'

"'Cucumetto?' cried Luigi and Teresa at the same moment.

"'Yes,' replied the brigadier; 'and as his head is valued at a thousand Roman crowns, there would have been five hundred for you, if you had helped us to catch him.' The two young persons exchanged looks. The brigadier had a moment's hope. Five hundred Roman crowns are three thousand lire, and three thousand lire are a fortune for two poor orphans who are going to be married.

"'Yes, it is very annoying,' said Vampa; 'but we have not seen him.'

"Then the carbineers scoured the country in different directions, but in vain; then, after a time, they disappeared. Vampa then removed the stone, and Cucumetto came out. Through the crevices in the granite he had seen the two young peasants talking with the carbineers, and guessed the subject of their parley. He had read in the countenances of Luigi and Teresa their steadfast resolution not to surrender him, and he drew from his pocket a purse full of gold, which he offered to them. But Vampa raised his head proudly; as to Teresa, her eyes sparkled when she thought of all the fine gowns and gay jewellery she could buy with this purse of gold.

"Cucumetto was a cunning fiend, and had assumed the form of a brigand instead of a serpent, and this look from Teresa showed to him that she was a worthy daughter of Eve, and he returned to the forest, pausing several times on his way, under the pretext of saluting his protectors.

"Several days elapsed, and they neither saw nor heard of Cucumetto. The time of the Carnival was at hand. The Count of San-Felice announced a grand masked ball, to which all that were distinguished in Rome were invited. Teresa had a great desire to see this ball. Luigi asked permission of his protector, the steward, that she and he might be present amongst the servants of the house. This was granted. The ball was given by the Count for the particular pleasure of his daughter Carmela, whom he adored. Carmela was precisely the age and figure of Teresa, and Teresa was as handsome as Carmela. On the evening of the ball Teresa was attired in her best, her most brilliant ornaments in her hair, and gayest glass beads, she was in the costume of the women of Frascati. Luigi wore the very picturesque garb of the Roman peasant at holiday time. They both mingled, as they had leave to do, with the servants and peasants.

"The *festa* was magnificent; not only was the villa brilliantly illuminated, but thousands of colored lanterns were suspended from the trees in the garden; and very soon the palace overflowed to the terraces, and the terraces to the garden-walks. At each cross-path was an orchestra, and tables spread with refreshments; the guests stopped, formed quadrilles, and danced in any part of the grounds they pleased. Carmela was attired like a woman of Sonnino. Her cap was embroidered with pearls, the pins in her hair were of gold and diamonds, her girdle was of Turkey silk, with large embroidered flowers, her bodice and skirt were of cashmere, her apron of Indian muslin, and the buttons of her corset were of jewels. Two of her companions were dressed, the one as a woman of Nettuno, and the other as a woman of La Riccia. Four young men of the richest and noblest families of Rome accompanied them with that Italian freedom which has not its parallel in any other country in the world. They were attired as peasants of Albano, Velletri, Civita-Castellana, and Sora. We need hardly add that these peasant costumes, like those of the young women, were brilliant with gold and jewels.

"Carmela wished to form a quadrille, but there was one lady wanting. Carmela looked all around her, but not one of the guests had a costume similar to her own, or those of her companions. The Count of San-Felice pointed out Teresa, who was hanging on Luigi's arm in a group of peasants.

"'Will you allow me, father?' said Carmela.

"'Certainly,' replied the count, 'are we not in Carnival time?'

"Carmela turned towards the young man who was talking with her, and saying a few words to him, pointed with her finger to Teresa. The young man looked, bowed in obedience, and then went to Teresa, and invited her to dance in a quadrille directed by the count's daughter. Teresa felt a flush pass over her face; she looked at Luigi, who could not refuse his assent. Luigi slowly relinquished Teresa's arm, which he had held beneath his own, and Teresa, accompanied by her elegant cavalier, took her appointed place with much agitation in the aristocratic quadrille. Certainly, in the eyes of an artist, the exact and strict costume of Teresa had a very different character from that of Carmela and her companions; and Teresa was frivolous and coquettish, and thus the embroidery and muslins, the cashmere waist-girdles, all dazzled her, and the reflection of sapphires and diamonds almost turned her giddy brain.

"Luigi felt a sensation hitherto unknown arising in his mind. It was like an acute pain which gnawed at his heart, and then thrilled through his whole body. He followed with his eye each movement of Teresa and her cavalier; when their hands touched, he felt as though he should swoon; every pulse beat with violence, and it seemed as though a bell were ringing in his ears. When they spoke, although Teresa listened timidly and with downcast eyes to the conversation of her cavalier, as Luigi could read in the ardent looks of the good-looking young man that his language was that of praise, it seemed as if the whole world was turning round with him, and all the voices of hell were whispering in his ears ideas of murder and assassination. Then fearing that his paroxysm might get the better of him, he clutched with one hand the branch of a tree against which he was leaning, and with the other convulsively grasped the dagger with a carved handle which was in his belt, and which, unwittingly, he drew from the scabbard from time to time.

"Luigi was jealous!

"He felt that, influenced by her ambitions and coquettish disposition, Teresa might escape him.

"The young peasant girl, at first timid and scared, soon recovered herself. We have said that Teresa was handsome, but this is not all; Teresa was endowed with all those wild graces which are so much more potent than our affected and studied elegancies. She had almost all the honors of the quadrille, and if she were envious of the Count of San-Felice's daughter, we will not undertake to say that Carmela was not jealous of her. And with overpowering compliments her handsome cavalier led her back to the place whence he had taken her, and where Luigi awaited her. Twice or thrice during the dance the young girl had glanced at Luigi, and each time she saw that he was pale and that his features were agitated, once even the blade of his knife, half drawn from its sheath, had dazzled her eyes with its sinister glare. Thus, it was almost tremblingly that she resumed her lover's arm. The quadrille had been most perfect, and it was evident there was a great demand for a repetition, Carmela alone objecting to it, but the Count of San-Felice besought his daughter so earnestly, that she acceded.

"One of the cavaliers then hastened to invite Teresa, without whom it was impossible for the quadrille to be formed, but the young girl had disappeared.

"The truth was, that Luigi had not felt the strength to support another such trial, and, half by persuasion and half by force, he had removed Teresa toward another part of the garden. Teresa had yielded in spite of herself, but when she looked at the agitated countenance of the young man, she understood by his silence and trembling voice that something strange was passing within him. She herself was not exempt from internal emotion, and without having done anything wrong, yet fully comprehended that Luigi was right in reproaching her. Why, she did not know, but yet she did not the less feel that these reproaches were merited.

"However, to Teresa's great astonishment, Luigi remained mute, and not a word escaped his lips the rest of the evening. When the chill of the night had driven away the guests from the gardens, and the gates of the villa were closed on them for the *festa* in-doors, he took Teresa quite away, and as he left her at her home, he said:

"'Teresa, what were you thinking of as you danced opposite the young Countess of San-Felice?'

"'I thought,' replied the young girl, with all the frankness of her nature, 'that I would give half my life for a costume such as she wore.'

"'And what said your cavalier to you?'

"'He said it only depended on myself to have it, and I had only one word to say.'

"'He was right,' said Luigi. 'Do you desire it as ardently as you say?'

"'Yes.'

"'Well, then, you shall have it!'

"The young girl, much astonished, raised her head to look at him, but his face was so gloomy and terrible that her words froze to her lips. As Luigi spoke thus, he left her. Teresa followed him with her eyes into the darkness as long as she could, and when he had quite disappeared, she went into the house with a sigh.

"That night a memorable event occurred, due, no doubt, to the imprudence of some servant who had neglected to extinguish the lights. The Villa of San-Felice took fire in the rooms adjoining the very apartment of the lovely Carmela. Awakened in the night by the light of the flames, she sprang out of bed, wrapped herself in a dressing-gown, and attempted to escape by the door, but the corridor by which she hoped to fly was already a prey to the flames. She then returned to her room, calling for help as loudly as she could, when suddenly her window, which was twenty feet from the ground, was opened, a young peasant jumped into the chamber, seized her in his arms, and with superhuman skill and strength conveyed her to the turf of the grass-plot, where she fainted. When she recovered, her father was by her side. All the servants surrounded her, offering her assistance. An entire wing of the villa was burnt down; but what of that, as long as Carmela was safe and uninjured?

"Her preserver was everywhere sought for, but he did not appear; he was inquired after, but no one had seen him. Carmela was greatly troubled that she had not recognized him.

"As the count was immensely rich, excepting the danger Carmela had run, and the marvellous manner in which she had escaped, made that appear to him rather a favor of Providence than a real misfortune, the loss occasioned by the conflagration was to him but a trifle.

"The next day, at the usual hour, the two young peasants were on the borders of the forest. Luigi arrived first. He came toward Teresa in high spirits, and seemed to have completely forgotten the events of the previous evening. The young girl was very pensive, but seeing Luigi so cheerful, she on her part assumed a smiling air, which was natural to her when she was not excited or in a passion.

"Luigi took her arm beneath his own, and led her to the door of the grotto. Then he paused. The young girl, perceiving that there was something extraordinary, looked at him steadfastly.

"'Teresa,' said Luigi, 'yesterday evening you told me you would give all the world to have a costume similar to that of the count's daughter.'

"'Yes,' replied Teresa with astonishment; 'but I was mad to utter such a wish.'

"'And I replied, "Very well, you shall have it."'"

"'Yes,' replied the young girl, whose astonishment increased at every word uttered by Luigi, 'but of course your reply was only to please me.'

"'I have promised no more than I have given you, Teresa,' said Luigi proudly. 'Go into the grotto and dress yourself.'

"At these words he drew away the stone, and showed Teresa the grotto, lighted up by two wax lights, which burnt on each side of a splendid mirror; on a rustic table, made by Luigi, were spread out the pearl necklace and the diamond pins, and on a chair at the side was laid the rest of the costume.

"Teresa uttered a cry of joy, and, without inquiring whence this attire came, or even thanking Luigi, darted into the grotto, transformed into a dressing-room.

"Luigi pushed the stone behind her, for on the crest of a small adjacent hill which cut off the view toward Palestrina, he saw a traveller on horseback, stopping a moment, as if uncertain of his road, and thus presenting against the blue sky that perfect outline which is peculiar to distant objects in southern climes. When he saw Luigi, he put his horse into a gallop and advanced toward him.

"Luigi was not mistaken. The traveller, who was going from Palestrina to Tivoli, had mistaken his way; the young man directed him; but as at a distance of a quarter of a mile the road again divided into three ways, and on reaching these the traveller might again stray from his route, he begged Luigi to be his guide.

"Luigi threw his cloak on the ground, placed his carbine on his shoulder, and freed from his heavy covering, preceded the traveller with the rapid step of a mountaineer, which a horse can scarcely keep up with. In ten minutes Luigi and the traveller reached the cross-roads. On arriving there, with an air as majestic as that of an emperor, he stretched his hand towards that one of the roads which the traveller was to follow.

"'That is your road, excellency, and now you cannot again mistake.'

"'And here is your recompense,' said the traveller, offering the young herdsman some small pieces of money.

"'Thank you,' said Luigi, drawing back his hand; 'I render a service, I do not sell it.'

"'Well,' replied the traveller, who seemed used to this difference between the servility of a man of the cities and the pride of the mountaineer, 'if you refuse wages, you will, perhaps, accept a gift.'

"'Ah, yes, that is another thing.'

"'Then,' said the traveller, 'take these two Venetian sequins and give them to your bride, to make herself a pair of earrings.'

"'And then do you take this poniard,' said the young herdsman; 'you will not find one better carved between Albano and Civita-Castellana.'

"'I accept it,' answered the traveller, 'but then the obligation will be on my side, for this poniard is worth more than two sequins.'

"'For a dealer perhaps; but for me, who engraved it myself, it is hardly worth a piastre.'

"'What is your name?' inquired the traveller.

"'Luigi Vampa,' replied the shepherd, with the same air as he would have replied, Alexander, King of Macedon. 'And yours?'

"'I,' said the traveller, 'am called Sinbad the Sailor.'"

Franz d'Épinay started with surprise.

"Sinbad the Sailor?" he said.

"Yes," replied the narrator; "that was the name which the traveller gave to Vampa as his own."

"Well, and what may you have to say against this name?" inquired Albert; "it is a very pretty name, and the adventures of the gentleman of that name amused me very much in my youth, I must confess."

Franz said no more. The name of Sinbad the Sailor, as may well be supposed, awakened in him a world of recollections, as had the name of the Count of Monte Cristo on the previous evening.

"Proceed!" said he to the host.

"Vampa put the two sequins haughtily into his pocket, and slowly returned by the way he had gone. As he came within two or three hundred paces of the grotto, he thought he heard a cry. He listened to know whence this sound could proceed. A moment afterwards he thought he heard his own name pronounced distinctly.

"The cry proceeded from the grotto. He bounded like a chamois, cocking his carbine as he went, and in a moment reached the summit of a hill opposite to that on which he had perceived the traveller. Three cries for help came more distinctly to his ear. He cast his eyes around him and saw a man carrying off Teresa, as Nessus, the centaur, carried Deianira.

"This man, who was hastening towards the wood, was already three-quarters of the way on the road from the grotto to the forest. Vampa measured the distance; the man was at least two hundred paces in advance of him, and there was not a chance of overtaking him. The young shepherd stopped, as if his feet had been rooted to the ground; then he put the butt of his carbine to his shoulder, took aim at the ravisher, followed him for a second in his track, and then fired.

"The ravisher stopped suddenly, his knees bent under him, and he fell with Teresa in his arms. The young girl rose instantly, but the man lay on the earth struggling in the agonies of death. Vampa then rushed towards Teresa; for at ten paces from the dying man her legs had failed her, and she had dropped on her knees, so that the young man feared that the ball that had brought down his enemy, had also wounded his betrothed.

"Fortunately, she was unscathed, and it was fright alone that had overcome Teresa. When Luigi had assured himself that she was safe and unharmed, he turned towards the wounded man. He had just expired, with clenched hands, his mouth in a spasm of agony, and his hair on end in the sweat of death. His eyes remained open and menacing. Vampa approached the corpse, and recognized Cucumetto.

"From the day on which the bandit had been saved by the two young peasants, he had been enamoured of Teresa, and had sworn she should be his. From that time he had watched them, and profiting by the moment when her lover had left her alone, had carried her off, and believed he at length had her in his power, when the ball, directed by the unerring skill of the young herdsman, had pierced his heart. Vampa gazed on him for a moment without betraying the slightest emotion; while, on the contrary, Teresa, shuddering in every limb, dared not approach the slain ruffian but by degrees, and threw a hesitating glance at the dead body over the shoulder of her lover. Suddenly Vampa turned toward his mistress:

"'Ah,' said he 'good, good! You are dressed; it is now my turn to dress myself.'

"Teresa was clothed from head to foot in the garb of the Count of San-Felice's daughter. Vampa took Cucumetto's body in his arms and conveyed it to the grotto, while in her turn Teresa remained outside. If a second traveller had passed, he would have seen a strange thing, a shepherdess watching her flock, clad in a cashmere grown, with ear-rings and necklace of pearls, diamond pins, and buttons of sapphires, emeralds, and rubies. He would, no doubt, have believed that he had returned to the times of Florian, and would have declared, on reaching Paris, that he had met an Alpine shepherdess seated at the foot of the Sabine Hill.

"At the end of a quarter of an hour Vampa quitted the grotto; his costume was no less elegant than that of Teresa. He wore a vest of garnet-colored velvet, with buttons of cut gold; a silk waistcoat covered with embroidery; a Roman scarf tied round his neck; a cartridge-box worked with gold, and red and green silk; sky-blue velvet breeches, fastened above the knee with diamond buckles; garters of deerskin, worked with a thousand arabesques, and a hat whereon hung ribbons of all colors; two watches hung from his girdle, and a splendid poniard was in his belt.

"Teresa uttered a cry of admiration. Vampa in this attire resembled a painting by Léopold Robert or Schnetz. He had assumed the entire costume of Cucumetto. The young man saw the effect produced on his betrothed, and a smile of pride passed over his lips.

"'Now,' he said to Teresa, 'are you ready to share my fortune, whatever it may be?'

"'Oh, yes!' exclaimed the young girl enthusiastically.

"'And follow me wherever I go?'

"'To the world's end.'

"'Then take my arm, and let us on; we have no time to lose.'

"The young girl did so without questioning her lover as to where he was conducting her, for he appeared to her at this moment as handsome, proud, and powerful as a god. They went towards the forest, and soon entered it.

"We need scarcely say that all the paths of the mountain were known to Vampa; he therefore went forward without a moment's hesitation, although there was no beaten track, but he knew his path by looking at the trees and bushes, and thus they kept on advancing for nearly an hour and a half. At the end of this time they had reached the thickest part of the forest. A torrent, whose bed was dry, led into a deep gorge. Vampa took this wild road, which, enclosed between two ridges, and shadowed by the tufted umbrage of the pines, seemed, but for the difficulties of its descent, that path to Avernus of which Virgil speaks. Teresa had become alarmed at the wild and deserted look of the plain around her, and pressed closely against her guide, not uttering a syllable; but as she saw him advance with even step and composed countenance, she endeavored to repress her emotion.

"Suddenly, about ten paces from them, a man advanced from behind a tree and aimed at Vampa.

"'Not another step,' he said, 'or you are a dead man.'

"'What, then,' said Vampa, raising his hand with a gesture of disdain, while Teresa, no longer able to restrain her alarm, clung closely to him, 'do wolves rend each other?'

"'Who are you?' inquired the sentinel.

"'I am Luigi Vampa, shepherd of the San-Felice farm.'

"'What do you want?'

"'I would speak with your companions who are in the glade at Rocca Bianca.'

"'Follow me, then,' said the sentinel; 'or, as you know your way, go first.'

"Vampa smiled disdainfully at this precaution on the part of the bandit, went before Teresa, and continued to advance with the same firm and easy step as before. At the end of ten minutes the bandit made them a sign to stop. The two young persons obeyed. Then the bandit thrice imitated the cry of a crow; a croak answered this signal.

"'Good!' said the sentry, 'you may now go on.'

"Luigi and Teresa again set forward; as they went on Teresa clung tremblingly to her lover at the sight of weapons and the glistening of carbines through the trees. The retreat of Rocca Bianca was at the top of a small mountain, which no doubt in former days had been a volcano an extinct volcano before the days when Remus and Romulus had deserted Alba to come and found the city of Rome.

"Teresa and Luigi reached the summit, and all at once found themselves in the presence of twenty bandits.

"'Here is a young man who seeks and wishes to speak to you,' said the sentinel.

"'What has he to say?' inquired the young man who was in command in the chief's absence.

"'I wish to say that I am tired of a shepherd's life,' was Vampa's reply.

"'Ah, I understand,' said the lieutenant; 'and you seek admittance into our ranks?'

"'Welcome!' cried several bandits from Ferrusino, Pampinara, and Anagni, who had recognized Luigi Vampa.

"'Yes, but I came to ask something more than to be your companion.'

"'And what may that be?' inquired the bandits with astonishment.

"'I come to ask to be your captain,' said the young man.

"The bandits shouted with laughter.

"'And what have you done to aspire to this honor?' demanded the lieutenant.

"'I have killed your chief, Cucumetto, whose dress I now wear; and I set fire to the villa San-Felice to procure a wedding-dress for my betrothed.'

"An hour afterwards Luigi Vampa was chosen captain, vice Cucumetto, deceased."

"Well, my dear Albert," said Franz, turning towards his friend; "what think you of citizen Luigi Vampa?"

"I say he is a myth," replied Albert, "and never had an existence."

"And what may a myth be?" inquired Pastrini.

"The explanation would be too long, my dear landlord," replied Franz.

"And you say that Signor Vampa exercises his profession at this moment in the environs of Rome?"

"And with a boldness of which no bandit before him ever gave an example."

"Then the police have vainly tried to lay hands on him?"

"Why, you see, he has a good understanding with the shepherds in the plains, the fishermen of the Tiber, and the smugglers of the coast. They seek for him in the mountains, and he is on the waters; they follow him on the waters, and he is on the open sea; then they pursue him, and he has suddenly taken refuge in the islands, at Giglio, Giannutri, or Monte Cristo; and when they hunt for him there, he reappears suddenly at Albano, Tivoli, or La Riccia."

"And how does he behave towards travellers?"

"Alas! his plan is very simple. It depends on the distance he may be from the city, whether he gives eight hours, twelve hours, or a day wherein to pay their ransom; and when that time has elapsed he allows another hour's grace. At the sixtieth minute of this hour, if the money is not forthcoming, he blows out the prisoner's brains with a pistol-shot, or plants his dagger in his heart, and that settles the account."

"Well, Albert," inquired Franz of his companion, "are you still disposed to go to the Colosseum by the outer wall?"

"Quite so," said Albert, "if the way be picturesque."

The clock struck nine as the door opened, and a coachman appeared.

"Excellencies," said he, "the coach is ready."

"Well, then," said Franz, "let us to the Colosseum."

"By the Porta del Popolo or by the streets, your excellencies?"

"By the streets, *morbleu!* by the streets!" cried Franz.

"Ah, my dear fellow," said Albert, rising, and lighting his third cigar, "really, I thought you had more courage."

So saying, the two young men went down the staircase, and got into the carriage.

Chapter 7

The Colosseum

Franz had so managed his route, that during the ride to the Colosseum they passed not a single ancient ruin, so that no preliminary impression interfered to mitigate the colossal proportions of the gigantic building they came to admire. The road selected was a continuation of the Via Sistina; then by cutting off the right angle of the street in which stands Santa Maria Maggiore and proceeding by the Via Urbana and San Pietro in Vincoli, the travellers would find themselves directly opposite the Colosseum.

This itinerary possessed another great advantage, that of leaving Franz at full liberty to indulge his deep reverie upon the subject of Signor Pastrini's story, in which his mysterious host of Monte Cristo was so strangely mixed up. Seated with folded arms in a corner of the carriage, he continued to ponder over the singular history he had so lately listened to, and to ask himself an interminable number of questions touching its various circumstances without, however, arriving at a satisfactory reply to any of them.

One fact more than the rest brought his friend "Sinbad the Sailor" back to his recollection, and that was the mysterious sort of intimacy that seemed to exist between the brigands and the sailors; and Pastrini's account of Vampa's having found refuge on board the vessels of smugglers and fishermen, reminded Franz of the two Corsican bandits he had found supping so amicably with the crew of the little yacht, which had even deviated from its course and touched at Porto-Vecchio for the sole purpose of landing them. The very name assumed by his host of Monte Cristo and again repeated by the landlord of the Hôtel de Londres, abundantly proved to him that his island friend was playing his philanthropic part on the shores of Piombino, Civita Vecchia, Ostia, and Gaëta, as on those of Corsica, Tuscany, and Spain; and further, Franz bethought him of having heard his singular entertainer speak both of Tunis and Palermo, proving thereby how largely his circle of acquaintances extended.

But however the mind of the young man might be absorbed in these reflections, they were at once dispersed at the sight of the dark frowning ruins of the stupendous Colosseum, through the various openings of which the pale moonlight played and flickered like the unearthly gleam from the eyes of the wandering dead. The carriage stopped near the Meta Sudans; the door was opened, and the young men, eagerly alighting, found themselves opposite a *cicerone*, who appeared to have sprung up from the ground, so unexpected was his appearance.

The usual guide from the hotel having followed them, they had paid two conductors, nor is it possible, at Rome, to avoid this abundant supply of guides; besides the ordinary *cicerone*, who seizes upon you directly you set foot in your hotel, and never quits you while you remain in the city, there is also a special *cicerone* belonging to each monument nay, almost to each part of a monument. It may, therefore, be easily imagined there is no scarcity of guides at the Colosseum, that wonder of all ages, which Martial thus eulogizes:

"Let Memphis cease to boast the barbarous miracles of her pyramids, and the wonders of Babylon be talked of no more among us; all must bow to the superiority of the gigantic labor of the Cæsars, and the many voices of Fame spread far and wide the surpassing merits of this incomparable monument."

As for Albert and Franz, they essayed not to escape from their *ciceronian* tyrants; and, indeed, it would have been so much the more difficult to break their bondage, as the guides alone are permitted to visit these monuments with torches in their hands. Thus, then, the young men made no attempt at resistance, but blindly and confidingly surrendered themselves into the care and custody of their conductors.

Franz had already made seven or eight similar excursions to the Colosseum, while his less favored companion trod for the first time in his life the classic ground forming the monument of Flavius Vespasian; and, to his credit be it spoken, his mind, even amid the glib loquacity of the guides, was duly and deeply touched with awe and enthusiastic admiration of all he saw; and certainly no adequate notion of these stupendous ruins can be formed save by such as have visited them, and more especially by moonlight, at which time the vast proportions of the building appear twice as large when viewed by the mysterious beams of a southern moonlit sky, whose rays are sufficiently clear and vivid to light the horizon with a glow equal to the soft twilight of a western clime.

Scarcely, therefore, had the reflective Franz walked a hundred steps beneath the interior porticoes of the ruin, when, abandoning Albert to the guides (who would by no means yield their prescriptive right of carrying their victims through the routine regularly laid down, and as regularly followed by them, but dragged the unconscious visitor to the various objects with a pertinacity that admitted of no appeal, beginning, as a matter of course, with the "Lions' Den", the "Hall of the Gladiators" and finishing with "Cæsar's Podium"), to escape a jargon and mechanical survey of the wonders by which he was surrounded, Franz ascended a half-dilapidated staircase, and, leaving them to follow their monotonous round, seated himself at the foot of a column, and immediately opposite a large aperture, which permitted him to enjoy a full and undisturbed view of the gigantic dimensions of the majestic ruin.

Franz had remained for nearly a quarter of an hour perfectly hidden by the shadow of the vast column at whose base he had found a resting-place, and from whence his eyes followed the motions of Albert and his guides, who, holding torches in their hands, had emerged from a vomitorium at the opposite extremity of the Colosseum, and then again disappeared down the steps conducting to the seats reserved for the Vestal virgins, resembling, as they glided along, some restless shades following the flickering glare of so many *ignes fatui*. All at once his ear caught a sound resembling that of a stone rolling down the staircase opposite the one by which he had himself ascended. There was nothing remarkable in the circumstance of a fragment of granite giving way and falling heavily below; but it seemed to him that the substance that fell gave way beneath the pressure of a foot, and also that someone, who endeavored as much as possible to prevent his footsteps from being heard, was approaching the spot where he sat.

Conjecture soon became certainty, for the figure of a man was distinctly visible to Franz, gradually emerging from the staircase opposite, upon which the moon was at that moment pouring a full tide of silvery brightness.

The stranger thus presenting himself was probably a person who, like Franz, preferred the enjoyment of solitude and his own thoughts to the frivolous gabble of the guides. And his appearance had nothing extraordinary in it; but the hesitation with which he proceeded, stopping and listening with anxious attention at every step he took, convinced Franz that he expected the arrival of some person.

By a sort of instinctive impulse, Franz withdrew as much as possible behind his pillar.

About ten feet from the spot where he and the stranger were, the roof had given way, leaving a large round opening, through which might be seen the blue vault of heaven, thickly studded with stars.

Around this opening, which had, possibly, for ages permitted a free entrance to the brilliant moonbeams that now illumined the vast pile, grew a quantity of creeping plants, whose delicate green branches stood out in bold relief against the clear azure of the firmament, while large masses of thick, strong fibrous shoots forced their way through the chasm, and hung floating to and fro, like so many waving strings.

The person whose mysterious arrival had attracted the attention of Franz stood in a kind of half-light, that rendered it impossible to distinguish his features, although his dress was easily made out. He wore a large brown mantle, one fold of which, thrown over his left shoulder, served likewise to mask the lower part of his countenance, while the upper part was completely hidden by his broad-brimmed hat. The lower part of his dress was more distinctly visible by the bright rays of the moon, which, entering through the broken ceiling, shed their refulgent beams on feet cased in elegantly made boots of polished leather, over which descended fashionably cut trousers of black cloth.

From the imperfect means Franz had of judging, he could only come to one conclusion, that the person whom he was thus watching certainly belonged to no inferior station of life.

Some few minutes had elapsed, and the stranger began to show manifest signs of impatience, when a slight noise was heard outside the aperture in the roof, and almost immediately a dark shadow seemed to obstruct the flood of light that had entered it, and the figure of a man was clearly seen gazing with eager scrutiny on the immense space beneath him; then, as his eye caught sight of him in the mantle, he grasped a floating mass of thickly matted boughs, and glided down by their help to within three or four feet of the ground, and then leaped lightly on his feet. The man who had performed this daring act with so much indifference wore the Transtevere costume.

"I beg your excellency's pardon for keeping you waiting," said the man, in the Roman dialect, "but I don't think I'm many minutes after my time, ten o'clock has just struck by the clock of Saint John Lateran."

"Say not a word about being late," replied the stranger in purest Tuscan; "'tis I who am too soon. But even if you had caused me to wait a little while, I should have felt quite sure that the delay was not occasioned by any fault of yours."

"Your excellency is perfectly right in so thinking," said the man; "I came here direct from the Castle of St. Angelo, and I had an immense deal of trouble before I could get a chance to speak to Beppo."

"And who is Beppo?"

"Oh, Beppo is employed in the prison, and I give him so much a year to let me know what is going on within his holiness's castle."

"Indeed! You are a provident person, I see."

"Why, you see, no one knows what may happen. Perhaps some of these days I may be entrapped, like poor Peppino and may be very glad to have some little nibbling mouse to gnaw the meshes of my net, and so help me out of prison."

"Briefly, what did you learn?"

"That two executions of considerable interest will take place the day after tomorrow at two o'clock, as is customary at Rome at the commencement of all great festivals. One of the culprits will be *mazzolato*; he is an atrocious villain, who murdered the priest who brought him up, and deserves not the smallest pity. The other sufferer is sentenced to be *decapitato*; and he, your excellency, is poor Peppino."

"The fact is, that you have inspired not only the pontifical government, but also the neighboring states, with such extreme fear, that they are glad of all opportunity of making an example."

"But Peppino did not even belong to my band; he was merely a poor shepherd, whose only crime consisted in furnishing us with provisions."

"Which makes him your accomplice to all intents and purposes. But mark the distinction with which he is treated; instead of being knocked on the head as you would be if once they caught hold of you, he is simply sentenced to be guillotined, by which means, too, the amusements of the day are diversified, and there is a spectacle to please every spectator."

"Without reckoning the wholly unexpected one I am preparing to surprise them with."

"My good friend," said the man in the cloak, "excuse me for saying that you seem to me precisely in the mood to commit some wild or extravagant act."

"Perhaps I am; but one thing I have resolved on, and that is, to stop at nothing to restore a poor devil to liberty, who has got into this scrape solely from having served me. I should hate and despise myself as a coward did I desert the brave fellow in his present extremity."

"And what do you mean to do?"

"To surround the scaffold with twenty of my best men, who, at a signal from me, will rush forward directly Peppino is brought for execution, and, by the assistance of their stilettos, drive back the guard, and carry off the prisoner."

"That seems to me as hazardous as uncertain, and convinces me that my scheme is far better than yours."

"And what is your excellency's project?"

"Just this. I will so advantageously bestow 2,000 piastres, that the person receiving them shall obtain a respite till next year for Peppino; and during that year, another skilfully placed 1,000 piastres will afford him the means of escaping from his prison."

"And do you feel sure of succeeding?"

"*Pardieu!*" exclaimed the man in the cloak, suddenly expressing himself in French.

"What did your excellency say?" inquired the other.

"I said, my good fellow, that I would do more single-handed by the means of gold than you and all your troop could effect with stilettos, pistols, carbines, and blunderbusses included. Leave me, then, to act, and have no fears for the result."

"At least, there can be no harm in myself and party being in readiness, in case your excellency should fail."

"None whatever. Take what precautions you please, if it is any satisfaction to you to do so; but rely upon my obtaining the reprieve I seek."

"Remember, the execution is fixed for the day after tomorrow, and that you have but one day to work in."

"And what of that? Is not a day divided into twenty-four hours, each hour into sixty minutes, and every minute sub-divided into sixty seconds? Now in 86,400 seconds very many things can be done."

"And how shall I know whether your excellency has succeeded or not."

"Oh, that is very easily arranged. I have engaged the three lower windows at the Café Rospoli; should I have obtained the requisite pardon for Peppino, the two outside windows will be hung with yellow damasks, and the centre with white, having a large cross in red marked on it."

"And whom will you employ to carry the reprieve to the officer directing the execution?"

"Send one of your men, disguised as a penitent friar, and I will give it to him. His dress will procure him the means of approaching the scaffold itself, and he will deliver the official order to the officer, who, in his turn, will hand it to the executioner; in the meantime, it will be as well to acquaint Peppino with what we have determined on, if it be only to prevent his dying of fear or losing his senses, because in either case a very useless expense will have been incurred."

"Your excellency," said the man, "you are fully persuaded of my entire devotion to you, are you not?"

"Nay, I flatter myself that there can be no doubt of it," replied the cavalier in the cloak.

"Well, then, only fulfil your promise of rescuing Peppino, and henceforward you shall receive not only devotion, but the most absolute obedience from myself and those under me that one human being can render to another."

"Have a care how far you pledge yourself, my good friend, for I may remind you of your promise at some, perhaps, not very distant period, when I, in my turn, may require your aid and influence."

"Let that day come sooner or later, your excellency will find me what I have found you in this my heavy trouble; and if from the other end of the world you but write me word to do such or such a thing, you may regard it as done, for done it shall be, on the word and faith of"

"Hush!" interrupted the stranger; "I hear a noise."

"'Tis some travellers, who are visiting the Colosseum by torchlight."

"'Twere better we should not be seen together; those guides are nothing but spies, and might possibly recognize you; and, however I may be honored by your friendship, my worthy friend, if once the extent of our intimacy were known, I am sadly afraid both my reputation and credit would suffer thereby."

"Well, then, if you obtain the reprieve?"

"The middle window at the Café Rospoli will be hung with white damask, bearing a red cross."

"And if you fail?"

"Then all three windows will have yellow draperies."

"And then?"

"And then, my good fellow, use your daggers in any way you please, and I further promise you to be there as a spectator of your prowess."

"We understand each other perfectly, then. Adieu, your excellency; depend upon me as firmly as I do upon you."

Saying these words, the Transteverin disappeared down the

staircase, while his companion, muffling his features more closely than before in the folds of his mantle, passed almost close to Franz, and descended to the arena by an outward flight of steps. The next minute Franz heard himself called by Albert, who made the lofty building re-echo with the sound of his friend's name. Franz, however, did not obey the summons till he had satisfied himself that the two men whose conversation he had overheard were at a sufficient distance to prevent his encountering them in his descent. In ten minutes after the strangers had departed, Franz was on the road to the Piazza di Spagna, listening with studied indifference to the learned dissertation delivered by Albert, after the manner of Pliny and Calpurnius, touching the iron-pointed nets used to prevent the ferocious beasts from springing on the spectators.

Franz let him proceed without interruption, and, in fact, did not hear what was said; he longed to be alone, and free to ponder over all that had occurred. One of the two men, whose mysterious meeting in the Colosseum he had so unintentionally witnessed, was an entire stranger to him, but not so the other; and though Franz had been unable to distinguish his features, from his being either wrapped in his mantle or obscured by the shadow, the tones of his voice had made too powerful an impression on him the first time he had heard them for him ever again to forget them, hear them when or where he might. It was more especially when this man was speaking in a manner half jesting, half bitter, that Franz's ear recalled most vividly the deep sonorous, yet well-pitched voice that had addressed him in the grotto of Monte Cristo, and which he heard for the second time amid the darkness and ruined grandeur of the Colosseum. And the more he thought, the more entire was his conviction, that the person who wore the mantle was no other than his former host and entertainer, "Sinbad the Sailor."

Under any other circumstances, Franz would have found it impossible to resist his extreme curiosity to know more of so singular a personage, and with that intent have sought to renew their short acquaintance; but in the present instance, the confidential nature of the conversation he had overheard made him, with propriety, judge that his appearance at such a time would be anything but agreeable. As we have seen, therefore, he permitted his former host to retire without attempting a recognition, but fully promising himself a rich indemnity for his present forbearance should chance afford him another opportunity.

In vain did Franz endeavor to forget the many perplexing thoughts which assailed him; in vain did he court the refreshment of sleep. Slumber refused to visit his eyelids and the night was passed in feverish contemplation of the chain of circumstances tending to prove the identity of the mysterious visitant to the Colosseum with the inhabitant of the grotto of Monte Cristo; and the more he thought, the firmer grew his opinion on the subject.

Worn out at length, he fell asleep at daybreak, and did not awake till late. Like a genuine Frenchman, Albert had employed his time in arranging for the evening's diversion; he had sent to engage a box at the Teatro Argentina; and Franz, having a number of letters to write, relinquished the carriage to Albert for the whole of the day.

At five o'clock Albert returned, delighted with his day's work; he had been occupied in leaving his letters of introduction, and had received in return more invitations to balls and routs than it would be possible for him to accept; besides this, he had seen (as he called it) all the remarkable sights at Rome. Yes, in a single day he had accomplished what his more serious-minded companion would have taken weeks to effect. Neither had he neglected to ascertain the name of the piece to be played that night at the Teatro Argentina, and also what performers appeared in it. The opera of *Parisina* was announced for representation, and the principal actors were Coselli, Moriani, and La Specchia.

The young men, therefore, had reason to consider themselves fortunate in having the opportunity of hearing one of the best works by the composer of *Lucia di Lammermoor*, supported by three of the most renowned vocalists of Italy.

Albert had never been able to endure the Italian theatres, with their orchestras from which it is impossible to see, and the absence of balconies, or open boxes; all these defects pressed hard on a man who had had his stall at the Bouffes, and had shared a lower box at the Opera. Still, in spite of this, Albert displayed his most dazzling and effective costumes each time he visited the theatres; but, alas, his elegant toilet was wholly thrown away, and one of the most worthy representatives of Parisian fashion had to carry with him the mortifying reflection that he had nearly overrun Italy without meeting with a single adventure.

Sometimes Albert would affect to make a joke of his want of success; but internally he was deeply wounded, and his self-love immensely piqued, to think that Albert de Morcerf, the most admired and most sought after of any young person of his day, should thus be passed over, and merely have his labor for his pains. And the thing was so much the more annoying, as, according to the characteristic modesty of a Frenchman, Albert had quitted Paris with the full conviction that he had only to show himself in Italy to carry all before him, and that upon his return he should astonish the Parisian world with the recital of his numerous love-affairs.

Alas, poor Albert! None of those interesting adventures fell in his way; the lovely Genoese, Florentines, and Neapolitans were all faithful, if not to their husbands, at least to their lovers, and thought not of changing even for the splendid appearance of Albert de Morcerf; and all he gained was the painful conviction that the ladies of Italy have this advantage over those of France, that they are faithful even in their infidelity.

Yet he could not restrain a hope that in Italy, as elsewhere, there might be an exception to the general rule.

Albert, besides being an elegant, well-looking young man, was also possessed of considerable talent and ability; moreover, he was a viscount a recently created one, certainly, but in the present day it is not necessary to go as far back as Noah in tracing a descent, and a genealogical tree is equally estimated, whether dated from 1399 or merely 1815; but to crown all these advantages, Albert de Morcerf commanded an income of 50,000 livres, a more than sufficient sum to render him a personage of considerable importance in Paris. It was therefore no small mortification to him to have visited most of the principal cities in Italy without having excited the most trifling observation.

Albert, however, hoped to indemnify himself for all these slights and indifferences during the Carnival, knowing full well that among the different states and kingdoms in which this festivity is celebrated, Rome is the spot where even the wisest and gravest throw off the usual rigidity of their lives, and deign to mingle in the follies of this time of liberty and relaxation. The Carnival was to commence on the morrow; therefore Albert had not an instant to lose in setting forth the programme of his hopes, expectations, and claims to notice.

With this design he had engaged a box in the most conspicuous part of the theatre, and exerted himself to set off his personal attractions by the aid of the most rich and elaborate toilet. The box taken by Albert was in the first circle; although each of the three tiers of boxes is deemed equally aristocratic, and is, for this reason, generally styled the "nobility's boxes," and although the box engaged for the two friends was sufficiently capacious to contain at least a dozen persons, it had cost less than would be paid at some of the French theatres for one admitting merely four occupants.

Another motive had influenced Albert's selection of his seat, who knew but that, thus advantageously placed, he might not in truth attract the notice of some fair Roman, and an introduction might ensue that would procure him the offer of a seat in a carriage, or a place in a princely balcony, from which he might behold the gayeties of the Carnival?

These united considerations made Albert more lively and anxious to please than he had hitherto been. Totally disregarding the business of the stage, he leaned from his box and began attentively scrutinizing the beauty of each pretty woman, aided by a powerful opera-glass; but, alas, this attempt to attract notice wholly failed; not even curiosity had been excited, and it was but too apparent that the lovely creatures, into whose good graces he was desirous of stealing, were all so much engrossed with themselves, their lovers, or their own thoughts, that they had not so much as noticed him or the manipulation of his glass.

The truth was, that the anticipated pleasures of the Carnival, with the "Holy Week" that was to succeed it, so filled every fair breast, as to prevent the least attention being bestowed even on the business of the stage. The actors made their entries and exits unobserved or unthought of; at certain conventional moments, the spectators would suddenly cease their conversation, or rouse themselves from their musings, to listen to some brilliant effort of Moriani's, a well-executed recitative by Coselli, or to join in loud applause at the wonderful powers of La Specchia; but that momentary excitement over, they quickly relapsed into their former state of preoccupation or interesting conversation.

Towards the close of the first act, the door of a box which had been hitherto vacant was opened; a lady entered to whom Franz had been introduced in Paris, where indeed, he had imagined she still was. The quick eye of Albert caught the involuntary start with which his friend beheld the new arrival, and, turning to him, he said hastily:

"Do you know the woman who has just entered that box?"

"Yes; what do you think of her?"

"Oh, she is perfectly lovely what a complexion! And such magnificent hair! Is she French?"

"No; a Venetian."

"And her name is "

"Countess G ."

"Ah, I know her by name!" exclaimed Albert; "she is said to possess as much wit and cleverness as beauty. I was to have been presented to her when I met her at Madame Villefort's ball."

"Shall I assist you in repairing your negligence?" asked Franz.

"My dear fellow, are you really on such good terms with her as to venture to take me to her box?"

"Why, I have only had the honor of being in her society and conversing with her three or four times in my life; but you know that even such an acquaintance as that might warrant my doing what you ask."

At that instant, the countess perceived Franz, and graciously waved her hand to him, to which he replied by a respectful inclination of the head. "Upon my word," said Albert, "you seem to be on excellent terms with the beautiful countess."

"You are mistaken in thinking so," returned Franz calmly; "but you merely fall into the same error which leads so many of our countrymen to commit the most egregious blunders, I mean that of judging the habits and customs of Italy and Spain by our Parisian notions; believe me, nothing is more fallacious than to form any estimate of the degree of intimacy you may suppose existing among persons by the familiar terms they seem upon; there is a similarity of feeling at this instant between ourselves and the countess nothing more."

"Is there, indeed, my good fellow? Pray tell me, is it sympathy of heart?"

"No; of taste," continued Franz gravely.

"And in what manner has this congeniality of mind been evinced?"

"By the countess's visiting the Colosseum, as we did last night, by moonlight, and nearly alone."

"You were with her, then?"

"I was."

"And what did you say to her?"

"Oh, we talked of the illustrious dead of whom that magnificent ruin is a glorious monument!"

"Upon my word," cried Albert, "you must have been a very entertaining companion alone, or all but alone, with a beautiful woman in such a place of sentiment as the Colosseum, and yet to find nothing better to talk about than the dead! All I can say is, if ever I should get such a chance, the living should be my theme."

"And you will probably find your theme ill-chosen."

"But," said Albert, breaking in upon his discourse, "never mind the past; let us only remember the present. Are you not going to keep your promise of introducing me to the fair subject of our remarks?"

"Certainly, directly the curtain falls on the stage."

"What a confounded long time this first act lasts. I believe, on my soul, that they never mean to finish it."

"Oh, yes, they will; only listen to that charming finale. How exquisitely Coselli sings his part."

"But what an awkward, inelegant fellow he is."

"Well, then, what do you say to La Specchia? Did you ever see anything more perfect than her acting?"

"Why, you know, my dear fellow, when one has been accustomed to Malibran and Sontag, such singers as these don't make the same impression on you they perhaps do on others."

"At least, you must admire Moriani's style and execution."

"I never fancied men of his dark, ponderous appearance singing with a voice like a woman's."

"My good friend," said Franz, turning to him, while Albert continued to point his glass at every box in the theatre, "you seem determined not to approve; you are really too difficult to please."

The curtain at length fell on the performances, to the infinite satisfaction of the Viscount of Morcerf, who seized his hat, rapidly passed his fingers through his hair, arranged his cravat and wristbands, and signified to Franz that he was waiting for him to lead the way.

Franz, who had mutely interrogated the countess, and received from her a gracious smile in token that he would be welcome, sought not to retard the gratification of Albert's eager impatience, but began at once the tour of the house, closely followed by Albert, who availed himself of the few minutes required to reach the opposite side of the theatre to settle the height and smoothness of his collar, and to arrange the lappets of his coat. This important task was just completed as they arrived at the countess's box.

At the knock, the door was immediately opened, and the young man who was seated beside the countess, in obedience to the Italian custom, instantly rose and surrendered his place to the strangers, who, in turn, would be expected to retire upon the arrival of other visitors.

Franz presented Albert as one of the most distinguished young men of the day, both as regarded his position in society and extraordinary talents; nor did he say more than the truth, for in Paris and the circle in which the viscount moved, he was looked upon and cited as a model of perfection. Franz added that his companion, deeply grieved at having been prevented the honor of being presented to the countess during her sojourn in Paris, was most anxious to make up for it, and had requested him (Franz) to remedy the past misfortune by conducting him to her box, and concluded by asking pardon for his presumption in having taken it upon himself to do so.

The countess, in reply, bowed gracefully to Albert, and extended her hand with cordial kindness to Franz; then, inviting Albert to take the vacant seat beside her, she recommended Franz to take the next best, if he wished to view the ballet, and pointed to the one behind her own chair.

Albert was soon deeply engrossed in discoursing upon Paris and Parisian matters, speaking to the countess of the various persons they both knew there. Franz perceived how completely he was in his element; and, unwilling to interfere with the pleasure he so evidently felt, took up Albert's glass, and began in his turn to survey the audience.

Sitting alone, in the front of a box immediately opposite, but situated on the third row, was a woman of exquisite beauty, dressed in a Greek costume, which evidently, from the ease and grace with which she wore it, was her national attire. Behind her, but in deep shadow, was the outline of a masculine figure; but the features of this latter personage it was not possible to distinguish. Franz could not forbear breaking in upon the apparently interesting conversation passing between the countess and Albert, to inquire of the former if she knew who was the fair Albanian opposite, since beauty such as hers was well worthy of being observed by either sex.

"All I can tell about her," replied the countess, "is, that she has been at Rome since the beginning of the season; for I saw her where she now sits the very first night of the season, and since then she has never missed a performance. Sometimes she is accompanied by the person who is now with her, and at others she is merely attended by a black servant."

"And what do you think of her personal appearance?"

"Oh, I consider her perfectly lovely she is just my idea of what Medora must have been."

Franz and the countess exchanged a smile, and then the latter resumed her conversation with Albert, while Franz returned to his previous survey of the house and company. The curtain rose on the ballet, which was one of those excellent specimens of the Italian school, admirably arranged and put on the stage by Henri, who has established for himself a great reputation throughout Italy for his taste and skill in the choreographic art one of those masterly productions of grace, method, and elegance in which the whole *corps de ballet*, from the principal dancers to the humblest supernumerary, are all engaged on the stage at the same time; and a hundred and fifty persons may be seen exhibiting the same attitude, or elevating the same arm or leg with a simultaneous movement, that would lead you to suppose that but one mind, one act of volition, influenced the moving mass.

The ballet was called *Poliska*.

However much the ballet might have claimed his attention, Franz was too deeply occupied with the beautiful Greek to take any note of it; while she seemed to experience an almost childlike delight in watching it, her eager, animated looks contrasting strongly with the utter indifference of her companion, who, during the whole time the piece lasted, never even moved, not even when the furious, crashing din produced by the trumpets, cymbals, and Chinese bells sounded their loudest from the orchestra. Of this he took no heed, but was, as far as appearances might be trusted, enjoying soft repose and bright celestial dreams.

The ballet at length came to a close, and the curtain fell amid the loud, unanimous plaudits of an enthusiastic and delighted audience.

Owing to the very judicious plan of dividing the two acts of the opera with a ballet, the pauses between the performances are very short, the singers in the opera having time to repose themselves and change their costume, when necessary, while the dancers are executing their pirouettes and exhibiting their graceful steps.

The overture to the second act began; and, at the first sound of the leader's bow across his violin, Franz observed the sleeper slowly arise and approach the Greek girl, who turned around to say a few words to him, and then, leaning forward again on the railing of her box, she became as absorbed as before in what was going on.

The countenance of the person who had addressed her remained so completely in the shade, that, though Franz tried his utmost, he could not distinguish a single feature. The curtain rose, and the attention of Franz was attracted by the actors; and his eyes turned from the box containing the Greek girl and her strange companion to watch the business of the stage.

Most of my readers are aware that the second act of *Parisina* opens with the celebrated and effective duet in which Parisina, while sleeping, betrays to Azzo the secret of her love for Ugo. The injured husband goes through all the emotions of jealousy, until conviction seizes on his mind, and then, in a frenzy of rage and indignation, he awakens his guilty wife to tell her that he knows her guilt and to threaten her with his vengeance.

This duet is one of the most beautiful, expressive and terrible conceptions that has ever emanated from the fruitful pen of Donizetti. Franz now listened to it for the third time; yet its notes, so tenderly expressive and fearfully grand as the wretched husband and wife give vent to their different griefs and passions, thrilled through the soul of Franz with an effect equal to his first emotions upon hearing it. Excited beyond his usual calm demeanor, Franz rose with the audience, and was about to join the loud, enthusiastic applause that followed; but suddenly his purpose was arrested, his hands fell by his sides, and the half-uttered "bravos" expired on his lips.

The occupant of the box in which the Greek girl sat appeared to share the universal admiration that prevailed; for he left his seat to stand up in front, so that, his countenance being fully revealed, Franz had no difficulty in recognizing him as the mysterious inhabitant of Monte Cristo, and the very same person he had encountered the preceding evening in the ruins of the Colosseum, and whose voice and figure had seemed so familiar to him.

All doubt of his identity was now at an end; his singular host evidently resided at Rome. The surprise and agitation occasioned by this full confirmation of Franz's former suspicion had no doubt imparted a corresponding expression to his features; for the countess, after gazing with a puzzled look at his face, burst into a fit of laughter, and begged to know what had happened.

"Countess," returned Franz, totally unheeding her raillery, "I asked you a short time since if you knew any particulars respecting the Albanian lady opposite; I must now beseech you to inform me who and what is her husband?"

"Nay," answered the countess, "I know no more of him than yourself."

"Perhaps you never before noticed him?"

"What a question so truly French! Do you not know that we Italians have eyes only for the man we love?"

"True," replied Franz.

"All I can say is," continued the countess, taking up the *lorgnette*, and directing it toward the box in question, "that the gentleman, whose history I am unable to furnish, seems to me as though he had just been dug up; he looks more like a corpse permitted by some friendly grave-digger to quit his tomb for a while, and revisit this earth of ours, than anything human. How ghastly pale he is!"

"Oh, he is always as colorless as you now see him," said Franz.

"Then you know him?" almost screamed the countess. "Oh, pray do, for heaven's sake, tell us all about is he a vampire, or a resuscitated corpse, or what?"

"I fancy I have seen him before; and I even think he recognizes me."

"And I can well understand," said the countess, shrugging up her beautiful shoulders, as though an involuntary shudder passed through her veins, "that those who have once seen that man will never be likely to forget him."

The sensation experienced by Franz was evidently not peculiar to himself; another, and wholly uninterested person, felt the same unaccountable awe and misgiving.

"Well." inquired Franz, after the countess had a second time directed her *lorgnette* at the box, "what do you think of our opposite neighbor?"

"Why, that he is no other than Lord Ruthven himself in a living form." drew a smile to Franz's countenance; although he could but allow that if anything was likely to induce belief in the existence of vampires, it would be the presence of such a man as the mysterious personage before him.

"I must positively find out who and what he is," said Franz, rising from his seat.

"No, no," cried the countess; "you must not leave me. I depend upon you to escort me home. Oh, indeed, I cannot permit you to go."

"Is it possible," whispered Franz, "that you entertain any fear?"

"I'll tell you," answered the countess. "Byron had the most

perfect belief in the existence of vampires, and even assured me that he had seen them. The description he gave me perfectly corresponds with the features and character of the man before us. Oh, he is the exact personification of what I have been led to expect! The coal-black hair, large bright, glittering eyes, in which a wild, unearthly fire seems burning, the same ghastly paleness. Then observe, too, that the woman with him is altogether unlike all others of her sex. She is a foreigner a stranger. Nobody knows who she is, or where she comes from. No doubt she belongs to the same horrible race he does, and is, like himself, a dealer in magical arts. I entreat of you not to go near him at least tonight; and if tomorrow your curiosity still continues as great, pursue your researches if you will; but tonight you neither can nor shall. For that purpose I mean to keep you all to myself."

Franz protested he could not defer his pursuit till the following day, for many reasons.

"Listen to me," said the countess, "and do not be so very headstrong. I am going home. I have a party at my house tonight, and therefore cannot possibly remain till the end of the opera. Now, I cannot for one instant believe you so devoid of gallantry as to refuse a lady your escort when she even condescends to ask you for it."

There was nothing else left for Franz to do but to take up his hat, open the door of the box, and offer the countess his arm. It was quite evident, by her manner, that her uneasiness was not feigned; and Franz himself could not resist a feeling of superstitious dread so much the stronger in him, as it arose from a variety of corroborative recollections, while the terror of the countess sprang from an instinctive belief, originally created in her mind by the wild tales she had listened to till she believed them truths. Franz could even feel her arm tremble as he assisted her into the carriage. Upon arriving at her hotel, Franz perceived that she had deceived him when she spoke of expecting company; on the contrary, her own return before the appointed hour seemed greatly to astonish the servants.

"Excuse my little subterfuge," said the countess, in reply to her companion's half-reproachful observation on the subject; "but that horrid man had made me feel quite uncomfortable, and I longed to be alone, that I might compose my startled mind."

Franz essayed to smile.

"Nay," said she, "do not smile; it ill accords with the expression of your countenance, and I am sure it does not spring from your heart. However, promise me one thing."

"What is it?"

"Promise me, I say."

"I will do anything you desire, except relinquish my determination of finding out who this man is. I have more reasons than you can imagine for desiring to know who he is, from whence he came, and whither he is going."

"Where he comes from I am ignorant; but I can readily tell you where he is going to, and that is down below, without the least doubt."

"Let us only speak of the promise you wished me to make," said Franz.

"Well, then, you must give me your word to return immediately to your hotel, and make no attempt to follow this man tonight. There are certain affinities between the persons we quit and those we meet afterwards. For heaven's sake, do not serve as a conductor between that man and me. Pursue your chase after him tomorrow as eagerly as you please; but never bring him near me, if you would not see me die of terror. And now, good-night; go to your rooms, and try to sleep away all recollections of this evening. For my own part, I am quite sure I shall not be able to close my eyes."

So saying, the countess quitted Franz, leaving him unable to decide whether she were merely amusing herself at his expense, or whether her fears and agitations were genuine.

Upon his return to the hotel, Franz found Albert in his dressing-gown and slippers, listlessly extended on a sofa, smoking a cigar.

"My dear fellow!" cried he, springing up, "is it really you? Why, I did not expect to see you before tomorrow."

"My dear Albert," replied Franz, "I am glad of this opportunity to tell you, once and forever, that you entertain a most erroneous notion concerning Italian women. I should have thought the continual failures you have met with in all your own love affairs might have taught you better by this time."

"Upon my soul, these women would puzzle the very Devil to read them aright. Why, here they give you their hand they press yours in return they keep up a whispering conversation permit you to accompany them home. Why, if a Parisian were to indulge in a quarter of these marks of flattering attention, her reputation would be gone forever."

"And the very reason why the women of this fine country, 'where sounds the *si*,' as Dante writes, put so little restraint on their words and actions, is because they live so much in public, and have really nothing to conceal. Besides, you must have perceived that the countess was really alarmed."

"At what? At the sight of that respectable gentleman sitting opposite to us in the same box with the lovely Greek girl? Now, for my part, I met them in the lobby after the conclusion of the piece; and hang me, if I can guess where you took your notions of the other world from. I can assure you that this hobgoblin of yours is a deuced fine-looking fellow admirably dressed. Indeed, I feel quite sure, from the cut of his clothes, they are made by a first-rate Paris tailor probably Blin or Humann. He was rather too pale, certainly; but then, you know, paleness is always looked upon as a strong proof of aristocratic descent and distinguished breeding."

Franz smiled; for he well remembered that Albert particularly prided himself on the entire absence of color in his own complexion.

"Well, that tends to confirm my own ideas," said Franz, "that the countess's suspicions were destitute alike of sense and reason. Did he speak in your hearing? and did you catch any of his words?"

"I did; but they were uttered in the Romaic dialect. I knew that from the mixture of Greek words. I don't know whether I ever told you that when I was at college I was rather rather strong in Greek."

"He spoke the Romaic language, did he?"

"I think so."

"That settles it," murmured Franz. "'Tis he, past all doubt."

"What do you say?"

"Nothing, nothing. But tell me, what were you thinking about when I came in?"

"Oh, I was arranging a little surprise for you."

"Indeed. Of what nature?"

"Why, you know it is quite impossible to procure a carriage."

"Certainly; and I also know that we have done all that human means afforded to endeavor to get one."

"Now, then, in this difficulty a bright idea has flashed across my brain."

Franz looked at Albert as though he had not much confidence in the suggestions of his imagination.

"I tell you what, M. Franz," cried Albert, "you deserve to be called out for such a misgiving and incredulous glance as that you were pleased to bestow on me just now."

"And I promise to give you the satisfaction of a gentleman if your scheme turns out as ingenious as you assert."

"Well, then, hearken to me."

"I listen."

"You agree, do you not, that obtaining a carriage is out of the question?"

"I do."

"Neither can we procure horses?"

"True; we have offered any sum, but have failed."

"Well, now, what do you say to a cart? I dare say such a thing might be had."

"Very possibly."

"And a pair of oxen?"

"As easily found as the cart."

"Then you see, my good fellow, with a cart and a couple of oxen our business can be managed. The cart must be tastefully ornamented; and if you and I dress ourselves as Neapolitan reapers, we may get up a striking tableau, after the manner of that splendid picture by Léopold Robert. It would add greatly to the effect if the countess would join us in the costume of a peasant from Puzzoli or Sorrento. Our group would then be quite complete, more especially as the countess is quite beautiful enough to represent a Madonna."

"Well," said Franz, "this time, M. Albert, I am bound to give you credit for having hit upon a most capital idea."

"And quite a national one, too," replied Albert with gratified pride. "A mere masque borrowed from our own festivities. Ha, ha, ye Romans! you thought to make us, unhappy strangers, trot at the heels of your processions, like so many lazzaroni, because no carriages or horses are to be had in your beggarly city. But you don't know us; when we can't have one thing we invent another."

"And have you communicated your triumphant idea to anybody?"

"Only to our host. Upon my return home I sent for him, and I then explained to him what I wished to procure. He assured me that nothing would be easier than to furnish all I desired. One thing I was sorry for; when I bade him have the horns of the oxen gilded, he told me there would not be time, as it would require three days to do that; so you see we must do without this little superfluity."

"And where is he now?"

"Who?"

"Our host."

"Gone out in search of our equipage, by tomorrow it might be too late."

"Then he will be able to give us an answer tonight."

"Oh, I expect him every minute."

At this instant the door opened, and the head of Signor Pastrini appeared. "*Permesso?*" inquired he.

"Certainly certainly," cried Franz. "Come in, my host."

"Now, then," asked Albert eagerly, "have you found the desired cart and oxen?"

"Better than that!" replied Signor Pastrini, with the air of a man perfectly well satisfied with himself.

"Take care, my worthy host," said Albert, "*better* is a sure enemy to *well*."

"Let your excellencies only leave the matter to me," returned Signor Pastrini in a tone indicative of unbounded self-confidence.

"But what *have* you done?" asked Franz. "Speak out, there's a worthy fellow."

"Your excellencies are aware," responded the landlord, swelling with importance, "that the Count of Monte Cristo is living on the same floor with yourselves!"

"I should think we did know it," exclaimed Albert, "since it is owing to that circumstance that we are packed into these small rooms, like two poor students in the back streets of Paris."

"When, then, the Count of Monte Cristo, hearing of the dilemma in which you are placed, has sent to offer you seats in his carriage and two places at his windows in the Palazzo Rospoli." The friends looked at each other with unutterable surprise.

"But do you think," asked Albert, "that we ought to accept such offers from a perfect stranger?"

"What sort of person is this Count of Monte Cristo?" asked Franz of his host.

"A very great nobleman, but whether Maltese or Sicilian I cannot exactly say; but this I know, that he is noble as a Borghese and rich as a gold mine."

"It seems to me," said Franz, speaking in an undertone to Albert, "that if this person merited the high panegyrics of our landlord, he would have conveyed his invitation through another channel, and not permitted it to be brought to us in this unceremonious way. He would have written or "

At this instant someone knocked at the door.

"Come in," said Franz.

A servant, wearing a livery of considerable style and richness, appeared at the threshold, and, placing two cards in the landlord's hands, who forthwith presented them to the two young men, he said:

"Please to deliver these, from the Count of Monte Cristo to Vicomte Albert de Morcerf and M. Franz d'Épinay. The Count of Monte Cristo," continued the servant, "begs these gentlemen's permission to wait upon them as their neighbor, and he will be honored by an intimation of what time they will please to receive him."

"Faith, Franz," whispered Albert, "there is not much to find fault with here."

"Tell the count," replied Franz, "that we will do ourselves the pleasure of calling on him."

The servant bowed and retired.

"That is what I call an elegant mode of attack," said Albert, "You were quite correct in what you said, Signor Pastrini. The Count of Monte Cristo is unquestionably a man of first-rate breeding and knowledge of the world."

"Then you accept his offer?" said the host.

"Of course we do," replied Albert. "Still, I must own I am sorry to be obliged to give up the cart and the group of reapers it would have produced such an effect! And were it not for the windows at the Palazzo Rospoli, by way of recompense for the loss of our beautiful scheme, I don't know but what I should have held on by my original plan. What say you, Franz?"

"Oh, I agree with you; the windows in the Palazzo Rospoli alone decided me."

The truth was, that the mention of two places in the Palazzo Rospoli had recalled to Franz the conversation he had overheard the preceding evening in the ruins of the Colosseum between the mysterious unknown and the Transteverin, in which the stranger in the cloak had undertaken to obtain the freedom of a condemned criminal; and if this muffled-up individual proved (as Franz felt sure he would) the same as the person he had just seen in the Teatro Argentina, then he should be able to establish his identity, and also to prosecute his researches respecting him with perfect facility and freedom.

Franz passed the night in confused dreams respecting the two meetings he had already had with his mysterious tormentor, and in waking speculations as to what the morrow would produce. The next day must clear up every doubt; and unless his near neighbor and would-be friend, the Count of Monte Cristo, possessed the ring of Gyges, and by its power was able to render himself invisible, it was very certain he could not escape this time.

Eight o'clock found Franz up and dressed, while Albert, who had not the same motives for early rising, was still soundly asleep. The first act of Franz was to summon his landlord, who presented himself with his accustomed obsequiousness.

"Pray, Signor Pastrini," asked Franz, "is not some execution appointed to take place today?"

"Yes, your excellency; but if your reason for inquiry is that you may procure a window to view it from, you are much too late."

"Oh, no," answered Franz, "I had no such intention; and even if I had felt a wish to witness the spectacle, I might have done so from Monte Pincio; could I not?"

"Ah!" exclaimed mine host, "I did not think it likely your excellency would have chosen to mingle with such a rabble as are always collected on that hill, which, indeed, they consider as exclusively belonging to themselves."

"Very possibly I may not go," answered Franz; "but in case I feel disposed, give me some particulars of today's executions."

"What particulars would your excellency like to hear?"

"Why, the number of persons condemned to suffer, their names, and description of the death they are to die."

"That happens just lucky, your excellency! Only a few minutes ago they brought me the *tavolettas*."

"What are they?"

"Sort of wooden tablets hung up at the corners of streets the evening before an execution, on which is pasted up a paper containing the names of the condemned persons, their crimes, and mode of punishment. The reason for so publicly announcing all this is, that all good and faithful Catholics may offer up their prayers for the unfortunate culprits, and, above all, beseech of Heaven to grant them a sincere repentance."

"And these tablets are brought to you that you may add your prayers to those of the faithful, are they?" asked Franz somewhat incredulously.

"Oh, dear, no, your excellency! I have not time for anybody's affairs but my own and those of my honorable guests; but I make an agreement with the man who pastes up the papers, and he brings them to me as he would the playbills, that in case any person staying at my hotel should like to witness an execution, he may obtain every requisite information concerning the time and place etc."

"Upon my word, that is a most delicate attention on your part, Signor Pastrini," cried Franz.

"Why, your excellency," returned the landlord, chuckling and rubbing his hands with infinite complacency, "I think I may take upon myself to say I neglect nothing to deserve the support and patronage of the noble visitors to this poor hotel."

"I see that plainly enough, my most excellent host, and you may rely upon me to proclaim so striking a proof of your attention to your guests wherever I go. Meanwhile, oblige me by a sight of one of these *tavolettas*."

"Nothing can be easier than to comply with your excellency's wish," said the landlord, opening the door of the chamber; "I have caused one to be placed on the landing, close by your apartment."

Then, taking the tablet from the wall, he handed it to Franz, who read as follows:

"'The public is informed that on Wednesday, February 23rd, being the first day of the Carnival, executions will take place in the Piazza del Popolo, by order of the Tribunal of the

Rota, of two persons, named Andrea Rondolo, and Peppino, otherwise called Rocca Priori; the former found guilty of the murder of a venerable and exemplary priest, named Don César Torlini, canon of the church of St. John Lateran; and the latter convicted of being an accomplice of the atrocious and sanguinary bandit, Luigi Vampa, and his band. The first-named malefactor will be *mazzolato*, the second culprit *decapitato*.

"'The prayers of all good Christians are entreated for these unfortunate men, that it may please God to awaken them to a sense of their guilt, and to grant them a hearty and sincere repentance for their crimes.'"

This was precisely what Franz had heard the evening before in the ruins of the Colosseum. No part of the programme differed, the names of the condemned persons, their crimes, and mode of punishment, all agreed with his previous information. In all probability, therefore, the Transteverin was no other than the bandit Luigi Vampa himself, and the man shrouded in the mantle the same he had known as "Sinbad the Sailor," but who, no doubt, was still pursuing his philanthropic expedition in Rome, as he had already done at Porto-Vecchio and Tunis.

Time was getting on, however, and Franz deemed it advisable to awaken Albert; but at the moment he prepared to proceed to his chamber, his friend entered the room in perfect costume for the day. The anticipated delights of the Carnival had so run in his head as to make him leave his pillow long before his usual hour.

"Now, my excellent Signor Pastrini," said Franz, addressing his landlord, "since we are both ready, do you think we may proceed at once to visit the Count of Monte Cristo?"

"Most assuredly," replied he. "The Count of Monte Cristo is always an early riser; and I can answer for his having been up these two hours."

"Then you really consider we shall not be intruding if we pay our respects to him directly?"

"Oh, I am quite sure. I will take all the blame on myself if you find I have led you into an error."

"Well, then, if it be so, are you ready, Albert?"

"Perfectly."

"Let us go and return our best thanks for his courtesy."

"Yes, let us do so."

The landlord preceded the friends across the landing, which was all that separated them from the apartments of the count, rang at the bell, and, upon the door being opened by a servant, said:

"*I signori Francesi.*"

The domestic bowed respectfully, and invited them to enter. They passed through two rooms, furnished in a luxurious manner they had not expected to see under the roof of Signor Pastrini, and were shown into an elegantly fitted-up drawing-room. The richest Turkey carpets covered the floor, and the softest and most inviting couches, easy-chairs, and sofas, offered their high-piled and yielding cushions to such as desired repose or refreshment. Splendid paintings by the first masters were ranged against the walls, intermingled with magnificent trophies of war, while heavy curtains of costly tapestry were suspended before the different doors of the room.

"If your excellencies will please to be seated," said the man, "I will let the count know that you are here."

And with these words he disappeared behind one of the tapestried *portières*. As the door opened, the sound of a *guzla* reached the ears of the young men, but was almost immediately lost, for the rapid closing of the door merely allowed one rich swell of harmony to enter. Franz and Albert looked inquiringly at each other, then at the gorgeous furnishings of the apartment. Everything seemed more magnificent at a second view than it had done at their first rapid survey.

"Well," said Franz to his friend, "what think you of all this?"

"Why, upon my soul, my dear fellow, it strikes me that our elegant and attentive neighbor must either be some successful stock-jobber who has speculated in the fall of the Spanish funds, or some prince travelling *incog.*"

"Hush, hush!" replied Franz; "we shall ascertain who and what he is he comes!"

As Franz spoke, he heard the sound of a door turning on its hinges, and almost immediately afterwards the tapestry was drawn aside, and the owner of all these riches stood before the two young men. Albert instantly rose to meet him, but Franz remained, in a manner, spellbound on his chair; for in the person of him who had just entered he recognized not only the mysterious visitant to the Colosseum, and the occupant of the box at the Teatro Argentina, but also his extraordinary host of Monte Cristo.

Chapter 8

La Mazzolata

G entlemen," said the Count of Monte Cristo as he entered, "I pray you excuse me for suffering my visit to be anticipated; but I feared to disturb you by presenting myself earlier at your apartments; besides, you sent me word that you would come to me, and I have held myself at your disposal."

"Franz and I have to thank you a thousand times, count," returned Albert; "you extricated us from a great dilemma, and we were on the point of inventing a very fantastic vehicle when your friendly invitation reached us."

"Indeed," returned the count, motioning the two young men to sit down. "It was the fault of that blockhead Pastrini, that I did not sooner assist you in your distress. He did not mention a syllable of your embarrassment to me, when he knows that, alone and isolated as I am, I seek every opportunity of making the acquaintance of my neighbors. As soon as I learned I could in any way assist you, I most eagerly seized the opportunity of offering my services."

The two young men bowed. Franz had, as yet, found nothing to say; he had come to no determination, and as nothing in the count's manner manifested the wish that he should recognize him, he did not know whether to make any allusion to the past, or wait until he had more proof; besides, although sure it was he who had been in the box the previous evening, he could not be equally positive that this was the man he had seen at the Colosseum. He resolved, therefore, to let things take their course without making any direct overture to the count. Moreover, he had this advantage, he was master of the count's secret, while the count had no hold on Franz, who had nothing to conceal. However, he resolved to lead the conversation to a subject which might possibly clear up his doubts.

"Count," said he, "you have offered us places in your carriage, and at your windows in the Rospoli Palace. Can you tell us where we can obtain a sight of the Piazza del Popolo?"

"Ah," said the count negligently, looking attentively at Morcerf, "is there not something like an execution upon the Piazza del Popolo?"

"Yes," returned Franz, finding that the count was coming to the point he wished.

"Stay, I think I told my steward yesterday to attend to this; perhaps I can render you this slight service also."

He extended his hand, and rang the bell thrice.

"Did you ever occupy yourself," said he to Franz, "with the employment of time and the means of simplifying the summoning your servants? I have. When I ring once, it is for my valet; twice, for my majordomo; thrice, for my steward, thus I do not waste a minute or a word. Here he is."

A man of about forty-five or fifty entered, exactly resembling the smuggler who had introduced Franz into the cavern; but he did not appear to recognize him. It was evident he had his orders.

"Monsieur Bertuccio," said the count, "you have procured me windows looking on the Piazza del Popolo, as I ordered you yesterday."

"Yes, excellency," returned the steward; "but it was very late."

"Did I not tell you I wished for one?" replied the count, frowning.

"And your excellency has one, which was let to Prince Lobanieff; but I was obliged to pay a hundred "

"That will do that will do, Monsieur Bertuccio; spare these gentlemen all such domestic arrangements. You have the window, that is sufficient. Give orders to the coachman; and be in readiness on the stairs to conduct us to it."

The steward bowed, and was about to quit the room.

"Ah!" continued the count, "be good enough to ask Pastrini if he has received the *tavoletta*, and if he can send us an account of the execution."

"There is no need to do that," said Franz, taking out his tablets; "for I saw the account, and copied it down."

"Very well, you can retire, M. Bertuccio; I need you no longer. Let us know when breakfast is ready. These gentlemen," added he, turning to the two friends, "will, I trust, do me the honor to breakfast with me?"

"But, my dear count," said Albert, "we shall abuse your kindness."

"Not at all; on the contrary, you will give me great pleasure. You will, one or other of you, perhaps both, return it to me at Paris. M. Bertuccio, lay covers for three."

He then took Franz's tablets out of his hand. "'We announce,' he read, in the same tone with which he would have read a newspaper, 'that today, the 23rd of February, will be executed Andrea Rondolo, guilty of murder on the person of the respected and venerated Don César Torlini, canon of the church of St. John Lateran, and Peppino, called Rocca Priori, convicted of complicity with the detestable bandit Luigi Vampa, and the men of his band.'

"Hum! 'The first will be *mazzolato*, the second *decapitato*.' Yes," continued the count, "it was at first arranged in this way; but I think since yesterday some change has taken place in the order of the ceremony."

"Really?" said Franz.

"Yes, I passed the evening at the Cardinal Rospigliosi's, and there mention was made of something like a pardon for one of the two men."

"For Andrea Rondolo?" asked Franz.

"No," replied the count, carelessly; "for the other (he glanced at the tablets as if to recall the name), for Peppino, called Rocca Priori. You are thus deprived of seeing a man guillotined; but the *mazzolata* still remains, which is a very curious punishment when seen for the first time, and even the second, while the other, as you must know, is very simple. The *mandaïa* never fails, never trembles, never strikes thirty times ineffectually, like the soldier who beheaded the Count of Chalais, and to whose tender mercy Richelieu had doubtless recommended the sufferer. Ah," added the count, in a contemptuous tone, "do not tell me of European punishments, they are in the infancy, or rather the old age, of cruelty."

"Really, count," replied Franz, "one would think that you had studied the different tortures of all the nations of the world."

"There are, at least, few that I have not seen," said the count coldly.

"And you took pleasure in beholding these dreadful spectacles?"

"My first sentiment was horror, the second indifference, the third curiosity."

"Curiosity that is a terrible word."

"Why so? In life, our greatest preoccupation is death; is it not then, curious to study the different ways by which the soul and body can part; and how, according to their different characters, temperaments, and even the different customs of their countries, different persons bear the transition from life to death, from existence to annihilation? As for myself, I can assure you of one thing, the more men you see die, the easier it becomes to die yourself; and in my opinion, death may be a torture, but it is not an expiation."

"I do not quite understand you," replied Franz; "pray explain your meaning, for you excite my curiosity to the highest pitch."

"Listen," said the count, and deep hatred mounted to his face, as the blood would to the face of any other. "If a man had by unheard-of and excruciating tortures destroyed your father, your mother, your betrothed, a being who, when torn from you, left a desolation, a wound that never closes, in your breast, do you think the reparation that society gives you is sufficient when it interposes the knife of the guillotine between the base of the occiput and the trapezal muscles of the murderer, and allows him who has caused us years of moral sufferings to escape with a few moments of physical pain?"

"Yes, I know," said Franz, "that human justice is insufficient to console us; she can give blood in return for blood, that is all; but you must demand from her only what it is in her power to grant."

"I will put another case to you," continued the count; "that where society, attacked by the death of a person, avenges death by death. But are there not a thousand tortures by which a man may be made to suffer without society taking the least cognizance of them, or offering him even the insufficient means of vengeance, of which we have just spoken? Are there not crimes for which the impalement of the Turks, the augers of the Persians, the stake and the brand of the Iroquois Indians, are inadequate tortures, and which are unpunished by society? Answer me, do not these crimes exist?"

"Yes," answered Franz; "and it is to punish them that duelling is tolerated."

"Ah, duelling," cried the count; "a pleasant manner, upon my soul, of arriving at your end when that end is vengeance! A man has carried off your mistress, a man has seduced your wife, a man has dishonored your daughter; he has rendered the whole life of one who had the right to expect from Heaven that portion of happiness God has promised to everyone of his creatures, an existence of misery and infamy; and you think you are avenged because you send a ball through the head, or pass a sword through the breast, of that man who has planted madness in your brain, and despair in your heart. And remember, moreover, that it is often he who comes off victorious from the strife, absolved of all crime in the eyes of the world. No, no," continued the count, "had I to avenge myself, it is not thus I would take revenge."

"Then you disapprove of duelling? You would not fight a duel?" asked Albert in his turn, astonished at this strange theory.

"Oh, yes," replied the count; "understand me, I would fight a duel for a trifle, for an insult, for a blow; and the more so that, thanks to my skill in all bodily exercises, and the indifference to danger I have gradually acquired, I should be almost certain to kill my man. Oh, I would fight for such a cause; but in return for a slow, profound, eternal torture, I would give back the same, were it possible; an eye for an eye, a tooth for a tooth, as the Orientalists say, our masters in everything, those favored creatures who have formed for themselves a life of dreams and a paradise of realities."

"But," said Franz to the count, "with this theory, which renders you at once judge and executioner of your own cause, it would be difficult to adopt a course that would forever prevent your falling under the power of the law. Hatred is blind, rage carries you away; and he who pours out vengeance runs the risk of tasting a bitter draught."

"Yes, if he be poor and inexperienced, not if he be rich and skilful; besides, the worst that could happen to him would be the punishment of which we have already spoken, and which the philanthropic French Revolution has substituted for being torn to pieces by horses or broken on the wheel. What matters this punishment, as long as he is avenged? On my word, I almost regret that in all probability this miserable Peppino will not be beheaded, as you might have had an opportunity then of seeing how short a time the punishment lasts, and whether it is worth even mentioning; but, really this is a most singular conversation for the Carnival, gentlemen; how did it arise? Ah, I recollect, you asked for a place at my window; you shall have it; but let us first sit down to table, for here comes the servant to inform us that breakfast is ready."

As he spoke, a servant opened one of the four doors of the apartment, saying:

"*Al suo commodo!*"

The two young men arose and entered the breakfast-room.

During the meal, which was excellent, and admirably served, Franz looked repeatedly at Albert, in order to observe the impressions which he doubted not had been made on him by the words of their entertainer; but whether with his usual carelessness he had paid but little attention to him, whether the explanation of the Count of Monte Cristo with regard to duelling had satisfied him, or whether the events which Franz knew of had had their effect on him alone, he remarked that his companion did not pay the least regard to them, but on the contrary ate like a man who for the last four or five months had been condemned to partake of Italian cookery that is, the worst in the world.

As for the count, he just touched the dishes; he seemed to fulfil the duties of a host by sitting down with his guests, and awaited their departure to be served with some strange or more delicate food. This brought back to Franz, in spite of himself, the recollection of the terror with which the count had inspired the Countess G , and her firm conviction that the man in the opposite box was a vampire.

At the end of the breakfast Franz took out his watch.

"Well," said the count, "what are you doing?"

"You must excuse us, count," returned Franz, "but we have still much to do."

"What may that be?"

"We have no masks, and it is absolutely necessary to procure them."

"Do not concern yourself about that; we have, I think, a private room in the Piazza del Popolo; I will have whatever costumes you choose brought to us, and you can dress there."

"After the execution?" cried Franz.

"Before or after, whichever you please."

"Opposite the scaffold?"

"The scaffold forms part of the *fête*."

"Count, I have reflected on the matter," said Franz, "I thank you for your courtesy, but I shall content myself with accepting a place in your carriage and at your window at the Rospoli Palace, and I leave you at liberty to dispose of my place at the Piazza del Popolo."

"But I warn you, you will lose a very curious sight," returned the count.

"You will describe it to me," replied Franz, "and the recital from your lips will make as great an impression on me as if I had witnessed it. I have more than once intended witnessing an execution, but I have never been able to make up my mind; and you, Albert?"

"I," replied the viscount, "I saw Castaing executed, but I think I was rather intoxicated that day, for I had quitted college the same morning, and we had passed the previous night at a tavern."

"Besides, it is no reason because you have not seen an execution at Paris, that you should not see one anywhere else; when you travel, it is to see everything. Think what a figure you will make when you are asked, 'How do they execute at Rome?' and you reply, 'I do not know!' And, besides, they say that the culprit is an infamous scoundrel, who killed with a log of wood a worthy canon who had brought him up like his own son. *Diable!* when a churchman is killed, it should be with a different weapon than a log, especially when he has behaved like a father. If you went to Spain, would you not see the bull-fights? Well, suppose it is a bull-fight you are going to see? Recollect the ancient Romans of the Circus, and the sports where they killed three hundred lions and a hundred men. Think of the eighty thousand applauding spectators, the sage matrons who took their daughters, and the charming Vestals who made with the thumb of their white hands the fatal sign that said, 'Come, despatch the dying.'"

"Shall you go, then, Albert?" asked Franz.

"*Ma foi*, yes; like you, I hesitated, but the count's eloquence decides me."

"Let us go, then," said Franz, "since you wish it; but on our way to the Piazza del Popolo, I wish to pass through the Corso. Is this possible, count?"

"On foot, yes, in a carriage, no."

"I will go on foot, then."

"Is it important that you should go that way?"

"Yes, there is something I wish to see."

"Well, we will go by the Corso. We will send the carriage to wait for us on the Piazza del Popolo, by the Via del Babuino, for I shall be glad to pass, myself, through the Corso, to see if some orders I have given have been executed."

"Excellency," said a servant, opening the door, "a man in the dress of a penitent wishes to speak to you."

"Ah! yes," returned the count, "I know who he is, gentlemen; will you return to the salon? you will find good cigars on the centre table. I will be with you directly."

The young men rose and returned into the salon, while the count, again apologizing, left by another door. Albert, who was a great smoker, and who had considered it no small sacrifice to be deprived of the cigars of the Café de Paris, approached the table, and uttered a cry of joy at perceiving some veritable *puros*.

"Well," asked Franz, "what think you of the Count of Monte Cristo?"

"What do I think?" said Albert, evidently surprised at such a question from his companion; "I think he is a delightful fellow, who does the honors of his table admirably; who has travelled much, read much, is, like Brutus, of the Stoic school, and moreover," added he, sending a volume of smoke up towards the ceiling, "that he has excellent cigars."

Such was Albert's opinion of the count, and as Franz well knew that Albert professed never to form an opinion except upon long reflection, he made no attempt to change it.

"But," said he, "did you observe one very singular thing?"

"What?"

"How attentively he looked at you."

"At me?"

"Yes."

Albert reflected. "Ah," replied he, sighing, "that is not very surprising; I have been more than a year absent from Paris, and my clothes are of a most antiquated cut; the count takes me for a provincial. The first opportunity you have, undeceive him, I beg, and tell him I am nothing of the kind."

Franz smiled; an instant after the count entered.

"I am now quite at your service, gentlemen," said he. "The carriage is going one way to the Piazza del Popolo, and we will go another; and, if you please, by the Corso. Take some more of these cigars, M. de Morcerf."

"With all my heart," returned Albert; "Italian cigars are horrible. When you come to Paris, I will return all this."

"I will not refuse; I intend going there soon, and since you allow me, I will pay you a visit. Come, we have not any time to lose, it is half-past twelve let us set off."

All three descended; the coachman received his master's orders, and drove down the Via del Babuino. While the three gentlemen walked along the Piazza di Spagna and the Via Frattina, which led directly between the Fiano and Rospoli palaces, Franz's attention was directed towards the windows of that last palace, for he had not forgotten the signal agreed upon between the man in the mantle and the Transtevere peasant.

"Which are your windows?" asked he of the count, with as much indifference as he could assume.

"The three last," returned he, with a negligence evidently unaffected, for he could not imagine with what intention the question was put.

Franz glanced rapidly towards the three windows. The side windows were hung with yellow damask, and the centre one with white damask and a red cross. The man in the mantle had kept his promise to the Transteverin, and there could now be no doubt that he was the count.

The three windows were still untenanted. Preparations were making on every side; chairs were placed, scaffolds were raised, and windows were hung with flags. The masks could not appear; the carriages could not move about; but the masks were visible behind the windows, the carriages, and the doors. Franz, Albert, and the count continued to descend the Corso. As they approached the Piazza del Popolo, the crowd became more dense, and above the heads of the multitude two objects were visible: the obelisk, surmounted by a cross, which marks the centre of the square, and in front of the obelisk, at the point where the three streets, del Babuino, del Corso, and di Ripetta, meet, the two uprights of the scaffold, between which glittered the curved knife of the *mandaïa*.

At the corner of the street they met the count's steward, who was awaiting his master. The window, let at an exorbitant price, which the count had doubtless wished to conceal from his guests, was on the second floor of the great palace, situated between the Via del Babuino and the Monte Pincio. It consisted, as we have said, of a small dressing-room, opening into a bedroom, and, when the door of communication was shut, the inmates were quite alone. On chairs were laid elegant masquerade costumes of blue and white satin.

"As you left the choice of your costumes to me," said the count to the two friends, "I have had these brought, as they will be the most worn this year; and they are most suitable, on account of the *confetti* (sweetmeats), as they do not show the flour."

Franz heard the words of the count but imperfectly, and he perhaps did not fully appreciate this new attention to their wishes; for he was wholly absorbed by the spectacle that the Piazza del Popolo presented, and by the terrible instrument that was in the centre.

It was the first time Franz had ever seen a guillotine, we say guillotine, because the Roman *mandaïa* is formed on almost the same model as the French instrument. The knife, which is shaped like a crescent, that cuts with the convex side, falls from a less height, and that is all the difference.

Two men, seated on the movable plank on which the victim is laid, were eating their breakfasts, while waiting for the criminal. Their repast consisted apparently of bread and sausages. One of them lifted the plank, took out a flask of wine, drank some, and then passed it to his companion. These two men were the executioner's assistants.

At this sight Franz felt the perspiration start forth upon his brow.

The prisoners, transported the previous evening from the Carceri Nuove to the little church of Santa Maria del Popolo, had passed the night, each accompanied by two priests, in a chapel closed by a grating, before which were two sentinels, who were relieved at intervals. A double line of carbineers, placed on each side of the door of the church, reached to the scaffold, and formed a circle around it, leaving a path about ten feet wide, and around the guillotine a space of nearly a hundred feet.

All the rest of the square was paved with heads. Many women held their infants on their shoulders, and thus the children had the best view. The Monte Pincio seemed a vast amphitheatre filled with spectators; the balconies of the two churches at the corner of the Via del Babuino and the Via di Ripetta were crammed; the steps even seemed a parti-colored sea, that was impelled towards the portico; every niche in the wall held its living statue. What the count said was true the most curious spectacle in life is that of death.

And yet, instead of the silence and the solemnity demanded by the occasion, laughter and jests arose from the crowd. It was evident that the execution was, in the eyes of the people, only the commencement of the Carnival.

Suddenly the tumult ceased, as if by magic, and the doors of the church opened. A brotherhood of penitents, clothed from head to foot in robes of gray sackcloth, with holes for the eyes, and holding in their hands lighted tapers, appeared first; the chief marched at the head.

Behind the penitents came a man of vast stature and proportions. He was naked, with the exception of cloth drawers at the left side of which hung a large knife in a sheath, and he bore on his right shoulder a heavy iron sledge-hammer.

This man was the executioner.

He had, moreover, sandals bound on his feet by cords.

Behind the executioner came, in the order in which they were to die, first Peppino and then Andrea. Each was accompanied by two priests. Neither had his eyes bandaged.

Peppino walked with a firm step, doubtless aware of what awaited him. Andrea was supported by two priests. Each of them, from time to time, kissed the crucifix a confessor held out to them.

At this sight alone Franz felt his legs tremble under him. He looked at Albert he was as white as his shirt, and mechanically cast away his cigar, although he had not half smoked it. The count alone seemed unmoved nay, more, a slight color seemed striving to rise in his pale cheeks. His nostrils dilated like those of a wild beast that scents its prey, and his lips, half opened, disclosed his white teeth, small and sharp like those of a jackal. And yet his features wore an expression of smiling tenderness, such as Franz had never before witnessed in them; his black eyes especially were full of kindness and pity.

However, the two culprits advanced, and as they approached their faces became visible. Peppino was a handsome young man of four or five-and-twenty, bronzed by the sun; he carried his head erect, and seemed on the watch to see on which side his liberator would appear. Andrea was short and fat; his visage, marked with brutal cruelty, did not indicate age; he might be thirty. In prison he had suffered his beard to grow; his head fell on his shoulder, his legs bent beneath him, and his movements were apparently automatic and unconscious.

"I thought," said Franz to the count, "that you told me there would be but one execution."

"I told you true," replied he coldly.

"And yet here are two culprits."

"Yes; but only one of these two is about to die; the other has many years to live."

"If the pardon is to come, there is no time to lose."

"And see, here it is," said the count. At the moment when Peppino reached the foot of the *mandaïa*, a priest arrived in some haste, forced his way through the soldiers, and, advancing to the chief of the brotherhood, gave him a folded paper. The piercing eye of Peppino had noticed all. The chief took the paper, unfolded it, and, raising his hand, "Heaven be praised, and his Holiness also," said he in a loud voice; "here is a pardon for one of the prisoners!"

"A pardon!" cried the people with one voice; "a pardon!"

At this cry Andrea raised his head.

"Pardon for whom?" cried he.

Peppino remained breathless.

"A pardon for Peppino, called Rocca Priori," said the principal friar. And he passed the paper to the officer commanding the carbineers, who read and returned it to him.

"For Peppino!" cried Andrea, who seemed roused from the torpor in which he had been plunged. "Why for him and not for me? We ought to die together. I was promised he should die with me. You have no right to put me to death alone. I will not die alone I will not!"

And he broke from the priests struggling and raving like a wild beast, and striving desperately to break the cords that bound his hands. The executioner made a sign, and his two assistants leaped from the scaffold and seized him.

"What is going on?" asked Franz of the count; for, as all the talk was in the Roman dialect, he had not perfectly understood it.

"Do you not see?" returned the count, "that this human creature who is about to die is furious that his fellow-sufferer does
not perish with him? and, were he able, he would rather tear
him to pieces with his teeth and nails than let him enjoy the
life he himself is about to be deprived of. Oh, man, man race of
crocodiles," cried the count, extending his clenched hands towards the crowd, "how well do I recognize you there, and that
at all times you are worthy of yourselves!"

Meanwhile Andrea and the two executioners were struggling
on the ground, and he kept exclaiming, "He ought to die! he
shall die! I will not die alone!"

"Look, look," cried the count, seizing the young men's hands;
"look, for on my soul it is curious. Here is a man who had
resigned himself to his fate, who was going to the scaffold to
die like a coward, it is true, but he was about to die without resistance. Do you know what gave him strength? do you know
what consoled him? It was, that another partook of his punishment that another partook of his anguish that another was
to die before him! Lead two sheep to the butcher's, two oxen
to the slaughterhouse, and make one of them understand that
his companion will not die; the sheep will bleat for pleasure,
the ox will bellow with joy. But man man, whom God created
in his own image man, upon whom God has laid his first, his
sole commandment, to love his neighbor man, to whom God
has given a voice to express his thoughts what is his first cry
when he hears his fellow-man is saved? A blasphemy. Honor to
man, this masterpiece of nature, this king of the creation!"

And the count burst into a laugh; a terrible laugh, that showed
he must have suffered horribly to be able thus to laugh.

However, the struggle still continued, and it was dreadful to
witness. The two assistants carried Andrea up to the scaffold;
the people all took part against Andrea, and twenty thousand
voices cried, "Put him to death! put him to death!"

Franz sprang back, but the count seized his arm, and held him
before the window.

"What are you doing?" said he. "Do you pity him? If you heard the cry of 'Mad dog!' you would take your gun you would unhesitatingly shoot the poor beast, who, after all, was only guilty of having been bitten by another dog. And yet you pity a man who, without being bitten by one of his race, has yet murdered his benefactor; and who, now unable to kill anyone, because his hands are bound, wishes to see his companion in captivity perish. No, no look, look!"

The recommendation was needless. Franz was fascinated by the horrible spectacle.

The two assistants had borne Andrea to the scaffold, and there, in spite of his struggles, his bites, and his cries, had forced him to his knees. During this time the executioner had raised his mace, and signed to them to get out of the way; the criminal strove to rise, but, ere he had time, the mace fell on his left temple. A dull and heavy sound was heard, and the man dropped like an ox on his face, and then turned over on his back.

The executioner let fall his mace, drew his knife, and with one stroke opened his throat, and mounting on his stomach, stamped violently on it with his feet. At every stroke a jet of blood sprang from the wound.

This time Franz could contain himself no longer, but sank, half fainting, into a seat.

Albert, with his eyes closed, was standing grasping the window-curtains.

The count was erect and triumphant, like the Avenging Angel!

Chapter 9

The Carnival at Rome

When Franz recovered his senses, he saw Albert drinking a glass of water, of which, to judge from his pallor, he stood in great need; and the count, who was assuming his masquerade costume. He glanced mechanically towards the piazza the scene was wholly changed; scaffold, executioners, victims, all had disappeared; only the people remained, full of noise and excitement. The bell of Monte Citorio, which only sounds on the pope's decease and the opening of the Carnival, was ringing a joyous peal.

"Well," asked he of the count, "what has, then, happened?"

"Nothing," replied the count; "only, as you see, the Carnival has commenced. Make haste and dress yourself."

"In fact," said Franz, "this horrible scene has passed away like a dream."

"It is but a dream, a nightmare, that has disturbed you."

"Yes, that I have suffered; but the culprit?"

"That is a dream also; only he has remained asleep, while you have awakened; and who knows which of you is the most fortunate?"

"But Peppino what has become of him?"

"Peppino is a lad of sense, who, unlike most men, who are happy in proportion as they are noticed, was delighted to see that the general attention was directed towards his companion. He profited by this distraction to slip away among the crowd, without even thanking the worthy priests who accompanied him. Decidedly man is an ungrateful and egotistical animal. But dress yourself; see, M. de Morcerf sets you the example."

Albert was drawing on the satin pantaloon over his black trousers and varnished boots.

"Well, Albert," said Franz, "do you feel much inclined to join the revels? Come, answer frankly."

"*Ma foi*, no," returned Albert. "But I am really glad to have seen such a sight; and I understand what the count said that when you have once habituated yourself to a similar spectacle, it is the only one that causes you any emotion."

"Without reflecting that this is the only moment in which you can study character," said the count; "on the steps of the scaffold death tears off the mask that has been worn through life, and the real visage is disclosed. It must be allowed that Andrea was not very handsome, the hideous scoundrel! Come, dress yourselves, gentlemen, dress yourselves."

Franz felt it would be ridiculous not to follow his two companions' example. He assumed his costume, and fastened on the mask that scarcely equalled the pallor of his own face. Their toilet finished, they descended; the carriage awaited them at the door, filled with sweetmeats and bouquets. They fell into the line of carriages.

It is difficult to form an idea of the perfect change that had taken place. Instead of the spectacle of gloomy and silent death, the Piazza del Popolo presented a spectacle of gay and noisy mirth and revelry. A crowd of masks flowed in from all sides, emerging from the doors, descending from the windows. From every street and every corner drove carriages filled with clowns, harlequins, dominoes, mummers, pantomimists, Transteverins, knights, and peasants, screaming, fighting, gesticulating, throwing eggs filled with flour, confetti, nosegays, attacking, with their sarcasms and their missiles, friends and foes, companions and strangers, indiscriminately, and no one took offence, or did anything but laugh.

Franz and Albert were like men who, to drive away a violent sorrow, have recourse to wine, and who, as they drink and become intoxicated, feel a thick veil drawn between the past and the present. They saw, or rather continued to see, the image of what they had witnessed; but little by little the general vertigo seized them, and they felt themselves obliged to take part in the noise and confusion.

A handful of confetti that came from a neighboring carriage, and which, while it covered Morcerf and his two companions with dust, pricked his neck and that portion of his face uncovered by his mask like a hundred pins, incited him to join in the general combat, in which all the masks around him were engaged. He rose in his turn, and seizing handfuls of confetti and sweetmeats, with which the carriage was filled, cast them with all the force and skill he was master of.

The strife had fairly begun, and the recollection of what they had seen half an hour before was gradually effaced from the young men's minds, so much were they occupied by the gay and glittering procession they now beheld.

As for the Count of Monte Cristo, he had never for an instant shown any appearance of having been moved. Imagine the large and splendid Corso, bordered from one end to the other with lofty palaces, with their balconies hung with carpets, and their windows with flags. At these balconies are three hundred thousand spectators Romans, Italians, strangers from all parts of the world, the united aristocracy of birth, wealth, and genius. Lovely women, yielding to the influence of the scene, bend over their balconies, or lean from their windows, and shower down confetti, which are returned by bouquets; the air seems darkened with the falling confetti and flying flowers. In the streets the lively crowd is dressed in the most fantastic costumes gigantic cabbages walk gravely about, buffaloes' heads bellow from men's shoulders, dogs walk on their hind legs; in the midst of all this a mask is lifted, and, as in Callot's Temptation of St. Anthony, a lovely face is exhibited, which we would fain follow, but from which we are separated by troops of fiends. This will give a faint idea of the Carnival at Rome.

At the second turn, the count stopped the carriage, and requested permission to withdraw, leaving the vehicle at their disposal. Franz looked up they were opposite the Rospoli Palace. At the centre window, the one hung with white damask with a red cross, was a blue domino, beneath which Franz's imagination easily pictured the beautiful Greek of the Argentina. "Gentlemen," said the count, springing out, "when you are tired of being actors, and wish to become spectators of this scene, you know you have places at my windows. In the meantime, dispose of my coachman, my carriage, and my servants." We have forgotten to mention, that the count's coachman was attired in a bear-skin, exactly resembling Odry's in *The Bear and the Pasha*; and the two footmen behind were dressed up as green monkeys, with spring masks, with which they made grimaces at everyone who passed.

Franz thanked the count for his attention. As for Albert, he was busily occupied throwing bouquets at a carriage full of Roman peasants that was passing near him. Unfortunately for him, the line of carriages moved on again, and while he descended the Piazza del Popolo, the other ascended towards the Palazzo di Venezia.

"Ah, my dear fellow," said he to Franz; "you did not see?"

"What?"

"There, that calash filled with Roman peasants."

"No."

"Well, I am convinced they are all charming women."

"How unfortunate that you were masked, Albert," said Franz; "here was an opportunity of making up for past disappointments."

"Oh," replied he, half laughing, half serious; "I hope the Carnival will not pass without some amends in one shape or the other."

But, in spite of Albert's hope, the day passed unmarked by any incident, excepting two or three encounters with the carriage full of Roman peasants. At one of these encounters, accidentally or purposely, Albert's mask fell off. He instantly rose and cast the remainder of the bouquets into the carriage. Doubtless one of the charming females Albert had detected beneath their coquettish disguise was touched by his gallantry; for, as the carriage of the two friends passed her, she threw a bunch of violets. Albert seized it, and as Franz had no reason to suppose it was meant for him, he suffered Albert to retain it. Albert placed it in his button-hole, and the carriage went triumphantly on.

"Well," said Franz to him; "there is the beginning of an adventure."

"Laugh if you please I really think so. So I will not abandon this bouquet."

"*Pardieu*," returned Franz, laughing, "in token of your ingratitude."

The jest, however, soon appeared to become earnest; for when Albert and Franz again encountered the carriage with the *contadini*, the one who had thrown the violets to Albert, clapped her hands when she beheld them in his button-hole.

"Bravo, bravo," said Franz; "things go wonderfully. Shall I leave you? Perhaps you would prefer being alone?"

"No," replied he; "I will not be caught like a fool at a first disclosure by a rendezvous under the clock, as they say at the opera-balls. If the fair peasant wishes to carry matters any further, we shall find her, or rather, she will find us tomorrow; then she will give me some sign or other, and I shall know what I have to do."

"On my word," said Franz, "you are as wise as Nestor and prudent as Ulysses, and your fair Circe must be very skilful or very powerful if she succeed in changing you into a beast of any kind."

Albert was right; the fair unknown had resolved, doubtless, to carry the intrigue no farther; for although the young men made several more turns, they did not again see the calash, which had turned up one of the neighboring streets. Then they returned to the Rospoli Palace; but the count and the blue domino had also disappeared; the two windows, hung with yellow damask, were still occupied by the persons whom the count had invited.

At this moment the same bell that had proclaimed the beginning of the mascherata sounded the retreat. The file on the Corso broke the line, and in a second all the carriages had disappeared. Franz and Albert were opposite the Via delle Muratte; the coachman, without saying a word, drove up it, passed along the Piazza di Spagna and the Rospoli Palace and stopped at the door of the hotel. Signor Pastrini came to the door to receive his guests.

Franz hastened to inquire after the count, and to express regret that he had not returned in sufficient time; but Pastrini reassured him by saying that the Count of Monte Cristo had ordered a second carriage for himself, and that it had gone at four o'clock to fetch him from the Rospoli Palace.

The count had, moreover, charged him to offer the two friends the key of his box at the Argentina. Franz questioned Albert as to his intentions; but Albert had great projects to put into execution before going to the theatre; and instead of making any answer, he inquired if Signor Pastrini could procure him a tailor.

"A tailor," said the host; "and for what?"

"To make us between now and tomorrow two Roman peasant costumes," returned Albert.

The host shook his head.

"To make you two costumes between now and tomorrow? I ask your excellencies' pardon, but this is quite a French demand; for the next week you will not find a single tailor who would consent to sew six buttons on a waistcoat if you paid him a crown a piece for each button."

"Then I must give up the idea?"

"No; we have them ready-made. Leave all to me; and tomorrow, when you awake, you shall find a collection of costumes with which you will be satisfied."

"My dear Albert," said Franz, "leave all to our host; he has already proved himself full of resources; let us dine quietly, and afterwards go and see *l'Italienne à Alger!*

"Agreed," returned Albert; "but remember, Signor Pastrini, that both my friend and myself attach the greatest importance to having tomorrow the costumes we have asked for."

The host again assured them they might rely on him, and that their wishes should be attended to; upon which Franz and Albert mounted to their apartments, and proceeded to disencumber themselves of their costumes. Albert, as he took off his dress, carefully preserved the bunch of violets; it was his token reserved for the morrow.

The two friends sat down to table; but they could not refrain from remarking the difference between the Count of Monte Cristo's table and that of Signor Pastrini. Truth compelled Franz, in spite of the dislike he seemed to have taken to the count, to confess that the advantage was not on Pastrini's side. During dessert, the servant inquired at what time they wished for the carriage. Albert and Franz looked at each other, fearing really to abuse the count's kindness. The servant understood them.

"His excellency the Count of Monte Cristo had," he said, "given positive orders that the carriage was to remain at their lordships' orders all day, and they could therefore dispose of it without fear of indiscretion."

They resolved to profit by the count's courtesy, and ordered the horses to be harnessed, while they substituted evening dress for that which they had on, and which was somewhat the worse for the numerous combats they had sustained.

This precaution taken, they went to the theatre, and installed themselves in the count's box. During the first act, the Countess G entered. Her first look was at the box where she had seen the count the previous evening, so that she perceived Franz and Albert in the place of the very person concerning whom she had expressed so strange an opinion to Franz. Her operaglass was so fixedly directed towards them, that Franz saw it would be cruel not to satisfy her curiosity; and, availing himself of one of the privileges of the spectators of the Italian theatres, who use their boxes to hold receptions, the two friends went to pay their respects to the countess. Scarcely had they entered, when she motioned to Franz to assume the seat of honor. Albert, in his turn, sat behind.

"Well," said she, hardly giving Franz time to sit down, "it seems you have nothing better to do than to make the acquaintance of this new Lord Ruthven, and you are already the best friends in the world."

"Without being so far advanced as that, my dear countess," returned Franz, "I cannot deny that we have abused his good nature all day."

"All day?"

"Yes; this morning we breakfasted with him; we rode in his carriage all day, and now we have taken possession of his box."

"You know him, then?"

"Yes, and no."

"How so?"

"It is a long story."

"Tell it to me."

"It would frighten you too much."

"So much the more reason."

"At least wait until the story has a conclusion."

"Very well; I prefer complete histories; but tell me how you made his acquaintance? Did anyone introduce you to him?"

"No; it was he who introduced himself to us."

"When?"

"Last night, after we left you."

"Through what medium?"

"The very prosaic one of our landlord."

"He is staying, then, at the Hôtel de Londres with you?"

"Not only in the same hotel, but on the same floor."

"What is his name; for, of course, you know?"

"The Count of Monte Cristo."

"That is not a family name?"

"No, it is the name of the island he has purchased."

"And he is a count?"

"A Tuscan count."

"Well, we must put up with that," said the countess, who was herself from one of the oldest Venetian families. "What sort of a man is he?"

"Ask the Vicomte de Morcerf."

"You hear, M. de Morcerf, I am referred to you," said the countess.

"We should be very hard to please, madam," returned Albert, "did we not think him delightful. A friend of ten years' standing could not have done more for us, or with a more perfect courtesy."

"Come," observed the countess, smiling, "I see my vampire is only some millionaire, who has taken the appearance of Lara in order to avoid being confounded with M. de Rothschild; and you have seen her?"

"Her?"

"The beautiful Greek of yesterday."

"No; we heard, I think, the sound of her *guzla*, but she remained perfectly invisible."

"When you say invisible," interrupted Albert, "it is only to keep up the mystery; for whom do you take the blue domino at the window with the white curtains?"

"Where was this window with white hangings?" asked the countess.

"At the Rospoli Palace."

"The count had three windows at the Rospoli Palace?"

"Yes. Did you pass through the Corso?"

"Yes."

"Well, did you notice two windows hung with yellow damask, and one with white damask with a red cross? Those were the count's windows."

"Why, he must be a nabob. Do you know what those three windows were worth?"

"Two or three hundred Roman crowns?"

"Two or three thousand."

"The deuce!"

"Does his island produce him such a revenue?"

"It does not bring him a bajocco."

"Then why did he purchase it?"

"For a whim."

"He is an original, then?"

"In reality," observed Albert, "he seemed to me somewhat eccentric; were he at Paris, and a frequenter of the theatres, I should say he was a poor devil literally mad. This morning he made two or three exits worthy of Didier or Anthony."

At this moment a fresh visitor entered, and, according to custom, Franz gave up his seat to him. This circumstance had, moreover, the effect of changing the conversation; an hour afterwards the two friends returned to their hotel.

Signor Pastrini had already set about procuring their disguises for the morrow; and he assured them that they would be perfectly satisfied. The next morning, at nine o'clock, he entered Franz's room, followed by a tailor, who had eight or ten Roman peasant costumes on his arm; they selected two exactly alike, and charged the tailor to sew on each of their hats about twenty yards of ribbon, and to procure them two of the long silk sashes of different colors with which the lower orders decorate themselves on fête days.

Albert was impatient to see how he looked in his new dress a jacket and breeches of blue velvet, silk stockings with clocks, shoes with buckles, and a silk waistcoat. This picturesque attire set him off to great advantage; and when he had bound the scarf around his waist, and when his hat, placed coquettishly on one side, let fall on his shoulder a stream of ribbons, Franz was forced to confess that costume has much to do with the physical superiority we accord to certain nations. The Turks used to be so picturesque with their long and flowing robes, but are they not now hideous with their blue frocks buttoned up to the chin, and their red caps, which make them look like a bottle of wine with a red seal? Franz complimented Albert, who looked at himself in the glass with an unequivocal smile of satisfaction. They were thus engaged when the Count of Monte Cristo entered.

"Gentlemen," said he, "although a companion is agreeable, perfect freedom is sometimes still more agreeable. I come to say that today, and for the remainder of the Carnival, I leave the carriage entirely at your disposal. The host will tell you I have three or four more, so that you will not inconvenience me in any way. Make use of it, I pray you, for your pleasure or your business."

The young men wished to decline, but they could find no good reason for refusing an offer which was so agreeable to them. The Count of Monte Cristo remained a quarter of an hour with them, conversing on all subjects with the greatest ease. He was, as we have already said, perfectly well acquainted with the literature of all countries. A glance at the walls of his salon proved to Franz and Albert that he was a connoisseur of pictures. A few words he let fall showed them that he was no stranger to the sciences, and he seemed much occupied with chemistry. The two friends did not venture to return the count the breakfast he had given them; it would have been too absurd to offer him in exchange for his excellent table the very inferior one of Signor Pastrini. They told him so frankly, and he received their excuses with the air of a man who appreciated their delicacy. Albert was charmed with the count's manners, and he was only prevented from recognizing him for a perfect gentleman by reason of his varied knowledge.

The permission to do what he liked with the carriage pleased him above all, for the fair peasants had appeared in a most elegant carriage the preceding evening, and Albert was not sorry to be upon an equal footing with them. At half-past one they descended, the coachman and footman had put on their livery over their disguises, which gave them a more ridiculous appearance than ever, and which gained them the applause of Franz and Albert. Albert had fastened the faded bunch of violets to his button-hole. At the first sound of the bell they hastened into the Corso by the Via Vittoria.

At the second turn, a bunch of fresh violets, thrown from a carriage filled with harlequins, indicated to Albert that, like himself and his friend, the peasants had changed their costume also; and whether it was the result of chance, or whether a similar feeling had possessed them both, while he had donned their costume, they had assumed his.

Albert placed the fresh bouquet in his button-hole, but he kept the faded one in his hand; and when he again met the calash, he raised it to his lips, an action which seemed greatly to amuse not only the fair lady who had thrown it, but her joyous companions also. The day was as gay as the preceding one, perhaps even more animated and noisy; the count appeared for an instant at his window, but when they again passed he had disappeared. It is almost needless to say that the flirtation between Albert and the fair peasant continued all day.

In the evening, on his return, Franz found a letter from the embassy, informing him that he would have the honor of being received by his holiness the next day. At each previous visit he had made to Rome, he had solicited and obtained the same favor; and incited as much by a religious feeling as by gratitude, he was unwilling to quit the capital of the Christian world without laying his respectful homage at the feet of one of St. Peter's successors who has set the rare example of all the virtues. He did not then think of the Carnival, for in spite of his condescension and touching kindness, one cannot incline one's self without awe before the venerable and noble old man called Gregory XVI.

On his return from the Vatican, Franz carefully avoided the Corso; he brought away with him a treasure of pious thoughts, to which the mad gayety of the maskers would have been profanation.

At ten minutes past five Albert entered overjoyed. The harlequin had reassumed her peasant's costume, and as she passed she raised her mask. She was charming. Franz congratulated Albert, who received his congratulations with the air of a man conscious that they are merited. He had recognized by certain unmistakable signs, that his fair *incognita* belonged to the aristocracy. He had made up his mind to write to her the next day. Franz remarked, while he gave these details, that Albert seemed to have something to ask of him, but that he was unwilling to ask it. He insisted upon it, declaring beforehand that he was willing to make any sacrifice the other wished.

Albert let himself be pressed just as long as friendship required, and then avowed to Franz that he would do him a great favor by allowing him to occupy the carriage alone the next day. Albert attributed to Franz's absence the extreme kindness of the fair peasant in raising her mask. Franz was not sufficiently egotistical to stop Albert in the middle of an adventure that promised to prove so agreeable to his curiosity and so flattering to his vanity. He felt assured that the perfect indiscretion of his friend would duly inform him of all that happened; and as, during three years that he had travelled all over Italy, a similar piece of good fortune had never fallen to his share, Franz was by no means sorry to learn how to act on such an occasion. He therefore promised Albert that he would content himself the morrow with witnessing the Carnival from the windows of the Rospoli Palace.

The next morning he saw Albert pass and repass, holding an enormous bouquet, which he doubtless meant to make the bearer of his amorous epistle. This belief was changed into certainty when Franz saw the bouquet (conspicuous by a circle of white camellias) in the hand of a charming harlequin dressed in rose-colored satin.

The evening was no longer joy, but delirium. Albert nothing doubted but that the fair unknown would reply in the same manner. Franz anticipated his wishes by saying that the noise fatigued him, and that he should pass the next day in writing and looking over his journal. Albert was not deceived, for the next evening Franz saw him enter triumphantly shaking a folded paper which he held by one corner.

"Well," said he, "was I mistaken?"

"She has answered you!" cried Franz.

"Read."

This word was pronounced in a manner impossible to describe. Franz took the letter, and read:

"Tuesday evening, at seven o'clock, descend from your carriage opposite the Via dei Pontefici, and follow the Roman peasant who snatches your torch from you. When you arrive at the first step of the church of San Giacomo, be sure to fasten a knot of rose-colored ribbons to the shoulder of your harlequin costume, in order that you may be recognized. Until then you will not see me. Constancy and Discretion."

"Well," asked he, when Franz had finished, "what do you think of that?"

"I think that the adventure is assuming a very agreeable appearance."

"I think so, also," replied Albert; "and I very much fear you will go alone to the Duke of Bracciano's ball."

Franz and Albert had received that morning an invitation from the celebrated Roman banker.

"Take care, Albert," said Franz. "All the nobility of Rome will be present, and if your fair *incognita* belong to the higher class of society, she must go there."

"Whether she goes there or not, my opinion is still the same," returned Albert. "You have read the letter?"

"Yes."

"You know how imperfectly the women of the *mezzo cito* are educated in Italy?" (This is the name of the lower class.)

"Yes."

"Well, read the letter again. Look at the writing, and find if you can, any blemish in the language or orthography." The writing was, in reality, charming, and the orthography irreproachable.

"You are born to good fortune," said Franz, as he returned the letter.

"Laugh as much as you will," replied Albert, "I am in love."

"You alarm me," cried Franz. "I see that I shall not only go alone to the Duke of Bracciano's, but also return to Florence alone."

"If my unknown be as amiable as she is beautiful," said Albert, "I shall fix myself at Rome for six weeks, at least. I adore Rome, and I have always had a great taste for archæology."

"Come, two or three more such adventures, and I do not despair of seeing you a member of the Academy."

Doubtless Albert was about to discuss seriously his right to the academic chair when they were informed that dinner was ready. Albert's love had not taken away his appetite. He hastened with Franz to seat himself, free to recommence the discussion after dinner. After dinner, the Count of Monte Cristo was announced. They had not seen him for two days. Signor Pastrini informed them that business had called him to Civita Vecchia. He had started the previous evening, and had only returned an hour since. He was charming. Whether he kept a watch over himself, or whether by accident he did not sound the acrimonious chords that in other circumstances had been touched, he was tonight like everybody else.

The man was an enigma to Franz. The count must feel sure that Franz recognized him; and yet he had not let fall a single word indicating any previous acquaintance between them.

On his side, however great Franz's desire was to allude to their former interview, the fear of being disagreeable to the man who had loaded him and his friend with kindness prevented him from mentioning it.

The count had learned that the two friends had sent to secure a box at the Argentina Theatre, and were told they were all let. In consequence, he brought them the key of his own at least such was the apparent motive of his visit. Franz and Albert made some difficulty, alleging their fear of depriving him of it; but the count replied that, as he was going to the Palli Theatre, the box at the Argentina Theatre would be lost if they did not profit by it. This assurance determined the two friends to accept it.

Franz had by degrees become accustomed to the count's pallor, which had so forcibly struck him at their first meeting. He could not refrain from admiring the severe beauty of his features, the only defect, or rather the principal quality of which was the pallor. Truly, a Byronic hero! Franz could not, we will not say see him, but even think of him without imagining his stern head upon Manfred's shoulders, or beneath Lara's helmet. His forehead was marked with the line that indicates the constant presence of bitter thoughts; he had the fiery eyes that seem to penetrate to the very soul, and the haughty and disdainful upper lip that gives to the words it utters a peculiar character that impresses them on the minds of those to whom they are addressed.

The count was no longer young. He was at least forty; and yet it was easy to understand that he was formed to rule the young men with whom he associated at present. And, to complete his resemblance with the fantastic heroes of the English poet, the count seemed to have the power of fascination. Albert was constantly expatiating on their good fortune in meeting such a man. Franz was less enthusiastic; but the count exercised over him also the ascendency a strong mind always acquires over a mind less domineering. He thought several times of the project the count had of visiting Paris; and he had no doubt but that, with his eccentric character, his character-istic face, and his colossal fortune, he would produce a great effect there. And yet he did not wish to be at Paris when the count was there.

The evening passed as evenings mostly pass at Italian the-atres; that is, not in listening to the music, but in paying visits and conversing. The Countess G wished to revive the subject of the count, but Franz announced he had something far newer to tell her, and, in spite of Albert's demonstrations of false modesty, he informed the countess of the great event which had preoccupied them for the last three days. As simi-lar intrigues are not uncommon in Italy, if we may credit travellers, the comtess did not manifest the least incredulity, but congratulated Albert on his success. They promised, upon separating, to meet at the Duke of Bracciano's ball, to which all Rome was invited.

The heroine of the bouquet kept her word; she gave Albert no sign of her existence the morrow or the day after.

At length Tuesday came, the last and most tumultuous day of the Carnival. On Tuesday, the theatres open at ten o'clock in the morning, as Lent begins after eight at night. On Tuesday, all those who through want of money, time, or enthusiasm, have not been to see the Carnival before, mingle in the gayety, and contribute to the noise and excitement. From two o'clock till five Franz and Albert followed in the *fête*, exchanging handfuls of *confetti* with the other carriages and the pedes-trians, who crowded amongst the horses' feet and the carriage wheels without a single accident, a single dispute, or a single fight.

The *fêtes* are veritable pleasure days to the Italians. The author of this history, who has resided five or six years in Italy, does not recollect to have ever seen a ceremony interrupted by one of those events so common in other countries. Albert was triumphant in his harlequin costume. A knot of rose-colored ribbons fell from his shoulder almost to the ground. In order that there might be no confusion, Franz wore his peasant's costume.

As the day advanced, the tumult became greater. There was not on the pavement, in the carriages, at the windows, a single tongue that was silent, a single arm that did not move. It was a human storm, made up of a thunder of cries, and a hail of sweetmeats, flowers, eggs, oranges, and nosegays.

At three o'clock the sound of fireworks, let off on the Piazza del Popolo and the Piazza di Venezia (heard with difficulty amid the din and confusion) announced that the races were about to begin.

The races, like the *moccoli*, are one of the episodes peculiar to the last days of the Carnival. At the sound of the fireworks the carriages instantly broke ranks, and retired by the adjacent streets. All these evolutions are executed with an inconceivable address and marvellous rapidity, without the police interfering in the matter. The pedestrians ranged themselves against the walls; then the trampling of horses and the clashing of steel were heard. A detachment of carbineers, fifteen abreast, galloped up the Corso in order to clear it for the *barberi*. When the detachment arrived at the Piazza di Venezia, a second volley of fireworks was discharged, to announce that the street was clear.

Almost instantly, in the midst of a tremendous and general outcry, seven or eight horses, excited by the shouts of three hundred thousand spectators, passed by like lightning. Then the Castle of Saint Angelo fired three cannon to indicate that number three had won.

Immediately, without any other signal, the carriages moved on, flowing on towards the Corso, down all the streets, like torrents pent up for a while, which again flow into the parent river; and the immense stream again continued its course between its two granite banks.

A new source of noise and movement was added to the crowd. The sellers of *moccoletti* entered on the scene. The *moccoli*, or *moccoletti*, are candles which vary in size from the pascal taper to the rushlight, and which give to each actor in the great final scene of the Carnival two very serious problems to grapple with, first, how to keep his own *moccoletto* alight; and secondly, how to extinguish the *moccoletti* of others. The *moccoletto* is like life: man has found but one means of transmitting it, and that one comes from God. But he has discovered a thousand means of taking it away, and the devil has somewhat aided him. The *moccoletto* is kindled by approaching it to a light. But who can describe the thousand means of extinguishing the *moccoletto*? the gigantic bellows, the monstrous extinguishers, the superhuman fans. Everyone hastened to purchase *moccoletti* Franz and Albert among the rest.

The night was rapidly approaching; and already, at the cry of "*Moccoletti!*" repeated by the shrill voices of a thousand vendors, two or three stars began to burn among the crowd. It was a signal. At the end of ten minutes fifty thousand lights glittered, descending from the Palazzo di Venezia to the Piazza del Popolo, and mounting from the Piazza del Popolo to the Palazzo di Venezia. It seemed like the *fête* of Jack-o'-lanterns.

It is impossible to form any idea of it without having seen it. Suppose that all the stars had descended from the sky and mingled in a wild dance on the face of the earth; the whole accompanied by cries that were never heard in any other part of the world. The *facchino* follows the prince, the Transteverin the citizen, everyone blowing, extinguishing, relighting. Had old Æolus appeared at this moment, he would have been proclaimed king of the *moccoli*, and Aquilo the heir-presumptive to the throne.

This battle of folly and flame continued for two hours; the Corso was light as day; the features of the spectators on the third and fourth stories were visible.

Every five minutes Albert took out his watch; at length it pointed to seven. The two friends were in the Via dei Pontefici. Albert sprang out, bearing his *moccoletto* in his hand. Two or three masks strove to knock his *moccoletto* out of his hand; but Albert, a first-rate pugilist, sent them rolling in the street, one after the other, and continued his course towards the church of San Giacomo.

The steps were crowded with masks, who strove to snatch each other's torches. Franz followed Albert with his eyes, and saw him mount the first step.

Instantly a mask, wearing the well-known costume of a peasant woman, snatched his *moccoletto* from him without his offering any resistance. Franz was too far off to hear what they said; but, without doubt, nothing hostile passed, for he saw Albert disappear arm-in-arm with the peasant girl. He watched them pass through the crowd for some time, but at length he lost sight of them in the Via Macello.

Suddenly the bell that gives the signal for the end of the Carnival sounded, and at the same instant all the *moccoletti* were extinguished as if by enchantment. It seemed as though one immense blast of the wind had extinguished everyone.

Franz found himself in utter darkness. No sound was audible save that of the carriages that were carrying the maskers home; nothing was visible save a few lights that burnt behind the windows.

The Carnival was over.

Chapter 10

The Catacombs of Saint Sebastian

Ihis whole life, perhaps, Franz had never before experienced so sudden an impression, so rapid a transition from gayety to sadness, as in this moment. It seemed as though Rome, under the magic breath of some demon of the night, had suddenly changed into a vast tomb. By a chance, which added yet more to the intensity of the darkness, the moon, which was on the wane, did not rise until eleven o'clock, and the streets which the young man traversed were plunged in the deepest obscurity.

The distance was short, and at the end of ten minutes his carriage, or rather the count's, stopped before the Hôtel de Londres.

Dinner was waiting, but as Albert had told him that he should not return so soon, Franz sat down without him. Signor Pastrini, who had been accustomed to see them dine together, inquired into the cause of his absence, but Franz merely replied that Albert had received on the previous evening an invitation which he had accepted.

The sudden extinction of the *moccoletti*, the darkness which had replaced the light, and the silence which had succeeded the turmoil, had left in Franz's mind a certain depression which was not free from uneasiness. He therefore dined very silently, in spite of the officious attention of his host, who presented himself two or three times to inquire if he wanted anything.

Franz resolved to wait for Albert as late as possible. He ordered the carriage, therefore, for eleven o'clock, desiring Signor Pastrini to inform him the moment that Albert returned to the hotel.

At eleven o'clock Albert had not come back. Franz dressed himself, and went out, telling his host that he was going to pass the night at the Duke of Bracciano's. The house of the Duke of Bracciano is one of the most delightful in Rome, the duchess, one of the last heiresses of the Colonnas, does its honors with the most consummate grace, and thus their *fêtes* have a European celebrity.

Franz and Albert had brought to Rome letters of introduction to them, and their first question on his arrival was to inquire the whereabouts of his travelling companion. Franz replied that he had left him at the moment they were about to extinguish the *moccoli*, and that he had lost sight of him in the Via Macello.

"Then he has not returned?" said the duke.

"I waited for him until this hour," replied Franz.

"And do you know whither he went?"

"No, not precisely; however, I think it was something very like a rendezvous."

"*Diavolo!*" said the duke, "this is a bad day, or rather a bad night, to be out late; is it not, countess?"

These words were addressed to the Countess G , who had just arrived, and was leaning on the arm of Signor Torlonia, the duke's brother.

"I think, on the contrary, that it is a charming night," replied the countess, "and those who are here will complain of but one thing, that of its too rapid flight."

"I am not speaking," said the duke with a smile, "of the persons who are here; the men run no other danger than that of falling in love with you, and the women of falling ill of jealousy at seeing you so lovely; I meant persons who were out in the streets of Rome."

"Ah," asked the countess, "who is out in the streets of Rome at this hour, unless it be to go to a ball?"

"Our friend, Albert de Morcerf, countess, whom I left in pursuit of his unknown about seven o'clock this evening," said Franz, "and whom I have not seen since."

"And don't you know where he is?"

"Not at all."

"Is he armed?"

"He is in masquerade."

"You should not have allowed him to go," said the duke to Franz; "you, who know Rome better than he does."

"You might as well have tried to stop number three of the *barberi*, who gained the prize in the race today," replied Franz; "and then moreover, what could happen to him?"

"Who can tell? The night is gloomy, and the Tiber is very near the Via Macello." Franz felt a shudder run through his veins at observing that the feeling of the duke and the countess was so much in unison with his own personal disquietude.

"I informed them at the hotel that I had the honor of passing the night here, duke," said Franz, "and desired them to come and inform me of his return."

"Ah," replied the duke, "here I think, is one of my servants who is seeking you."

The duke was not mistaken; when he saw Franz, the servant

came up to him.

"Your excellency," he said, "the master of the Hôtel de Londres has sent to let you know that a man is waiting for you with a letter from the Viscount of Morcerf."

"A letter from the viscount!" exclaimed Franz.

"Yes."

"And who is the man?"

"I do not know."

"Why did he not bring it to me here?"

"The messenger did not say."

"And where is the messenger?"

"He went away directly he saw me enter the ball-room to find you."

"Oh," said the countess to Franz, "go with all speed poor young man! Perhaps some accident has happened to him."

"I will hasten," replied Franz.

"Shall we see you again to give us any information?" inquired the countess.

"Yes, if it is not any serious affair, otherwise I cannot answer as to what I may do myself."

"Be prudent, in any event," said the countess.

"Oh! pray be assured of that."

Franz took his hat and went away in haste. He had sent away his carriage with orders for it to fetch him at two o'clock; fortunately the Palazzo Bracciano, which is on one side in the Corso, and on the other in the Square of the Holy Apostles, is hardly ten minutes' walk from the Hôtel de Londres.

As he came near the hotel, Franz saw a man in the middle of the street. He had no doubt that it was the messenger from Albert. The man was wrapped up in a large cloak. He went up to him, but, to his extreme astonishment, the stranger first addressed him.

"What wants your excellency of me?" inquired the man, retreating a step or two, as if to keep on his guard.

"Are not you the person who brought me a letter," inquired Franz, "from the Viscount of Morcerf?"

"Your excellency lodges at Pastrini's hotel?"

"I do."

"Your excellency is the travelling companion of the viscount?"

"I am."

"Your excellency's name "

"Is the Baron Franz d'Épinay."

"Then it is to your excellency that this letter is addressed."

"Is there any answer?" inquired Franz, taking the letter from him.

"Yes your friend at least hopes so."

"Come upstairs with me, and I will give it to you."

"I prefer waiting here," said the messenger, with a smile.

"And why?"

"Your excellency will know when you have read the letter."

"Shall I find you here, then?"

"Certainly."

Franz entered the hotel. On the staircase he met Signor Pastrini. "Well?" said the landlord.

"Well what?" responded Franz.

"You have seen the man who desired to speak with you from your friend?" he asked of Franz.

"Yes, I have seen him," he replied, "and he has handed this letter to me. Light the candles in my apartment, if you please." The innkeeper gave orders to a servant to go before Franz with a light. The young man had found Signor Pastrini looking very much alarmed, and this had only made him the more anxious to read Albert's letter; and so he went instantly towards the waxlight, and unfolded it. It was written and signed by Albert. Franz read it twice before he could comprehend what it contained. It was thus worded:

"My dear Fellow,

"The moment you have received this, have the kindness to take the letter of credit from my pocket-book, which you will find in the square drawer of the *secrétaire*; add your own to it, if it be not sufficient. Run to Torlonia, draw from him instantly four thousand piastres, and give them to the bearer. It is urgent that I should have this money without delay. I do not say more, relying on you as you may rely on me.

"Your friend,

"Albert de Morcerf.

"P.S. I now believe in Italian *banditti*."

Below these lines were written, in a strange hand, the following in Italian:

"*Se alle sei della mattina le quattro mille piastre non sono nelle mie mani, alla sette il Conte Alberto avrà cessato di vivere.*

"Luigi Vampa."

"*If by six in the morning the four thousand piastres are not in my hands, by seven o'clock the Count Albert will have ceased to live.*"

This second signature explained everything to Franz, who now understood the objection of the messenger to coming up into the apartment; the street was safer for him. Albert, then, had fallen into the hands of the famous bandit chief, in whose existence he had for so long a time refused to believe.

There was no time to lose. He hastened to open the *secrétaire*, and found the pocket-book in the drawer, and in it the letter of credit. There were in all six thousand piastres, but of these six thousand Albert had already expended three thousand.

As to Franz, he had no letter of credit, as he lived at Florence, and had only come to Rome to pass seven or eight days; he had brought but a hundred louis, and of these he had not more than fifty left. Thus seven or eight hundred piastres were wanting to them both to make up the sum that Albert required. True, he might in such a case rely on the kindness of Signor Torlonia. He was, therefore, about to return to the Palazzo Bracciano without loss of time, when suddenly a luminous idea crossed his mind.

He remembered the Count of Monte Cristo. Franz was about to ring for Signor Pastrini, when that worthy presented himself.

"My dear sir," he said, hastily, "do you know if the count is within?"

"Yes, your excellency; he has this moment returned."

"Is he in bed?"

"I should say no."

"Then ring at his door, if you please, and request him to be so kind as to give me an audience."

Signor Pastrini did as he was desired, and returning five minutes after, he said:

"The count awaits your excellency."

Franz went along the corridor, and a servant introduced him to the count. He was in a small room which Franz had not yet seen, and which was surrounded with divans. The count came towards him.

"Well, what good wind blows you hither at this hour?" said he; "have you come to sup with me? It would be very kind of you."

"No; I have come to speak to you of a very serious matter."

"A serious matter," said the count, looking at Franz with the earnestness usual to him; "and what may it be?"

"Are we alone?"

"Yes," replied the count, going to the door, and returning. Franz gave him Albert's letter.

"Read that," he said.

The count read it.

"Well, well!" said he.

"Did you see the postscript?"

"I did, indeed.

"'*Se alle sei della mattina le quattro mille piastre non sono nelle mie mani, alla sette il conte Alberto avrà cessato di vivere.*

"'Luigi Vampa.'"

"What think you of that?" inquired Franz.

"Have you the money he demands?"

"Yes, all but eight hundred piastres."

The count went to his *secrétaire*, opened it, and pulling out a drawer filled with gold, said to Franz, "I hope you will not offend me by applying to anyone but myself."

"You see, on the contrary, I come to you first and instantly," replied Franz.

"And I thank you; have what you will;" and he made a sign to

Franz to take what he pleased.

"Is it absolutely necessary, then, to send the money to Luigi Vampa?" asked the young man, looking fixedly in his turn at the count.

"Judge for yourself," replied he. "The postscript is explicit."

"I think that if you would take the trouble of reflecting, you could find a way of simplifying the negotiation," said Franz.

"How so?" returned the count, with surprise.

"If we were to go together to Luigi Vampa, I am sure he would not refuse you Albert's freedom."

"What influence can I possibly have over a bandit?"

"Have you not just rendered him a service that can never be forgotten?"

"What is that?"

"Have you not saved Peppino's life?"

"Well, well," said the count, "who told you that?"

"No matter; I know it." The count knit his brows, and remained silent an instant.

"And if I went to seek Vampa, would you accompany me?"

"If my society would not be disagreeable."

"Be it so. It is a lovely night, and a walk without Rome will do us both good."

"Shall I take any arms?"

"For what purpose?"

"Any money?"

"It is useless. Where is the man who brought the letter?"

"In the street."

"He awaits the answer?"

"Yes."

"I must learn where we are going. I will summon him hither."

"It is useless; he would not come up."

"To your apartments, perhaps; but he will not make any difficulty at entering mine."

The count went to the window of the apartment that looked on to the street, and whistled in a peculiar manner. The man in the mantle quitted the wall, and advanced into the middle of the street. "*Salite!*" said the count, in the same tone in which he would have given an order to his servant. The messenger obeyed without the least hesitation, but rather with alacrity, and, mounting the steps at a bound, entered the hotel; five seconds afterwards he was at the door of the room.

"Ah, it is you, Peppino," said the count. But Peppino, instead of answering, threw himself on his knees, seized the count's hand, and covered it with kisses. "Ah," said the count, "you have, then, not forgotten that I saved your life; that is strange, for it is a week ago."

"No, excellency; and never shall I forget it," returned Peppino, with an accent of profound gratitude.

"Never? That is a long time; but it is something that you believe so. Rise and answer."

Peppino glanced anxiously at Franz.

"Oh, you may speak before his excellency," said he; "he is one of my friends. You allow me to give you this title?" continued the count in French, "it is necessary to excite this man's confidence."

"You can speak before me," said Franz; "I am a friend of the count's."

"Good!" returned Peppino. "I am ready to answer any questions your excellency may address to me."

"How did the Viscount Albert fall into Luigi's hands?"

"Excellency, the Frenchman's carriage passed several times the one in which was Teresa."

"The chief's mistress?"

"Yes. The Frenchman threw her a bouquet; Teresa returned it all this with the consent of the chief, who was in the carriage."

"What?" cried Franz, "was Luigi Vampa in the carriage with the Roman peasants?"

"It was he who drove, disguised as the coachman," replied Peppino.

"Well?" said the count.

"Well, then, the Frenchman took off his mask; Teresa, with the chief's consent, did the same. The Frenchman asked for a rendezvous; Teresa gave him one only, instead of Teresa, it was Beppo who was on the steps of the church of San Giacomo."

"What!" exclaimed Franz, "the peasant girl who snatched his *mocoletto* from him"

"Was a lad of fifteen," replied Peppino. "But it was no disgrace to your friend to have been deceived; Beppo has taken in plenty of others."

"And Beppo led him outside the walls?" said the count.

"Exactly so; a carriage was waiting at the end of the Via Macello. Beppo got in, inviting the Frenchman to follow him, and he did not wait to be asked twice. He gallantly offered the right-hand seat to Beppo, and sat by him. Beppo told him he was going to take him to a villa a league from Rome; the Frenchman assured him he would follow him to the end of the world. The coachman went up the Via di Ripetta and the Porta San Paolo; and when they were two hundred yards outside, as the Frenchman became somewhat too forward, Beppo put a brace of pistols to his head, the coachman pulled up and did the same. At the same time, four of the band, who were concealed on the banks of the Almo, surrounded the carriage. The Frenchman made some resistance, and nearly strangled Beppo; but he could not resist five armed men, and was forced to yield. They made him get out, walk along the banks of the river, and then brought him to Teresa and Luigi, who were waiting for him in the catacombs of St. Sebastian."

"Well," said the count, turning towards Franz, "it seems to me that this is a very likely story. What do you say to it?"

"Why, that I should think it very amusing," replied Franz, "if it had happened to anyone but poor Albert."

"And, in truth, if you had not found me here," said the count, "it might have proved a gallant adventure which would have cost your friend dear; but now, be assured, his alarm will be the only serious consequence."

"And shall we go and find him?" inquired Franz.

"Oh, decidedly, sir. He is in a very picturesque place do you know the catacombs of St. Sebastian?"

"I was never in them; but I have often resolved to visit them."

"Well, here is an opportunity made to your hand, and it would be difficult to contrive a better. Have you a carriage?"

"No."

"That is of no consequence; I always have one ready, day and night."

"Always ready?"

"Yes. I am a very capricious being, and I should tell you that sometimes when I rise, or after my dinner, or in the middle of the night, I resolve on starting for some particular point, and away I go."

The count rang, and a footman appeared.

"Order out the carriage," he said, "and remove the pistols which are in the holsters. You need not awaken the coachman; Ali will drive."

In a very short time the noise of wheels was heard, and the carriage stopped at the door. The count took out his watch.

"Half-past twelve," he said. "We might start at five o'clock and be in time, but the delay may cause your friend to pass an uneasy night, and therefore we had better go with all speed to extricate him from the hands of the infidels. Are you still resolved to accompany me?"

"More determined than ever."

"Well, then, come along."

Franz and the count went downstairs, accompanied by Peppino. At the door they found the carriage. Ali was on the box, in whom Franz recognized the dumb slave of the grotto of Monte Cristo. Franz and the count got into the carriage. Peppino placed himself beside Ali, and they set off at a rapid pace. Ali had received his instructions, and went down the Corso, crossed the Campo Vaccino, went up the Strada San Gregorio, and reached the gates of St. Sebastian. Then the porter raised some difficulties, but the Count of Monte Cristo produced a permit from the governor of Rome, allowing him to leave or enter the city at any hour of the day or night; the portcullis was therefore raised, the porter had a louis for his trouble, and they went on their way.

The road which the carriage now traversed was the ancient Appian Way, and bordered with tombs. From time to time, by the light of the moon, which began to rise, Franz imagined that he saw something like a sentinel appear at various points among the ruins, and suddenly retreat into the darkness on a signal from Peppino.

A short time before they reached the Baths of Caracalla the carriage stopped, Peppino opened the door, and the count and Franz alighted.

"In ten minutes," said the count to his companion, "we shall be there."

He then took Peppino aside, gave him an order in a low voice, and Peppino went away, taking with him a torch, brought with them in the carriage. Five minutes elapsed, during which Franz saw the shepherd going along a narrow path that led over the irregular and broken surface of the Campagna; and finally he disappeared in the midst of the tall red herbage, which seemed like the bristling mane of an enormous lion.

"Now," said the count, "let us follow him."

Franz and the count in their turn then advanced along the same path, which, at the distance of a hundred paces, led them over a declivity to the bottom of a small valley. They then perceived two men conversing in the obscurity.

"Ought we to go on?" asked Franz of the count; "or should we pause?"

"Let us go on; Peppino will have warned the sentry of our coming."

One of the two men was Peppino, and the other a bandit on the lookout. Franz and the count advanced, and the bandit saluted them.

"Your excellency," said Peppino, addressing the count, "if you will follow me, the opening of the catacombs is close at hand."

"Go on, then," replied the count. They came to an opening behind a clump of bushes and in the midst of a pile of rocks, by which a man could scarcely pass. Peppino glided first into this crevice; after they got along a few paces the passage widened. Peppino passed, lighted his torch, and turned to see if they came after him. The count first reached an open space and Franz followed him closely. The passageway sloped in a gentle descent, enlarging as they proceeded; still Franz and the count were compelled to advance in a stooping posture, and were scarcely able to proceed abreast of one another. They went on a hundred and fifty paces in this way, and then were stopped by, "Who comes there?" At the same time they saw the reflection of a torch on a carbine barrel.

"A friend!" responded Peppino; and, advancing alone towards the sentry, he said a few words to him in a low tone; and then he, like the first, saluted the nocturnal visitors, making a sign that they might proceed.

Behind the sentinel was a staircase with twenty steps. Franz and the count descended these, and found themselves in a mortuary chamber. Five corridors diverged like the rays of a star, and the walls, dug into niches, which were arranged one above the other in the shape of coffins, showed that they were at last in the catacombs. Down one of the corridors, whose extent it was impossible to determine, rays of light were visible. The count laid his hand on Franz's shoulder.

"Would you like to see a camp of bandits in repose?" he inquired.

"Exceedingly," replied Franz.

"Come with me, then. Peppino, put out the torch." Peppino obeyed, and Franz and the count were in utter darkness, except that fifty paces in advance of them a reddish glare, more evident since Peppino had put out his torch, was visible along the wall.

They advanced silently, the count guiding Franz as if he had the singular faculty of seeing in the dark. Franz himself, however, saw his way more plainly in proportion as he went on towards the light, which served in some manner as a guide. Three arcades were before them, and the middle one was used as a door. These arcades opened on one side into the corridor where the count and Franz were, and on the other into a large square chamber, entirely surrounded by niches similar to those of which we have spoken.

In the midst of this chamber were four stones, which had formerly served as an altar, as was evident from the cross which still surmounted them. A lamp, placed at the base of a pillar, lighted up with its pale and flickering flame the singular scene which presented itself to the eyes of the two visitors concealed in the shadow.

A man was seated with his elbow leaning on the column, and was reading with his back turned to the arcades, through the openings of which the new-comers contemplated him. This was the chief of the band, Luigi Vampa. Around him, and in groups, according to their fancy, lying in their mantles, or with their backs against a sort of stone bench, which went all round the columbarium, were to be seen twenty brigands or more, each having his carbine within reach. At the other end, silent, scarcely visible, and like a shadow, was a sentinel, who was walking up and down before a grotto, which was only distinguishable because in that spot the darkness seemed more dense than elsewhere.

When the count thought Franz had gazed sufficiently on this picturesque tableau, he raised his finger to his lips, to warn him to be silent, and, ascending the three steps which led to the corridor of the columbarium, entered the chamber by the middle arcade, and advanced towards Vampa, who was so intent on the book before him that he did not hear the noise of his footsteps.

"Who comes there?" cried the sentinel, who was less abstracted, and who saw by the lamp-light a shadow approaching his chief. At this challenge, Vampa rose quickly, drawing at the same moment a pistol from his girdle. In a moment all the bandits were on their feet, and twenty carbines were levelled at the count.

"Well," said he in a voice perfectly calm, and no muscle of his countenance disturbed, "well, my dear Vampa, it appears to me that you receive a friend with a great deal of ceremony."

"Ground arms," exclaimed the chief, with an imperative sign of the hand, while with the other he took off his hat respectfully; then, turning to the singular personage who had caused this scene, he said, "Your pardon, your excellency, but I was so far from expecting the honor of a visit, that I did not really recognize you."

"It seems that your memory is equally short in everything, Vampa," said the count, "and that not only do you forget people's faces, but also the conditions you make with them."

"What conditions have I forgotten, your excellency?" inquired the bandit, with the air of a man who, having committed an error, is anxious to repair it.

"Was it not agreed," asked the count, "that not only my person, but also that of my friends, should be respected by you?"

"And how have I broken that treaty, your excellency?"

"You have this evening carried off and conveyed hither the Viscount Albert de Morcerf. Well," continued the count, in a tone that made Franz shudder, "this young gentleman is one of *my friends* this young gentleman lodges in the same hotel as myself this young gentleman has been up and down the Corso for eight hours in my private carriage, and yet, I repeat to you, you have carried him off, and conveyed him hither, and," added the count, taking the letter from his pocket, "you have set a ransom on him, as if he were an utter stranger."

"Why did you not tell me all this you?" inquired the brigand chief, turning towards his men, who all retreated before his look. "Why have you caused me thus to fail in my word towards a gentleman like the count, who has all our lives in his hands? By heavens! if I thought one of you knew that the young gentleman was the friend of his excellency, I would blow his brains out with my own hand!"

"Well," said the count, turning towards Franz, "I told you there was some mistake in this."

"Are you not alone?" asked Vampa with uneasiness.

"I am with the person to whom this letter was addressed, and to whom I desired to prove that Luigi Vampa was a man of his word. Come, your excellency," the count added, turning to Franz, "here is Luigi Vampa, who will himself express to you his deep regret at the mistake he has committed."

Franz approached, the chief advancing several steps to meet him.

"Welcome among us, your excellency," he said to him; "you heard what the count just said, and also my reply; let me add that I would not for the four thousand piastres at which I had fixed your friend's ransom, that this had happened."

"But," said Franz, looking round him uneasily, "where is the viscount? I do not see him."

"Nothing has happened to him, I hope," said the count frowningly.

"The prisoner is there," replied Vampa, pointing to the hollow space in front of which the bandit was on guard, "and I will go myself and tell him he is free."

The chief went towards the place he had pointed out as Albert's prison, and Franz and the count followed him.

"What is the prisoner doing?" inquired Vampa of the sentinel.

"*Ma foi*, captain," replied the sentry, "I do not know; for the last hour I have not heard him stir."

"Come in, your excellency," said Vampa. The count and Franz ascended seven or eight steps after the chief, who drew back a bolt and opened a door. Then, by the gleam of a lamp, similar to that which lighted the columbarium, Albert was to be seen wrapped up in a cloak which one of the bandits had lent him, lying in a corner in profound slumber.

"Come," said the count, smiling with his own peculiar smile, "not so bad for a man who is to be shot at seven o'clock tomorrow morning."

Vampa looked at Albert with a kind of admiration; he was not insensible to such a proof of courage.

"You are right, your excellency," he said; "this must be one of your friends."

Then going to Albert, he touched him on the shoulder, saying,

THE COUNT OF MONTE CRISTO

"Will your excellency please to awaken?"

Albert stretched out his arms, rubbed his eyelids, and opened his eyes.

"Oh," said he, "is it you, captain? You should have allowed me to sleep. I had such a delightful dream. I was dancing the galop at Torlonia's with the Countess G ." Then he drew his watch from his pocket, that he might see how time sped.

"Half-past one only?" said he. "Why the devil do you rouse me at this hour?"

"To tell you that you are free, your excellency."

"My dear fellow," replied Albert, with perfect ease of mind, "remember, for the future, Napoleon's maxim, 'Never awaken me but for bad news;' if you had let me sleep on, I should have finished my galop, and have been grateful to you all my life. So, then, they have paid my ransom?"

"No, your excellency."

"Well, then, how am I free?"

"A person to whom I can refuse nothing has come to demand you."

"Come hither?"

"Yes, hither."

"Really? Then that person is a most amiable person."

Albert looked around and perceived Franz. "What," said he, "is it you, my dear Franz, whose devotion and friendship are thus displayed?"

"No, not I," replied Franz, "but our neighbor, the Count of Monte Cristo."

"Oh, my dear count," said Albert gayly, arranging his cravat and wristbands, "you are really most kind, and I hope you will consider me as under eternal obligations to you, in the first place for the carriage, and in the next for this visit," and he put out his hand to the count, who shuddered as he gave his own, but who nevertheless did give it.

The bandit gazed on this scene with amazement; he was evidently accustomed to see his prisoners tremble before him, and yet here was one whose gay temperament was not for a moment altered; as for Franz, he was enchanted at the way in which Albert had sustained the national honor in the presence of the bandit.

"My dear Albert," he said, "if you will make haste, we shall yet have time to finish the night at Torlonia's. You may conclude your interrupted galop, so that you will owe no ill-will to Signor Luigi, who has, indeed, throughout this whole affair acted like a gentleman."

"You are decidedly right, and we may reach the Palazzo by two o'clock. Signor Luigi," continued Albert, "is there any formality to fulfil before I take leave of your excellency?"

"None, sir," replied the bandit, "you are as free as air."

"Well, then, a happy and merry life to you. Come, gentlemen, come."

And Albert, followed by Franz and the count, descended the staircase, crossed the square chamber, where stood all the bandits, hat in hand.

"Peppino," said the brigand chief, "give me the torch."

"What are you going to do?" inquired the count.

"I will show you the way back myself," said the captain; "that is the least honor that I can render to your excellency."

And taking the lighted torch from the hands of the herdsman, he preceded his guests, not as a servant who performs an act of civility, but like a king who precedes ambassadors. On reaching the door, he bowed.

"And now, your excellency," added he, "allow me to repeat my apologies, and I hope you will not entertain any resentment at what has occurred."

"No, my dear Vampa," replied the count; "besides, you compensate for your mistakes in so gentlemanly a way, that one almost feels obliged to you for having committed them."

"Gentlemen," added the chief, turning towards the young men, "perhaps the offer may not appear very tempting to you; but if you should ever feel inclined to pay me a second visit, wherever I may be, you shall be welcome."

Franz and Albert bowed. The count went out first, then Albert.

Franz paused for a moment.

"Has your excellency anything to ask me?" said Vampa with a smile.

"Yes, I have," replied Franz; "I am curious to know what work you were perusing with so much attention as we entered."

"Cæsar's *Commentaries*," said the bandit, "it is my favorite work."

"Well, are you coming?" asked Albert.

"Yes," replied Franz, "here I am," and he, in his turn, left the caves. They advanced to the plain.

"Ah, your pardon," said Albert, turning round; "will you allow me, captain?"

And he lighted his cigar at Vampa's torch.

"Now, my dear count," he said, "let us on with all the speed we may. I am enormously anxious to finish my night at the Duke of Bracciano's."

They found the carriage where they had left it. The count said a word in Arabic to Ali, and the horses went on at great speed.

It was just two o'clock by Albert's watch when the two friends entered into the dancing-room. Their return was quite an event, but as they entered together, all uneasiness on Albert's account ceased instantly.

"Madame," said the Viscount of Morcerf, advancing towards the countess, "yesterday you were so condescending as to promise me a galop; I am rather late in claiming this gracious promise, but here is my friend, whose character for veracity you well know, and he will assure you the delay arose from no fault of mine."

And as at this moment the orchestra gave the signal for the waltz, Albert put his arm round the waist of the countess, and disappeared with her in the whirl of dancers.

In the meanwhile Franz was considering the singular shudder that had passed over the Count of Monte Cristo at the moment when he had been, in some sort, forced to give his hand to Albert.

Chapter 11

The Rendezvous

The first words that Albert uttered to his friend, on the following morning, contained a request that Franz would accompany him on a visit to the count; true, the young man had warmly and energetically thanked the count on the previous evening; but services such as he had rendered could never be too often acknowledged. Franz, who seemed attracted by some invisible influence towards the count, in which terror was strangely mingled, felt an extreme reluctance to permit his friend to be exposed alone to the singular fascination that this mysterious personage seemed to exercise over him, and therefore made no objection to Albert's request, but at once accompanied him to the desired spot, and, after a short delay, the count joined them in the salon.

"My dear count," said Albert, advancing to meet him, "permit me to repeat the poor thanks I offered last night, and to assure you that the remembrance of all I owe to you will never be effaced from my memory; believe me, as long as I live, I shall never cease to dwell with grateful recollection on the prompt and important service you rendered me; and also to remember that to you I am indebted even for my life."

"My very good friend and excellent neighbor," replied the count, with a smile, "you really exaggerate my trifling exertions. You owe me nothing but some trifle of 20,000 francs, which you have been saved out of your travelling expenses, so that there is not much of a score between us; but you must really permit me to congratulate you on the ease and unconcern with which you resigned yourself to your fate, and the perfect indifference you manifested as to the turn events might take."

"Upon my word," said Albert, "I deserve no credit for what I could not help, namely, a determination to take everything as I found it, and to let those bandits see, that although men get into troublesome scrapes all over the world, there is no nation but the French that can smile even in the face of grim Death himself. All that, however, has nothing to do with my obligations to you, and I now come to ask you whether, in my own person, my family, or connections, I can in any way serve you? My father, the Comte de Morcerf, although of Spanish origin, possesses considerable influence, both at the court of France and Madrid, and I unhesitatingly place the best services of myself, and all to whom my life is dear, at your disposal."

"Monsieur de Morcerf," replied the count, "your offer, far from surprising me, is precisely what I expected from you, and I accept it in the same spirit of hearty sincerity with which it is made; nay, I will go still further, and say that I had previously made up my mind to ask a great favor at your hands."

"Oh, pray name it."

"I am wholly a stranger to Paris it is a city I have never yet seen."

"Is it possible," exclaimed Albert, "that you have reached your present age without visiting the finest capital in the world? I can scarcely credit it."

"Nevertheless, it is quite true; still, I agree with you in thinking that my present ignorance of the first city in Europe is a reproach to me in every way, and calls for immediate correction; but, in all probability, I should have performed so important, so necessary a duty, as that of making myself acquainted with the wonders and beauties of your justly celebrated capital, had I known any person who would have introduced me into the fashionable world, but unfortunately I possessed no acquaintance there, and, of necessity, was compelled to abandon the idea."

"So distinguished an individual as yourself," cried Albert, "could scarcely have required an introduction."

"You are most kind; but as regards myself, I can find no merit I possess, save that, as a millionaire, I might have become a partner in the speculations of M. Aguado and M. Rothschild; but as my motive in travelling to your capital would not have been for the pleasure of dabbling in stocks, I stayed away till some favorable chance should present itself of carrying my wish into execution. Your offer, however, smooths all difficulties, and I have only to ask you, my dear M. de Morcerf" (these words were accompanied by a most peculiar smile), "whether you undertake, upon my arrival in France, to open to me the doors of that fashionable world of which I know no more than a Huron or a native of Cochin-China?"

"Oh, that I do, and with infinite pleasure," answered Albert; "and so much the more readily as a letter received this morning from my father summons me to Paris, in consequence of a treaty of marriage (my dear Franz, do not smile, I beg of you) with a family of high standing, and connected with the very cream of Parisian society."

"Connected by marriage, you mean," said Franz, laughingly.

"Well, never mind how it is," answered Albert, "it comes to the same thing in the end. Perhaps by the time you return to Paris, I shall be quite a sober, staid father of a family! A most edifying representative I shall make of all the domestic virtues don't you think so? But as regards your wish to visit our fine city, my dear count, I can only say that you may command me and mine to any extent you please."

"Then it is settled," said the count, "and I give you my solemn assurance that I only waited an opportunity like the present to realize plans that I have long meditated."

Franz did not doubt that these plans were the same concerning which the count had dropped a few words in the grotto of Monte Cristo, and while the count was speaking the young man watched him closely, hoping to read something of his purpose in his face, but his countenance was inscrutable especially when, as in the present case, it was veiled in a sphinx-like smile.

"But tell me now, count," exclaimed Albert, delighted at the idea of having to chaperon so distinguished a person as Monte Cristo; "tell me truly whether you are in earnest, or if this project of visiting Paris is merely one of the chimerical and uncertain air castles of which we make so many in the course of our lives, but which, like a house built on the sand, is liable to be blown over by the first puff of wind?"

"I pledge you my honor," returned the count, "that I mean to do as I have said; both inclination and positive necessity compel me to visit Paris."

"When do you propose going thither?"

"Have you made up your mind when you shall be there yourself?"

"Certainly I have; in a fortnight or three weeks' time, that is to say, as fast as I can get there!"

"Nay," said the Count; "I will give you three months ere I join

you; you see I make an ample allowance for all delays and difficulties.

"And in three months' time," said Albert, "you will be at my
house?"

"Shall we make a positive appointment for a particular day
and hour?" inquired the count; "only let me warn you that I
am proverbial for my punctilious exactitude in keeping my
engagements."

"Day for day, hour for hour," said Albert; "that will suit me to a
dot."

"So be it, then," replied the count, and extending his hand towards a calendar, suspended near the chimney-piece, he said,
"today is the 21st of February;" and drawing out his watch,
added, "it is exactly half-past ten o'clock. Now promise me to
remember this, and expect me the 21st of May at the same
hour in the forenoon."

"Capital!" exclaimed Albert; "your breakfast shall be waiting."

"Where do you live?"

"No. 27, Rue du Helder."

"Have you bachelor's apartments there? I hope my coming
will not put you to any inconvenience."

"I reside in my father's house, but occupy a pavilion at the farther side of the courtyard, entirely separated from the main
building."

"Quite sufficient," replied the count, as, taking out his tablets,
he wrote down "No. 27, Rue du Helder, 21st May, half-past ten
in the morning."

"Now then," said the count, returning his tablets to his pocket,
"make yourself perfectly easy; the hand of your time-piece
will not be more accurate in marking the time than myself."

"Shall I see you again ere my departure?" asked Albert.

"That depends; when do you leave?"

"Tomorrow evening, at five o'clock."

"In that case I must say adieu to you, as I am compelled to go to
Naples, and shall not return hither before Saturday evening or
Sunday morning. And you, baron," pursued the count, address-

ing Franz, "do you also depart tomorrow?"

"Yes."

"For France?"

"No, for Venice; I shall remain in Italy for another year or two."

"Then we shall not meet in Paris?"

"I fear I shall not have that honor."

"Well, since we must part," said the count, holding out a hand to each of the young men, "allow me to wish you both a safe and pleasant journey."

It was the first time the hand of Franz had come in contact with that of the mysterious individual before him, and unconsciously he shuddered at its touch, for it felt cold and icy as that of a corpse.

"Let us understand each other," said Albert; "it is agreed is it not? that you are to be at No. 27, in the Rue du Helder, on the 21st of May, at half-past ten in the morning, and your word of honor passed for your punctuality?"

"The 21st of May, at half-past ten in the morning, Rue du Helder, No. 27," replied the count.

The young men then rose, and bowing to the count, quitted the room.

"What is the matter?" asked Albert of Franz, when they had returned to their own apartments; "you seem more than commonly thoughtful."

"I will confess to you, Albert," replied Franz, "the count is a very singular person, and the appointment you have made to meet him in Paris fills me with a thousand apprehensions."

"My dear fellow," exclaimed Albert, "what can there possibly be in that to excite uneasiness? Why, you must have lost your senses."

"Whether I am in my senses or not," answered Franz, "that is the way I feel."

"Listen to me, Franz," said Albert; "I am glad that the occasion has presented itself for saying this to you, for I have noticed how cold you are in your bearing towards the count, while he, on the other hand, has always been courtesy itself to us. Have you anything particular against him?"

"Possibly."

"Did you ever meet him previously to coming hither?"

"I have."

"And where?"

"Will you promise me not to repeat a single word of what I am about to tell you?"

"I promise."

"Upon your honor?"

"Upon my honor."

"Then listen to me."

Franz then related to his friend the history of his excursion to the Island of Monte Cristo and of his finding a party of smugglers there, and the two Corsican bandits with them. He dwelt with considerable force and energy on the almost magical hospitality he had received from the count, and the magnificence of his entertainment in the grotto of the *Thousand and One Nights*.

He recounted, with circumstantial exactitude, all the particulars of the supper, the hashish, the statues, the dream, and how, at his awakening, there remained no proof or trace of all these events, save the small yacht, seen in the distant horizon driving under full sail toward Porto-Vecchio.

Then he detailed the conversation overheard by him at the Colosseum, between the count and Vampa, in which the count had promised to obtain the release of the bandit Peppino, an engagement which, as our readers are aware, he most faithfully fulfilled.

At last he arrived at the adventure of the preceding night, and the embarrassment in which he found himself placed by not having sufficient cash by six or seven hundred piastres to make up the sum required, and finally of his application to the count and the picturesque and satisfactory result that followed. Albert listened with the most profound attention.

"Well," said he, when Franz had concluded, "what do you find to object to in all you have related? The count is fond of travelling, and, being rich, possesses a vessel of his own. Go but to Portsmouth or Southampton, and you will find the harbors crowded with the yachts belonging to such of the English as can afford the expense, and have the same liking for this amusement. Now, by way of having a resting-place during his excursions, avoiding the wretched cookery which has been trying its best to poison me during the last four months, while you have manfully resisted its effects for as many years, and obtaining a bed on which it is possible to slumber, Monte Cristo has furnished for himself a temporary abode where you first found him; but, to prevent the possibility of the Tuscan government taking a fancy to his enchanted palace, and thereby depriving him of the advantages naturally expected from so large an outlay of capital, he has wisely enough purchased the island, and taken its name. Just ask yourself, my good fellow, whether there are not many persons of our acquaintance who assume the names of lands and properties they never in their lives were masters of?"

"But," said Franz, "the Corsican bandits that were among the crew of his vessel?"

"Why, really the thing seems to me simple enough. Nobody knows better than yourself that the bandits of Corsica are not rogues or thieves, but purely and simply fugitives, driven by some sinister motive from their native town or village, and that their fellowship involves no disgrace or stigma; for my own part, I protest that, should I ever go to Corsica, my first visit, ere even I presented myself to the mayor or prefect, should be to the bandits of Colomba, if I could only manage to find them; for, on my conscience, they are a race of men I admire greatly."

"Still," persisted Franz, "I suppose you will allow that such men as Vampa and his band are regular villains, who have no other motive than plunder when they seize your person. How do you explain the influence the count evidently possessed over those ruffians?"

"My good friend, as in all probability I own my present safety to that influence, it would ill become me to search too closely into its source; therefore, instead of condemning him for his intimacy with outlaws, you must give me leave to excuse any little irregularity there may be in such a connection; not altogether for preserving my life, for my own idea was that it never was in much danger, but certainly for saving me 4,000 piastres, which, being translated, means neither more nor less than 24,000 livres of our money a sum at which, most assuredly, I should never have been estimated in France, proving most indisputably," added Albert with a laugh, "that no prophet is honored in his own country."

"Talking of countries," replied Franz, "of what country is the count, what is his native tongue, whence does he derive his immense fortune, and what were those events of his early life a life as marvellous as unknown that have tinctured his succeeding years with so dark and gloomy a misanthropy? Certainly these are questions that, in your place, I should like to have answered."

"My dear Franz," replied Albert, "when, upon receipt of my letter, you found the necessity of asking the count's assistance, you promptly went to him, saying, 'My friend Albert de Morcerf is in danger; help me to deliver him.' Was not that nearly what you said?"

"It was."

"Well, then, did he ask you, 'Who is M. Albert de Morcerf? how does he come by his name his fortune? what are his means of existence? what is his birthplace? of what country is he a native?' Tell me, did he put all these questions to you?"

"I confess he asked me none."

"No; he merely came and freed me from the hands of Signor Vampa, where, I can assure you, in spite of all my outward appearance of ease and unconcern, I did not very particularly care to remain. Now, then, Franz, when, for services so promptly and unhesitatingly rendered, he but asks me in return to do for him what is done daily for any Russian prince or Italian nobleman who may pass through Paris merely to introduce him into society would you have me refuse? My good fellow, you must have lost your senses to think it possible I could act with such cold-blooded policy."

And this time it must be confessed that, contrary to the usual state of affairs in discussions between the young men, the effective arguments were all on Albert's side.

"Well," said Franz with a sigh, "do as you please my dear viscount, for your arguments are beyond my powers of refutation. Still, in spite of all, you must admit that this Count of Monte Cristo is a most singular personage."

"He is a philanthropist," answered the other; "and no doubt his motive in visiting Paris is to compete for the Monthyon prize, given, as you are aware, to whoever shall be proved to have most materially advanced the interests of virtue and humanity. If my vote and interest can obtain it for him, I will readily give him the one and promise the other. And now, my dear Franz, let us talk of something else. Come, shall we take our luncheon, and then pay a last visit to St. Peter's?"

Franz silently assented; and the following afternoon, at half-past five o'clock, the young men parted. Albert de Morcerf to return to Paris, and Franz d'Épinay to pass a fortnight at Venice.

But, ere he entered his travelling carriage, Albert, fearing that his expected guest might forget the engagement he had entered into, placed in the care of a waiter at the hotel a card to be delivered to the Count of Monte Cristo, on which, beneath the name of Viscount Albert de Morcerf, he had written in pencil:

"27, *Rue du Helder, on the* 21*st May, half-past ten* A.M."

Chapter 12

The Guests

I n the house in the Rue du Helder, where Albert had invited the Count of Monte Cristo, everything was being prepared on the morning of the 21st of May to do honor to the occasion. Albert de Morcerf inhabited a pavilion situated at the corner of a large court, and directly opposite another building, in which were the servants' apartments. Two windows only of the pavilion faced the street; three other windows looked into the court, and two at the back into the garden.

Between the court and the garden, built in the heavy style of the imperial architecture, was the large and fashionable dwelling of the Count and Countess of Morcerf.

A high wall surrounded the whole of the property, surmounted at intervals by vases filled with flowers, and broken in the centre by a large gate of gilded iron, which served as the carriage entrance. A small door, close to the lodge of the *concierge*, gave ingress and egress to the servants and masters when they were on foot.

It was easy to discover that the delicate care of a mother, unwilling to part from her son, and yet aware that a young man of the viscount's age required the full exercise of his liberty, had chosen this habitation for Albert. There were not lacking, however, evidences of what we may call the intelligent egoism of a youth who is charmed with the indolent, careless life of an only son, and who lives as it were in a gilded cage. By means of the two windows looking into the street, Albert could see all that passed; the sight of what is going on is necessary to young men, who always want to see the world traverse their horizon, even if that horizon is only a public thoroughfare. Then, should anything appear to merit a more minute examination, Albert de Morcerf could follow up his researches by means of a small gate, similar to that close to the *concierge's* door, and which merits a particular description.

It was a little entrance that seemed never to have been opened since the house was built, so entirely was it covered with dust and dirt; but the well-oiled hinges and locks told quite another story. This door was a mockery to the *concierge*, from whose vigilance and jurisdiction it was free, and, like that famous portal in the *Arabian Nights*, opening at the "*Sesame*" of Ali Baba, it was wont to swing backward at a cabalistic word or a concerted tap from without from the sweetest voices or whitest fingers in the world.

At the end of a long corridor, with which the door communicated, and which formed the antechamber, was, on the right, Albert's breakfast-room, looking into the court, and on the left the salon, looking into the garden. Shrubs and creeping plants covered the windows, and hid from the garden and court these two apartments, the only rooms into which, as they were on the ground floor, the prying eyes of the curious could penetrate.

On the floor above were similar rooms, with the addition of a third, formed out of the antechamber; these three rooms were a salon, a boudoir, and a bedroom. The salon downstairs was only an Algerian divan, for the use of smokers. The boudoir upstairs communicated with the bedchamber by an invisible door on the staircase; it was evident that every precaution had been taken. Above this floor was a large *atelier*, which had been increased in size by pulling down the partitions a pandemonium, in which the artist and the dandy strove for pre-eminence.

There were collected and piled up all Albert's successive caprices, hunting-horns, bass-viols, flutes a whole orchestra, for Albert had had not a taste but a fancy for music; easels, palettes, brushes, pencils for music had been succeeded by painting; foils, boxing-gloves, broadswords, and single-sticks for, following the example of the fashionable young men of the time, Albert de Morcerf cultivated, with far more perseverance than music and drawing, the three arts that complete a dandy's education, i.e., fencing, boxing, and single-stick; and it was here that he received Grisier, Cooks, and Charles Leboucher.

The rest of the furniture of this privileged apartment consisted of old cabinets, filled with Chinese porcelain and Japanese vases, Lucca della Robbia *faïences*, and Palissy platters; of old armchairs, in which perhaps had sat Henry IV. or Sully, Louis XIII. or Richelieu for two of these armchairs, adorned with a carved shield, on which were engraved the fleur-de-lis of France on an azure field, evidently came from the Louvre, or, at least, some royal residence.

Over these dark and sombre chairs were thrown splendid stuffs, dyed beneath Persia's sun, or woven by the fingers of the women of Calcutta or of Chandernagor. What these stuffs did there, it was impossible to say; they awaited, while gratifying the eyes, a destination unknown to their owner himself; in the meantime they filled the place with their golden and silky reflections.

In the centre of the room was a Roller and Blanchet "baby grand" piano in rosewood, but holding the potentialities of an orchestra in its narrow and sonorous cavity, and groaning beneath the weight of the *chefs-d'œuvre* of Beethoven, Weber, Mozart, Haydn, Grétry, and Porpora.

On the walls, over the doors, on the ceiling, were swords, daggers, Malay creeses, maces, battle-axes; gilded, damasked, and inlaid suits of armor; dried plants, minerals, and stuffed birds, their flame-colored wings outspread in motionless flight, and their beaks forever open. This was Albert's favorite lounging place.

However, the morning of the appointment, the young man had established himself in the small salon downstairs. There, on a table, surrounded at some distance by a large and luxurious divan, every species of tobacco known, from the yellow tobacco of Petersburg to the black of Sinai, and so on along the scale from Maryland and Porto Rico, to Latakia, was exposed in pots of crackled earthenware of which the Dutch are so fond; beside them, in boxes of fragrant wood, were ranged, according to their size and quality, puros, regalias, havanas, and manillas; and, in an open cabinet, a collection of German pipes, of chibouques, with their amber mouth-pieces ornamented with coral, and of narghiles, with their long tubes of morocco, awaiting the caprice or the sympathy of the smokers.

Albert had himself presided at the arrangement, or, rather, the symmetrical derangement, which, after coffee, the guests at a breakfast of modern days love to contemplate through the vapor that escapes from their mouths, and ascends in long and fanciful wreaths to the ceiling.

At a quarter to ten, a valet entered; he composed, with a little groom named John, and who only spoke English, all Albert's establishment, although the cook of the hotel was always at his service, and on great occasions the count's *chasseur* also. This valet, whose name was Germain, and who enjoyed the entire confidence of his young master, held in one hand a number of papers, and in the other a packet of letters, which he gave to Albert. Albert glanced carelessly at the different missives, selected two written in a small and delicate hand, and enclosed in scented envelopes, opened them and perused their contents with some attention.

"How did these letters come?" said he.

"One by the post, Madame Danglars' footman left the other."

"Let Madame Danglars know that I accept the place she offers me in her box. Wait; then, during the day, tell Rosa that when I leave the Opera I will sup with her as she wishes. Take her six bottles of different wine Cyprus, sherry, and Malaga, and a barrel of Ostend oysters; get them at Borel's, and be sure you say they are for me."

"At what o'clock, sir, do you breakfast?"

"What time is it now?"

"A quarter to ten."

"Very well, at half past ten. Debray will, perhaps, be obliged to go to the minister and besides" (Albert looked at his tablets), "it is the hour I told the count, 21st May, at half past ten; and though I do not much rely upon his promise, I wish to be punctual. Is the countess up yet?"

"If you wish, I will inquire."

"Yes, ask her for one of her *liqueur* cellarets, mine is incomplete; and tell her I shall have the honor of seeing her about three o'clock, and that I request permission to introduce someone to her."

The valet left the room. Albert threw himself on the divan, tore off the cover of two or three of the papers, looked at the theatre announcements, made a face seeing they gave an opera, and not a ballet; hunted vainly amongst the advertisements for a new tooth-powder of which he had heard, and threw down, one after the other, the three leading papers of Paris, muttering,

"These papers become more and more stupid every day."

A moment after, a carriage stopped before the door, and the servant announced M. Lucien Debray. A tall young man, with light hair, clear gray eyes, and thin and compressed lips, dressed in a blue coat with beautifully carved gold buttons, a white neckcloth, and a tortoiseshell eye-glass suspended by a silken thread, and which, by an effort of the superciliary and zygomatic muscles, he fixed in his eye, entered, with a half-official air, without smiling or speaking.

"Good-morning, Lucien, good-morning," said Albert; "your punctuality really alarms me. What do I say? punctuality! You, whom I expected last, you arrive at five minutes to ten, when the time fixed was half-past! Has the ministry resigned?"

"No, my dear fellow," returned the young man, seating himself on the divan; "reassure yourself; we are tottering always, but we never fall, and I begin to believe that we shall pass into a state of immobility, and then the affairs of the Peninsula will completely consolidate us."

"Ah, true; you drive Don Carlos out of Spain."

"No, no, my dear fellow, do not confound our plans. We take him to the other side of the French frontier, and offer him hospitality at Bourges."

"At Bourges?"

"Yes, he has not much to complain of; Bourges is the capital of Charles VII. Do you not know that all Paris knew it yesterday, and the day before it had already transpired on the Bourse, and M. Danglars (I do not know by what means that man contrives to obtain intelligence as soon as we do) made a million!"

"And you another order, for I see you have a blue ribbon at your button-hole."

"Yes; they sent me the order of Charles III.," returned Debray carelessly.

"Come, do not affect indifference, but confess you were pleased to have it."

"Oh, it is very well as a finish to the toilet. It looks very neat on a black coat buttoned up."

"And makes you resemble the Prince of Wales or the Duke of Reichstadt."

"It is for that reason you see me so early."

"Because you have the order of Charles III., and you wish to announce the good news to me?"

"No, because I passed the night writing letters, five-and-twenty despatches. I returned home at daybreak, and strove to sleep; but my head ached and I got up to have a ride for an hour. At the Bois de Boulogne, *ennui* and hunger attacked me at once, two enemies who rarely accompany each other, and who are yet leagued against me, a sort of Carlo-republican alliance. I then recollected you gave a breakfast this morning, and here I am. I am hungry, feed me; I am bored, amuse me."

"It is my duty as your host," returned Albert, ringing the bell, while Lucien turned over, with his gold-mounted cane, the papers that lay on the table. "Germain, a glass of sherry and a biscuit. In the meantime, my dear Lucien, here are cigars contraband, of course try them, and persuade the minister to sell us such instead of poisoning us with cabbage leaves."

"*Peste!* I will do nothing of the kind; the moment they come from government you would find them execrable. Besides, that does not concern the home but the financial department. Address yourself to M. Humann, section of the indirect contributions, corridor A., No. 26."

"On my word," said Albert, "you astonish me by the extent of your knowledge. Take a cigar."

"Really, my dear Albert," replied Lucien, lighting a manilla at a rose-colored taper that burnt in a beautifully enamelled stand "how happy you are to have nothing to do. You do not know your own good fortune!"

"And what would you do, my dear diplomatist," replied Morcerf, with a slight degree of irony in his voice, "if you did nothing? What? private secretary to a minister, plunged at once into European cabals and Parisian intrigues; having kings, and, better still, queens, to protect, parties to unite, elections to direct; making more use of your cabinet with your pen and your telegraph than Napoleon did of his battle-fields with his sword and his victories; possessing five-and-twenty thousand francs a year, besides your place; a horse, for which Château-Renaud offered you four hundred louis, and which you would not part with; a tailor who never disappoints you; with the opera, the jockey-club, and other diversions, can you not amuse yourself? Well, I will amuse you."

"How?"

"By introducing to you a new acquaintance."

"A man or a woman?"

"A man."

"I know so many men already."

"But you do not know this man."

"Where does he come from the end of the world?"

"Farther still, perhaps."

"The deuce! I hope he does not bring our breakfast with him."

"Oh, no; our breakfast comes from my father's kitchen. Are you hungry?"

"Humiliating as such a confession is, I am. But I dined at M. de Villefort's, and lawyers always give you very bad dinners. You would think they felt some remorse; did you ever remark that?"

"Ah, depreciate other persons' dinners; you ministers give such splendid ones."

"Yes; but we do not invite people of fashion. If we were not forced to entertain a parcel of country boobies because they think and vote with us, we should never dream of dining at home, I assure you."

"Well, take another glass of sherry and another biscuit."

"Willingly. Your Spanish wine is excellent. You see we were quite right to pacify that country."

"Yes; but Don Carlos?"

"Well, Don Carlos will drink Bordeaux, and in ten years we will marry his son to the little queen."

"You will then obtain the Golden Fleece, if you are still in the ministry."

"I think, Albert, you have adopted the system of feeding me on smoke this morning."

"Well, you must allow it is the best thing for the stomach; but I hear Beauchamp in the next room; you can dispute together, and that will pass away the time."

"About what?"

"About the papers."

"My dear friend," said Lucien with an air of sovereign contempt, "do I ever read the papers?"

"Then you will dispute the more."

"M. Beauchamp," announced the servant. "Come in, come in," said Albert, rising and advancing to meet the young man. "Here is Debray, who detests you without reading you, so he says."

"He is quite right," returned Beauchamp; "for I criticise him without knowing what he does. Good-day, commander!"

"Ah, you know that already," said the private secretary, smiling and shaking hands with him.

"*Pardieu!*"

"And what do they say of it in the world?"

"In which world? we have so many worlds in the year of grace 1838."

"In the entire political world, of which you are one of the leaders."

"They say that it is quite fair, and that sowing so much red, you ought to reap a little blue."

"Come, come, that is not bad!" said Lucien. "Why do you not join our party, my dear Beauchamp? With your talents you would make your fortune in three or four years."

"I only await one thing before following your advice; that is, a minister who will hold office for six months. My dear Albert, one word, for I must give poor Lucien a respite. Do we breakfast or dine? I must go to the Chamber, for our life is not an idle one."

"You only breakfast; I await two persons, and the instant they arrive we shall sit down to table."

Chapter 13

The Breakfast

nd what sort of persons do you expect to breakfast?" said Beauchamp.

"A gentleman, and a diplomatist."

"Then we shall have to wait two hours for the gentleman, and three for the diplomatist. I shall come back to dessert; keep me some strawberries, coffee, and cigars. I shall take a cutlet on my way to the Chamber."

"Do not do anything of the sort; for were the gentleman a Montmorency, and the diplomatist a Metternich, we will breakfast at eleven; in the meantime, follow Debray's example, and take a glass of sherry and a biscuit."

"Be it so; I will stay; I must do something to distract my thoughts."

"You are like Debray, and yet it seems to me that when the minister is out of spirits, the opposition ought to be joyous."

"Ah, you do not know with what I am threatened. I shall hear this morning that M. Danglars make a speech at the Chamber of Deputies, and at his wife's this evening I shall hear the tragedy of a peer of France. The devil take the constitutional government, and since we had our choice, as they say, at least, how could we choose that?"

"I understand; you must lay in a stock of hilarity."

"Do not run down M. Danglars' speeches," said Debray; "he votes for you, for he belongs to the opposition."

"*Pardieu*, that is exactly the worst of all. I am waiting until you send him to speak at the Luxembourg, to laugh at my ease."

"My dear friend," said Albert to Beauchamp, "it is plain that the affairs of Spain are settled, for you are most desperately out of humor this morning. Recollect that Parisian gossip has spoken of a marriage between myself and Mlle. Eugénie Danglars; I cannot in conscience, therefore, let you run down the speeches of a man who will one day say to me, 'Vicomte, you know I give my daughter two millions.'"

"Ah, this marriage will never take place," said Beauchamp. "The king has made him a baron, and can make him a peer, but he cannot make him a gentleman, and the Count of Morcerf is too aristocratic to consent, for the paltry sum of two million francs, to a *mésalliance*. The Viscount of Morcerf can only wed a marchioness."

"But two million francs make a nice little sum," replied Morcerf.

"It is the social capital of a theatre on the boulevard, or a railroad from the Jardin des Plantes to La Râpée."

"Never mind what he says, Morcerf," said Debray, "do you marry her. You marry a money-bag label, it is true; well, but what does that matter? It is better to have a blazon less and a figure more on it. You have seven martlets on your arms; give three to your wife, and you will still have four; that is one more than M. de Guise had, who so nearly became King of France, and whose cousin was Emperor of Germany."

"On my word, I think you are right, Lucien," said Albert absently.

"To be sure; besides, every millionaire is as noble as a bastard that is, he can be."

"Do not say that, Debray," returned Beauchamp, laughing, "for here is Château-Renaud, who, to cure you of your mania for paradoxes, will pass the sword of Renaud de Montauban, his ancestor, through your body."

"He will sully it then," returned Lucien; "for I am low very low."

"Oh, heavens," cried Beauchamp, "the minister quotes Béranger, what shall we come to next?"

"M. de Château-Renaud M. Maximilian Morrel," said the servant, announcing two fresh guests.

"Now, then, to breakfast," said Beauchamp; "for, if I remember, you told me you only expected two persons, Albert."

"Morrel," muttered Albert "Morrel who is he?"

But before he had finished, M. de Château-Renaud, a handsome young man of thirty, gentleman all over, that is, with the figure of a Guiche and the wit of a Mortemart, took Albert's hand.

"My dear Albert," said he, "let me introduce to you M. Maximilian Morrel, captain of Spahis, my friend; and what is more however the man speaks for himself my preserver. Salute my hero, viscount."

And he stepped on one side to give place to a young man of refined and dignified bearing, with large and open brow, piercing eyes, and black moustache, whom our readers have already seen at Marseilles, under circumstances sufficiently dramatic not to be forgotten. A rich uniform, half French, half Oriental, set off his graceful and stalwart figure, and his broad chest was decorated with the order of the Legion of Honor. The young officer bowed with easy and elegant politeness.

"Monsieur," said Albert with affectionate courtesy, "the count of Château-Renaud knew how much pleasure this introduction would give me; you are his friend, be ours also."

"Well said," interrupted Château-Renaud; "and pray that, if you should ever be in a similar predicament, he may do as much for you as he did for me."

"What has he done?" asked Albert.

"Oh, nothing worth speaking of," said Morrel; "M. de Château-Renaud exaggerates."

"Not worth speaking of?" cried Château-Renaud; "life is not worth speaking of! that is rather too philosophical, on my word, Morrel. It is very well for you, who risk your life every day, but for me, who only did so once "

"We gather from all this, baron, that Captain Morrel saved your life."

"Exactly so."

"On what occasion?" asked Beauchamp.

"Beauchamp, my good fellow, you know I am starving," said Debray: "do not set him off on some long story."

"Well, I do not prevent your sitting down to table," replied Beauchamp, "Château-Renaud can tell us while we eat our breakfast."

"Gentlemen," said Morcerf, "it is only a quarter past ten, and I expect someone else."

"Ah, true, a diplomatist!" observed Debray.

"Diplomat or not, I don't know; I only know that he charged himself on my account with a mission, which he terminated so entirely to my satisfaction, that had I been king, I should have instantly created him knight of all my orders, even had I been able to offer him the Golden Fleece and the Garter."

"Well, since we are not to sit down to table," said Debray, "take a glass of sherry, and tell us all about it."

"You all know that I had the fancy of going to Africa."

"It is a road your ancestors have traced for you," said Albert gallantly.

"Yes? but I doubt that your object was like theirs to rescue the Holy Sepulchre."

"You are quite right, Beauchamp," observed the young aristocrat. "It was only to fight as an amateur. I cannot bear duelling ever since two seconds, whom I had chosen to arrange an affair, forced me to break the arm of one of my best friends, one whom you all know poor Franz d'Épinay."

"Ah, true," said Debray, "you did fight some time ago; about what?"

"The devil take me, if I remember," returned Château-Renaud. "But I recollect perfectly one thing, that, being unwilling to let such talents as mine sleep, I wished to try upon the Arabs the new pistols that had been given to me. In consequence I embarked for Oran, and went from thence to Constantine, where I arrived just in time to witness the raising of the siege. I retreated with the rest, for eight-and-forty hours. I endured the rain during the day, and the cold during the night tolerably well, but the third morning my horse died of cold. Poor brute accustomed to be covered up and to have a stove in the stable, the Arabian finds himself unable to bear ten degrees of cold in Arabia."

"That's why you want to purchase my English horse," said Debray, "you think he will bear the cold better."

"You are mistaken, for I have made a vow never to return to Africa."

"You were very much frightened, then?" asked Beauchamp.

"Well, yes, and I had good reason to be so," replied Château-Renaud. "I was retreating on foot, for my horse was dead. Six Arabs came up, full gallop, to cut off my head. I shot two with my double-barrelled gun, and two more with my pistols, but I was then disarmed, and two were still left; one seized me by the hair (that is why I now wear it so short, for no one knows what may happen), the other swung a yataghan, and I already felt the cold steel on my neck, when this gentleman whom you see here charged them, shot the one who held me by the hair, and cleft the skull of the other with his sabre. He had assigned himself the task of saving a man's life that day; chance caused that man to be myself. When I am rich I will order a statue of Chance from Klagmann or Marochetti."

"Yes," said Morrel, smiling, "it was the 5th of September, the anniversary of the day on which my father was miraculously preserved; therefore, as far as it lies in my power, I endeavor to celebrate it by some "

"Heroic action," interrupted Château-Renaud. "I was chosen. But that is not all after rescuing me from the sword, he rescued me from the cold, not by sharing his cloak with me, like St. Martin, but by giving me the whole; then from hunger by sharing with me guess what?"

"A Strasbourg pie?" asked Beauchamp.

"No, his horse; of which we each of us ate a slice with a hearty appetite. It was very hard."

"The horse?" said Morcerf, laughing.

"No, the sacrifice," returned Château-Renaud; "ask Debray if he would sacrifice his English steed for a stranger?"

"Not for a stranger," said Debray, "but for a friend I might, perhaps."

"I divined that you would become mine, count," replied Morrel; "besides, as I had the honor to tell you, heroism or not, sacrifice or not, that day I owed an offering to bad fortune in recompense for the favors good fortune had on other days granted to us."

"The history to which M. Morrel alludes," continued Château-Renaud, "is an admirable one, which he will tell you some day when you are better acquainted with him; today let us fill our stomachs, and not our memories. What time do you breakfast, Albert?"

"At half-past ten."

"Precisely?" asked Debray, taking out his watch.

"Oh, you will give me five minutes' grace," replied Morcerf, "for I also expect a preserver."

"Of whom?"

"Of myself," cried Morcerf; "*parbleu!* do you think I cannot be saved as well as anyone else, and that there are only Arabs who cut off heads? Our breakfast is a philanthropic one, and we shall have at table at least, I hope so two benefactors of humanity."

"What shall we do?" said Debray; "we have only one Monthyon prize."

"Well, it will be given to someone who has done nothing to deserve it," said Beauchamp; "that is the way the Academy mostly escapes from the dilemma."

"And where does he come from?" asked Debray. "You have already answered the question once, but so vaguely that I venture to put it a second time."

"Really," said Albert, "I do not know; when I invited him three months ago, he was then at Rome, but since that time who knows where he may have gone?"

"And you think him capable of being exact?" demanded Debray.

"I think him capable of everything."

"Well, with the five minutes' grace, we have only ten left."

"I will profit by them to tell you something about my guest."

"I beg pardon," interrupted Beauchamp; "are there any materials for an article in what you are going to tell us?"

"Yes, and for a most curious one."

"Go on, then, for I see I shall not get to the Chamber this morning, and I must make up for it."

"I was at Rome during the last Carnival."

"We know that," said Beauchamp.

"Yes, but what you do not know is that I was carried off by bandits."

"There are no bandits," cried Debray.

"Yes there are, and most hideous, or rather most admirable ones, for I found them ugly enough to frighten me."

"Come, my dear Albert," said Debray, "confess that your cook is behindhand, that the oysters have not arrived from Ostend or Marennes, and that, like Madame de Maintenon, you are going to replace the dish by a story. Say so at once; we are sufficiently well-bred to excuse you, and to listen to your history, fabulous as it promises to be."

"And I say to you, fabulous as it may seem, I tell it as a true one from beginning to end. The brigands had carried me off, and conducted me to a gloomy spot, called the Catacombs of Saint Sebastian."

"I know it," said Château-Renaud; "I narrowly escaped catching a fever there."

"And I did more than that," replied Morcerf, "for I caught one. I was informed that I was prisoner until I paid the sum of 4,000 Roman crowns about 24,000 francs. Unfortunately, I had not above 1,500. I was at the end of my journey and of my credit. I wrote to Franz and were he here he would confirm every word I wrote then to Franz that if he did not come with the four thousand crowns before six, at ten minutes past I should have gone to join the blessed saints and glorious martyrs in whose company I had the honor of being; and Signor Luigi Vampa, such was the name of the chief of these bandits, would have scrupulously kept his word."

"But Franz did come with the four thousand crowns," said Château-Renaud. "A man whose name is Franz d'Épinay or Albert de Morcerf has not much difficulty in procuring them."

"No, he arrived accompanied simply by the guest I am going to present to you."

"Ah, this gentleman is a Hercules killing Cacus, a Perseus freeing Andromeda."

"No, he is a man about my own size."

"Armed to the teeth?"

"He had not even a knitting-needle."

"But he paid your ransom?"

"He said two words to the chief and I was free."

"And they apologized to him for having carried you off?" said Beauchamp.

"Just so."

"Why, he is a second Ariosto."

"No, his name is the Count of Monte Cristo."

"There is no Count of Monte Cristo" said Debray.

"I do not think so," added Château-Renaud, with the air of a man who knows the whole of the European nobility perfectly. "Does anyone know anything of a Count of Monte Cristo?"

"He comes possibly from the Holy Land, and one of his ancestors possessed Calvary, as the Mortemarts did the Dead Sea."

"I think I can assist your researches," said Maximilian. "Monte Cristo is a little island I have often heard spoken of by the old sailors my father employed a grain of sand in the centre of the Mediterranean, an atom in the infinite."

"Precisely!" cried Albert. "Well, he of whom I speak is the lord and master of this grain of sand, of this atom; he has purchased the title of count somewhere in Tuscany."

"He is rich, then?"

"I believe so."

"But that ought to be visible."

"That is what deceives you, Debray."

"I do not understand you."

"Have you read the *Arabian Nights*?"

"What a question!"

"Well, do you know if the persons you see there are rich or poor, if their sacks of wheat are not rubies or diamonds? They seem like poor fishermen, and suddenly they open some mysterious cavern filled with the wealth of the Indies."

"Which means?"

"Which means that my Count of Monte Cristo is one of those fishermen. He has even a name taken from the book, since he calls himself Sinbad the Sailor, and has a cave filled with gold."

"And you have seen this cavern, Morcerf?" asked Beauchamp.

"No, but Franz has; for heaven's sake, not a word of this before him. Franz went in with his eyes blindfolded, and was waited on by mutes and by women to whom Cleopatra was a painted strumpet. Only he is not quite sure about the women, for they did not come in until after he had taken hashish, so that what he took for women might have been simply a row of statues."

The two young men looked at Morcerf as if to say, "Are you mad, or are you laughing at us?"

"And I also," said Morrel thoughtfully, "have heard something like this from an old sailor named Penelon."

"Ah," cried Albert, "it is very lucky that M. Morrel comes to aid me; you are vexed, are you not, that he thus gives a clew to the labyrinth?"

"My dear Albert," said Debray, "what you tell us is so extraordinary."

"Ah, because your ambassadors and your consuls do not tell you of them they have no time. They are too much taken up with interfering in the affairs of their countrymen who travel."

"Now you get angry, and attack our poor agents. How will you have them protect you? The Chamber cuts down their salaries every day, so that now they have scarcely any. Will you be ambassador, Albert? I will send you to Constantinople."

"No, lest on the first demonstration I make in favor of Mehemet Ali, the Sultan send me the bowstring, and make my secretaries strangle me."

"You say very true," responded Debray.

"Yes," said Albert, "but this has nothing to do with the existence of the Count of Monte Cristo."

"*Pardieu!* everyone exists."

"Doubtless, but not in the same way; everyone has not black slaves, a princely retinue, an arsenal of weapons that would do credit to an Arabian fortress, horses that cost six thousand francs apiece, and Greek mistresses."

"Have you seen the Greek mistress?"

"I have both seen and heard her. I saw her at the theatre, and heard her one morning when I breakfasted with the count."

"He eats, then?"

"Yes; but so little, it can hardly be called eating."

"He must be a vampire."

"Laugh, if you will; the Countess G , who knew Lord Ruthven, declared that the count was a vampire."

"Ah, capital," said Beauchamp. "For a man not connected with newspapers, here is the pendant to the famous sea-serpent of the *Constitutionnel.*"

"Wild eyes, the iris of which contracts or dilates at pleasure," said Debray; "facial angle strongly developed, magnificent forehead, livid complexion, black beard, sharp and white teeth, politeness unexceptionable."

"Just so, Lucien," returned Morcerf; "you have described him feature for feature. Yes, keen and cutting politeness. This man has often made me shudder; and one day when we were viewing an execution, I thought I should faint, more from hearing the cold and calm manner in which he spoke of every description of torture, than from the sight of the executioner and the culprit."

"Did he not conduct you to the ruins of the Colosseum and suck your blood?" asked Beauchamp.

"Or, having delivered you, make you sign a flaming parchment, surrendering your soul to him as Esau did his birthright?"

"Rail on, rail on at your ease, gentlemen," said Morcerf, somewhat piqued. "When I look at you Parisians, idlers on the Boulevard de Gand or the Bois de Boulogne, and think of this man, it seems to me we are not of the same race."

"I am highly flattered," returned Beauchamp.

"At the same time," added Château-Renaud, "your Count of Monte Cristo is a very fine fellow, always excepting his little arrangements with the Italian banditti."

"There are no Italian banditti," said Debray.

"No vampire," cried Beauchamp.

"No Count of Monte Cristo" added Debray. "There is half-past ten striking, Albert."

"Confess you have dreamed this, and let us sit down to breakfast," continued Beauchamp.

But the sound of the clock had not died away when Germain announced, "His excellency the Count of Monte Cristo." The involuntary start everyone gave proved how much Morcerf's narrative had impressed them, and Albert himself could not wholly refrain from manifesting sudden emotion. He had not heard a carriage stop in the street, or steps in the antechamber; the door had itself opened noiselessly. The count appeared, dressed with the greatest simplicity, but the most fastidious dandy could have found nothing to cavil at in his toilet. Every article of dress hat, coat, gloves, and boots was from the first makers. He seemed scarcely five-and-thirty. But what struck everybody was his extreme resemblance to the portrait Debray had drawn. The count advanced, smiling, into the centre of the room, and approached Albert, who hastened towards him holding out his hand in a ceremonial manner.

"Punctuality," said Monte Cristo, "is the politeness of kings, according to one of your sovereigns, I think; but it is not the same with travellers. However, I hope you will excuse the two or three seconds I am behindhand; five hundred leagues are not to be accomplished without some trouble, and especially in France, where, it seems, it is forbidden to beat the postilions."

"My dear count," replied Albert, "I was announcing your visit to some of my friends, whom I had invited in consequence of the promise you did me the honor to make, and whom I now present to you. They are the Count of Château-Renaud, whose nobility goes back to the twelve peers, and whose ancestors had a place at the Round Table; M. Lucien Debray, private secretary to the minister of the interior; M. Beauchamp, an editor of a paper, and the terror of the French government, but of whom, in spite of his national celebrity, you perhaps have not heard in Italy, since his paper is prohibited there; and M. Maximilian Morrel, captain of Spahis."

At this name the count, who had hitherto saluted everyone with courtesy, but at the same time with coldness and formality, stepped a pace forward, and a slight tinge of red colored his pale cheeks.

"You wear the uniform of the new French conquerors, monsieur," said he; "it is a handsome uniform."

No one could have said what caused the count's voice to vibrate so deeply, and what made his eye flash, which was in general so clear, lustrous, and limpid when he pleased.

"You have never seen our Africans, count?" said Albert.

"Never," replied the count, who was by this time perfectly master of himself again.

"Well, beneath this uniform beats one of the bravest and noblest hearts in the whole army."

"Oh, M. de Morcerf," interrupted Morrel.

"Let me go on, captain. And we have just heard," continued Albert, "of a new deed of his, and so heroic a one, that, although I have seen him today for the first time, I request you to allow me to introduce him as my friend."

At these words it was still possible to observe in Monte Cristo the concentrated look, changing color, and slight trembling of the eyelid that show emotion.

"Ah, you have a noble heart," said the count; "so much the better."

This exclamation, which corresponded to the count's own thought rather than to what Albert was saying, surprised everybody, and especially Morrel, who looked at Monte Cristo with wonder. But, at the same time, the intonation was so soft that, however strange the speech might seem, it was impossible to be offended at it.

"Why should he doubt it?" said Beauchamp to Château-Renaud.

"In reality," replied the latter, who, with his aristocratic glance and his knowledge of the world, had penetrated at once all that was penetrable in Monte Cristo, "Albert has not deceived us, for the count is a most singular being. What say you, Morrel!"

"*Ma foi*, he has an open look about him that pleases me, in spite of the singular remark he has made about me."

"Gentlemen," said Albert, "Germain informs me that breakfast is ready. My dear count, allow me to show you the way." They passed silently into the breakfast-room, and everyone took his place.

"Gentlemen," said the count, seating himself, "permit me to make a confession which must form my excuse for any improprieties I may commit. I am a stranger, and a stranger to such a degree, that this is the first time I have ever been at Paris. The French way of living is utterly unknown to me, and up to the present time I have followed the Eastern customs, which are entirely in contrast to the Parisian. I beg you, therefore, to excuse if you find anything in me too Turkish, too Italian, or too Arabian. Now, then, let us breakfast."

"With what an air he says all this," muttered Beauchamp; "decidedly he is a great man."

"A great man in his own country," added Debray.

"A great man in every country, M. Debray," said Château-Renaud.

The count was, it may be remembered, a most temperate guest. Albert remarked this, expressing his fears lest, at the outset, the Parisian mode of life should displease the traveller in the most essential point.

"My dear count," said he, "I fear one thing, and that is, that the fare of the Rue du Helder is not so much to your taste as that of the Piazza di Spagna. I ought to have consulted you on the point, and have had some dishes prepared expressly."

"Did you know me better," returned the count, smiling, "you would not give one thought of such a thing for a traveller like myself, who has successively lived on macaroni at Naples, polenta at Milan, olla podrida at Valencia, pilau at Constantinople, curry in India, and swallows' nests in China. I eat everywhere, and of everything, only I eat but little; and today, that you reproach me with my want of appetite, is my day of appetite, for I have not eaten since yesterday morning."

"What," cried all the guests, "you have not eaten for four-and-twenty hours?"

"No," replied the count; "I was forced to go out of my road to obtain some information near Nîmes, so that I was somewhat late, and therefore I did not choose to stop."

"And you ate in your carriage?" asked Morcerf.

"No, I slept, as I generally do when I am weary without having the courage to amuse myself, or when I am hungry without feeling inclined to eat."

"But you can sleep when you please, monsieur?" said Morrel.

"Yes."

"You have a recipe for it?"

"An infallible one."

"That would be invaluable to us in Africa, who have not always any food to eat, and rarely anything to drink."

"Yes," said Monte Cristo; "but, unfortunately, a recipe excellent for a man like myself would be very dangerous applied to an army, which might not awake when it was needed."

"May we inquire what is this recipe?" asked Debray.

"Oh, yes," returned Monte Cristo; "I make no secret of it. It is a mixture of excellent opium, which I fetched myself from Canton in order to have it pure, and the best hashish which grows in the East that is, between the Tigris and the Euphrates. These two ingredients are mixed in equal proportions, and formed into pills. Ten minutes after one is taken, the effect is produced. Ask Baron Franz d'Épinay; I think he tasted them one day."

"Yes," replied Morcerf, "he said something about it to me."

"But," said Beauchamp, who, as became a journalist, was very incredulous, "you always carry this drug about you?"

"Always."

"Would it be an indiscretion to ask to see those precious pills?" continued Beauchamp, hoping to take him at a disadvantage.

"No, monsieur," returned the count; and he drew from his pocket a marvellous casket, formed out of a single emerald and closed by a golden lid which unscrewed and gave passage to a small greenish colored pellet about the size of a pea. This ball had an acrid and penetrating odor. There were four or five more in the emerald, which would contain about a dozen. The casket passed around the table, but it was more to examine the admirable emerald than to see the pills that it passed from hand to hand.

"And is it your cook who prepares these pills?" asked Beauchamp.

"Oh, no, monsieur," replied Monte Cristo; "I do not thus betray my enjoyments to the vulgar. I am a tolerable chemist, and prepare my pills myself."

"This is a magnificent emerald, and the largest I have ever seen," said Château-Renaud, "although my mother has some remarkable family jewels."

"I had three similar ones," returned Monte Cristo. "I gave one to the Sultan, who mounted it in his sabre; another to our holy father the Pope, who had it set in his tiara, opposite to one nearly as large, though not so fine, given by the Emperor Napoleon to his predecessor, Pius VII. I kept the third for myself, and I had it hollowed out, which reduced its value, but rendered it more commodious for the purpose I intended."

Everyone looked at Monte Cristo with astonishment; he spoke with so much simplicity that it was evident he spoke the truth, or that he was mad. However, the sight of the emerald made them naturally incline to the former belief.

"And what did these two sovereigns give you in exchange for these magnificent presents?" asked Debray.

"The Sultan, the liberty of a woman," replied the Count; "the Pope, the life of a man; so that once in my life I have been as powerful as if heaven had brought me into the world on the steps of a throne."

"And it was Peppino you saved, was it not?" cried Morcerf; "it was for him that you obtained pardon?"

"Perhaps," returned the count, smiling.

"My dear count, you have no idea what pleasure it gives me to hear you speak thus," said Morcerf. "I had announced you beforehand to my friends as an enchanter of the *Arabian Nights*, a wizard of the Middle Ages; but the Parisians are so subtle in paradoxes that they mistake for caprices of the imagination the most incontestable truths, when these truths do not form a part of their daily existence. For example, here is Debray who reads, and Beauchamp who prints, every day, 'A member of the Jockey Club has been stopped and robbed on the Boulevard;' 'four persons have been assassinated in the Rue St. Denis' or 'the Faubourg St. Germain;' 'ten, fifteen, or twenty thieves, have been arrested in a *café* on the Boulevard du Temple, or in the Thermes de Julien,' and yet these same men deny the existence of the bandits in the Maremma, the Campagna di Romana, or the Pontine Marshes. Tell them yourself that I was taken by bandits, and that without your generous intercession I should now have been sleeping in the Catacombs of St. Sebastian, instead of receiving them in my humble abode in the Rue du Helder."

"Ah," said Monte Cristo "you promised me never to mention that circumstance."

"It was not I who made that promise," cried Morcerf; "it must have been someone else whom you have rescued in the same manner, and whom you have forgotten. Pray speak of it, for I shall not only, I trust, relate the little I do know, but also a great deal I do not know."

"It seems to me," returned the count, smiling, "that you played a sufficiently important part to know as well as myself what happened."

"Well, you promise me, if I tell all I know, to relate, in your turn, all that I do not know?"

"That is but fair," replied Monte Cristo.

"Well," said Morcerf, "for three days I believed myself the object of the attentions of a masque, whom I took for a descendant of Tullia or Poppæa, while I was simply the object of the attentions of a *contadina*, and I say *contadina* to avoid saying peasant girl. What I know is, that, like a fool, a greater fool than he of whom I spoke just now, I mistook for this peasant girl a young bandit of fifteen or sixteen, with a beardless chin and slim waist, and who, just as I was about to imprint a chaste salute on his lips, placed a pistol to my head, and, aided by seven or eight others, led, or rather dragged me, to the Catacombs of St. Sebastian, where I found a highly educated brigand chief perusing Cæsar's *Commentaries*, and who deigned to leave off reading to inform me, that unless the next morning, before six o'clock, four thousand piastres were paid into his account at his banker's, at a quarter past six I should have ceased to exist. The letter is still to be seen, for it is in Franz d'Épinay's possession, signed by me, and with a postscript of

M. Luigi Vampa. This is all I know, but I know not, count, how you contrived to inspire so much respect in the bandits of Rome who ordinarily have so little respect for anything. I assure you, Franz and I were lost in admiration."

"Nothing more simple," returned the count. "I had known the famous Vampa for more than ten years. When he was quite a child, and only a shepherd, I gave him a few gold pieces for showing me my way, and he, in order to repay me, gave me a poniard, the hilt of which he had carved with his own hand, and which you may have seen in my collection of arms. In after years, whether he had forgotten this interchange of presents, which ought to have cemented our friendship, or whether he did not recollect me, he sought to take me, but, on the contrary, it was I who captured him and a dozen of his band. I might have handed him over to Roman justice, which is somewhat expeditious, and which would have been particularly so with him; but I did nothing of the sort I suffered him and his band to depart."

"With the condition that they should sin no more," said Beauchamp, laughing. "I see they kept their promise."

"No, monsieur," returned Monte Cristo "upon the simple condition that they should respect myself and my friends. Perhaps what I am about to say may seem strange to you, who are socialists, and vaunt humanity and your duty to your neighbor, but I never seek to protect a society which does not protect me, and which I will even say, generally occupies itself about me only to injure me; and thus by giving them a low place in my esteem, and preserving a neutrality towards them, it is society and my neighbor who are indebted to me."

"Bravo," cried Château-Renaud; "you are the first man I ever met sufficiently courageous to preach egotism. Bravo, count, bravo!"

"It is frank, at least," said Morrel. "But I am sure that the count does not regret having once deviated from the principles he has so boldly avowed."

"How have I deviated from those principles, monsieur?" asked

Monte Cristo, who could not help looking at Morrel with so much intensity, that two or three times the young man had been unable to sustain that clear and piercing glance.

"Why, it seems to me," replied Morrel, "that in delivering M. de Morcerf, whom you did not know, you did good to your neighbor and to society."

"Of which he is the brightest ornament," said Beauchamp, drinking off a glass of champagne.

"My dear count," cried Morcerf, "you are at fault you, one of the most formidable logicians I know and you must see it clearly proved that instead of being an egotist, you are a philanthropist. Ah, you call yourself Oriental, a Levantine, Maltese, Indian, Chinese; your family name is Monte Cristo; Sinbad the Sailor is your baptismal appellation, and yet the first day you set foot in Paris you instinctively display the greatest virtue, or rather the chief defect, of us eccentric Parisians, that is, you assume the vices you have not, and conceal the virtues you possess."

"My dear vicomte," returned Monte Cristo, "I do not see, in all I have done, anything that merits, either from you or these gentlemen, the pretended eulogies I have received. You were no stranger to me, for I knew you from the time I gave up two rooms to you, invited you to breakfast with me, lent you one of my carriages, witnessed the Carnival in your company, and saw with you from a window in the Piazza del Popolo the execution that affected you so much that you nearly fainted. I will appeal to any of these gentlemen, could I leave my guest in the hands of a hideous bandit, as you term him? Besides, you know, I had the idea that you could introduce me into some of the Paris salons when I came to France. You might some time ago have looked upon this resolution as a vague project, but today you see it was a reality, and you must submit to it under penalty of breaking your word."

"I will keep it," returned Morcerf; "but I fear that you will be much disappointed, accustomed as you are to picturesque events and fantastic horizons. Amongst us you will not meet with any of those episodes with which your adventurous existence has so familiarized you; our Chimborazo is Mortmartre, our Himalaya is Mount Valérien, our Great Desert is the plain of Grenelle, where they are now boring an artesian well to water the caravans. We have plenty of thieves, though not so many as is said; but these thieves stand in far more dread of a policeman than a lord. France is so prosaic, and Paris so civilized a city, that you will not find in its eighty-five departments I say eighty-five, because I do not include Corsica you will not find, then, in these eighty-five departments a single hill on which there is not a telegraph, or a grotto in which the commissary of police has not put up a gaslamp. There is but one service I can render you, and for that I place myself entirely at your orders, that is, to present, or make my friends present, you everywhere; besides, you have no need of anyone to introduce you with your name, and your fortune, and your talent" (Monte Cristo bowed with a somewhat ironical smile) "you can present yourself everywhere, and be well received. I can be useful in one way only if knowledge of Parisian habits, of the means of rendering yourself comfortable, or of the bazaars, can assist, you may depend upon me to find you a fitting dwelling here. I do not dare offer to share my apartments with you, as I shared yours at Rome I, who do not profess egotism, but am yet egotist *par excellence*; for, except myself, these rooms would not hold a shadow more, unless that shadow were feminine."

"Ah," said the count, "that is a most conjugal reservation; I recollect that at Rome you said something of a projected marriage. May I congratulate you?"

"The affair is still in projection."

"And he who says in 'projection,' means already decided," said Debray.

"No," replied Morcerf, "my father is most anxious about it; and I hope, ere long, to introduce you, if not to my wife, at least to my betrothed Mademoiselle Eugénie Danglars."

"Eugénie Danglars," said Monte Cristo; "tell me, is not her

father Baron Danglars?"

"Yes," returned Morcerf, "a baron of a new creation."

"What matter," said Monte Cristo "if he has rendered the State services which merit this distinction?"

"Enormous ones," answered Beauchamp. "Although in reality a Liberal, he negotiated a loan of six millions for Charles X., in 1829, who made him a baron and chevalier of the Legion of Honor; so that he wears the ribbon, not, as you would think, in his waistcoat-pocket, but at his button-hole."

"Ah," interrupted Morcerf, laughing, "Beauchamp, Beauchamp, keep that for the *Corsaire* or the *Charivari*, but spare my future father-in-law before me." Then, turning to Monte Cristo, "You just now spoke his name as if you knew the baron?"

"I do not know him," returned Monte Cristo; "but I shall probably soon make his acquaintance, for I have a credit opened with him by the house of Richard & Blount, of London, Arstein & Eskeles of Vienna, and Thomson & French at Rome." As he pronounced the two last names, the count glanced at Maximilian Morrel. If the stranger expected to produce an effect on Morrel, he was not mistaken Maximilian started as if he had been electrified.

"Thomson & French," said he; "do you know this house, monsieur?"

"They are my bankers in the capital of the Christian world," returned the count quietly. "Can my influence with them be of any service to you?"

"Oh, count, you could assist me perhaps in researches which have been, up to the present, fruitless. This house, in past years, did ours a great service, and has, I know not for what reason, always denied having rendered us this service."

"I shall be at your orders," said Monte Cristo bowing.

"But," continued Morcerf, "*à propos* of Danglars, we have strangely wandered from the subject. We were speaking of a suitable habitation for the Count of Monte Cristo. Come, gentlemen, let us all propose some place. Where shall we lodge this new guest in our great capital?"

"Faubourg Saint-Germain," said Château-Renaud. "The count will find there a charming hotel, with a court and garden."

"Bah! Château-Renaud," returned Debray, "you only know your dull and gloomy Faubourg Saint-Germain; do not pay any attention to him, count live in the Chaussée d'Antin, that's the real centre of Paris."

"Boulevard de l'Opéra," said Beauchamp; "the second floor a house with a balcony. The count will have his cushions of silver cloth brought there, and as he smokes his chibouque, see all Paris pass before him."

"You have no idea, then, Morrel?" asked Château-Renaud; "you do not propose anything."

"Oh, yes," returned the young man, smiling; "on the contrary, I have one, but I expected the count would be tempted by one of the brilliant proposals made him, yet as he has not replied to any of them, I will venture to offer him a suite of apartments in a charming hotel, in the Pompadour style, that my sister has inhabited for a year, in the Rue Meslay."

"You have a sister?" asked the count.

"Yes, monsieur, a most excellent sister."

"Married?"

"Nearly nine years."

"Happy?" asked the count again.

"As happy as it is permitted to a human creature to be," replied Maximilian. "She married the man she loved, who remained faithful to us in our fallen fortunes Emmanuel Herbaut." Monte Cristo smiled imperceptibly.

"I live there during my leave of absence," continued Maximilian; "and I shall be, together with my brother-in-law Emmanuel, at the disposition of the Count, whenever he thinks fit to honor us."

"One minute," cried Albert, without giving Monte Cristo the time to reply. "Take care, you are going to immure a traveller, Sinbad the Sailor, a man who comes to see Paris; you are going to make a patriarch of him."

"Oh, no," said Morrel; "my sister is five-and-twenty, my brother-in-law is thirty, they are gay, young, and happy. Besides, the count will be in his own house, and only see them when he thinks fit to do so."

"Thanks, monsieur," said Monte Cristo; "I shall content myself with being presented to your sister and her husband, if you will do me the honor to introduce me; but I cannot accept the offer of anyone of these gentlemen, since my habitation is already prepared."

"What," cried Morcerf; "you are, then, going to a hotel that will be very dull for you."

"Was I so badly lodged at Rome?" said Monte Cristo smiling.

"*Parbleu!* at Rome you spent fifty thousand piastres in furnishing your apartments, but I presume that you are not disposed to spend a similar sum every day."

"It is not that which deterred me," replied Monte Cristo; "but as I determined to have a house to myself, I sent on my valet de chambre, and he ought by this time to have bought the house and furnished it."

"But you have, then, a valet de chambre who knows Paris?" said Beauchamp.

"It is the first time he has ever been in Paris. He is black, and cannot speak," returned Monte Cristo.

"It is Ali!" cried Albert, in the midst of the general surprise.

"Yes, Ali himself, my Nubian mute, whom you saw, I think, at Rome."

"Certainly," said Morcerf; "I recollect him perfectly. But how could you charge a Nubian to purchase a house, and a mute to furnish it? he will do everything wrong."

"Undeceive yourself, monsieur," replied Monte Cristo; "I am quite sure, that, on the contrary, he will choose everything as I wish. He knows my tastes, my caprices, my wants. He has been here a week, with the instinct of a hound, hunting by himself. He will arrange everything for me. He knew, that I should arrive today at ten o'clock; he was waiting for me at nine at the Barrière de Fontainebleau. He gave me this paper; it contains the number of my new abode; read it yourself," and Monte Cristo passed a paper to Albert.

"Ah, that is really original," said Beauchamp.

"And very princely," added Château-Renaud.

"What, do you not know your house?" asked Debray.

"No," said Monte Cristo; "I told you I did not wish to be behind my time; I dressed myself in the carriage, and descended at the viscount's door." The young men looked at each other; they did not know if it was a comedy Monte Cristo was playing, but every word he uttered had such an air of simplicity, that it was impossible to suppose what he said was false besides, why should he tell a falsehood?

"We must content ourselves, then," said Beauchamp, "with rendering the count all the little services in our power. I, in my quality of journalist, open all the theatres to him."

"Thanks, monsieur," returned Monte Cristo, "my steward has orders to take a box at each theatre."

"Is your steward also a Nubian?" asked Debray.

"No, he is a countryman of yours, if a Corsican is a countryman of anyone's. But you know him, M. de Morcerf."

"Is it that excellent M. Bertuccio, who understands hiring windows so well?"

"Yes, you saw him the day I had the honor of receiving you; he has been a soldier, a smuggler in fact, everything. I would not be quite sure that he has not been mixed up with the police for some trifle a stab with a knife, for instance."

"And you have chosen this honest citizen for your steward," said Debray. "Of how much does he rob you every year?"

"On my word," replied the count, "not more than another. I am sure he answers my purpose, knows no impossibility, and so I keep him."

"Then," continued Château-Renaud, "since you have an establishment, a steward, and a hotel in the Champs-Élysées, you only want a mistress." Albert smiled. He thought of the fair Greek he had seen in the count's box at the Argentina and Valle theatres.

"I have something better than that," said Monte Cristo; "I have a slave. You procure your mistresses from the opera, the Vaudeville, or the Variétés; I purchased mine at Constantinople; it cost me more, but I have nothing to fear."

"But you forget," replied Debray, laughing, "that we are Franks by name and franks by nature, as King Charles said, and that the moment she puts her foot in France your slave becomes free."

"Who will tell her?"

"The first person who sees her."

"She only speaks Romaic."

"That is different."

"But at least we shall see her," said Beauchamp, "or do you keep eunuchs as well as mutes?"

"Oh, no," replied Monte Cristo; "I do not carry brutalism so far. Everyone who surrounds me is free to quit me, and when they leave me will no longer have any need of me or anyone else; it is for that reason, perhaps, that they do not quit me."

They had long since passed to dessert and cigars.

"My dear Albert," said Debray, rising, "it is half-past two. Your guest is charming, but you leave the best company to go into the worst sometimes. I must return to the minister's. I will tell him of the count, and we shall soon know who he is."

"Take care," returned Albert; "no one has been able to accomplish that."

"Oh, we have three millions for our police; it is true they are almost always spent beforehand, but, no matter, we shall still have fifty thousand francs to spend for this purpose."

"And when you know, will you tell me?"

"I promise you. *Au revoir*, Albert. Gentlemen, good morning."

As he left the room, Debray called out loudly, "My carriage."

"Bravo," said Beauchamp to Albert; "I shall not go to the Chamber, but I have something better to offer my readers than a speech of M. Danglars."

"For heaven's sake, Beauchamp," returned Morcerf, "do not deprive me of the merit of introducing him everywhere. Is he not peculiar?"

"He is more than that," replied Château-Renaud; "he is one of the most extraordinary men I ever saw in my life. Are you coming, Morrel?"

"Directly I have given my card to the count, who has promised to pay us a visit at Rue Meslay, No. 14."

"Be sure I shall not fail to do so," returned the count, bowing.

And Maximilian Morrel left the room with the Baron de Château-Renaud, leaving Monte Cristo alone with Morcerf.

Chapter 14

The Presentation

When Albert found himself alone with Monte Cristo, "My dear count," said he, "allow me to commence my services as cicerone by showing you a specimen of a bachelor's apartment. You, who are accustomed to the palaces of Italy, can amuse yourself by calculating in how many square feet a young man who is not the worst lodged in Paris can live. As we pass from one room to another, I will open the windows to let you breathe."

Monte Cristo had already seen the breakfast-room and the salon on the ground floor. Albert led him first to his *atelier*, which was, as we have said, his favorite apartment. Monte Cristo quickly appreciated all that Albert had collected here old cabinets, Japanese porcelain, Oriental stuffs, Venetian glass, arms from all parts of the world everything was familiar to him; and at the first glance he recognized their date, their country, and their origin.

Morcerf had expected he should be the guide; on the contrary, it was he who, under the count's guidance, followed a course of archæology, mineralogy, and natural history.

They descended to the first floor; Albert led his guest into the salon. The salon was filled with the works of modern artists; there were landscapes by Dupré, with their long reeds and tall trees, their lowing oxen and marvellous skies; Delacroix's Arabian cavaliers, with their long white burnouses, their shining belts, their damasked arms, their horses, who tore each other with their teeth while their riders contended fiercely with their maces; *aquarelles* of Boulanger, representing Notre Dame de Paris with that vigor that makes the artist the rival of the poet; there were paintings by Diaz, who makes his flowers more beautiful than flowers, his suns more brilliant than the sun; designs by Decamp, as vividly colored as those of Salvator Rosa, but more poetic; *pastels* by Giraud and Müller, representing children like angels and women with the features of a virgin; sketches torn from the album of Dauzats' "Travels in the East," that had been made in a few seconds on the saddle of a camel, or beneath the dome of a mosque in a word, all that modern art can give in exchange and as recompense for the art lost and gone with ages long since past.

Albert expected to have something new this time to show to the traveller, but, to his great surprise, the latter, without seeking for the signatures, many of which, indeed, were only initials, named instantly the author of every picture in such a manner that it was easy to see that each name was not only known to him, but that each style associated with it had been appreciated and studied by him. From the salon they passed into the bedchamber; it was a model of taste and simple elegance. A single portrait, signed by Léopold Robert, shone in its carved and gilded frame. This portrait attracted the Count of

Monte Cristo's attention, for he made three rapid steps in the chamber, and stopped suddenly before it.

It was the portrait of a young woman of five or six-and-twenty, with a dark complexion, and light and lustrous eyes, veiled beneath long lashes. She wore the picturesque costume of the Catalan fisherwomen, a red and black bodice, and golden pins in her hair. She was looking at the sea, and her form was outlined on the blue ocean and sky. The light was so faint in the room that Albert did not perceive the pallor that spread itself over the count's visage, or the nervous heaving of his chest and shoulders. Silence prevailed for an instant, during which Monte Cristo gazed intently on the picture.

"You have there a most charming mistress, viscount," said the count in a perfectly calm tone; "and this costume a ball costume, doubtless becomes her admirably."

"Ah, monsieur," returned Albert, "I would never forgive you this mistake if you had seen another picture beside this. You do not know my mother; she it is whom you see here. She had her portrait painted thus six or eight years ago. This costume is a fancy one, it appears, and the resemblance is so great that I think I still see my mother the same as she was in 1830. The countess had this portrait painted during the count's absence. She doubtless intended giving him an agreeable surprise; but, strange to say, this portrait seemed to displease my father, and the value of the picture, which is, as you see, one of the best works of Léopold Robert, could not overcome his dislike to it. It is true, between ourselves, that M. de Morcerf is one of the most assiduous peers at the Luxembourg, a general renowned for theory, but a most mediocre amateur of art. It is different with my mother, who paints exceedingly well, and who, unwilling to part with so valuable a picture, gave it to me to put here, where it would be less likely to displease M. de Morcerf, whose portrait, by Gros, I will also show you. Excuse my talking of family matters, but as I shall have the honor of introducing you to the count, I tell you this to prevent you making any allusions to this picture. The picture seems to have a malign influence, for my mother rarely comes here without looking at it, and still more rarely does she look at it without weeping. This disagreement is the only one that has ever taken place between the count and countess, who are still as much united, although married more than twenty years, as on the first day of their wedding."

Monte Cristo glanced rapidly at Albert, as if to seek a hidden meaning in his words, but it was evident the young man uttered them in the simplicity of his heart.

"Now," said Albert, "that you have seen all my treasures, allow me to offer them to you, unworthy as they are. Consider yourself as in your own house, and to put yourself still more at your ease, pray accompany me to the apartments of M. de Morcerf, he whom I wrote from Rome an account of the services you rendered me, and to whom I announced your promised visit, and I may say that both the count and countess anxiously desire to thank you in person. You are somewhat *blasé* I know, and family scenes have not much effect on Sinbad the Sailor, who has seen so many others. However, accept what I propose to you as an initiation into Parisian life a life of politeness, visiting, and introductions."

Monte Cristo bowed without making any answer; he accepted the offer without enthusiasm and without regret, as one of those conventions of society which every gentleman looks upon as a duty. Albert summoned his servant, and ordered him to acquaint M. and Madame de Morcerf of the arrival of the Count of Monte Cristo. Albert followed him with the count. When they arrived at the antechamber, above the door was visible a shield, which, by its rich ornaments and its harmony with the rest of the furniture, indicated the importance the owner attached to this blazon. Monte Cristo stopped and examined it attentively.

"Azure seven merlets, or, placed bender," said he. "These are, doubtless, your family arms? Except the knowledge of blazons, that enables me to decipher them, I am very ignorant of heraldry I, a count of a fresh creation, fabricated in Tuscany by the aid of a commandery of St. Stephen, and who would not have taken the trouble had I not been told that when you travel much it is necessary. Besides, you must have something on the panels of your carriage, to escape being searched by the custom-house officers. Excuse my putting such a question to you."

"It is not indiscreet," returned Morcerf, with the simplicity of conviction. "You have guessed rightly. These are our arms, that is, those of my father, but they are, as you see, joined to another shield, which has gules, a silver tower, which are my mother's. By her side I am Spanish, but the family of Morcerf is French, and, I have heard, one of the oldest of the south of France."

"Yes," replied Monte Cristo "these blazons prove that. Almost all the armed pilgrims that went to the Holy Land took for their arms either a cross, in honor of their mission, or birds of passage, in sign of the long voyage they were about to undertake, and which they hoped to accomplish on the wings of faith. One of your ancestors had joined the Crusades, and supposing it to be only that of St. Louis, that makes you mount to the thirteenth century, which is tolerably ancient."

"It is possible," said Morcerf; "my father has in his study a genealogical tree which will tell you all that, and on which I made commentaries that would have greatly edified d'Hozier and Jaucourt. At present I no longer think of it, and yet I must tell you that we are beginning to occupy ourselves greatly with these things under our popular government."

"Well, then, your government would do well to choose from the past something better than the things that I have noticed on your monuments, and which have no heraldic meaning whatever. As for you, viscount," continued Monte Cristo to Morcerf, "you are more fortunate than the government, for your arms are really beautiful, and speak to the imagination. Yes, you are at once from Provence and Spain; that explains, if the portrait you showed me be like, the dark hue I so much admired on the visage of the noble Catalan."

It would have required the penetration of Œdipus or the Sphinx to have divined the irony the count concealed beneath these words, apparently uttered with the greatest politeness. Morcerf thanked him with a smile, and pushed open the door above which were his arms, and which, as we have said, opened into the salon. In the most conspicuous part of the salon was another portrait. It was that of a man, from five to eight-and-thirty, in the uniform of a general officer, wearing the double epaulet of heavy bullion, that indicates superior rank, the ribbon of the Legion of Honor around his neck, which showed he was a commander, and on the right breast, the star of a grand officer of the order of the Saviour, and on the left that of the grand cross of Charles III., which proved that the person represented by the picture had served in the wars of Greece and Spain, or, what was just the same thing as regarded decorations, had fulfilled some diplomatic mission in the two countries.

Monte Cristo was engaged in examining this portrait with no less care than he had bestowed upon the other, when another door opened, and he found himself opposite to the Count of Morcerf in person.

He was a man of forty to forty-five years, but he seemed at least fifty, and his black moustache and eyebrows contrasted strangely with his almost white hair, which was cut short, in the military fashion. He was dressed in plain clothes, and wore at his button-hole the ribbons of the different orders to which he belonged.

He entered with a tolerably dignified step, and some little haste. Monte Cristo saw him advance towards him without making a single step. It seemed as if his feet were rooted to the ground, and his eyes on the Count of Morcerf.

"Father," said the young man, "I have the honor of presenting to you the Count of Monte Cristo, the generous friend whom I had the good fortune to meet in the critical situation of which I have told you."

"You are most welcome, monsieur," said the Count of Morcerf, saluting Monte Cristo with a smile, "and monsieur has rendered our house, in preserving its only heir, a service which insures him our eternal gratitude."

As he said these words, the count of Morcerf pointed to a chair, while he seated himself in another opposite the window.

Monte Cristo, in taking the seat Morcerf offered him, placed himself in such a manner as to remain concealed in the shadow of the large velvet curtains, and read on the careworn and livid features of the count a whole history of secret griefs written in each wrinkle time had planted there.

"The countess," said Morcerf, "was at her toilet when she was informed of the visit she was about to receive. She will, however, be in the salon in ten minutes."

"It is a great honor to me," returned Monte Cristo, "to be thus, on the first day of my arrival in Paris, brought in contact with a man whose merit equals his reputation, and to whom fortune has for once been equitable, but has she not still on the plains of Mitidja, or in the mountains of Atlas, a marshal's staff to offer you?"

"Oh," replied Morcerf, reddening slightly, "I have left the service, monsieur. Made a peer at the Restoration, I served through the first campaign under the orders of Marshal Bourmont. I could, therefore, expect a higher rank, and who knows what might have happened had the elder branch remained on the throne? But the Revolution of July was, it seems, sufficiently glorious to allow itself to be ungrateful, and it was so for all services that did not date from the imperial period. I tendered my resignation, for when you have gained your epaulets on the battle-field, you do not know how to manœuvre on the slippery grounds of the salons. I have hung up my sword, and cast myself into politics. I have devoted myself to industry; I study the useful arts. During the twenty years I served, I often wished to do so, but I had not the time."

"These are the ideas that render your nation superior to any other," returned Monte Cristo. "A gentleman of high birth, possessor of an ample fortune, you have consented to gain your promotion as an obscure soldier, step by step this is uncommon; then become general, peer of France, commander of the Legion of Honor, you consent to again commence a second apprenticeship, without any other hope or any other desire than that of one day becoming useful to your fellow-creatures; this, indeed, is praiseworthy, nay, more, it is sublime."

Albert looked on and listened with astonishment; he was not used to see Monte Cristo give vent to such bursts of enthusiasm.

"Alas," continued the stranger, doubtless to dispel the slight cloud that covered Morcerf's brow, "we do not act thus in Italy; we grow according to our race and our species, and we pursue the same lines, and often the same uselessness, all our lives."

"But, monsieur," said the Count of Morcerf, "for a man of your merit, Italy is not a country, and France opens her arms to receive you; respond to her call. France will not, perhaps, be always ungrateful. She treats her children ill, but she always welcomes strangers."

"Ah, father," said Albert with a smile, "it is evident you do not know the Count of Monte Cristo; he despises all honors, and contents himself with those written on his passport."

"That is the most just remark," replied the stranger, "I ever heard made concerning myself."

"You have been free to choose your career," observed the Count of Morcerf, with a sigh; "and you have chosen the path strewed with flowers."

"Precisely, monsieur," replied Monte Cristo with one of those smiles that a painter could never represent or a physiologist analyze.

"If I did not fear to fatigue you," said the general, evidently charmed with the count's manners, "I would have taken you to the Chamber; there is a debate very curious to those who are strangers to our modern senators."

"I shall be most grateful, monsieur, if you will, at some future time, renew your offer, but I have been flattered with the hope of being introduced to the countess, and I will therefore wait."

"Ah, here is my mother," cried the viscount.

Monte Cristo, turned round hastily, and saw Madame de Morcerf at the entrance of the salon, at the door opposite to that by which her husband had entered, pale and motionless; when Monte Cristo turned round, she let fall her arm, which for some unknown reason had been resting on the gilded doorpost. She had been there some moments, and had heard the last words of the visitor. The latter rose and bowed to the countess, who inclined herself without speaking.

"Ah! good heavens, madame," said the count, "are you ill, or is it the heat of the room that affects you?"

"Are you ill, mother?" cried the viscount, springing towards her.

She thanked them both with a smile.

"No," returned she, "but I feel some emotion on seeing, for the first time, the man without whose intervention we should have been in tears and desolation. Monsieur," continued the countess, advancing with the majesty of a queen, "I owe to you the life of my son, and for this I bless you. Now, I thank you for the pleasure you give me in thus affording me the opportunity of thanking you as I have blessed you, from the bottom of my heart."

The count bowed again, but lower than before; he was even paler than Mercédès.

"Madame," said he, "the count and yourself recompense too generously a simple action. To save a man, to spare a father's feelings, or a mother's sensibility, is not to do a good action, but a simple deed of humanity."

At these words, uttered with the most exquisite sweetness and politeness, Madame de Morcerf replied:

"It is very fortunate for my son, monsieur, that he found such a friend, and I thank God that things are thus."

And Mercédès raised her fine eyes to heaven with so fervent an expression of gratitude, that the count fancied he saw tears in them. M. de Morcerf approached her.

"Madame," said he. "I have already made my excuses to the count for quitting him, and I pray you to do so also. The sitting commences at two; it is now three, and I am to speak."

"Go, then, and monsieur and I will strive our best to forget your absence," replied the countess, with the same tone of deep feeling. "Monsieur," continued she, turning to Monte Cristo, "will you do us the honor of passing the rest of the day with us?"

"Believe me, madame, I feel most grateful for your kindness, but I got out of my travelling carriage at your door this morning, and I am ignorant how I am installed in Paris, which I scarcely know; this is but a trifling inquietude, I know, but one that may be appreciated."

"We shall have the pleasure another time," said the countess; "you promise that?"

Monte Cristo inclined himself without answering, but the gesture might pass for assent.

"I will not detain you, monsieur," continued the countess; "I would not have our gratitude become indiscreet or importunate."

"My dear Count," said Albert, "I will endeavor to return your politeness at Rome, and place my coupé at your disposal until your own be ready."

"A thousand thanks for your kindness, viscount," returned the Count of Monte Cristo "but I suppose that M. Bertuccio has suitably employed the four hours and a half I have given him, and that I shall find a carriage of some sort ready at the door."

Albert was used to the count's manner of proceeding; he knew that, like Nero, he was in search of the impossible, and nothing astonished him, but wishing to judge with his own eyes how far the count's orders had been executed, he accompanied him to the door of the house. Monte Cristo was not deceived. As soon as he appeared in the Count of Morcerf's antechamber, a footman, the same who at Rome had brought the count's card to the two young men, and announced his visit, sprang into the vestibule, and when he arrived at the door the illustrious traveller found his carriage awaiting him. It was a *coupé* of Koller's building, and with horses and harness for which Drake had, to the knowledge of all the lions of Paris, refused on the previous day seven hundred guineas.

"Monsieur," said the count to Albert, "I do not ask you to accompany me to my house, as I can only show you a habitation fitted up in a hurry, and I have, as you know, a reputation to keep up as regards not being taken by surprise. Give me, therefore, one more day before I invite you; I shall then be certain not to fail in my hospitality."

"If you ask me for a day, count, I know what to anticipate; it will not be a house I shall see, but a palace. You have decidedly some genius at your control."

"*Ma foi*, spread that idea," replied the Count of Monte Cristo, putting his foot on the velvet-lined steps of his splendid carriage, "and that will be worth something to me among the ladies."

As he spoke, he sprang into the vehicle, the door was closed, but not so rapidly that Monte Cristo failed to perceive the almost imperceptible movement which stirred the curtains of the apartment in which he had left Madame de Morcerf.

When Albert returned to his mother, he found her in the boudoir reclining in a large velvet armchair, the whole room so obscure that only the shining spangle, fastened here and there to the drapery, and the angles of the gilded frames of the pictures, showed with some degree of brightness in the gloom. Albert could not see the face of the countess, as it was covered with a thin veil she had put on her head, and which fell over her features in misty folds, but it seemed to him as though her voice had altered. He could distinguish amid the perfumes of the roses and heliotropes in the flower-stands, the sharp and fragrant odor of volatile salts, and he noticed in one of the chased cups on the mantle-piece the countess's smelling-bottle, taken from its shagreen case, and exclaimed in a tone of uneasiness, as he entered:

"My dear mother, have you been ill during my absence?"

"No, no, Albert, but you know these roses, tuberoses, and orange-flowers throw out at first, before one is used to them, such violent perfumes."

"Then, my dear mother," said Albert, putting his hand to the bell, "they must be taken into the antechamber. You are really ill, and just now were so pale as you came into the room"

"Was I pale, Albert?"

"Yes; a pallor that suits you admirably, mother, but which did not the less alarm my father and myself."

"Did your father speak of it?" inquired Mercédès eagerly.

"No, madame; but do you not remember that he spoke of the fact to you?"

"Yes, I do remember," replied the countess.

A servant entered, summoned by Albert's ring of the bell.

"Take these flowers into the anteroom or dressing-room," said the viscount; "they make the countess ill."

The footman obeyed his orders. A long pause ensued, which lasted until all the flowers were removed.

"What is this name of Monte Cristo?" inquired the countess, when the servant had taken away the last vase of flowers, "is it a family name, or the name of the estate, or a simple title?"

"I believe, mother, it is merely a title. The count purchased an island in the Tuscan archipelago, and, as he told you today, has founded a commandery. You know the same thing was done for Saint Stephen of Florence, Saint George Constantinian of Parma, and even for the Order of Malta. Except this, he has no pretension to nobility, and calls himself a chance count, although the general opinion at Rome is that the count is a man of very high distinction."

"His manners are admirable," said the countess, "at least, as far as I could judge in the few minutes he remained here."

"They are perfect mother, so perfect, that they surpass by far all I have known in the leading aristocracy of the three proudest nobilities of Europe the English, the Spanish, and the German."

The countess paused a moment; then, after a slight hesitation, she resumed.

"You have seen, my dear Albert I ask the question as a mother you have seen M. de Monte Cristo in his house, you are quick-sighted, have much knowledge of the world, more tact than is usual at your age, do you think the count is really what he appears to be?"

"What does he appear to be?"

"Why, you have just said, a man of high distinction."

"I told you, my dear mother, he was esteemed such."

"But what is your own opinion, Albert?"

"I must tell you that I have not come to any decided opinion respecting him, but I think him a Maltese."

"I do not ask you of his origin but what he is."

"Ah! what he is; that is quite another thing. I have seen so many remarkable things in him, that if you would have me really say what I think, I shall reply that I really do look upon him as one of Byron's heroes, whom misery has marked with a fatal brand; some Manfred, some Lara, some Werner, one of those wrecks, as it were, of some ancient family, who, disinherited of their patrimony, have achieved one by the force of their adventurous genius, which has placed them above the laws of society."

"You say "

"I say that Monte Cristo is an island in the midst of the Mediterranean, without inhabitants or garrison, the resort of smugglers of all nations, and pirates of every flag. Who knows whether or not these industrious worthies do not pay to their feudal lord some dues for his protection?"

"That is possible," said the countess, reflecting.

"Never mind," continued the young man, "smuggler or not, you must agree, mother dear, as you have seen him, that the Count of Monte Cristo is a remarkable man, who will have the greatest success in the salons of Paris. Why, this very morning, in my rooms, he made his *entrée* amongst us by striking every man of us with amazement, not even excepting Château-Renaud."

"And what do you suppose is the count's age?" inquired Mer-cédès, evidently attaching great importance to this question.

"Thirty-five or thirty-six, mother."

"So young, it is impossible," said Mercédès, replying at the same time to what Albert said as well as to her own private reflection.

"It is the truth, however. Three or four times he has said to me, and certainly without the slightest premeditation, 'at such a period I was five years old, at another ten years old, at another twelve,' and I, induced by curiosity, which kept me alive to these details, have compared the dates, and never found him inaccurate. The age of this singular man, who is of no age, is then, I am certain, thirty-five. Besides, mother, remark how vivid his eye, how raven-black his hair, and his brow, though so pale, is free from wrinkles, he is not only vigorous, but also young."

The countess bent her head, as if beneath a heavy wave of bit-ter thoughts.

"And has this man displayed a friendship for you, Albert?" she asked with a nervous shudder.

"I am inclined to think so."

"And do you like him?"

"Why, he pleases me in spite of Franz d'Épinay, who tries to convince me that he is a being returned from the other world."

The countess shuddered.

"Albert," she said, in a voice which was altered by emotion, "I have always put you on your guard against new acquaint-ances. Now you are a man, and are able to give me advice; yet I repeat to you, Albert, be prudent."

"Why, my dear mother, it is necessary, in order to make your advice turn to account, that I should know beforehand what I have to distrust. The count never plays, he only drinks pure water tinged with a little sherry, and is so rich that he can-not, without intending to laugh at me, try to borrow money. What, then, have I to fear from him?"

"You are right," said the countess, "and my fears are weakness, especially when directed against a man who has saved your life. How did your father receive him, Albert? It is necessary that we should be more than complaisant to the count. M. de Morcerf is sometimes occupied, his business makes him reflective, and he might, without intending it "

"Nothing could be in better taste than my father's demeanor, madame," said Albert; "nay, more, he seemed greatly flattered at two or three compliments which the count very skilfully and agreeably paid him with as much ease as if he had known him these thirty years. Each of these little tickling arrows must have pleased my father," added Albert with a laugh. "And thus they parted the best possible friends, and M. de Morcerf even wished to take him to the Chamber to hear the speakers."

The countess made no reply. She fell into so deep a reverie that her eyes gradually closed. The young man, standing up before her, gazed upon her with that filial affection which is so tender and endearing with children whose mothers are still young and handsome. Then, after seeing her eyes closed, and hearing her breathe gently, he believed she had dropped asleep, and left the apartment on tiptoe, closing the door after him with the utmost precaution.

"This devil of a fellow," he muttered, shaking his head; "I said at the time he would create a sensation here, and I measure his effect by an infallible thermometer. My mother has noticed him, and he must therefore, perforce, be remarkable."

He went down to the stables, not without some slight annoyance, when he remembered that the Count of Monte Cristo had laid his hands on a "turnout" which sent his bays down to second place in the opinion of connoisseurs.

"Most decidedly," said he, "men are not equal, and I must beg my father to develop this theorem in the Chamber of Peers."

Chapter 15

Monsieur Bertuccio

Meanwhile the count had arrived at his house; it had taken him six minutes to perform the distance, but these six minutes were sufficient to induce twenty young men who knew the price of the equipage they had been unable to purchase themselves, to put their horses in a gallop in order to see the rich foreigner who could afford to give 20,000 francs apiece for his horses.

The house Ali had chosen, and which was to serve as a town residence to Monte Cristo, was situated on the right hand as you ascend the Champs-Élysées. A thick clump of trees and shrubs rose in the centre, and masked a portion of the front; around this shrubbery two alleys, like two arms, extended right and left, and formed a carriage-drive from the iron gates to a double portico, on every step of which stood a porcelain vase, filled with flowers. This house, isolated from the rest, had, besides the main entrance, another in the Rue de Ponthieu. Even before the coachman had hailed the *concierge*, the massy gates rolled on their hinges they had seen the Count coming, and at Paris, as everywhere else, he was served with the rapidity of lightning. The coachman entered and traversed the half-circle without slackening his speed, and the gates were closed ere the wheels had ceased to sound on the gravel. The carriage stopped at the left side of the portico, two men presented themselves at the carriage-window; the one was Ali, who, smiling with an expression of the most sincere joy, seemed amply repaid by a mere look from Monte Cristo. The other bowed respectfully, and offered his arm to assist the count in descending.

"Thanks, M. Bertuccio," said the count, springing lightly up the three steps of the portico; "and the notary?"

"He is in the small salon, excellency," returned Bertuccio.

"And the cards I ordered to be engraved as soon as you knew the number of the house?"

"Your excellency, it is done already. I have been myself to the best engraver of the Palais Royal, who did the plate in my presence. The first card struck off was taken, according to your orders, to the Baron Danglars, Rue de la Chaussée d'Antin, No. 7; the others are on the mantle-piece of your excellency's bedroom."

"Good; what o'clock is it?"

"Four o'clock."

Monte Cristo gave his hat, cane, and gloves to the same French footman who had called his carriage at the Count of Morcerf's, and then he passed into the small salon, preceded by Bertuccio, who showed him the way.

"These are but indifferent marbles in this antechamber," said Monte Cristo. "I trust all this will soon be taken away."

Bertuccio bowed. As the steward had said, the notary awaited him in the small salon. He was a simple-looking lawyer's clerk, elevated to the extraordinary dignity of a provincial scrivener.

"You are the notary empowered to sell the country house that I wish to purchase, monsieur?" asked Monte Cristo.

"Yes, count," returned the notary.

"Is the deed of sale ready?"

"Yes, count."

"Have you brought it?"

"Here it is."

"Very well; and where is this house that I purchase?" asked the count carelessly, addressing himself half to Bertuccio, half to the notary. The steward made a gesture that signified, "I do not know." The notary looked at the count with astonishment.

"What!" said he, "does not the count know where the house he purchases is situated?"

"No," returned the count.

"The count does not know?"

"How should I know? I have arrived from Cadiz this morning. I have never before been at Paris, and it is the first time I have ever even set my foot in France."

"Ah, that is different; the house you purchase is at Auteuil."

At these words Bertuccio turned pale.

"And where is Auteuil?" asked the count.

"Close by here, monsieur," replied the notary "a little beyond Passy; a charming situation, in the heart of the Bois de Boulogne."

"So near as that?" said the Count; "but that is not in the country. What made you choose a house at the gates of Paris, M. Bertuccio?"

"I," cried the steward with a strange expression. "His excellency did not charge me to purchase this house. If his excellency will recollect if he will think "

"Ah, true," observed Monte Cristo; "I recollect now. I read the advertisement in one of the papers, and was tempted by the false title, 'a country house.'"

"It is not yet too late," cried Bertuccio, eagerly; "and if your excellency will intrust me with the commission, I will find you a better at Enghien, at Fontenay-aux-Roses, or at Bellevue."

"Oh, no," returned Monte Cristo negligently; "since I have this, I will keep it."

"And you are quite right," said the notary, who feared to lose his fee. "It is a charming place, well supplied with spring-water and fine trees; a comfortable habitation, although abandoned for a long time, without reckoning the furniture, which, although old, is yet valuable, now that old things are so much sought after. I suppose the count has the tastes of the day?"

"To be sure," returned Monte Cristo; "it is very convenient, then?"

"It is more it is magnificent."

"*Peste!* let us not lose such an opportunity," returned Monte Cristo. "The deed, if you please, Mr. Notary."

And he signed it rapidly, after having first run his eye over that part of the deed in which were specified the situation of the house and the names of the proprietors.

"Bertuccio," said he, "give fifty-five thousand francs to monsieur."

The steward left the room with a faltering step, and returned with a bundle of bank-notes, which the notary counted like a man who never gives a receipt for money until after he is sure it is all there.

"And now," demanded the count, "are all the forms complied with?"

"All, sir."

"Have you the keys?"

"They are in the hands of the concierge, who takes care of the house, but here is the order I have given him to install the count in his new possessions."

"Very well;" and Monte Cristo made a sign with his hand to the notary, which said, "I have no further need of you; you may go."

"But," observed the honest notary, "the count is, I think, mistaken; it is only fifty thousand francs, everything included."

"And your fee?"

"Is included in this sum."

"But have you not come from Auteuil here?"

"Yes, certainly."

"Well, then, it is but fair that you should be paid for your loss of time and trouble," said the count; and he made a gesture of polite dismissal.

The notary left the room backwards, and bowing down to the ground; it was the first time he had ever met a similar client.

"See this gentleman out," said the count to Bertuccio. And the steward followed the notary out of the room.

Scarcely was the count alone, when he drew from his pocket a book closed with a lock, and opened it with a key which he wore round his neck, and which never left him. After having sought for a few minutes, he stopped at a leaf which had several notes, and compared them with the deed of sale, which lay on the table, and recalling his *souvenirs*

"'Auteuil, Rue de la Fontaine, No. 28;' it is indeed the same," said he; "and now, am I to rely upon an avowal extorted by religious or physical terror? However, in an hour I shall know all. Bertuccio!" cried he, striking a light hammer with a pliant handle on a small gong. "Bertuccio!"

The steward appeared at the door.

"Monsieur Bertuccio," said the count, "did you never tell me that you had travelled in France?"

"In some parts of France yes, excellency."

"You know the environs of Paris, then?"

"No, excellency, no," returned the steward, with a sort of nervous trembling, which Monte Cristo, a connoisseur in all emotions, rightly attributed to great disquietude.

"It is unfortunate," returned he, "that you have never visited the environs, for I wish to see my new property this evening, and had you gone with me, you could have given me some useful information."

"To Auteuil!" cried Bertuccio, whose copper complexion became livid "I go to Auteuil?"

"Well, what is there surprising in that? When I live at Auteuil, you must come there, as you belong to my service."

Bertuccio hung down his head before the imperious look of his master, and remained motionless, without making any answer.

"Why, what has happened to you? are you going to make me ring a second time for the carriage?" asked Monte Cristo, in the same tone that Louis XIV. pronounced the famous, "I have been almost obliged to wait." Bertuccio made but one bound to the antechamber, and cried in a hoarse voice:

"His excellency's horses!"

Monte Cristo wrote two or three notes, and, as he sealed the last, the steward appeared.

"Your excellency's carriage is at the door," said he.

"Well, take your hat and gloves," returned Monte Cristo.

"Am I to accompany you, your excellency?" cried Bertuccio.

"Certainly, you must give the orders, for I intend residing at the house."

It was unexampled for a servant of the count's to dare to dispute an order of his, so the steward, without saying a word, followed his master, who got into the carriage, and signed to him to follow, which he did, taking his place respectfully on the front seat.

Chapter 16

The House at Auteuil

Monte Cristo noticed, as they descended the staircase, that Bertuccio signed himself in the Corsican manner; that is, had formed the sign of the cross in the air with his thumb, and as he seated himself in the carriage, muttered a short prayer. Anyone but a man of exhaustless thirst for knowledge would have had pity on seeing the steward's extraordinary repugnance for the count's projected drive without the walls; but the count was too curious to let Bertuccio off from this little journey. In twenty minutes they were at Auteuil; the steward's emotion had continued to augment as they entered the village. Bertuccio, crouched in the corner of the carriage, began to examine with a feverish anxiety every house they passed.

"Tell them to stop at Rue de la Fontaine, No. 28," said the count, fixing his eyes on the steward, to whom he gave this order.

Bertuccio's forehead was covered with perspiration; however, he obeyed, and, leaning out of the window, he cried to the coachman, "Rue de la Fontaine, No. 28." No. 28 was situated at the extremity of the village; during the drive night had set in, and darkness gave the surroundings the artificial appearance of a scene on the stage. The carriage stopped, the footman sprang off the box and opened the door.

"Well," said the count, "you do not get out, M. Bertuccio you are going to stay in the carriage, then? What are you thinking of this evening?"

Bertuccio sprang out, and offered his shoulder to the count, who, this time, leaned upon it as he descended the three steps of the carriage.

"Knock," said the count, "and announce me."

Bertuccio knocked, the door opened, and the concierge appeared.

"What is it?" asked he.

"It is your new master, my good fellow," said the footman. And he held out to the concierge the notary's order.

"The house is sold, then?" demanded the concierge; "and this gentleman is coming to live here?"

"Yes, my friend," returned the count; "and I will endeavor to give you no cause to regret your old master."

"Oh, monsieur," said the concierge, "I shall not have much cause to regret him, for he came here but seldom; it is five years since he was here last, and he did well to sell the house, for it did not bring him in anything at all."

"What was the name of your old master?" said Monte Cristo.

"The Marquis of Saint-Méran. Ah, I am sure he has not sold the house for what he gave for it."

"The Marquis of Saint-Méran!" returned the count. "The name is not unknown to me; the Marquis of Saint-Méran!" and he appeared to meditate.

"An old gentleman," continued the concierge, "a staunch follower of the Bourbons; he had an only daughter, who married M. de Villefort, who had been the king's attorney at Nîmes, and afterwards at Versailles."

Monte Cristo glanced at Bertuccio, who became whiter than the wall against which he leaned to prevent himself from falling.

"And is not this daughter dead?" demanded Monte Cristo; "I fancy I have heard so."

"Yes, monsieur, one-and-twenty years ago; and since then we have not seen the poor marquis three times."

"Thanks, thanks," said Monte Cristo, judging from the steward's utter prostration that he could not stretch the cord further without danger of breaking it. "Give me a light."

"Shall I accompany you, monsieur?"

"No, it is unnecessary; Bertuccio will show me a light."

And Monte Cristo accompanied these words by the gift of two gold pieces, which produced a torrent of thanks and blessings from the concierge.

"Ah, monsieur," said he, after having vainly searched on the mantle-piece and the shelves, "I have not got any candles."

"Take one of the carriage-lamps, Bertuccio," said the count, "and show me the apartments."

The steward obeyed in silence, but it was easy to see, from the manner in which the hand that held the light trembled, how much it cost him to obey. They went over a tolerably large ground floor; a first floor consisted of a salon, a bathroom, and two bedrooms; near one of the bedrooms they came to a winding staircase that led down to the garden.

"Ah, here is a private staircase," said the count; "that is convenient. Light me, M. Bertuccio, and go first; we will see where it leads to."

"Monsieur," replied Bertuccio, "it leads to the garden."

"And, pray, how do you know that?"

"It ought to do so, at least."

"Well, let us be sure of that."

Bertuccio sighed, and went on first; the stairs did, indeed, lead to the garden. At the outer door the steward paused.

"Go on, Monsieur Bertuccio," said the count.

But he who was addressed stood there, stupefied, bewildered, stunned; his haggard eyes glanced around, as if in search of the traces of some terrible event, and with his clenched hands he seemed striving to shut out horrible recollections.

"Well!" insisted the Count.

"No, no," cried Bertuccio, setting down the lantern at the angle of the interior wall. "No, monsieur, it is impossible; I can go no farther."

"What does this mean?" demanded the irresistible voice of Monte Cristo.

"Why, you must see, your excellency," cried the steward, "that this is not natural; that, having a house to purchase, you purchase it exactly at Auteuil, and that, purchasing it at Auteuil, this house should be No. 28, Rue de la Fontaine. Oh, why did I not tell you all? I am sure you would not have forced me to come. I hoped your house would have been some other one than this; as if there was not another house at Auteuil than that of the assassination!"

"What, what!" cried Monte Cristo, stopping suddenly, "what words do you utter? Devil of a man, Corsican that you are always mysteries or superstitions. Come, take the lantern, and let us visit the garden; you are not afraid of ghosts with me, I hope?"

Bertuccio raised the lantern, and obeyed. The door, as it opened, disclosed a gloomy sky, in which the moon strove vainly to struggle through a sea of clouds that covered her with billows of vapor which she illumined for an instant, only to sink into obscurity. The steward wished to turn to the left.

"No, no, monsieur," said Monte Cristo. "What is the use of following the alleys? Here is a beautiful lawn; let us go on straight forwards."

Bertuccio wiped the perspiration from his brow, but obeyed; however, he continued to take the left hand. Monte Cristo, on the contrary, took the right hand; arrived near a clump of trees, he stopped. The steward could not restrain himself.

"Move, monsieur move away, I entreat you; you are exactly in the spot!"

"What spot?"

"Where he fell."

"My dear Monsieur Bertuccio," said Monte Cristo, laughing, "control yourself; we are not at Sartène or at Corte. This is not a Corsican *maquis* but an English garden; badly kept, I own, but still you must not calumniate it for that."

"Monsieur, I implore you do not stay there!"

"I think you are going mad, Bertuccio," said the count coldly. "If that is the case, I warn you, I shall have you put in a lunatic asylum."

"Alas! excellency," returned Bertuccio, joining his hands, and shaking his head in a manner that would have excited the count's laughter, had not thoughts of a superior interest occupied him, and rendered him attentive to the least revelation of this timorous conscience. "Alas! excellency, the evil has arrived!"

"M. Bertuccio," said the count, "I am very glad to tell you, that while you gesticulate, you wring your hands and roll your eyes like a man possessed by a devil who will not leave him; and I have always observed, that the devil most obstinate to be expelled is a secret. I knew you were a Corsican. I knew you were gloomy, and always brooding over some old history of the vendetta; and I overlooked that in Italy, because in Italy those things are thought nothing of. But in France they are considered in very bad taste; there are gendarmes who occupy themselves with such affairs, judges who condemn, and scaffolds which avenge."

Bertuccio clasped his hands, and as, in all these evolutions, he did not let fall the lantern, the light showed his pale and altered countenance. Monte Cristo examined him with the same look that, at Rome, he had bent upon the execution of Andrea, and then, in a tone that made a shudder pass through the veins of the poor steward

"The Abbé Busoni, then told me an untruth," said he, "when, after his journey in France, in 1829, he sent you to me, with a letter of recommendation, in which he enumerated all your valuable qualities. Well, I shall write to the abbé; I shall hold him responsible for his *protégé's* misconduct, and I shall soon know all about this assassination. Only I warn you, that when I reside in a country, I conform to all its code, and I have no wish to put myself within the compass of the French laws for your sake."

"Oh, do not do that, excellency; I have always served you faithfully," cried Bertuccio, in despair. "I have always been an honest man, and, as far as lay in my power, I have done good."

"I do not deny it," returned the count; "but why are you thus agitated. It is a bad sign; a quiet conscience does not occasion such paleness in the cheeks, and such fever in the hands of a man."

"But, your excellency," replied Bertuccio hesitatingly, "did not the Abbé Busoni, who heard my confession in the prison at Nîmes, tell you that I had a heavy burden upon my conscience?"

"Yes; but as he said you would make an excellent steward, I concluded you had stolen that was all."

"Oh, your excellency!" returned Bertuccio in deep contempt.

"Or, as you are a Corsican, that you had been unable to resist the desire of making a 'stiff,' as you call it."

"Yes, my good master," cried Bertuccio, casting himself at the count's feet, "it was simply vengeance nothing else."

"I understand that, but I do not understand what it is that galvanizes you in this manner."

"But, monsieur, it is very natural," returned Bertuccio, "since it was in this house that my vengeance was accomplished."

"What! my house?"

"Oh, your excellency, it was not yours, then."

"Whose, then? The Marquis de Saint-Méran, I think, the concierge said. What had you to revenge on the Marquis de Saint-Méran?"

"Oh, it was not on him, monsieur; it was on another."

"This is strange," returned Monte Cristo, seeming to yield to his reflections, "that you should find yourself without any preparation in a house where the event happened that causes you so much remorse."

"Monsieur," said the steward, "it is fatality, I am sure. First, you purchase a house at Auteuil this house is the one where I have committed an assassination; you descend to the garden by the same staircase by which he descended; you stop at the spot where he received the blow; and two paces farther is the grave in which he had just buried his child. This is not chance, for chance, in this case, is too much like Providence."

"Well, amiable Corsican, let us suppose it is Providence. I always suppose anything people please, and, besides, you must concede something to diseased minds. Come, collect yourself, and tell me all."

"I have related it but once, and that was to the Abbé Busoni. Such things," continued Bertuccio, shaking his head, "are only related under the seal of confession."

"Then," said the count, "I refer you to your confessor. Turn Chartreux or Trappist, and relate your secrets, but, as for me, I do not like anyone who is alarmed by such phantasms, and I do not choose that my servants should be afraid to walk in the garden of an evening. I confess I am not very desirous of a visit from the commissary of police, for, in Italy, justice is only paid when silent in France she is paid only when she speaks. *Peste!* I thought you somewhat Corsican, a great deal smuggler, and an excellent steward; but I see you have other strings to your bow. You are no longer in my service, Monsieur Bertuccio."

"Oh, your excellency, your excellency!" cried the steward, struck with terror at this threat, "if that is the only reason I cannot remain in your service, I will tell all, for if I quit you, it will only be to go to the scaffold."

"That is different," replied Monte Cristo; "but if you intend to tell an untruth, reflect it were better not to speak at all."

"No, monsieur, I swear to you, by my hopes of salvation, I will tell you all, for the Abbé Busoni himself only knew a part of my secret; but, I pray you, go away from that plane-tree. The moon is just bursting through the clouds, and there, standing where you do, and wrapped in that cloak that conceals your figure, you remind me of M. de Villefort."

"What!" cried Monte Cristo, "it was M. de Villefort?"

"Your excellency knows him?"

"The former royal attorney at Nîmes?"

"Yes."

"Who married the Marquis of Saint-Méran's daughter?"

"Yes."

"Who enjoyed the reputation of being the most severe, the most upright, the most rigid magistrate on the bench?"

"Well, monsieur," said Bertuccio, "this man with this spotless reputation"

"Well?"

"Was a villain."

"Bah," replied Monte Cristo, "impossible!"

"It is as I tell you."

"Ah, really," said Monte Cristo. "Have you proof of this?"

"I had it."

"And you have lost it; how stupid!"

"Yes; but by careful search it might be recovered."

"Really," returned the count, "relate it to me, for it begins to interest me."

And the count, humming an air from *Lucia*, went to sit down on a bench, while Bertuccio followed him, collecting his thoughts. Bertuccio remained standing before him.

Chapter 17

The Vendetta

At what point shall I begin my story, your excellency?" asked Bertuccio.

"Where you please," returned Monte Cristo, "since I know nothing at all of it."

"I thought the Abbé Busoni had told your excellency."

"Some particulars, doubtless, but that is seven or eight years ago, and I have forgotten them."

"Then I can speak without fear of tiring your excellency."

"Go on, M. Bertuccio; you will supply the want of the evening papers."

"The story begins in 1815."

"Ah," said Monte Cristo, "1815 is not yesterday."

"No, monsieur, and yet I recollect all things as clearly as if they had happened but then. I had a brother, an elder brother, who was in the service of the emperor; he had become lieutenant in a regiment composed entirely of Corsicans. This brother was my only friend; we became orphans I at five, he at eighteen. He brought me up as if I had been his son, and in 1814 he married. When the emperor returned from the Island of Elba, my brother instantly joined the army, was slightly wounded at Waterloo, and retired with the army beyond the Loire."

"But that is the history of the Hundred Days, M. Bertuccio," said the count; "unless I am mistaken, it has been already written."

"Excuse me, excellency, but these details are necessary, and you promised to be patient."

"Go on; I will keep my word."

"One day we received a letter. I should tell you that we lived in the little village of Rogliano, at the extremity of Cap Corse. This letter was from my brother. He told us that the army was disbanded, and that he should return by Châteauroux, Clermont-Ferrand, Le Puy, and Nîmes; and, if I had any money, he prayed me to leave it for him at Nîmes, with an innkeeper with whom I had dealings."

"In the smuggling line?" said Monte Cristo.

"Eh, your excellency? Everyone must live."

"Certainly; go on."

"I loved my brother tenderly, as I told your excellency, and I resolved not to send the money, but to take it to him myself. I possessed a thousand francs. I left five hundred with Assunta, my sister-in-law, and with the other five hundred I set off for Nîmes. It was easy to do so, and as I had my boat and a lading to take in at sea, everything favored my project. But, after we had taken in our cargo, the wind became contrary, so that we were four or five days without being able to enter the Rhône. At last, however, we succeeded, and worked up to Arles. I left the boat between Bellegarde and Beaucaire, and took the road to Nîmes."

"We are getting to the story now?"

"Yes, your excellency; excuse me, but, as you will see, I only tell you what is absolutely necessary. Just at this time the famous massacres took place in the south of France. Three brigands, called Trestaillon, Truphemy, and Graffan, pub-licly assassinated everybody whom they suspected of Bona-partism. You have doubtless heard of these massacres, your excellency?"

"Vaguely; I was far from France at that period. Go on."

"As I entered Nîmes, I literally waded in blood; at every step you encountered dead bodies and bands of murderers, who killed, plundered, and burned. At the sight of this slaughter and devastation I became terrified, not for myself for I, a sim-ple Corsican fisherman, had nothing to fear; on the contrary, that time was most favorable for us smugglers but for my brother, a soldier of the empire, returning from the army of the Loire, with his uniform and his epaulets, there was every-thing to apprehend. I hastened to the innkeeper. My misgiv-ings had been but too true. My brother had arrived the previ-ous evening at Nîmes, and, at the very door of the house where he was about to demand hospitality, he had been assassinated. I did all in my power to discover the murderers, but no one durst tell me their names, so much were they dreaded. I then thought of that French justice of which I had heard so much, and which feared nothing, and I went to the king's attorney."

"And this king's attorney was named Villefort?" asked Monte Cristo carelessly.

"Yes, your excellency; he came from Marseilles, where he had been deputy procureur. His zeal had procured him advance-ment, and he was said to be one of the first who had informed the government of the departure from the Island of Elba."

"Then," said Monte Cristo "you went to him?"

"'Monsieur,' I said, 'my brother was assassinated yesterday in the streets of Nîmes, I know not by whom, but it is your duty to find out. You are the representative of justice here, and it is for justice to avenge those she has been unable to protect.'

"'Who was your brother?' asked he.

"'A lieutenant in the Corsican battalion.'

"'A soldier of the usurper, then?'

"'A soldier of the French army.'

"'Well,' replied he, 'he has smitten with the sword, and he has perished by the sword.'

"'You are mistaken, monsieur,' I replied; 'he has perished by the poniard.'

"'What do you want me to do?' asked the magistrate.

"'I have already told you avenge him.'

"'On whom?'

"'On his murderers.'

"'How should I know who they are?'

"'Order them to be sought for.'

"'Why, your brother has been involved in a quarrel, and killed in a duel. All these old soldiers commit excesses which were tolerated in the time of the emperor, but which are not suffered now, for the people here do not like soldiers of such disorderly conduct.'

"'Monsieur,' I replied, 'it is not for myself that I entreat your interference I should grieve for him or avenge him, but my poor brother had a wife, and were anything to happen to me, the poor creature would perish from want, for my brother's pay alone kept her. Pray, try and obtain a small government pension for her.'

"'Every revolution has its catastrophes,' returned M. de Villefort; 'your brother has been the victim of this. It is a misfortune, and government owes nothing to his family. If we are to judge by all the vengeance that the followers of the usurper exercised on the partisans of the king, when, in their turn, they were in power, your brother would be today, in all probability, condemned to death. What has happened is quite natural, and in conformity with the law of reprisals.'

"'What,' cried I, 'do you, a magistrate, speak thus to me?'

"'All these Corsicans are mad, on my honor,' replied M. de Villefort; 'they fancy that their countryman is still emperor. You have mistaken the time, you should have told me this two months ago, it is too late now. Go now, at once, or I shall have you put out.'

"I looked at him an instant to see if there was anything to hope from further entreaty. But he was a man of stone. I approached him, and said in a low voice, 'Well, since you know the Corsicans so well, you know that they always keep their word. You think that it was a good deed to kill my brother, who was a Bonapartist, because you are a royalist. Well, I, who am a Bonapartist also, declare one thing to you, which is, that I will kill you. From this moment I declare the vendetta against you, so protect yourself as well as you can, for the next time we meet your last hour has come.' And before he had recovered from his surprise, I opened the door and left the room."

"Well, well," said Monte Cristo, "such an innocent looking person as you are to do those things, M. Bertuccio, and to a king's attorney at that! But did he know what was meant by the terrible word 'vendetta'?"

"He knew so well, that from that moment he shut himself in his house, and never went out unattended, seeking me high and low. Fortunately, I was so well concealed that he could not find me. Then he became alarmed, and dared not stay any longer at Nîmes, so he solicited a change of residence, and, as he was in reality very influential, he was nominated to Versailles. But, as you know, a Corsican who has sworn to avenge himself cares not for distance, so his carriage, fast as it went, was never above half a day's journey before me, who followed him on foot. The most important thing was, not to kill him only for I had an opportunity of doing so a hundred times but to kill him without being discovered at least, without being arrested. I no longer belonged to myself, for I had my sister-in-law to protect and provide for.

"For three months I watched M. de Villefort, for three months he took not a step out-of-doors without my following him. At length I discovered that he went mysteriously to Auteuil. I followed him thither, and I saw him enter the house where we now are, only, instead of entering by the great door that looks into the street, he came on horseback, or in his carriage, left the one or the other at the little inn, and entered by the gate you see there."

Monte Cristo made a sign with his head to show that he could discern in the darkness the door to which Bertuccio alluded.

"As I had nothing more to do at Versailles, I went to Auteuil, and gained all the information I could. If I wished to surprise him, it was evident this was the spot to lie in wait for him. The house belonged, as the concierge informed your excellency, to M. de Saint-Méran, Villefort's father-in-law. M. de Saint-Méran lived at Marseilles, so that this country house was useless to him, and it was reported to be let to a young widow, known only by the name of 'the Baroness.'

"One evening, as I was looking over the wall, I saw a young and handsome woman who was walking alone in that garden, which was not overlooked by any windows, and I guessed that she was awaiting M. de Villefort. When she was sufficiently near for me to distinguish her features, I saw she was from eighteen to nineteen, tall and very fair. As she had a loose muslin dress on and as nothing concealed her figure, I saw she would ere long become a mother. A few moments after, the little door was opened and a man entered. The young woman hastened to meet him. They threw themselves into each other's arms, embraced tenderly, and returned together to the house. The man was M. de Villefort; I fully believed that when he went out in the night he would be forced to traverse the whole of the garden alone."

"And," asked the count, "did you ever know the name of this woman?"

"No, excellency," returned Bertuccio; "you will see that I had no time to learn it."

"Go on."

"That evening," continued Bertuccio, "I could have killed the procureur, but as I was not sufficiently acquainted with the neighborhood, I was fearful of not killing him on the spot, and that if his cries were overheard I might be taken; so I put it off until the next occasion, and in order that nothing should escape me, I took a chamber looking into the street bordered by the wall of the garden. Three days after, about seven o'clock in the evening, I saw a servant on horseback leave the house at full gallop, and take the road to Sèvres. I concluded that he was going to Versailles, and I was not deceived. Three hours later, the man returned covered with dust, his errand was performed, and two minutes after, another man on foot, muffled in a mantle, opened the little door of the garden, which he closed after him. I descended rapidly; although I had not seen Villefort's face, I recognized him by the beating of my heart. I crossed the street, and stopped at a post placed at the angle of the wall, and by means of which I had once before looked into the garden.

"This time I did not content myself with looking, but I took my knife out of my pocket, felt that the point was sharp, and sprang over the wall. My first care was to run to the door; he had left the key in it, taking the simple precaution of turning it twice in the lock. Nothing, then, preventing my escape by this means, I examined the grounds. The garden was long and narrow; a stretch of smooth turf extended down the middle, and at the corners were clumps of trees with thick and massy foliage, that made a background for the shrubs and flowers. In order to go from the door to the house, or from the house to the door, M. de Villefort would be obliged to pass by one of these clumps of trees.

"It was the end of September; the wind blew violently. The faint glimpses of the pale moon, hidden momentarily by masses of dark clouds that were sweeping across the sky, whitened the gravel walks that led to the house, but were unable to pierce the obscurity of the thick shrubberies, in which a man could conceal himself without any fear of discovery. I hid myself in the one nearest to the path Villefort must take, and scarcely was I there when, amidst the gusts of wind, I fancied I heard groans; but you know, or rather you do not know, your excellency, that he who is about to commit an assassination fancies that he hears low cries perpetually ringing in his ears. Two hours passed thus, during which I imagined I heard moans repeatedly. Midnight struck. As the last stroke died away, I saw a faint light shine through the windows of the private staircase by which we have just descended. The door opened, and the man in the mantle reappeared.

"The terrible moment had come, but I had so long been prepared for it that my heart did not fail in the least. I drew my knife from my pocket again, opened it, and made ready to strike. The man in the mantle advanced towards me, but as he drew near I saw that he had a weapon in his hand. I was afraid, not of a struggle, but of a failure. When he was only a few paces from me, I saw that what I had taken for a weapon was only a spade. I was still unable to divine for what reason M. de Villefort had this spade in his hands, when he stopped close to the thicket where I was, glanced round, and began to dig a hole in the earth. I then perceived that he was hiding something under his mantle, which he laid on the grass in order to dig more freely. Then, I confess, curiosity mingled with hatred; I wished to see what Villefort was going to do there, and I remained motionless, holding my breath. Then an idea crossed my mind, which was confirmed when I saw the procureur lift from under his mantle a box, two feet long, and six or eight inches deep. I let him place the box in the hole he had made, then, while he stamped with his feet to remove all traces of his occupation, I rushed on him and plunged my knife into his breast, exclaiming:

"'I am Giovanni Bertuccio; thy death for my brother's; thy treasure for his widow; thou seest that my vengeance is more complete than I had hoped.'

"I know not if he heard these words; I think he did not, for he fell without a cry. I felt his blood gush over my face, but I was intoxicated, I was delirious, and the blood refreshed, instead of burning me. In a second I had disinterred the box; then, that it might not be known I had done so, I filled up the hole, threw the spade over the wall, and rushed through the door, which I double-locked, carrying off the key."

"Ah," said Monte Cristo "it seems to me this was nothing but murder and robbery."

"No, your excellency," returned Bertuccio; "it was a vendetta followed by restitution."

"And was the sum a large one?"

"It was not money."

"Ah, I recollect," replied the count; "did you not say something of an infant?"

"Yes, excellency; I hastened to the river, sat down on the bank, and with my knife forced open the lock of the box. In a fine linen cloth was wrapped a new-born child. Its purple visage, and its violet-colored hands showed that it had perished from suffocation, but as it was not yet cold, I hesitated to throw it into the water that ran at my feet. After a moment I fancied that I felt a slight pulsation of the heart, and as I had been assistant at the hospital at Bastia, I did what a doctor would have done I inflated the lungs by blowing air into them, and at the expiration of a quarter of an hour, it began to breathe, and cried feebly. In my turn I uttered a cry, but a cry of joy.

"'God has not cursed me then,' I cried, 'since he permits me to save the life of a human creature, in exchange for the life I have taken away.'"

"And what did you do with the child?" asked Monte Cristo. "It was an embarrassing load for a man seeking to escape."

"I had not for a moment the idea of keeping it, but I knew that at Paris there was an asylum where they receive such creatures. As I passed the city gates I declared that I had found the child on the road, and I inquired where the asylum was; the box confirmed my statement, the linen proved that the infant belonged to wealthy parents, the blood with which I was covered might have proceeded from the child as well as from anyone else. No objection was raised, but they pointed out the asylum, which was situated at the upper end of the Rue d'Enfer, and after having taken the precaution of cutting the linen in two pieces, so that one of the two letters which marked it was on the piece wrapped around the child, while the other remained in my possession, I rang the bell, and fled with all speed. A fortnight after I was at Rogliano, and I said to Assunta:

"'Console thyself, sister; Israel is dead, but he is avenged.'

"She demanded what I meant, and when I had told her all, 'Giovanni,' said she, 'you should have brought this child with you; we would have replaced the parents it has lost, have called it Benedetto, and then, in consequence of this good action, God would have blessed us.' In reply I gave her the half of the linen I had kept in order to reclaim him if we became rich."

"What letters were marked on the linen?" said Monte Cristo.

"An H and an N, surmounted by a baron's coronet."

"By heaven, M. Bertuccio, you make use of heraldic terms; where did you study heraldry?"

"In your service, excellency, where everything is learned."

"Go on, I am curious to know two things."

"What are they, your excellency?"

"What became of this little boy? for I think you told me it was a boy, M. Bertuccio."

"No excellency, I do not recollect telling you that."

"I thought you did; I must have been mistaken."

"No, you were not, for it was in reality a little boy. But your excellency wished to know two things; what was the second?"

"The second was the crime of which you were accused when you asked for a confessor, and the Abbé Busoni came to visit you at your request in the prison at Nîmes."

"The story will be very long, excellency."

"What matter? you know I take but little sleep, and I do not suppose you are very much inclined for it either." Bertuccio bowed, and resumed his story.

"Partly to drown the recollections of the past that haunted me, partly to supply the wants of the poor widow, I eagerly returned to my trade of smuggler, which had become more easy since that relaxation of the laws which always follows a revolution. The southern districts were ill-watched in particular, in consequence of the disturbances that were perpetually breaking out in Avignon, Nîmes, or Uzès. We profited by this respite on the part of the government to make friends everywhere. Since my brother's assassination in the streets of Nîmes, I had never entered the town; the result was that the innkeeper with whom we were connected, seeing that we would no longer come to him, was forced to come to us, and had established a branch to his inn, on the road from Belle-garde to Beaucaire, at the sign of the Pont du Gard. We had thus, at Aigues-Mortes, Martigues, or Bouc, a dozen places where we left our goods, and where, in case of necessity, we concealed ourselves from the gendarmes and custom-house officers. Smuggling is a profitable trade, when a certain degree of vigor and intelligence is employed; as for myself, brought up in the mountains, I had a double motive for fearing the gendarmes and custom-house officers, as my appearance be-fore the judges would cause an inquiry, and an inquiry always looks back into the past. And in my past life they might find something far more grave than the selling of smuggled cigars, or barrels of brandy without a permit. So, preferring death to capture, I accomplished the most astonishing deeds, and which, more than once, showed me that the too great care we take of our bodies is the only obstacle to the success of those projects which require rapid decision, and vigorous and de-termined execution. In reality, when you have once devoted your life to your enterprises, you are no longer the equal of other men, or, rather, other men are no longer your equals, and whosoever has taken this resolution, feels his strength and re-sources doubled."

"Philosophy, M. Bertuccio," interrupted the count; "you have done a little of everything in your life."

"Oh, excellency!"

"No, no; but philosophy at half-past ten at night is somewhat late; yet I have no other observation to make, for what you say is correct, which is more than can be said for all philosophy."

"My journeys became more and more extensive and more productive. Assunta took care of all, and our little fortune increased. One day as I was setting off on an expedition, 'Go,' said she; 'at your return I will give you a surprise.' I ques-tioned her, but in vain; she would tell me nothing, and I departed. Our expedition lasted nearly six weeks; we had been to Lucca to take in oil, to Leghorn for English cottons, and we ran our cargo without opposition, and returned home full of joy. When I entered the house, the first thing I beheld in the middle of Assunta's chamber was a cradle that might be called sumptuous compared with the rest of the furniture, and in it a baby seven or eight months old. I uttered a cry of joy; the only moments of sadness I had known since the assassination of the procureur were caused by the recollection that I had abandoned this child. For the assassination itself I had never felt any remorse. Poor Assunta had guessed all. She had profited by my absence, and furnished with the half of the linen, and having written down the day and hour at which I had deposited the child at the asylum, had set off for Paris, and had reclaimed it. No objection was raised, and the infant was given up to her. Ah, I confess, your excellency, when I saw this poor creature sleeping peacefully in its cradle, I felt my eyes filled with tears. 'Ah, Assunta,' cried I, 'you are an excellent woman, and Heaven will bless you.'"

"This," said Monte Cristo, "is less correct than your philosophy, it is only faith."

"Alas, your excellency is right," replied Bertuccio, "and God made this infant the instrument of our punishment. Never did a perverse nature declare itself more prematurely, and yet it was not owing to any fault in his bringing up. He was a most lovely child, with large blue eyes, of that deep color that harmonizes so well with the blond complexion; only his hair, which was too light, gave his face a most singular expression, and added to the vivacity of his look, and the malice of his smile.

"Unfortunately, there is a proverb which says that 'red is either altogether good or altogether bad.' The proverb was but too correct as regarded Benedetto, and even in his infancy he manifested the worst disposition. It is true that the indulgence of his foster-mother encouraged him. This child, for whom my poor sister would go to the town, five or six leagues off, to purchase the earliest fruits and the most tempting sweetmeats, preferred to Palma grapes or Genoese preserves, the chestnuts stolen from a neighbor's orchard, or the dried apples in his loft, when he could eat as well of the nuts and apples that grew in my garden.

"One day, when Benedetto was about five or six, our neighbor Wasilio, who, according to the custom of the country, never locked up his purse or his valuables for, as your excellency knows, there are no thieves in Corsica complained that he had lost a louis out of his purse; we thought he must have made a mistake in counting his money, but he persisted in the accuracy of his statement. One day, Benedetto, who had been gone from the house since morning, to our great anxiety, did not return until late in the evening, dragging a monkey after him, which he said he had found chained to the foot of a tree. For more than a month past, the mischievous child, who knew not what to wish for, had taken it into his head to have a monkey. A boatman, who had passed by Rogliano, and who had several of these animals, whose tricks had greatly diverted him, had, doubtless, suggested this idea to him. 'Monkeys are not found in our woods chained to trees,' said I; 'confess how you obtained this animal.' Benedetto maintained the truth of what he had said, and accompanied it with details that did more honor to his imagination than to his veracity. I became angry; he began to laugh, I threatened to strike him, and he made two steps backwards. 'You cannot beat me,' said he; 'you have no right, for you are not my father.'

"We never knew who had revealed this fatal secret, which we had so carefully concealed from him; however, it was this answer, in which the child's whole character revealed itself, that almost terrified me, and my arm fell without touching him.

"The boy triumphed, and this victory rendered him so audacious, that all the money of Assunta, whose affection for him seemed to increase as he became more unworthy of it, was spent in caprices she knew not how to contend against, and follies she had not the courage to prevent. When I was at

Rogliano everything went on properly, but no sooner was my back turned than Benedetto became master, and everything went ill. When he was only eleven, he chose his companions from among the young men of eighteen or twenty, the worst characters in Bastia, or, indeed, in Corsica, and they had already, for some mischievous pranks, been several times threatened with a prosecution. I became alarmed, as any prosecution might be attended with serious consequences. I was compelled, at this period, to leave Corsica on an important expedition; I reflected for a long time, and with the hope of averting some impending misfortune, I resolved that Benedetto should accompany me.

"I hoped that the active and laborious life of a smuggler, with the severe discipline on board, would have a salutary effect on his character, which was now well-nigh, if not quite, corrupt. I spoke to Benedetto alone, and proposed to him to accompany me, endeavoring to tempt him by all the promises most likely to dazzle the imagination of a child of twelve. He heard me patiently, and when I had finished, burst out laughing.

"'Are you mad, uncle?' (he called me by this name when he was in good humor); 'do you think I am going to change the life I lead for your mode of existence my agreeable indolence for the hard and precarious toil you impose on yourself, exposed to the bitter frost at night, and the scorching heat by day, compelled to conceal yourself, and when you are perceived, receive a volley of bullets, all to earn a paltry sum? Why, I have as much money as I want; mother Assunta always furnishes me when I ask for it! You see that I should be a fool to accept your offer.'

"The arguments, and his audacity, perfectly stupefied me. Benedetto rejoined his associates, and I saw him from a distance point me out to them as a fool."

"Sweet child," murmured Monte Cristo.

"Oh, had he been my own son," replied Bertuccio, "or even my nephew, I would have brought him back to the right road, for the knowledge that you are doing your duty gives you strength, but the idea that I was striking a child whose father I had killed, made it impossible for me to punish him. I gave my sister, who constantly defended the unfortunate boy, good advice, and as she confessed that she had several times missed money to a considerable amount, I showed her a safe place in which to conceal our little treasure for the future. My mind was already made up. Benedetto could read, write, and cipher perfectly, for when the fit seized him, he learned more in a day than others in a week. My intention was to enter him as a clerk in some ship, and without letting him know anything of my plan, to convey him some morning on board; by this means his future treatment would depend upon his own conduct. I set off for France, after having fixed upon the plan. Our cargo was to be landed in the Gulf of Lyons, and this was a difficult thing to do because it was then the year 1829. The most perfect tranquillity was restored, and the vigilance of the custom-house officers was redoubled, and their strictness was increased at this time, in consequence of the fair at Beaucaire.

"Our expedition made a favorable beginning. We anchored our vessel which had a double hold, where our goods were concealed amidst a number of other vessels that bordered the banks of the Rhône from Beaucaire to Arles. On our arrival we began to discharge our cargo in the night, and to convey it into the town, by the help of the innkeeper with whom we were connected.

"Whether success rendered us imprudent, or whether we were betrayed, I know not; but one evening, about five o'clock, our little cabin-boy came breathlessly, to inform us that he had seen a detachment of custom-house officers advancing in our direction. It was not their proximity that alarmed us, for detachments were constantly patrolling along the banks of the Rhône, but the care, according to the boy's account, that they took to avoid being seen. In an instant we were on the alert, but it was too late; our vessel was surrounded, and amongst the custom-house officers I observed several gendarmes, and, as terrified at the sight of their uniforms as I was brave at the sight of any other, I sprang into the hold, opened a port, and dropped into the river, dived, and only rose at intervals to breathe, until I reached a ditch that had recently been made from the Rhône to the canal that runs from Beaucaire to Aigues-Mortes. I was now safe, for I could swim along the ditch without being seen, and I reached the canal in safety. I had designedly taken this direction. I have already told your excellency of an innkeeper from Nîmes who had set up a little tavern on the road from Bellegarde to Beaucaire."

"Yes," said Monte Cristo "I perfectly recollect him; I think he was your colleague."

"Precisely," answered Bertuccio; "but he had, seven or eight years before this period, sold his establishment to a tailor at Marseilles, who, having almost ruined himself in his old trade, wished to make his fortune in another. Of course, we made the same arrangements with the new landlord that we had with the old; and it was of this man that I intended to ask shelter."

"What was his name?" inquired the count, who seemed to become somewhat interested in Bertuccio's story.

"Gaspard Caderousse; he had married a woman from the village of Carconte, and whom we did not know by any other name than that of her village. She was suffering from malarial fever, and seemed dying by inches. As for her husband, he was a strapping fellow of forty, or five-and-forty, who had more than once, in time of danger, given ample proof of his presence of mind and courage."

"And you say," interrupted Monte Cristo "that this took place towards the year "

"1829, your excellency."

"In what month?"

"June."

"The beginning or the end?"

"The evening of the 3rd."

"Ah," said Monte Cristo "the evening of the 3rd of June, 1829. Go on."

"It was from Caderousse that I intended demanding shelter,

and, as we never entered by the door that opened onto the road, I resolved not to break through the rule, so climbing over the garden-hedge, I crept amongst the olive and wild fig trees, and fearing that Caderousse might have some guest, I entered a kind of shed in which I had often passed the night, and which was only separated from the inn by a partition, in which holes had been made in order to enable us to watch an opportunity of announcing our presence.

"My intention was, if Caderousse was alone, to acquaint him with my presence, finish the meal the custom-house officers had interrupted, and profit by the threatened storm to return to the Rhône, and ascertain the state of our vessel and its crew. I stepped into the shed, and it was fortunate I did so, for at that moment Caderousse entered with a stranger.

"I waited patiently, not to overhear what they said, but because I could do nothing else; besides, the same thing had occurred often before. The man who was with Caderousse was evidently a stranger to the South of France; he was one of those merchants who come to sell jewellery at the Beaucaire fair, and who during the month the fair lasts, and during which there is so great an influx of merchants and customers from all parts of Europe, often have dealings to the amount of 100,000 to 150,000 francs. Caderousse entered hastily. Then, seeing that the room was, as usual, empty, and only guarded by the dog, he called to his wife, 'Hello, Carconte,' said he, 'the worthy priest has not deceived us; the diamond is real.'

"An exclamation of joy was heard, and the staircase creaked beneath a feeble step. 'What do you say?' asked his wife, pale as death.

"'I say that the diamond is real, and that this gentleman, one of the first jewellers of Paris, will give us 50,000 francs for it. Only, in order to satisfy himself that it really belongs to us, he wishes you to relate to him, as I have done already, the miraculous manner in which the diamond came into our possession. In the meantime please to sit down, monsieur, and I will fetch you some refreshment.'

"The jeweller examined attentively the interior of the inn and the apparent poverty of the persons who were about to sell him a diamond that seemed to have come from the casket of a prince.

"'Relate your story, madame,' said he, wishing, no doubt, to profit by the absence of the husband, so that the latter could not influence the wife's story, to see if the two recitals tallied.

"'Oh,' returned she, 'it was a gift of heaven. My husband was a great friend, in 1814 or 1815, of a sailor named Edmond Dantès. This poor fellow, whom Caderousse had forgotten, had not forgotten him, and at his death he bequeathed this diamond to him.'

"'But how did he obtain it?' asked the jeweller; 'had he it before he was imprisoned?'

"'No, monsieur; but it appears that in prison he made the acquaintance of a rich Englishman, and as in prison he fell sick, and Dantès took the same care of him as if he had been his brother, the Englishman, when he was set free, gave this stone to Dantès, who, less fortunate, died, and, in his turn, left it to us, and charged the excellent abbé, who was here this morning, to deliver it.'

"'The same story,' muttered the jeweller; 'and improbable as it seemed at first, it may be true. There's only the price we are not agreed about.'

"'How not agreed about?' said Caderousse. 'I thought we agreed for the price I asked.'

"'That is,' replied the jeweller, 'I offered 40,000 francs.'

'Forty thousand,' cried La Carconte; 'we will not part with it for that sum. The abbé told us it was worth 50,000 without the setting.'

"'What was the abbé's name?' asked the indefatigable questioner.

"'The Abbé Busoni,' said La Carconte.

"'He was a foreigner?'

"'An Italian from the neighborhood of Mantua, I believe.'

"'Let me see this diamond again,' replied the jeweller; 'the first time you are often mistaken as to the value of a stone.'

"Caderousse took from his pocket a small case of black shag-reen, opened, and gave it to the jeweller. At the sight of the diamond, which was as large as a hazel-nut, La Carconte's eyes sparkled with cupidity."

"And what did you think of this fine story, eavesdropper?" said Monte Cristo; "did you credit it?"

"Yes, your excellency. I did not look on Caderousse as a bad man, and I thought him incapable of committing a crime, or even a theft."

"That did more honor to your heart than to your experience, M. Bertuccio. Had you known this Edmond Dantès, of whom they spoke?"

"No, your excellency, I had never heard of him before, and never but once afterwards, and that was from the Abbé Busoni himself, when I saw him in the prison at Nîmes."

"Go on."

"The jeweller took the ring, and drawing from his pocket a pair of steel pliers and a small set of copper scales, he took the stone out of its setting, and weighed it carefully.

"'I will give you 45,000,' said he, 'but not a sou more; besides, as that is the exact value of the stone, I brought just that sum with me.'

"'Oh, that's no matter,' replied Caderousse, 'I will go back with you to fetch the other 5,000 francs.'

"'No,' returned the jeweller, giving back the diamond and the ring to Caderousse, 'no, it is worth no more, and I am sorry I offered so much, for the stone has a flaw in it, which I had not seen. However, I will not go back on my word, and I will give 45,000.'

"'At least, replace the diamond in the ring,' said La Carconte sharply.

"'Ah, true,' replied the jeweller, and he reset the stone.

"'No matter,' observed Caderousse, replacing the box in his pocket, 'someone else will purchase it.'

"'Yes,' continued the jeweller; 'but someone else will not be so easy as I am, or content himself with the same story. It is not natural that a man like you should possess such a diamond. He will inform against you. You will have to find the Abbé Busoni; and abbés who give diamonds worth two thousand louis are rare. The law would seize it, and put you in prison; if at the end of three or four months you are set at liberty, the ring will be lost, or a false stone, worth three francs, will be given you, instead of a diamond worth 50,000 or perhaps 55,000 francs; from which you must allow that one runs considerable risk in purchasing.'

"Caderousse and his wife looked eagerly at each other.

"'No,' said Caderousse, 'we are not rich enough to lose 5,000 francs.'

"'As you please, my dear sir,' said the jeweller; 'I had, however, as you see, brought you the money in bright coin.' And he drew from his pocket a handful of gold, and held it sparkling before the dazzled eyes of the innkeeper, and in the other hand he held a packet of bank-notes.

"There was evidently a severe struggle in the mind of Caderousse; it was plain that the small shagreen case, which he turned over and over in his hand, did not seem to him commensurate in value to the enormous sum which fascinated his gaze. He turned towards his wife.

"'What do you think of this?' he asked in a low voice.

"'Let him have it let him have it,' she said. 'If he returns to Beaucaire without the diamond, he will inform against us, and, as he says, who knows if we shall ever again see the Abbé Busoni? in all probability we shall never see him.'

"'Well, then, so I will!' said Caderousse; 'so you may have the diamond for 45,000 francs. But my wife wants a gold chain, and I want a pair of silver buckles.'

"The jeweller drew from his pocket a long flat box, which contained several samples of the articles demanded. 'Here,' he said, 'I am very straightforward in my dealings take your choice.'

"The woman selected a gold chain worth about five louis, and the husband a pair of buckles, worth perhaps fifteen francs.

"'I hope you will not complain now?' said the jeweller.

"'The abbé told me it was worth 50,000 francs,' muttered Caderousse.

"'Come, come give it to me! What a strange fellow you are,' said the jeweller, taking the diamond from his hand. 'I give you 45,000 francs that is, 2,500 livres of income, a fortune such as I wish I had myself, and you are not satisfied!'

"'And the five-and-forty thousand francs,' inquired Caderousse in a hoarse voice, 'where are they? Come let us see them.'

"'Here they are,' replied the jeweller, and he counted out upon the table 15,000 francs in gold, and 30,000 francs in banknotes.

"'Wait while I light the lamp,' said La Carconte; 'it is growing dark, and there may be some mistake.' In fact, night had come on during this conversation, and with night the storm which had been threatening for the last half-hour. The thunder growled in the distance; but it was apparently not heard by the jeweller, Caderousse, or La Carconte, absorbed as they were all three with the demon of gain. I myself felt; a strange kind of fascination at the sight of all this gold and all these bank-notes; it seemed to me that I was in a dream, and, as it always happens in a dream, I felt myself riveted to the spot. Caderousse counted and again counted the gold and the notes, then handed them to his wife, who counted and counted them again in her turn. During this time, the jeweller made the diamond play and sparkle in the lamplight, and the gem threw out jets of light which made him unmindful of those which precursors of the storm began to play in at the windows.

"'Well,' inquired the jeweller, 'is the cash all right?'

"'Yes,' said Caderousse. 'Give me the pocket-book, La Carconte, and find a bag somewhere.'

"La Carconte went to a cupboard, and returned with an old leathern pocket-book and a bag. From the former she took some greasy letters, and put in their place the bank-notes, and from the bag took two or three crowns of six livres each, which, in all probability, formed the entire fortune of the miserable couple.

"'There,' said Caderousse; 'and now, although you have wronged us of perhaps 10,000 francs, will you have your supper with us? I invite you with good-will.'

"'Thank you,' replied the jeweller, 'it must be getting late, and I must return to Beaucaire my wife will be getting uneasy.' He drew out his watch, and exclaimed, '*Morbleu!* nearly nine o'clock why, I shall not get back to Beaucaire before midnight! Good-night, my friends. If the Abbé Busoni should by any accident return, think of me.'

"'In another week you will have left Beaucaire,' remarked Caderousse, 'for the fair ends in a few days.'

"'True, but that makes no difference. Write to me at Paris, to M. Joannes, in the Palais Royal, arcade Pierre, No. 45. I will make the journey on purpose to see him, if it is worth while.'

"At this moment there was a tremendous clap of thunder, accompanied by a flash of lightning so vivid, that it quite eclipsed the light of the lamp.

"'See here,' exclaimed Caderousse. 'You cannot think of going out in such weather as this.'

"'Oh, I am not afraid of thunder,' said the jeweller.

"'And then there are robbers,' said La Carconte. 'The road is never very safe during fair time.'

"'Oh, as to the robbers,' said Joannes, 'here is something for them,' and he drew from his pocket a pair of small pistols, loaded to the muzzle. 'Here,' said he, 'are dogs who bark and bite at the same time, they are for the two first who shall have a longing for your diamond, Friend Caderousse.'

"Caderousse and his wife again interchanged a meaning look. It seemed as though they were both inspired at the same time with some horrible thought. 'Well, then, a good journey to you,' said Caderousse.

"'Thanks,' replied the jeweller. He then took his cane, which he had placed against an old cupboard, and went out. At the moment when he opened the door, such a gust of wind came in that the lamp was nearly extinguished. 'Oh,' said he, 'this is very nice weather, and two leagues to go in such a storm.'

"'Remain,' said Caderousse. 'You can sleep here.'

"'Yes; do stay,' added La Carconte in a tremulous voice; 'we will take every care of you.'

"'No; I must sleep at Beaucaire. So, once more, good-night.' Caderousse followed him slowly to the threshold. 'I can see neither heaven nor earth,' said the jeweller, who was outside the door. 'Do I turn to the right, or to the left hand?'

"'To the right,' said Caderousse. 'You cannot go wrong the road is bordered by trees on both sides.'

"'Good all right,' said a voice almost lost in the distance.

"'Close the door,' said La Carconte; 'I do not like open doors when it thunders.'

"'Particularly when there is money in the house, eh?' answered Caderousse, double-locking the door.

"He came into the room, went to the cupboard, took out the bag and pocket-book, and both began, for the third time, to count their gold and bank-notes. I never saw such an expression of cupidity as the flickering lamp revealed in those two countenances. The woman, especially, was hideous; her usual feverish tremulousness was intensified, her countenance had become livid, and her eyes resembled burning coals.

"'Why,' she inquired in a hoarse voice, 'did you invite him to sleep here tonight?'

"'Why?' said Caderousse with a shudder; 'why, that he might not have the trouble of returning to Beaucaire.'

"'Ah,' responded the woman, with an expression impossible to describe; 'I thought it was for something else.'

"'Woman, woman why do you have such ideas?' cried Caderousse; 'or, if you have them, why don't you keep them to yourself?'

"'Well,' said La Carconte, after a moment's pause, 'you are not a man.'

"'What do you mean?' added Caderousse.

"'If you had been a man, you would not have let him go from

here.'

"'Woman!'

"'Or else he should not have reached Beaucaire.'

"'Woman!'

"'The road takes a turn he is obliged to follow it while alongside of the canal there is a shorter road.'

"'Woman! you offend the good God. There listen!'

And at this moment there was a tremendous peal of thunder, while the livid lightning illumined the room, and the thunder, rolling away in the distance, seemed to withdraw unwillingly from the cursed abode. 'Mercy!' said Caderousse, crossing himself.

"At the same moment, and in the midst of the terrifying silence which usually follows a clap of thunder, they heard a knocking at the door. Caderousse and his wife started and looked aghast at each other.

"'Who's there?' cried Caderousse, rising, and drawing up in a heap the gold and notes scattered over the table, and which he covered with his two hands.

"'It is I,' shouted a voice.

"'And who are you?'

"'Eh, *pardieu!* Joannes, the jeweller.'

"'Well, and you said I offended the good God,' said La Carconte with a horrid smile. 'Why, the good God sends him back again.' Caderousse sank pale and breathless into his chair.

"La Carconte, on the contrary, rose, and going with a firm step towards the door, opened it, saying, as she did so:

"'Come in, dear M. Joannes.'

"'*Ma foi,*' said the jeweller, drenched with rain, 'I am not destined to return to Beaucaire tonight. The shortest follies are best, my dear Caderousse. You offered me hospitality, and I accept it, and have returned to sleep beneath your friendly roof.'

"Caderousse stammered out something, while he wiped away the sweat that started to his brow. La Carconte double-locked the door behind the jeweller."

Chapter 18

The Rain of Blood

As the jeweller returned to the apartment, he cast around him a scrutinizing glance but there was nothing to excite suspicion, if it did not exist, or to confirm it, if it were already awakened. Caderousse's hands still grasped the gold and bank-notes, and La Carconte called up her sweetest smiles while welcoming the reappearance of their guest.

"'Well, well,' said the jeweller, 'you seem, my good friends, to have had some fears respecting the accuracy of your money, by counting it over so carefully directly I was gone.'

"'Oh, no,' answered Caderousse, 'that was not my reason, I can assure you; but the circumstances by which we have become possessed of this wealth are so unexpected, as to make us scarcely credit our good fortune, and it is only by placing the actual proof of our riches before our eyes that we can persuade ourselves that the whole affair is not a dream.'

"The jeweller smiled. 'Have you any other guests in your house?' inquired he.

"'Nobody but ourselves,' replied Caderousse; 'the fact is, we do not lodge travellers indeed, our tavern is so near the town, that nobody would think of stopping here.'

"'Then I am afraid I shall very much inconvenience you.'

"'Inconvenience us? Not at all, my dear sir,' said La Carconte in her most gracious manner. 'Not at all, I assure you.'

"'But where will you manage to stow me?'

"'In the chamber overhead.'

"'Surely that is where you yourselves sleep?'

"'Never mind that; we have a second bed in the adjoining room.'

"Caderousse stared at his wife with much astonishment.

"The jeweller, meanwhile, was humming a song as he stood warming his back at the fire La Carconte had kindled to dry the wet garments of her guest; and this done, she next occupied herself in arranging his supper, by spreading a napkin at the end of the table, and placing on it the slender remains of their dinner, to which she added three or four fresh-laid eggs. Caderousse had once more parted with his treasure the bank-notes were replaced in the pocket-book, the gold put back into the bag, and the whole carefully locked in the cupboard. He then began pacing the room with a pensive and gloomy air, glancing from time to time at the jeweller, who stood reeking with the steam from his wet clothes, and merely changing his place on the warm hearth, to enable the whole of his garments to be dried.

"'There,' said La Carconte, as she placed a bottle of wine on the table, 'supper is ready whenever you are.'

"'And you?' asked Joannes.

"'I don't want any supper,' said Caderousse.

"'We dined so very late,' hastily interposed La Carconte.

"'Then it seems I am to eat alone,' remarked the jeweller.

"'Oh, we shall have the pleasure of waiting upon you,' answered La Carconte, with an eager attention she was not accustomed to manifest even to guests who paid for what they took.

"From time to time Caderousse darted on his wife keen, searching glances, but rapid as the lightning flash. The storm still continued.

"'There, there,' said La Carconte; 'do you hear that? upon my word, you did well to come back.'

"'Nevertheless,' replied the jeweller, 'if by the time I have finished my supper the tempest has at all abated, I shall make another start.'

"'It's the mistral,' said Caderousse, 'and it will be sure to last till tomorrow morning.' He sighed heavily.

"'Well,' said the jeweller, as he placed himself at table, 'all I can say is, so much the worse for those who are abroad.'

"'Yes,' chimed in La Carconte, 'they will have a wretched night of it.'

"The jeweller began eating his supper, and the woman, who was ordinarily so querulous and indifferent to all who approached her, was suddenly transformed into the most smiling and attentive hostess. Had the unhappy man on whom she lavished her assiduities been previously acquainted with her, so sudden an alteration might well have excited suspicion in his mind, or at least have greatly astonished him. Caderousse, meanwhile, continued to pace the room in gloomy silence, sedulously avoiding the sight of his guest; but as soon as the stranger had completed his repast, the agitated innkeeper went eagerly to the door and opened it.

"'I believe the storm is over,' said he.

"But as if to contradict his statement, at that instant a violent clap of thunder seemed to shake the house to its very foundation, while a sudden gust of wind, mingled with rain, extinguished the lamp he held in his hand.

"Trembling and awe-struck, Caderousse hastily shut the door

and returned to his guest, while La Carconte lighted a candle by the smouldering ashes that glimmered on the hearth.

"'You must be tired,' said she to the jeweller; 'I have spread a pair of white sheets on your bed; go up when you are ready, and sleep well.'

"Joannes stayed for a while to see whether the storm seemed to abate in its fury, but a brief space of time sufficed to assure him that, instead of diminishing, the violence of the rain and thunder momentarily increased; resigning himself, therefore, to what seemed inevitable, he bade his host good-night, and mounted the stairs. He passed over my head and I heard the flooring creak beneath his footsteps. The quick, eager glance of La Carconte followed him as he ascended, while Caderousse, on the contrary, turned his back, and seemed most anxiously to avoid even glancing at him.

"All these circumstances did not strike me as painfully at the time as they have since done; in fact, all that had happened (with the exception of the story of the diamond, which certainly did wear an air of improbability), appeared natural enough, and called for neither apprehension nor mistrust; but, worn out as I was with fatigue, and fully purposing to proceed onwards directly the tempest abated, I determined to obtain a few hours' sleep. Overhead I could accurately distinguish every movement of the jeweller, who, after making the best arrangements in his power for passing a comfortable night, threw himself on his bed, and I could hear it creak and groan beneath his weight.

"Insensibly my eyelids grew heavy, deep sleep stole over me, and having no suspicion of anything wrong, I sought not to shake it off. I looked into the kitchen once more and saw Caderousse sitting by the side of a long table upon one of the low wooden stools which in country places are frequently used instead of chairs; his back was turned towards me, so that I could not see the expression of his countenance neither should I have been able to do so had he been placed differently, as his head was buried between his two hands. La Carconte continued to gaze on him for some time, then shrugging her shoulders, she took her seat immediately opposite to him.

"At this moment the expiring embers threw up a fresh flame from the kindling of a piece of wood that lay near, and a bright light flashed over the room. La Carconte still kept her eyes fixed on her husband, but as he made no sign of changing his position, she extended her hard, bony hand, and touched him on the forehead.

"Caderousse shuddered. The woman's lips seemed to move, as though she were talking; but because she merely spoke in an undertone, or my senses were dulled by sleep, I did not catch a word she uttered. Confused sights and sounds seemed to float before me, and gradually I fell into a deep, heavy slumber. How long I had been in this unconscious state I know not, when I was suddenly aroused by the report of a pistol, followed by a fearful cry. Weak and tottering footsteps resounded across the chamber above me, and the next instant a dull, heavy weight seemed to fall powerless on the staircase. I had not yet fully recovered consciousness, when again I heard groans, mingled with half-stifled cries, as if from persons engaged in a deadly struggle. A cry more prolonged than the others and ending in a series of groans effectually roused me from my drowsy lethargy. Hastily raising myself on one arm, I looked around, but all was dark; and it seemed to me as if the rain must have penetrated through the flooring of the room above, for some kind of moisture appeared to fall, drop by drop, upon my forehead, and when I passed my hand across my brow, I felt that it was wet and clammy.

"To the fearful noises that had awakened me had succeeded the most perfect silence unbroken, save by the footsteps of a man walking about in the chamber above. The staircase creaked, he descended into the room below, approached the fire and lit a candle.

"The man was Caderousse he was pale and his shirt was all bloody. Having obtained the light, he hurried upstairs again, and once more I heard his rapid and uneasy footsteps.

"A moment later he came down again, holding in his hand the small shagreen case, which he opened, to assure himself it contained the diamond, seemed to hesitate as to which pocket he should put it in, then, as if dissatisfied with the security of either pocket, he deposited it in his red handkerchief, which he carefully rolled round his head.

"After this he took from his cupboard the bank-notes and gold he had put there, thrust the one into the pocket of his trousers, and the other into that of his waistcoat, hastily tied up a small bundle of linen, and rushing towards the door, disappeared in the darkness of the night.

"Then all became clear and manifest to me, and I reproached myself with what had happened, as though I myself had done the guilty deed. I fancied that I still heard faint moans, and imagining that the unfortunate jeweller might not be quite dead, I determined to go to his relief, by way of atoning in some slight degree, not for the crime I had committed, but for that which I had not endeavored to prevent. For this purpose I applied all the strength I possessed to force an entrance from the cramped spot in which I lay to the adjoining room. The poorly fastened boards which alone divided me from it yielded to my efforts, and I found myself in the house. Hastily snatching up the lighted candle, I hurried to the staircase; about midway a body was lying quite across the stairs. It was that of La Carconte. The pistol I had heard had doubtless been fired at her. The shot had frightfully lacerated her throat, leaving two gaping wounds from which, as well as the mouth, the blood was pouring in floods. She was stone dead. I strode past her, and ascended to the sleeping chamber, which presented an appearance of the wildest disorder. The furniture had been knocked over in the deadly struggle that had taken place there, and the sheets, to which the unfortunate jeweller had doubtless clung, were dragged across the room. The murdered man lay on the floor, his head leaning against the wall, and about him was a pool of blood which poured forth from three large wounds in his breast; there was a fourth gash, in which a long table knife was plunged up to the handle.

"I stumbled over some object; I stooped to examine it was the second pistol, which had not gone off, probably from the powder being wet. I approached the jeweller, who was not quite dead, and at the sound of my footsteps and the creaking of the floor, he opened his eyes, fixed them on me with an anxious and inquiring gaze, moved his lips as though trying to speak, then, overcome by the effort, fell back and expired.

"This appalling sight almost bereft me of my senses, and finding that I could no longer be of service to anyone in the house, my only desire was to fly. I rushed towards the staircase, clutching my hair, and uttering a groan of horror.

"Upon reaching the room below, I found five or six customhouse officers, and two or three gendarmes all heavily armed. They threw themselves upon me. I made no resistance; I was no longer master of my senses. When I strove to speak, a few inarticulate sounds alone escaped my lips.

"As I noticed the significant manner in which the whole party pointed to my blood-stained garments, I involuntarily surveyed myself, and then I discovered that the thick warm drops that had so bedewed me as I lay beneath the staircase must have been the blood of La Carconte. I pointed to the spot where I had concealed myself.

"'What does he mean?' asked a gendarme.

"One of the officers went to the place I directed.

"'He means,' replied the man upon his return, 'that he got in that way;' and he showed the hole I had made when I broke through.

"Then I saw that they took me for the assassin. I recovered force and energy enough to free myself from the hands of those who held me, while I managed to stammer forth:

"'I did not do it! Indeed, indeed I did not!'

"A couple of gendarmes held the muzzles of their carbines against my breast.

"'Stir but a step,' said they, 'and you are a dead man.'

"'Why should you threaten me with death,' cried I, 'when I

have already declared my innocence?'

"'Tush, tush,' cried the men; 'keep your innocent stories to tell to the judge at Nîmes. Meanwhile, come along with us; and the best advice we can give you is to do so unresistingly.'

"Alas, resistance was far from my thoughts. I was utterly over-powered by surprise and terror; and without a word I suffered myself to be handcuffed and tied to a horse's tail, and thus they took me to Nîmes.

"I had been tracked by a customs-officer, who had lost sight of me near the tavern; feeling certain that I intended to pass the night there, he had returned to summon his comrades, who just arrived in time to hear the report of the pistol, and to take me in the midst of such circumstantial proofs of my guilt as rendered all hopes of proving my innocence utterly futile. One only chance was left me, that of beseeching the magistrate before whom I was taken to cause every inquiry to be made for the Abbé Busoni, who had stopped at the inn of the Pont du Gard on that morning.

"If Caderousse had invented the story relative to the diamond, and there existed no such person as the Abbé Busoni, then, indeed, I was lost past redemption, or, at least, my life hung upon the feeble chance of Caderousse himself being appre-hended and confessing the whole truth.

"Two months passed away in hopeless expectation on my part, while I must do the magistrate the justice to say that he used every means to obtain information of the person I declared could exculpate me if he would. Caderousse still evaded all pursuit, and I had resigned myself to what seemed my inevitable fate. My trial was to come on at the approach-ing assizes; when, on the 8th of September that is to say, precisely three months and five days after the events which had perilled my life the Abbé Busoni, whom I never ventured to believe I should see, presented himself at the prison doors, saying he understood one of the prisoners wished to speak to him; he added, that having learned at Marseilles the particu-lars of my imprisonment, he hastened to comply with my desire.

"You may easily imagine with what eagerness I welcomed him, and how minutely I related the whole of what I had seen and heard. I felt some degree of nervousness as I entered upon the history of the diamond, but, to my inexpressible astonishment, he confirmed it in every particular, and to my equal surprise, he seemed to place entire belief in all I said.

"And then it was that, won by his mild charity, seeing that he was acquainted with all the habits and customs of my own country, and considering also that pardon for the only crime of which I was really guilty might come with a double power from lips so benevolent and kind, I besought him to receive my confession, under the seal of which I recounted the Auteuil affair in all its details, as well as every other transaction of my life. That which I had done by the impulse of my best feelings produced the same effect as though it had been the result of calculation. My voluntary confession of the assassination at Auteuil proved to him that I had not committed that of which I stood accused. When he quitted me, he bade me be of good courage, and to rely upon his doing all in his power to convince my judges of my innocence.

"I had speedy proofs that the excellent abbé was engaged in my behalf, for the rigors of my imprisonment were alleviated by many trifling though acceptable indulgences, and I was told that my trial was to be postponed to the assizes following those now being held.

"In the interim it pleased Providence to cause the apprehension of Caderousse, who was discovered in some distant country, and brought back to France, where he made a full confession, refusing to make the fact of his wife's having suggested and arranged the murder any excuse for his own guilt. The wretched man was sentenced to the galleys for life, and I was immediately set at liberty."

"And then it was, I presume," said Monte Cristo "that you came to me as the bearer of a letter from the Abbé Busoni?"

"It was, your excellency; the benevolent abbé took an evident interest in all that concerned me.

"'Your mode of life as a smuggler,' said he to me one day, 'will be the ruin of you; if you get out, don't take it up again.'

"'But how,' inquired I, 'am I to maintain myself and my poor sister?'

"'A person, whose confessor I am,' replied he, 'and who entertains a high regard for me, applied to me a short time since to procure him a confidential servant. Would you like such a post? If so, I will give you a letter of introduction to him.'

"'Oh, father,' I exclaimed, 'you are very good.'

"'But you must swear solemnly that I shall never have reason to repent my recommendation.'

"I extended my hand, and was about to pledge myself by any promise he would dictate, but he stopped me.

"'It is unnecessary for you to bind yourself by any vow,' said he; 'I know and admire the Corsican nature too well to fear you. Here, take this,' continued he, after rapidly writing the few lines I brought to your excellency, and upon receipt of which you deigned to receive me into your service, and proudly I ask whether your excellency has ever had cause to repent having done so?"

"No," replied the count; "I take pleasure in saying that you have served me faithfully, Bertuccio; but you might have shown more confidence in me."

"I, your excellency?"

"Yes; you. How comes it, that having both a sister and an adopted son, you have never spoken to me of either?"

"Alas, I have still to recount the most distressing period of my life. Anxious as you may suppose I was to behold and comfort my dear sister, I lost no time in hastening to Corsica, but when I arrived at Rogliano I found a house of mourning, the consequences of a scene so horrible that the neighbors remember and speak of it to this day. Acting by my advice, my poor sister had refused to comply with the unreasonable demands of Benedetto, who was continually tormenting her for money, as long as he believed there was a sou left in her possession. One morning he threatened her with the severest consequences if she did not supply him with what he desired, and disappeared and remained away all day, leaving the kind-hearted Assunta, who loved him as if he were her own child, to weep over his conduct and bewail his absence. Evening came, and still, with all the patient solicitude of a mother, she watched for his return.

"As the eleventh hour struck, he entered with a swaggering air, attended by two of the most dissolute and reckless of his boon companions. She stretched out her arms to him, but they seized hold of her, and one of the three none other than the accursed Benedetto exclaimed:

"'Put her to torture and she'll soon tell us where her money is.'

"It unfortunately happened that our neighbor, Wasilio, was at Bastia, leaving no person in his house but his wife; no human creature beside could hear or see anything that took place within our dwelling. Two held poor Assunta, who, unable to conceive that any harm was intended to her, smiled in the face of those who were soon to become her executioners. The third proceeded to barricade the doors and windows, then returned, and the three united in stifling the cries of terror incited by the sight of these preparations, and then dragged Assunta feet foremost towards the brazier, expecting to wring from her an avowal of where her supposed treasure was secreted. In the struggle her clothes caught fire, and they were obliged to let go their hold in order to preserve themselves from sharing the same fate. Covered with flames, Assunta rushed wildly to the door, but it was fastened; she flew to the windows, but they were also secured; then the neighbors heard frightful shrieks; it was Assunta calling for help. The cries died away in groans, and next morning, as soon as Wasilio's wife could muster up courage to venture abroad, she caused the door of our dwelling to be opened by the public authorities, when Assunta, although dreadfully burnt, was found still breathing; every drawer and closet in the house had been forced open, and the money stolen. Benedetto never again appeared at Rogliano, neither have I since that day either seen or heard anything concerning him.

"It was subsequently to these dreadful events that I waited on your excellency, to whom it would have been folly to have mentioned Benedetto, since all trace of him seemed entirely lost; or of my sister, since she was dead."

"And in what light did you view the occurrence?" inquired Monte Cristo.

"As a punishment for the crime I had committed," answered Bertuccio. "Oh, those Villeforts are an accursed race!"

"Truly they are," murmured the count in a lugubrious tone.

"And now," resumed Bertuccio, "your excellency may, perhaps, be able to comprehend that this place, which I revisit for the first time this garden, the actual scene of my crime must have given rise to reflections of no very agreeable nature, and produced that gloom and depression of spirits which excited the notice of your excellency, who was pleased to express a desire to know the cause. At this instant a shudder passes over me as I reflect that possibly I am now standing on the very grave in which lies M. de Villefort, by whose hand the ground was dug to receive the corpse of his child."

"Everything is possible," said Monte Cristo, rising from the bench on which he had been sitting; "even," he added in an inaudible voice, "even that the procureur be not dead. The Abbé Busoni did right to send you to me," he went on in his ordinary tone, "and you have done well in relating to me the whole of your history, as it will prevent my forming any erroneous opinions concerning you in future. As for that Benedetto, who so grossly belied his name, have you never made any effort to trace out whither he has gone, or what has become of him?"

"No; far from wishing to learn whither he has betaken himself, I should shun the possibility of meeting him as I would a wild beast. Thank God, I have never heard his name mentioned by any person, and I hope and believe he is dead."

"Do not think so, Bertuccio," replied the count; "for the wicked are not so easily disposed of, for God seems to have them under his special watch-care to make of them instruments of his vengeance."

"So be it," responded Bertuccio, "all I ask of heaven is that I may never see him again. And now, your excellency," he added, bowing his head, "you know everything you are my judge on earth, as the Almighty is in heaven; have you for me no words of consolation?"

"My good friend, I can only repeat the words addressed to you by the Abbé Busoni. Villefort merited punishment for what he had done to you, and, perhaps, to others. Benedetto, if still living, will become the instrument of divine retribution in some way or other, and then be duly punished in his turn. As far as you yourself are concerned, I see but one point in which you are really guilty. Ask yourself, wherefore, after rescuing the infant from its living grave, you did not restore it to its mother? There was the crime, Bertuccio that was where you became really culpable."

"True, excellency, that was the crime, the real crime, for in that I acted like a coward. My first duty, directly I had succeeded in recalling the babe to life, was to restore it to its mother; but, in order to do so, I must have made close and careful inquiry, which would, in all probability, have led to my own apprehension; and I clung to life, partly on my sister's account, and partly from that feeling of pride inborn in our hearts of desiring to come off untouched and victorious in the execution of our vengeance. Perhaps, too, the natural and instinctive love of life made me wish to avoid endangering my own. And then, again, I am not as brave and courageous as was my poor brother."

Bertuccio hid his face in his hands as he uttered these words, while Monte Cristo fixed on him a look of inscrutable meaning. After a brief silence, rendered still more solemn by the time and place, the count said, in a tone of melancholy wholly unlike his usual manner:

"In order to bring this conversation to a fitting termination (the last we shall ever hold upon this subject), I will repeat to you some words I have heard from the lips of the Abbé Busoni. For all evils there are two remedies time and silence. And now leave me, Monsieur Bertuccio, to walk alone here in the garden. The very circumstances which inflict on you, as a principal in the tragic scene enacted here, such painful emotions, are to me, on the contrary, a source of something like contentment, and serve but to enhance the value of this dwelling in my estimation. The chief beauty of trees consists in the deep shadow of their umbrageous boughs, while fancy pictures a moving multitude of shapes and forms flitting and passing beneath that shade. Here I have a garden laid out in such a way as to afford the fullest scope for the imagination, and furnished with thickly grown trees, beneath whose leafy screen a visionary like myself may conjure up phantoms at will. This to me, who expected but to find a blank enclosure surrounded by a straight wall, is, I assure you, a most agreeable surprise. I have no fear of ghosts, and I have never heard it said that so much harm had been done by the dead during six thousand years as is wrought by the living in a single day. Retire within, Bertuccio, and tranquillize your mind. Should your confessor be less indulgent to you in your dying moments than you found the Abbé Busoni, send for me, if I am still on earth, and I will soothe your ears with words that shall effectually calm and soothe your parting soul ere it goes forth to traverse the ocean called eternity."

Bertuccio bowed respectfully, and turned away, sighing heavily. Monte Cristo, left alone, took three or four steps onwards, and murmured:

"Here, beneath this plane-tree, must have been where the infant's grave was dug. There is the little door opening into the garden. At this corner is the private staircase communicating with the sleeping apartment. There will be no necessity for me to make a note of these particulars, for there, before my eyes, beneath my feet, all around me, I have the plan sketched with all the living reality of truth."

After making the tour of the garden a second time, the count re-entered his carriage, while Bertuccio, who perceived the thoughtful expression of his master's features, took his seat beside the driver without uttering a word. The carriage proceeded rapidly towards Paris.

That same evening, upon reaching his abode in the Champs-Élysées, the Count of Monte Cristo went over the whole building with the air of one long acquainted with each nook or corner. Nor, although preceding the party, did he once mistake one door for another, or commit the smallest error when choosing any particular corridor or staircase to conduct him to a place or suite of rooms he desired to visit. Ali was his principal attendant during this nocturnal survey. Having given various orders to Bertuccio relative to the improvements and alterations he desired to make in the house, the Count, drawing out his watch, said to the attentive Nubian:

"It is half-past eleven o'clock; Haydée will soon be here. Have the French attendants been summoned to await her coming?"

Ali extended his hands towards the apartments destined for the fair Greek, which were so effectually concealed by means of a tapestried entrance, that it would have puzzled the most curious to have divined their existence. Ali, having pointed to the apartments, held up three fingers of his right hand, and then, placing it beneath his head, shut his eyes, and feigned to sleep.

"I understand," said Monte Cristo, well acquainted with Ali's pantomime; "you mean to tell me that three female attendants await their new mistress in her sleeping-chamber."

Ali, with considerable animation, made a sign in the affirmative.

"Madame will be tired tonight," continued Monte Cristo, "and will, no doubt, wish to rest. Desire the French attendants not to weary her with questions, but merely to pay their respectful duty and retire. You will also see that the Greek servants hold no communication with those of this country."

He bowed. Just at that moment voices were heard hailing the concierge. The gate opened, a carriage rolled down the avenue, and stopped at the steps. The count hastily descended, presented himself at the already opened carriage door, and held out his hand to a young woman, completely enveloped in a green silk mantle heavily embroidered with gold. She raised the hand extended towards her to her lips, and kissed it with a mixture of love and respect. Some few words passed between them in that sonorous language in which Homer makes his gods converse. The young woman spoke with an expression of deep tenderness, while the count replied with an air of gentle gravity.

Preceded by Ali, who carried a rose-colored flambeau in his hand, the young lady, who was no other than the lovely Greek who had been Monte Cristo's companion in Italy, was conducted to her apartments, while the count retired to the pavilion reserved for himself. In another hour every light in the house was extinguished, and it might have been thought that all its inmates slept.

Chapter 19

Unlimited Credit

About two o'clock the following day a calash, drawn by a pair of magnificent English horses, stopped at the door of Monte Cristo and a person, dressed in a blue coat, with buttons of a similar color, a white waistcoat, over which was displayed a massive gold chain, brown trousers, and a quantity of black hair descending so low over his eyebrows as to leave it doubtful whether it were not artificial so little did its jetty glossiness assimilate with the deep wrinkles stamped on his features a person, in a word, who, although evidently past fifty, desired to be taken for not more than forty, bent forwards from the carriage door, on the panels of which were emblazoned the armorial bearings of a baron, and directed his groom to inquire at the porter's lodge whether the Count of Monte Cristo resided there, and if he were within.

While waiting, the occupant of the carriage surveyed the house, the garden as far as he could distinguish it, and the livery of servants who passed to and fro, with an attention so close as to be somewhat impertinent. His glance was keen but showed cunning rather than intelligence; his lips were straight, and so thin that, as they closed, they were drawn in over the teeth; his cheek-bones were broad and projecting, a never-failing proof of audacity and craftiness; while the flatness of his forehead, and the enlargement of the back of his skull, which rose much higher than his large and coarsely shaped ears, combined to form a physiognomy anything but prepossessing, save in the eyes of such as considered that the owner of so splendid an equipage must needs be all that was admirable and enviable, more especially when they gazed on the enormous diamond that glittered in his shirt, and the red ribbon that depended from his button-hole.

The groom, in obedience to his orders, tapped at the window of the porter's lodge, saying:

"Pray, does not the Count of Monte Cristo live here?"

"His excellency does reside here," replied the concierge; "but " added he, glancing an inquiring look at Ali. Ali returned a sign in the negative.

"But what?" asked the groom.

"His excellency does not receive visitors today."

"Then here is my master's card, the Baron Danglars. You will take it to the count, and say that, although in haste to attend the Chamber, my master came out of his way to have the honor of calling upon him."

"I never speak to his excellency," replied the concierge; "the valet de chambre will carry your message."

The groom returned to the carriage.

"Well?" asked Danglars.

The man, somewhat crest-fallen by the rebuke he had received, repeated what the concierge had said.

"Bless me," murmured Baron Danglars, "this must surely be a prince instead of a count by their styling him 'excellency,' and only venturing to address him by the medium of his valet de chambre. However, it does not signify; he has a letter of credit on me, so I must see him when he requires his money."

Then, throwing himself back in his carriage, Danglars called out to his coachman, in a voice that might be heard across the road, "To the Chamber of Deputies."

Apprised in time of the visit paid him, Monte Cristo had, from behind the blinds of his pavilion, as minutely observed the baron, by means of an excellent lorgnette, as Danglars himself had scrutinized the house, garden, and servants.

"That fellow has a decidedly bad countenance," said the count in a tone of disgust, as he shut up his glass into its ivory case. "How comes it that all do not retreat in aversion at sight of that flat, receding, serpent-like forehead, round, vulture-shaped head, and sharp-hooked nose, like the beak of a buzzard? Ali," cried he, striking at the same time on the brazen gong. Ali appeared. "Summon Bertuccio," said the count. Almost immediately Bertuccio entered the apartment.

"Did your excellency desire to see me?" inquired he.

"I did," replied the count. "You no doubt observed the horses standing a few minutes since at the door?"

"Certainly, your excellency. I noticed them for their remarkable beauty."

"Then how comes it," said Monte Cristo with a frown, "that, when I desired you to purchase for me the finest pair of horses to be found in Paris, there is another pair, fully as fine as mine, not in my stables?"

At the look of displeasure, added to the angry tone in which the count spoke, Ali turned pale and held down his head.

"It is not your fault, my good Ali," said the count in the Arabic language, and with a gentleness none would have thought him capable of showing, either in voice or face "it is not your fault. You do not understand the points of English horses."

The countenance of poor Ali recovered its serenity.

"Permit me to assure your excellency," said Bertuccio, "that the horses you speak of were not to be sold when I purchased yours."

Monte Cristo shrugged his shoulders. "It seems, sir steward," said he, "that you have yet to learn that all things are to be sold to such as care to pay the price."

"His excellency is not, perhaps, aware that M. Danglars gave 16,000 francs for his horses?"

"Very well. Then offer him double that sum; a banker never loses an opportunity of doubling his capital."

"Is your excellency really in earnest?" inquired the steward.

Monte Cristo regarded the person who durst presume to doubt his words with the look of one equally surprised and displeased.

"I have to pay a visit this evening," replied he. "I desire that these horses, with completely new harness, may be at the door with my carriage."

Bertuccio bowed, and was about to retire; but when he reached the door, he paused, and then said, "At what o'clock does your excellency wish the carriage and horses to be ready?"

"At five o'clock," replied the count.

"I beg your excellency's pardon," interposed the steward in a deprecating manner, "for venturing to observe that it is already two o'clock."

"I am perfectly aware of that fact," answered Monte Cristo calmly. Then, turning towards Ali, he said, "Let all the horses in my stables be led before the windows of your young lady, that she may select those she prefers for her carriage. Request her also to oblige me by saying whether it is her pleasure to dine with me; if so, let dinner be served in her apartments.

Now, leave me, and desire my valet de chambre to come hither."

Scarcely had Ali disappeared when the valet entered the chamber.

"Monsieur Baptistin," said the count, "you have been in my service one year, the time I generally give myself to judge of the merits or demerits of those about me. You suit me very well."

Baptistin bowed low.

"It only remains for me to know whether I also suit you?"

"Oh, your excellency!" exclaimed Baptistin eagerly.

"Listen, if you please, till I have finished speaking," replied Monte Cristo. "You receive 1,500 francs per annum for your services here more than many a brave subaltern, who continually risks his life for his country, obtains. You live in a manner far superior to many clerks who work ten times harder than you do for their money. Then, though yourself a servant, you have other servants to wait upon you, take care of your clothes, and see that your linen is duly prepared for you. Again, you make a profit upon each article you purchase for my toilet, amounting in the course of a year to a sum equalling your wages."

"Nay, indeed, your excellency."

"I am not condemning you for this, Monsieur Baptistin; but let your profits end here. It would be long indeed ere you would find so lucrative a post as that you have now the good fortune to fill. I neither ill-use nor ill-treat my servants by word or action. An error I readily forgive, but wilful negligence or forgetfulness, never. My commands are ordinarily short, clear, and precise; and I would rather be obliged to repeat my words twice, or even three times, than they should be misunderstood. I am rich enough to know whatever I desire to know, and I can promise you I am not wanting in curiosity. If, then, I should learn that you had taken upon yourself to speak of me to anyone favorably or unfavorably, to comment on my actions, or watch my conduct, that very instant you would quit my service. You may now retire. I never caution my servants a second time remember that."

Baptistin bowed, and was proceeding towards the door.

"I forgot to mention to you," said the count, "that I lay yearly aside a certain sum for each servant in my establishment; those whom I am compelled to dismiss lose (as a matter of course) all participation in this money, while their portion goes to the fund accumulating for those domestics who remain with me, and among whom it will be divided at my death. You have been in my service a year, your fund has already begun to accumulate let it continue to do so."

This address, delivered in the presence of Ali, who, not understanding one word of the language in which it was spoken, stood wholly unmoved, produced an effect on M. Baptistin only to be conceived by such as have occasion to study the character and disposition of French domestics.

"I assure your excellency," said he, "that at least it shall be my study to merit your approbation in all things, and I will take M. Ali as my model."

"By no means," replied the count in the most frigid tones; "Ali has many faults mixed with most excellent qualities. He cannot possibly serve you as a pattern for your conduct, not being, as you are, a paid servant, but a mere slave a dog, who, should he fail in his duty towards me, I should not discharge from my service, but kill."

Baptistin opened his eyes with astonishment.

"You seem incredulous," said Monte Cristo, who repeated to Ali in the Arabic language what he had just been saying to Baptistin in French.

The Nubian smiled assentingly to his master's words, then, kneeling on one knee, respectfully kissed the hand of the count. This corroboration of the lesson he had just received put the finishing stroke to the wonder and stupefaction of M. Baptistin. The count then motioned the valet de chambre to retire, and to Ali to follow to his study, where they conversed long and earnestly together. As the hand of the clock pointed to five the count struck thrice upon his gong. When Ali was wanted one stroke was given, two summoned Baptistin, and three Bertuccio. The steward entered.

"My horses," said Monte Cristo.

"They are at the door harnessed to the carriage as your excellency desired. Does your excellency wish me to accompany him?"

"No, the coachman, Ali, and Baptistin will go."

The count descended to the door of his mansion, and beheld his carriage drawn by the very pair of horses he had so much admired in the morning as the property of Danglars. As he passed them he said:

"They are extremely handsome certainly, and you have done well to purchase them, although you were somewhat remiss not to have procured them sooner."

"Indeed, your excellency, I had very considerable difficulty in obtaining them, and, as it is, they have cost an enormous price."

"Does the sum you gave for them make the animals less beautiful," inquired the count, shrugging his shoulders.

"Nay, if your excellency is satisfied, it is all that I could wish. Whither does your excellency desire to be driven?"

"To the residence of Baron Danglars, Rue de la Chaussée d'Antin."

This conversation had passed as they stood upon the terrace, from which a flight of stone steps led to the carriage-drive. As Bertuccio, with a respectful bow, was moving away, the count called him back.

"I have another commission for you, M. Bertuccio," said he; "I am desirous of having an estate by the seaside in Normandy for instance, between Le Havre and Boulogne. You see I give you a wide range. It will be absolutely necessary that the place you may select have a small harbor, creek, or bay, into which my corvette can enter and remain at anchor. She draws only fifteen feet. She must be kept in constant readiness to sail immediately I think proper to give the signal. Make the requisite inquiries for a place of this description, and when you have met with an eligible spot, visit it, and if it possess the advantages desired, purchase it at once in your own name. The corvette must now, I think, be on her way to Fécamp, must she not?"

"Certainly, your excellency; I saw her put to sea the same evening we quitted Marseilles."

"And the yacht."

"Was ordered to remain at Martigues."

"'Tis well. I wish you to write from time to time to the captains in charge of the two vessels so as to keep them on the alert."

"And the steamboat?"

"She is at Châlons?"

"Yes."

"The same orders for her as for the two sailing vessels."

"Very good."

"When you have purchased the estate I desire, I want constant relays of horses at ten leagues apart along the northern and southern road."

"Your excellency may depend upon me."

The Count made a gesture of satisfaction, descended the terrace steps, and sprang into his carriage, which was whirled along swiftly to the banker's house.

Danglars was engaged at that moment, presiding over a railroad committee. But the meeting was nearly concluded when the name of his visitor was announced. As the count's title sounded on his ear he rose, and addressing his colleagues, who were members of one or the other Chamber, he said:

"Gentlemen, pardon me for leaving you so abruptly; but a most ridiculous circumstance has occurred, which is this, Thomson & French, the Roman bankers, have sent to me a certain person calling himself the Count of Monte Cristo, and have given him an unlimited credit with me. I confess this is the drollest thing I have ever met with in the course of my extensive foreign transactions, and you may readily suppose it has greatly roused my curiosity. I took the trouble this morning to call on the pretended count if he were a real count he wouldn't be so rich. But, would you believe it, 'He was not receiving.' So the master of Monte Cristo gives himself airs befitting a great millionaire or a capricious beauty. I made inquiries, and found that the house in the Champs-Élysées is his own property, and certainly it was very decently kept up. But," pursued Danglars with one of his sinister smiles, "an order for unlimited credit calls for something like caution on the part of the banker to whom that order is given. I am very anxious to see this man. I suspect a hoax is intended, but the instigators of it little knew whom they had to deal with. 'They laugh best who laugh last!'"

Having delivered himself of this pompous address, uttered with a degree of energy that left the baron almost out of breath, he bowed to the assembled party and withdrew to his drawing-room, whose sumptuous furnishings of white and gold had caused a great sensation in the Chaussée d'Antin. It was to this apartment he had desired his guest to be shown, with the purpose of overwhelming him at the sight of so much luxury. He found the count standing before some copies of Albano and Fattore that had been passed off to the banker as originals; but which, mere copies as they were, seemed to feel their degradation in being brought into juxtaposition with the gaudy colors that covered the ceiling.

The count turned round as he heard the entrance of Danglars into the room. With a slight inclination of the head, Danglars signed to the count to be seated, pointing significantly to a gilded armchair, covered with white satin embroidered with gold. The count sat down.

"I have the honor, I presume, of addressing M. de Monte Cristo."

The count bowed.

"And I of speaking to Baron Danglars, chevalier of the Legion of Honor, and member of the Chamber of Deputies?"

Monte Cristo repeated all the titles he had read on the baron's card.

Danglars felt the irony and compressed his lips.

"You will, I trust, excuse me, monsieur, for not calling you by your title when I first addressed you," he said, "but you are aware that we are living under a popular form of government, and that I am myself a representative of the liberties of the people."

"So much so," replied Monte Cristo, "that while you call yourself baron you are not willing to call anybody else count."

"Upon my word, monsieur," said Danglars with affected carelessness, "I attach no sort of value to such empty distinctions; but the fact is, I was made baron, and also chevalier of the Legion of Honor, in return for services rendered, but "

"But you have discarded your titles after the example set you by Messrs. de Montmorency and Lafayette? That was a noble example to follow, monsieur."

"Why," replied Danglars, "not entirely so; with the servants, you understand."

"I see; to your domestics you are 'my lord,' the journalists style you 'monsieur,' while your constituents call you 'citizen.' These are distinctions very suitable under a constitutional government. I understand perfectly."

Again Danglars bit his lips; he saw that he was no match for Monte Cristo in an argument of this sort, and he therefore hastened to turn to subjects more congenial.

"Permit me to inform you, Count," said he, bowing, "that I have received a letter of advice from Thomson & French, of Rome."

"I am glad to hear it, baron, for I must claim the privilege of addressing you after the manner of your servants. I have acquired the bad habit of calling persons by their titles from living in a country where barons are still barons by right of birth. But as regards the letter of advice, I am charmed to find that it has reached you; that will spare me the troublesome and disagreeable task of coming to you for money myself. You have received a regular letter of advice?"

"Yes," said Danglars, "but I confess I didn't quite comprehend its meaning."

"Indeed?"

"And for that reason I did myself the honor of calling upon you, in order to beg for an explanation."

"Go on, monsieur. Here I am, ready to give you any explanation you desire."

"Why," said Danglars, "in the letter I believe I have it about me" here he felt in his breast-pocket "yes, here it is. Well, this letter gives the Count of Monte Cristo unlimited credit on our house."

"Well, baron, what is there difficult to understand about that?"

"Merely the term *unlimited* nothing else, certainly."

"Is not that word known in France? The people who wrote are Anglo-Germans, you know."

"Oh, as for the composition of the letter, there is nothing to be said; but as regards the competency of the document, I certainly have doubts."

"Is it possible?" asked the count, assuming all air and tone of the utmost simplicity and candor. "Is it possible that Thomson & French are not looked upon as safe and solvent bankers? Pray tell me what you think, baron, for I feel uneasy, I can assure you, having some considerable property in their hands."

"Thomson & French are perfectly solvent," replied Danglars, with an almost mocking smile; "but the word *unlimited*, in financial affairs, is so extremely vague."

"Is, in fact, unlimited," said Monte Cristo.

"Precisely what I was about to say," cried Danglars. "Now what is vague is doubtful; and it was a wise man who said, 'when in doubt, keep out.'"

"Meaning to say," rejoined Monte Cristo, "that however Thomson & French may be inclined to commit acts of imprudence and folly, the Baron Danglars is not disposed to follow their example."

"Not at all."

"Plainly enough; Messrs. Thomson & French set no bounds to their engagements while those of M. Danglars have their limits; he is a wise man, according to his own showing."

"Monsieur," replied the banker, drawing himself up with a haughty air, "the extent of my resources has never yet been questioned."

"It seems, then, reserved for me," said Monte Cristo coldly, "to be the first to do so."

"By what right, sir?"

"By right of the objections you have raised, and the explanations you have demanded, which certainly must have some motive."

Once more Danglars bit his lips. It was the second time he had been worsted, and this time on his own ground. His forced politeness sat awkwardly upon him, and approached almost to impertinence. Monte Cristo on the contrary, preserved a graceful suavity of demeanor, aided by a certain degree of simplicity he could assume at pleasure, and thus possessed the advantage.

"Well, sir," resumed Danglars, after a brief silence, "I will endeavor to make myself understood, by requesting you to inform me for what sum you propose to draw upon me?"

"Why, truly," replied Monte Cristo, determined not to lose an inch of the ground he had gained, "my reason for desiring an 'unlimited' credit was precisely because I did not know how much money I might need."

The banker thought the time had come for him to take the upper hand. So throwing himself back in his armchair, he said, with an arrogant and purse-proud air:

"Let me beg of you not to hesitate in naming your wishes; you will then be convinced that the resources of the house of Danglars, however limited, are still equal to meeting the largest demands; and were you even to require a million "

"I beg your pardon," interposed Monte Cristo.

"I said a million," replied Danglars, with the confidence of ignorance.

"But could I do with a million?" retorted the count. "My dear sir, if a trifle like that could suffice me, I should never have given myself the trouble of opening an account. A million? Excuse my smiling when you speak of a sum I am in the habit of carrying in my pocket-book or dressing-case."

And with these words Monte Cristo took from his pocket a small case containing his visiting-cards, and drew forth two orders on the treasury for 500,000 francs each, payable at sight to the bearer. A man like Danglars was wholly inaccessible to any gentler method of correction. The effect of the present revelation was stunning; he trembled and was on the verge of apoplexy. The pupils of his eyes, as he gazed at Monte Cristo dilated horribly.

"Come, come," said Monte Cristo, "confess honestly that you have not perfect confidence in Thomson & French. I understand, and foreseeing that such might be the case, I took, in spite of my ignorance of affairs, certain precautions. See, here are two similar letters to that you have yourself received; one from the house of Arstein & Eskeles of Vienna, to Baron Rothschild, the other drawn by Baring of London, upon M. Lafitte. Now, sir, you have but to say the word, and I will spare you all uneasiness by presenting my letter of credit to one or other of these two firms."

The blow had struck home, and Danglars was entirely vanquished; with a trembling hand he took the two letters from the count, who held them carelessly between finger and thumb, and proceeded to scrutinize the signatures, with a minuteness that the count might have regarded as insulting, had it not suited his present purpose to mislead the banker.

"Oh, sir," said Danglars, after he had convinced himself of the authenticity of the documents he held, and rising as if to salute the power of gold personified in the man before him, "three letters of unlimited credit! I can be no longer mistrustful, but you must pardon me, my dear count, for confessing to some degree of astonishment."

"Nay," answered Monte Cristo, with the most gentlemanly air, "'tis not for such trifling sums as these that your banking house is to be incommoded. Then, you can let me have some money, can you not?"

"Whatever you say, my dear count; I am at your orders."

"Why," replied Monte Cristo, "since we mutually understand each other for such I presume is the case?" Danglars bowed assentingly. "You are quite sure that not a lurking doubt or suspicion lingers in your mind?"

"Oh, my dear count," exclaimed Danglars, "I never for an instant entertained such a feeling towards you."

"No, you merely wished to be convinced, nothing more; but now that we have come to so clear an understanding, and that all distrust and suspicion are laid at rest, we may as well fix a sum as the probable expenditure of the first year, suppose we say six millions to "

"Six millions!" gasped Danglars "so be it."

"Then, if I should require more," continued Monte Cristo in a careless manner, "why, of course, I should draw upon you; but my present intention is not to remain in France more than a year, and during that period I scarcely think I shall exceed the sum I mentioned. However, we shall see. Be kind enough, then, to send me 500,000 francs tomorrow. I shall be at home till midday, or if not, I will leave a receipt with my steward."

"The money you desire shall be at your house by ten o'clock tomorrow morning, my dear count," replied Danglars. "How would you like to have it? in gold, silver, or notes?"

"Half in gold, and the other half in bank-notes, if you please," said the count, rising from his seat.

"I must confess to you, count," said Danglars, "that I have hitherto imagined myself acquainted with the degree of all the great fortunes of Europe, and still wealth such as yours has been wholly unknown to me. May I presume to ask whether you have long possessed it?"

"It has been in the family a very long while," returned Monte Cristo, "a sort of treasure expressly forbidden to be touched for a certain period of years, during which the accumulated interest has doubled the capital. The period appointed by the testator for the disposal of these riches occurred only a short time ago, and they have only been employed by me within the last few years. Your ignorance on the subject, therefore, is easily accounted for. However, you will be better informed as to me and my possessions ere long."

And the count, while pronouncing these latter words, accompanied them with one of those ghastly smiles that used to strike terror into poor Franz d'Épinay.

"With your tastes, and means of gratifying them," continued Danglars, "you will exhibit a splendor that must effectually put us poor miserable millionaires quite in the shade. If I mistake not you are an admirer of paintings, at least I judged so from the attention you appeared to be bestowing on mine when I entered the room. If you will permit me, I shall be happy to show you my picture gallery, composed entirely of works by the ancient masters warranted as such. Not a modern picture among them. I cannot endure the modern school of painting."

"You are perfectly right in objecting to them, for this one great fault that they have not yet had time to become old."

"Or will you allow me to show you several fine statues by Thorwaldsen, Bartoloni, and Canova? all foreign artists, for, as you may perceive, I think but very indifferently of our French sculptors."

"You have a right to be unjust to them, monsieur; they are your compatriots."

"But all this may come later, when we shall be better known to each other. For the present, I will confine myself (if perfectly agreeable to you) to introducing you to the Baroness Danglars excuse my impatience, my dear count, but a client like you is almost like a member of the family."

Monte Cristo bowed, in sign that he accepted the proffered honor; Danglars rang and was answered by a servant in a showy livery.

"Is the baroness at home?" inquired Danglars.

"Yes, my lord," answered the man.

"And alone?"

"No, my lord, madame has visitors."

"Have you any objection to meet any persons who may be with madame, or do you desire to preserve a strict *incognito*?"

"No, indeed," replied Monte Cristo with a smile, "I do not arrogate to myself the right of so doing."

"And who is with madame? M. Debray?" inquired Danglars, with an air of indulgence and good-nature that made Monte Cristo smile, acquainted as he was with the secrets of the banker's domestic life.

"Yes, my lord," replied the servant, "M. Debray is with madame."

Danglars nodded his head; then, turning to Monte Cristo, said, "M. Lucien Debray is an old friend of ours, and private secretary to the Minister of the Interior. As for my wife, I must tell you, she lowered herself by marrying me, for she belongs to one of the most ancient families in France. Her maiden name was De Servières, and her first husband was Colonel the Marquis of Nargonne."

"I have not the honor of knowing Madame Danglars; but I have already met M. Lucien Debray."

"Ah, indeed?" said Danglars; "and where was that?"

"At the house of M. de Morcerf."

"Ah! you are acquainted with the young viscount, are you?"

"We were together a good deal during the Carnival at Rome."

"True, true," cried Danglars. "Let me see; have I not heard talk of some strange adventure with bandits or thieves hid in ruins, and of his having had a miraculous escape? I forget how, but I know he used to amuse my wife and daughter by telling them about it after his return from Italy."

"Her ladyship is waiting to receive you, gentlemen," said the servant, who had gone to inquire the pleasure of his mistress.

"With your permission," said Danglars, bowing, "I will precede you, to show you the way."

"By all means," replied Monte Cristo; "I follow you."

Chapter 20

The Dappled Grays

The baron, followed by the count, traversed a long series of apartments, in which the prevailing characteristics were heavy magnificence and the gaudiness of ostentatious wealth, until he reached the boudoir of Madame Danglars a small octagonal-shaped room, hung with pink satin, covered with white Indian muslin. The chairs were of ancient workmanship and materials; over the doors were painted sketches of shepherds and shepherdesses, after the style and manner of Boucher; and at each side pretty medallions in crayons, harmonizing well with the furnishings of this charming apartment, the only one throughout the great mansion in which any distinctive taste prevailed. The truth was, it had been entirely overlooked in the plan arranged and followed out by M. Danglars and his architect, who had been selected to aid the baron in the great work of improvement solely because he was the most fashionable and celebrated decorator of the day. The decorations of the boudoir had then been left entirely to Madame Danglars and Lucien Debray. M. Danglars, however, while possessing a great admiration for the antique, as it was understood during the time of the Directory, entertained the most sovereign contempt for the simple elegance of his wife's favorite sitting-room, where, by the way, he was never permitted to intrude, unless, indeed, he excused his own appearance by ushering in some more agreeable visitor than himself; and even then he had rather the air and manner of a person who was himself introduced, than that of being the presenter of another, his reception being cordial or frigid, in proportion as the person who accompanied him chanced to please or displease the baroness.

Madame Danglars (who, although past the first bloom of youth, was still strikingly handsome) was now seated at the piano, a most elaborate piece of cabinet and inlaid work, while Lucien Debray, standing before a small work-table, was turning over the pages of an album.

Lucien had found time, preparatory to the count's arrival, to relate many particulars respecting him to Madame Danglars.

It will be remembered that Monte Cristo had made a lively impression on the minds of all the party assembled at the breakfast given by Albert de Morcerf; and although Debray was not in the habit of yielding to such feelings, he had never been able to shake off the powerful influence excited in his mind by the impressive look and manner of the count, consequently the description given by Lucien to the baroness bore the highly-colored tinge of his own heated imagination. Already excited by the wonderful stories related of the count by de Morcerf, it is no wonder that Madame Danglars eagerly listened to, and fully credited, all the additional circumstances detailed by Debray. This posing at the piano and over the album was only a little ruse adopted by way of precaution. A most gracious welcome and unusual smile were bestowed on M. Danglars; the count, in return for his gentlemanly bow, received a formal though graceful courtesy, while Lucien exchanged with the count a sort of distant recognition, and with Danglars a free and easy nod.

"Baroness," said Danglars, "give me leave to present to you the Count of Monte Cristo, who has been most warmly recommended to me by my correspondents at Rome. I need but mention one fact to make all the ladies in Paris court his notice, and that is, that he has come to take up his abode in Paris for a year, during which brief period he proposes to spend six millions of money. That means balls, dinners, and lawn parties without end, in all of which I trust the count will remember us, as he may depend upon it we shall him, in our own humble entertainments."

In spite of the gross flattery and coarseness of this address, Madame Danglars could not forbear gazing with considerable interest on a man capable of expending six millions in twelve months, and who had selected Paris for the scene of his princely extravagance.

"And when did you arrive here?" inquired she.

"Yesterday morning, madame."

"Coming, as usual, I presume, from the extreme end of the

globe? Pardon me at least, such I have heard is your custom."

"Nay, madame. This time I have merely come from Cadiz."

"You have selected a most unfavorable moment for your first visit. Paris is a horrible place in summer. Balls, parties, and *fêtes* are over; the Italian opera is in London; the French opera everywhere except in Paris. As for the Théatre Français, you know, of course, that it is nowhere. The only amusements left us are the indifferent races at the Champ-de-Mars and Satory. Do you propose entering any horses at either of these races, count?"

"I shall do whatever they do at Paris, madame, if I have the good fortune to find someone who will initiate me into the prevalent ideas of amusement."

"Are you fond of horses, count?"

"I have passed a considerable part of my life in the East, madame, and you are doubtless aware that the Orientals value only two things the fine breeding of their horses and the beauty of their women."

"Nay, count," said the baroness, "it would have been somewhat more gallant to have placed the ladies first."

"You see, madame, how rightly I spoke when I said I required a preceptor to guide me in all my sayings and doings here."

At this instant the favorite attendant of Madame Danglars entered the boudoir; approaching her mistress, she spoke some words in an undertone. Madame Danglars turned very pale, then exclaimed:

"I cannot believe it; the thing is impossible."

"I assure you, madame," replied the woman, "it is as I have said."

Turning impatiently towards her husband, Madame Danglars demanded, "Is this true?"

"Is what true, madame?" inquired Danglars, visibly agitated.

"What my maid tells me."

"But what does she tell you?"

"That when my coachman was about to harness the horses to my carriage, he discovered that they had been removed from the stables without his knowledge. I desire to know what is the meaning of this?"

"Be kind enough, madame, to listen to me," said Danglars.

"Oh, yes; I will listen, monsieur, for I am most curious to hear what explanation you will give. These two gentlemen shall decide between us; but, first, I will state the case to them. Gentlemen," continued the baroness, "among the ten horses in the stables of Baron Danglars, are two that belong exclusively to me a pair of the handsomest and most spirited creatures to be found in Paris. But to you, at least, M. Debray, I need not give a further description, because to you my beautiful pair of dappled grays were well known. Well, I had promised Madame de Villefort the loan of my carriage to drive tomorrow to the Bois; but when my coachman goes to fetch the grays from the stables they are gone positively gone. No doubt M. Danglars has sacrificed them to the selfish consideration of gaining some thousands of paltry francs. Oh, what a detestable crew they are, these mercenary speculators!"

"Madame," replied Danglars, "the horses were not sufficiently quiet for you; they were scarcely four years old, and they made me extremely uneasy on your account."

"Nonsense," retorted the baroness; "you could not have entertained any alarm on the subject, because you are perfectly well aware that I have had for a month in my service the very best coachman in Paris. But, perhaps, you have disposed of the coachman as well as the horses?"

"My dear love, pray do not say any more about them, and I promise you another pair exactly like them in appearance, only more quiet and steady."

The baroness shrugged her shoulders with an air of ineffable contempt, while her husband, affecting not to observe this unconjugal gesture, turned towards Monte Cristo and said, "Upon my word, count, I am quite sorry not to have met you sooner. You are setting up an establishment, of course?"

"Why, yes," replied the count.

"I should have liked to have made you the offer of these horses.

I have almost given them away, as it is; but, as I before said, I was anxious to get rid of them upon any terms. They were only fit for a young man."

"I am much obliged by your kind intentions towards me," said Monte Cristo; "but this morning I purchased a very excellent pair of carriage-horses, and I do not think they were dear. There they are. Come, M. Debray, you are a connoisseur, I believe, let me have your opinion upon them."

As Debray walked towards the window, Danglars approached his wife.

"I could not tell you before others," said he in a low tone, "the reason of my parting with the horses; but a most enormous price was offered me this morning for them. Some madman or fool, bent upon ruining himself as fast as he can, actually sent his steward to me to purchase them at any cost; and the fact is, I have gained 16,000 francs by the sale of them. Come, don't look so angry, and you shall have 4,000 francs of the money to do what you like with, and Eugénie shall have 2,000. There, what do you think now of the affair? Wasn't I right to part with the horses?"

Madame Danglars surveyed her husband with a look of withering contempt.

"Great heavens?" suddenly exclaimed Debray.

"What is it?" asked the baroness.

"I cannot be mistaken; there are your horses! The very animals we were speaking of, harnessed to the count's carriage!"

"My dappled grays?" demanded the baroness, springing to the window. "'Tis indeed they!" said she.

Danglars looked absolutely stupefied.

"How very singular," cried Monte Cristo with well-feigned astonishment.

"I cannot believe it," murmured the banker. Madame Danglars whispered a few words in the ear of Debray, who approached Monte Cristo, saying, "The baroness wishes to know what you paid her husband for the horses."

"I scarcely know," replied the count; "it was a little surprise prepared for me by my steward, and cost me well, somewhere about 30,000 francs."

Debray conveyed the count's reply to the baroness. Poor Danglars looked so crest-fallen and discomfited that Monte Cristo assumed a pitying air towards him.

"See," said the count, "how very ungrateful women are. Your kind attention, in providing for the safety of the baroness by disposing of the horses, does not seem to have made the least impression on her. But so it is; a woman will often, from mere wilfulness, prefer that which is dangerous to that which is safe. Therefore, in my opinion, my dear baron, the best and easiest way is to leave them to their fancies, and allow them to act as they please, and then, if any mischief follows, why, at least, they have no one to blame but themselves."

Danglars made no reply; he was occupied in anticipations of the coming scene between himself and the baroness, whose frowning brow, like that of Olympic Jove, predicted a storm. Debray, who perceived the gathering clouds, and felt no desire to witness the explosion of Madame Danglars' rage, suddenly recollected an appointment, which compelled him to take his leave; while Monte Cristo, unwilling by prolonging his stay to destroy the advantages he hoped to obtain, made a farewell bow and departed, leaving Danglars to endure the angry reproaches of his wife.

"Excellent," murmured Monte Cristo to himself, as he came away. "All has gone according to my wishes. The domestic peace of this family is henceforth in my hands. Now, then, to play another master-stroke, by which I shall gain the heart of both husband and wife delightful! Still," added he, "amid all this, I have not yet been presented to Mademoiselle Eugénie Danglars, whose acquaintance I should have been glad to make. But," he went on with his peculiar smile, "I am here in Paris, and have plenty of time before me by and by will do for that."

With these reflections he entered his carriage and returned home. Two hours afterwards, Madame Danglars received a most flattering epistle from the count, in which he entreated her to receive back her favorite "dappled grays," protesting that he could not endure the idea of making his entry into the Parisian world of fashion with the knowledge that his splendid equipage had been obtained at the price of a lovely woman's regrets. The horses were sent back wearing the same harness she had seen on them in the morning; only, by the count's orders, in the centre of each rosette that adorned either side of their heads, had been fastened a large diamond.

To Danglars Monte Cristo also wrote, requesting him to excuse the whimsical gift of a capricious millionaire, and to beg the baroness to pardon the Eastern fashion adopted in the return of the horses.

During the evening, Monte Cristo quitted Paris for Auteuil, accompanied by Ali. The following day, about three o'clock, a single blow struck on the gong summoned Ali to the presence of the count.

"Ali," observed his master, as the Nubian entered the chamber, "you have frequently explained to me how more than commonly skilful you are in throwing the lasso, have you not?"

Ali drew himself up proudly, and then returned a sign in the affirmative.

"I thought I did not mistake. With your lasso you could stop an ox?"

Again Ali repeated his affirmative gesture.

"Or a tiger?"

Ali bowed his head in token of assent.

"A lion even?"

Ali sprung forwards, imitating the action of one throwing the lasso, then of a strangled lion.

"I understand," said Monte Cristo; "you wish to tell me you have hunted the lion?"

Ali smiled with triumphant pride as he signified that he had indeed both chased and captured many lions.

"But do you believe you could arrest the progress of two horses rushing forwards with ungovernable fury?"

The Nubian smiled.

"It is well," said Monte Cristo. "Then listen to me. Ere long a carriage will dash past here, drawn by the pair of dappled gray horses you saw me with yesterday; now, at the risk of your own life, you must manage to stop those horses before my door."

Ali descended to the street, and marked a straight line on the pavement immediately at the entrance of the house, and then pointed out the line he had traced to the count, who was watching him. The count patted him gently on the shoulder, his usual mode of praising Ali, who, pleased and gratified with the commission assigned him, walked calmly towards a projecting stone forming the angle of the street and house, and, seating himself thereon, began to smoke his chibouque, while Monte Cristo re-entered his dwelling, perfectly assured of the success of his plan.

Still, as five o'clock approached, and the carriage was momentarily expected by the count, the indication of more than common impatience and uneasiness might be observed in his manner. He stationed himself in a room commanding a view of the street, pacing the chamber with restless steps, stopping merely to listen from time to time for the sound of approaching wheels, then to cast an anxious glance on Ali; but the regularity with which the Nubian puffed forth the smoke of his chibouque proved that he at least was wholly absorbed in the enjoyment of his favorite occupation.

Suddenly a distant sound of rapidly advancing wheels was heard, and almost immediately a carriage appeared, drawn by a pair of wild, ungovernable horses, while the terrified coachman strove in vain to restrain their furious speed.

In the vehicle was a young woman and a child of about seven or eight clasped in each other's arms. Terror seemed to have deprived them even of the power of uttering a cry. The carriage creaked and rattled as it flew over the rough stones, and the slightest obstacle under the wheels would have caused disaster; but it kept on in the middle of the road, and those who saw it pass uttered cries of terror.

Ali suddenly cast aside his chibouque, drew the lasso from his pocket, threw it so skilfully as to catch the forelegs of the near horse in its triple fold, and suffered himself to be dragged on for a few steps by the violence of the shock, then the animal fell over on the pole, which snapped, and therefore prevented the other horse from pursuing its way. Gladly availing himself of this opportunity, the coachman leaped from his box; but Ali had promptly seized the nostrils of the second horse, and held them in his iron grasp, till the beast, snorting with pain, sunk beside his companion.

All this was achieved in much less time than is occupied in the recital. The brief space had, however, been sufficient for a man, followed by a number of servants, to rush from the house before which the accident had occurred, and, as the coachman opened the door of the carriage, to take from it a lady who was convulsively grasping the cushions with one hand, while with the other she pressed to her bosom the young boy, who had lost consciousness. Monte Cristo carried them both to the salon, and deposited them on a sofa.

"Compose yourself, madame," said he; "all danger is over." The woman looked up at these words, and, with a glance far more expressive than any entreaties could have been, pointed to her child, who still continued insensible. "I understand the nature of your alarms, madame," said the count, carefully examining the child, "but I assure you there is not the slightest occasion for uneasiness; your little charge has not received the least injury; his insensibility is merely the effects of terror, and will soon pass."

"Are you quite sure you do not say so to tranquillize my fears? See how deadly pale he is! My child, my darling Edward; speak to your mother open your dear eyes and look on me once again! Oh, sir, in pity send for a physician; my whole fortune shall not be thought too much for the recovery of my boy."

With a calm smile and a gentle wave of the hand, Monte Cristo signed to the distracted mother to lay aside her apprehensions; then, opening a casket that stood near, he drew forth a phial of Bohemian glass incrusted with gold, containing a liquid of the color of blood, of which he let fall a single drop on the child's lips. Scarcely had it reached them, ere the boy, though still pale as marble, opened his eyes, and eagerly gazed around him. At this, the delight of the mother was almost frantic.

"Where am I?" exclaimed she; "and to whom am I indebted for so happy a termination to my late dreadful alarm?"

"Madame," answered the count, "you are under the roof of one who esteems himself most fortunate in having been able to save you from a further continuance of your sufferings."

"My wretched curiosity has brought all this about," pursued the lady. "All Paris rung with the praises of Madame Danglars' beautiful horses, and I had the folly to desire to know whether they really merited the high praise given to them."

"Is it possible," exclaimed the count with well-feigned astonishment, "that these horses belong to the baroness?"

"They do, indeed. May I inquire if you are acquainted with Madame Danglars?"

"I have that honor; and my happiness at your escape from the danger that threatened you is redoubled by the consciousness that I have been the unwilling and the unintentional cause of all the peril you have incurred. I yesterday purchased these horses of the baron; but as the baroness evidently regretted parting with them, I ventured to send them back to her, with a request that she would gratify me by accepting them from my hands."

"You are, then, doubtless, the Count of Monte Cristo, of whom Hermine has talked to me so much?"

"You have rightly guessed, madame," replied the count.

"And I am Madame Héloïse de Villefort."

The count bowed with the air of a person who hears a name for the first time.

"How grateful will M. de Villefort be for all your goodness; how thankfully will he acknowledge that to you alone he owes the existence of his wife and child! Most certainly, but for the prompt assistance of your intrepid servant, this dear child and myself must both have perished."

"Indeed, I still shudder at the fearful danger you were placed in."

"I trust you will allow me to recompense worthily the devotion of your man."

"I beseech you, madame," replied Monte Cristo "not to spoil Ali, either by too great praise or rewards. I cannot allow him to acquire the habit of expecting to be recompensed for every trifling service he may render. Ali is my slave, and in saving your life he was but discharging his duty to me."

"Nay," interposed Madame de Villefort, on whom the authoritative style adopted by the count made a deep impression, "nay, but consider that to preserve my life he has risked his own."

"His life, madame, belongs not to him; it is mine, in return for my having myself saved him from death."

Madame de Villefort made no further reply; her mind was utterly absorbed in the contemplation of the person who, from the first instant she saw him, had made so powerful an impression on her.

During the evident preoccupation of Madame de Villefort, Monte Cristo scrutinized the features and appearance of the boy she kept folded in her arms, lavishing on him the most tender endearments. The child was small for his age, and unnaturally pale. A mass of straight black hair, defying all attempts to train or curl it, fell over his projecting forehead, and hung down to his shoulders, giving increased vivacity to eyes already sparkling with a youthful love of mischief and fondness for every forbidden enjoyment. His mouth was large, and the lips, which had not yet regained their color, were particularly thin; in fact, the deep and crafty look, giving a predominant expression to the child's face, belonged rather to a boy of twelve or fourteen than to one so young. His first movement was to free himself by a violent push from the encircling arms of his mother, and to rush forward to the casket from whence the count had taken the phial of elixir; then, without asking permission of anyone, he proceeded, in all the wilfulness of a spoiled child unaccustomed to restrain either whims or caprices, to pull the corks out of all the bottles.

"Touch nothing, my little friend," cried the count eagerly; "some of those liquids are not only dangerous to taste, but even to inhale."

Madame de Villefort became very pale, and, seizing her son's arm, drew him anxiously toward her; but, once satisfied of his safety, she also cast a brief but expressive glance on the casket, which was not lost upon the count. At this moment Ali entered. At sight of him Madame de Villefort uttered an expression of pleasure, and, holding the child still closer towards her, she said:

"Edward, dearest, do you see that good man? He has shown very great courage and resolution, for he exposed his own life to stop the horses that were running away with us, and would certainly have dashed the carriage to pieces. Thank him, then, my child, in your very best manner; for, had he not come to our aid, neither you nor I would have been alive to speak our thanks."

The child stuck out his lips and turned away his head in a disdainful manner, saying, "He's too ugly."

The count smiled as if the child bade fair to realize his hopes, while Madame de Villefort reprimanded her son with a gentleness and moderation very far from conveying the least idea of a fault having been committed.

"This lady," said the Count, speaking to Ali in the Arabic language, "is desirous that her son should thank you for saving both their lives; but the boy refuses, saying you are too ugly."

Ali turned his intelligent countenance towards the boy, on whom he gazed without any apparent emotion; but the spasmodic working of the nostrils showed to the practiced eye of Monte Cristo that the Arab had been wounded to the heart.

"Will you permit me to inquire," said Madame de Villefort, as she arose to take her leave, "whether you usually reside here?" "No, I do not," replied Monte Cristo; "it is a small place I have purchased quite lately. My place of abode is No. 30, Avenue des Champs-Élysées; but I see you have quite recovered from your fright, and are, no doubt, desirous of returning home. Anticipating your wishes, I have desired the same horses you came with to be put to one of my carriages, and Ali, he whom you think so very ugly," continued he, addressing the boy with a smiling air, "will have the honor of driving you home, while your coachman remains here to attend to the necessary repairs of your calash. As soon as that important business is concluded, I will have a pair of my own horses harnessed to convey it direct to Madame Danglars."

"I dare not return with those dreadful horses," said Madame de Villefort.

"You will see," replied Monte Cristo, "that they will be as different as possible in the hands of Ali. With him they will be gentle and docile as lambs."

Ali had, indeed, given proof of this; for, approaching the animals, who had been got upon their legs with considerable difficulty, he rubbed their foreheads and nostrils with a sponge soaked in aromatic vinegar, and wiped off the sweat and foam that covered their mouths. Then, commencing a loud whistling noise, he rubbed them well all over their bodies for several minutes; then, undisturbed by the noisy crowd collected round the broken carriage, Ali quietly harnessed the pacified animals to the count's chariot, took the reins in his hands, and mounted the box, when to the utter astonishment of those who had witnessed the ungovernable spirit and maddened speed of the same horses, he was actually compelled to apply his whip in no very gentle manner before he could induce them to start; and even then all that could be obtained from the celebrated "dappled grays," now changed into a couple of dull, sluggish, stupid brutes, was a slow, pottering pace, kept up with so much difficulty that Madame de Villefort was more than two hours returning to her residence in the

Faubourg Saint-Honoré.

Scarcely had the first congratulations upon her marvellous escape been gone through when she wrote the following letter to Madame Danglars:

"Dear Hermine, I have just had a wonderful escape from the most imminent danger, and I owe my safety to the very Count of Monte Cristo we were talking about yesterday, but whom I little expected to see today. I remember how unmercifully I laughed at what I considered your eulogistic and exaggerated praises of him; but I have now ample cause to admit that your enthusiastic description of this wonderful man fell far short of his merits. Your horses got as far as Ranelagh, when they darted forward like mad things, and galloped away at so fearful a rate, that there seemed no other prospect for myself and my poor Edward but that of being dashed to pieces against the first object that impeded their progress, when a strange-looking man, an Arab, a negro, or a Nubian, at least a black of some nation or other at a signal from the count, whose domestic he is, suddenly seized and stopped the infuriated animals, even at the risk of being trampled to death himself; and certainly he must have had a most wonderful escape. The count then hastened to us, and took us into his house, where he speedily recalled my poor Edward to life. He sent us home in his own carriage. Yours will be returned to you tomorrow. You will find your horses in bad condition, from the results of this accident; they seem thoroughly stupefied, as if sulky and vexed at having been conquered by man. The count, however, has commissioned me to assure you that two or three days' rest, with plenty of barley for their sole food during that time, will bring them back to as fine, that is as terrifying, a condition as they were in yesterday.

Adieu! I cannot return you many thanks for the drive of yesterday; but, after all, I ought not to blame you for the misconduct of your horses, more especially as it procured me the pleasure of an introduction to the Count of Monte Cristo, and certainly that illustrious personage, apart from the millions he is said to be so very anxious to dispose of, seemed to me one of those curiously interesting problems I, for one, delight in solving at any risk, even if it were to necessitate another drive to the Bois behind your horses.

Edward endured the accident with miraculous courage he did not utter a single cry, but fell lifeless into my arms; nor did a tear fall from his eyes after it was over. I doubt not you will consider these praises the result of blind maternal affection, but there is a soul of iron in that delicate, fragile body. Valentine sends many affectionate remembrances to your dear Eugénie. I embrace you with all my heart.

Héloïse de Villefort.

P.S. Do pray contrive some means for me to meet the Count of Monte Cristo at your house. I must and will see him again. I have just made M. de Villefort promise to call on him, and I hope the visit will be returned.

That night the adventure at Auteuil was talked of everywhere. Albert related it to his mother; Château-Renaud recounted it at the Jockey Club, and Debray detailed it at length in the salons of the minister; even Beauchamp accorded twenty lines in his journal to the relation of the count's courage and gallantry, thereby celebrating him as the greatest hero of the day in the eyes of all the feminine members of the aristocracy. Vast was the crowd of visitors and inquiring friends who left their names at the residence of Madame de Villefort, with the design of renewing their visit at the right moment, of hearing from her lips all the interesting circumstances of this most romantic adventure.

As for M. de Villefort, he fulfilled the predictions of Héloïse to the letter, donned his dress suit, drew on a pair of white gloves, ordered the servants to attend the carriage dressed in their full livery, and drove that same night to No. 30 in the Avenue des Champs-Élysées.